Library of Southern Civilization
Lewis P. Simpson, Editor

THE FREE FLAG OF CUBA

THE LOST NOVEL OF
LUCY HOLCOMBE PICKENS

Edited, with an Introduction, by
Orville Vernon Burton *and* Georganne B. Burton

Louisiana State University Press *Baton Rouge*

Manufactured in the United States of America
First printing
Cloth   11   10   09   08   07   06   05   04   03   02
5   4   3   2   1

Paper   11   10   09   08   07   06   05   04   03   02
5   4   3   2   1

Designer: Barbara Neely Bourgoyne
Typeface: Minion
Typesetter: Coghill Composition, Inc.
Printer and binder: Thomson-Shore, Inc.

Library of Congress Cataloging-in-Publication Data

Pickens, Lucy Petaway Holcombe.
  The free flag of Cuba : the lost novel of Lucy Holcombe Pickens / edited, with an
introduction, by Orville Vernon Burton and Georganne B. Burton.
    p.   cm. — (Library of Southern civilization)
  Includes bibliographical references.
  ISBN 0-8071-2831-7 (alk. paper) — ISBN 0-8071-2834-1 (pbk. : alk. paper)
  1. Cuba—History—Insurrection, 1849–1851—Fiction.   2. López, Narcisco,
1797–1851—Fiction.   I. Burton, Orville Vernon.   II. Burton, Georganne B.,
1946– .   III. Title.   IV. Series.

PS2583.P44F74   2002
813'.3—dc21   2002011068

The paper in this book meets the guidelines for permanence and
durability of the Committee on Production Guidelines for Book
Longevity of the Council on Library Resources. ♾

To our daughter, Maya

CONTENTS

ACKNOWLEDGMENTS

WE WOULD LIKE TO acknowledge all the helpful comments of Sonya Michel, Kristin Hoganson, Nina Baym, participants of the University of Illinois at Urbana-Champaign Southern Reading Group, and members of the Southern Intellectual History Circle, especially commentators Emily Bingham and Carla Peterson, who gave us the ideas on reconciliation. University of Illinois librarian Carol Penka helped us track down the few existing copies and fragments of *The Free Flag of Cuba*. John Stagg offered information on early filibustering. Gary Mormino ("Tampa Slim") contributed his expertise on etymology. For various assistance with research, we would like to thank Masatomo Ayabe, Henry Kamerling, George Peseley, Marco Robinson, and Rose Stremlau, and we thank Matt Chaney for his help. Maureen Hewitt showed us the importance of real quality in an editor; thank you, Maureen. Thanks also to George Roupe at LSU, a remarkable copy editor. We appreciate the support of the Research Board at the University of Illinois.

INTRODUCTION

ACCORDING TO THE PRESS, Lucy Holcombe Pickens (1832–1899) was "one of the most famous women of the South, and one whose name will live in history."[1] Such hyperbole followed Lucy all her life.[2] Her admirers declared her the most beautiful and charming of ladies. Her detractors proclaimed her the most cunning and shallow. South Carolina novelist Elizabeth Boatwright Coker presents her as a flamboyant major character in the novel *India Allan.*[3] Mary Chesnut, the South's most famous diarist, presents several unflattering pictures of "Lucy Long-tongue."[4] Numisma-

1. Belle Walsh, "Mrs. F. W. Pickens Dead," Charleston *News and Courier,* August 9, 1899, 15. Scholarly articles about Lucy Holcombe Pickens include Emily L. Bull, "Lucy Pickens: First Lady of the South Carolina Confederacy," *Proceedings of the South Carolina Historical Association, 1981* (1982), 5–18; Marli F. Weiner, "Pickens, Lucy Petway Holcombe," in *American National Biography,* ed. John A. Garraty and Mark C. Carnes (New York: Oxford University Press, 1999), 17:473–74; Francis B. Simkins, "Pickens, Lucy Petway Holcombe," in *Notable American Women, 1607–1950: A Biographical Dictionary,* ed. Edward T. James, Janet Wilson James, and Paul S. Boyer (Cambridge, Mass.: Belknap Press of Harvard University Press, 1971), 3:64–65; Lori M. Glover, "Bound by Words: Letters in the Life of Lucy Holcombe Pickens, 1857–1861" (master's thesis, Clemson University, 1992). Holcombe is discussed in Orville Vernon Burton's *In My Father's House Are Many Mansions: Family and Community in Edgefield, South Carolina* (Chapel Hill: University of North Carolina Press, 1985) and in the biography of her husband by John B. Edmunds, Jr., *Francis W. Pickens and the Politics of Destruction* (Chapel Hill: University of North Carolina Press, 1986).

2. For example, she is even credited with inventing iced tea. Amy Geier, "Book, Gala Pay Tribute to S.C.,'s First Ladies," Charleston *Post and Courier,* February 7, 2001, 5B.

3. Elizabeth Boatwright Coker, *India Allen* (New York: E. P. Dutton & Co., 1953).

4. C. Vann Woodward, ed., *Mary Chesnut's Civil War* (New Haven: Yale University Press, 1981), 329. Lucy Pickens is also mentioned on pages 40, 136, 275, 284, 285, 297, 316–17, 323, 324, 328, 332, 338, 340, 342, 358, 369, 375, 392, 395, 397, 423, 454, 455, 537. Neither did Chesnut like the genre of literary domestic novels, which she considered "piety and pie-making." Michael O'Brien, "The Flight down the Middle Walk: Mary Chesnut and the

tists know her as the only woman pictured on Confederate currency, and Civil War buffs know her as the wife of South Carolina secession governor Francis Wilkinson Pickens.[5] An extravagant and flirtatious hostess, this "uncrowned Queen of the Southern Confederate States" was confidant to many southern political leaders. More renowned for her beauty than for her intelligence, she held both in abundance.

The Holcombe family scrapbook tells of a novel Lucy Holcombe had written as a young woman. The use of a pseudonym, and the misspelling of that pseudonym (Hardeman in the family album, Hardiman in reference works such as Lyle H. Wright's bibliography of American fiction), made the novel difficult to locate. One librarian's response has been typical: "I have been unable to locate a copy."[6] But this lost novel is now found. *The Free Flag of Cuba; or, The Martyrdom of Lopez: A Tale of the Liberating Expedition of 1851* by H. M. Hardimann was written by Lucy Petway Holcombe of Texas, the future Lucy Pickens of South Carolina.[7]

Forms of Observance," in *Haunted Bodies: Gender and Southern Texts,* ed. Anne Goodwyn Jones and Susan V. Donaldson (Charlottesville: University Press of Virginia, 1997), 114.

5. H. D. Allen, "The Paper Money of the Confederate States with Historical Data," *The Numismatist* 31, no. 7 (July 1918): 287–311. As of this writing, the Confederate one hundred dollar bill featuring Lucy Pickens could be viewed at www.csacurrency.com/csacur/cs209215.htm.

6. The family history was put together by Lucy's great-grandnephew. Jack Thorndyke Greer, "Leaves from a Family Album," 45, in Francis W. Pickens Papers, South Caroliniana Library at the University of South Carolina (hereinafter cited as FWP Papers, SCL). Papers of Francis W. Pickens are also located in the Library of Congress, the South Carolina Archives, the Southern Historical Collection at the University of North Carolina in Chapel Hill (hereinafter cited as Pickens-Dugas Papers, SHC), and the Perkins Library at Duke University, Durham, North Carolina. Wright misspells the pseudonym in *American Fiction, 1851–1875: A Contribution toward a Bibliography* (San Marino, Calif.: Huntington Library, 1965). The librarian's quote is from the Head of Public Services for Reader Services, Perkins Library, Duke University, to Ms. Phyllis Giese, June 22, 1990.

7. H. M. Hardimann, *The Free Flag of Cuba; or, The Martyrdom of López: A Tale of the Liberating Expedition of 1851* (New York: DeWitt & Davenport, 1854). The fiction included in Wright's bibliography can be viewed at some libraries on microfilm produced by Research Publications; *The Free Flag of Cuba* is identified as no. 1097, on reel H-7. The novel is also listed under the name of H. M. Hardiman [*sic*] in *The Bibliography of American Imprints to 1901* (New York: K. G. Saur, 1993), 48:266.The South Caroliniana Library at the University of South Carolina received a copy of the novel in 1961 from Lucy Pickens's granddaughter, Lucy Dugas. Although the card catalog shows that a copy of the book is at the South Caroliniana Library, this copy includes only select pages: 99–100, 117–120, 123–130, 135–142, 145–

The publisher, DeWitt and Davenport of Nassau Street, New York, was a well-known publisher of popular romantic fiction of the day.[8] The book, 19 cm in height and issued in brown printed wrappers with publisher's advertisements, then cost fifty cents.

Holcombe wrote with factual accuracy about the geography, soldiers, and history of the López expedition into Cuba.[9] It happens that Holcombe wrote the first filibustering novel about Cuba. One filibustering novel that precedes Holcombe's is on Texas (1826), and others would follow, usually on Mexico.[10] Holcombe's writing is fluent and articulate, though it is characterized by such overblown descriptions as were com-

---

166, 169–70. A very short section of the novel written in Holcombe's penmanship is in the Francis W. Pickens Papers, Perkins Library, Duke University. A complete copy of the book may be in the holdings of the New York Historical Society.

8. Later, both Robert DeWitt and James Davenport were staunchly pro-Union during the Civil War. Madeleine B. Stern, ed., *Publishers for Mass Entertainment in Nineteenth Century America.* (Boston: G. K. Hall & Co, 1980), 93–96; "Robert M. DeWitt," *American Bookseller* 2 (June 1, 1877): 327–28. According to Elizabeth Moss, southern domestic fiction was usually published in the North. Elizabeth Moss, *Domestic Novelists in the Old South: Defenders of Southern Culture* (Baton Rouge: Louisiana State University Press, 1992), 11.

9. Our analysis relies heavily on the thorough account of the López expedition by its foremost authority, Tom Chaffin, *Fatal Glory: Narciso López and the First Clandestine U.S. War against Cuba* (Charlottesville: University Press of Virginia, 1996). James M. McPherson, provides a good summary in *Battle Cry of Freedom: The Civil War Era* (New York: Oxford University Press, 1988), 105–8. Holcombe's account is also consistent with those of Robert Granville Caldwell, *The López Expeditions to Cuba, 1848–1851* (Princeton: Princeton University Press, 1915); Phillip S. Foner, *A History of Cuba and Its Relationship with the United States*, vol. 2, *1845–1895* (New York: International, 1963); Hugh Thomas, *Cuba: The Pursuit of Freedom* (New York: Harper & Row, 1971), 207–32; Gonzalo de Quesada and Henry Davenport Northrop, *Cuba's Great Struggle for Freedom . . .* , 18–21, 142–50, 263, 288–300, 340–56; Ramiro Guerra y Sánchez, *Manual de historia de Cuba: Económica, socia, y política* (La Habana: Consejo Nacional de Cultura, 1962), i–xxi, 412–85, 511.

10. Brady Harrison, "The Young Americans: Emerson, Walker, and the Early Literature of American Empire," *American Studies* 40, no. 3 (Fall 1999): 75–97. In the 1800s *filibuster* usually referred to an invasion of another country for the purpose of conquest. It refers both to such expeditions and those who undertook them. The first filibustering novel was Timothy Flint's *Francis Berrian; or, The Mexican Patriot* (Boston: Cummings, Hilliard, 1826); other examples are Bret Harte's *The Crusade of the Excelsior* (1877) and Richard Harding Davis's *Soldiers of Fortune* (1897) and *Captain Macklin: His Memoirs* (1902). Robert E. May discusses *Captain Macklin* in "Young American Males and Filibustering in the Age of Manifest Destiny: The United States Army as a Cultural Mirror," *Journal of American History* 78, no. 3 (December 1991): 885–86.

mon in the mid-1800s. Her novel is full of distinct and interesting characters, and she uses their gallery of voices to argue her concerns. The
novel demonstrates a connection between gender issues and filibustering,
and it also sheds light on other nineteenth-century issues such as patriotism, race, and the role of southern women in their society. The López
expedition was an abject failure, and Holcombe's novel, in an uncanny
and fascinating way, presages the mythology of the Lost Cause. Readers
will note time and again the irony and mythology in Holcombe's story.
As another historian has so aptly put it, "Myth and irony are powerful
forces to be reckoned with" in antebellum southern culture.[11]

This novel is an important window to understanding the world view
of a young aristocratic southern woman who would become influential
during the Civil War. In her perception of the world, people fit into
clearly defined roles. Men were brave and "manly." Married women were
wise and long-suffering. Unmarried women were beautiful and engaging.
Slaves were in a separate category, not gendered men or women, but
human beings nevertheless—shrewd, perhaps funny, definitely companionable and loyal. The enslaved laboring on the land were outside Holcombe's field of vision. Within these roles Holcombe gives her female
characters maneuverability denied her male characters. Following a familiar model in nineteenth-century writing, Holcombe presents two
main female characters, best friends, whom Holcombe uses to confront
some of the contradictions of women's lives. Both are attractive and desirable, but one pushes against the boundaries established for her as a
woman.

Lucy Holcombe herself was pushing against boundaries in writing her
novel. With an intense desire to affect political policy, Holcombe needed
an outlet, and writing was the most effective means available to her.[12] As

11. Steven M. Stowe, *Intimacy and Power in the Old South: Ritual in the Lives of the
Planters* (Baltimore: Johns Hopkins University Press, 1987), xiii.

12. Steven Stowe's study of the southern elite found that men and women "were each
thought not only to possess specific forms of language, but also to be incapable of moving
beyond the aptitudes for thinking and feeling that these forms signified" (*Intimacy and
Power*, 2–3). In this novel, it seems, Holcombe moves beyond such aptitudes. Her polemics
also fit into the political pamphleteering of the age. Some women supported causes with
parades and by raising money. Elizabeth R. Varon, *We Mean to Be Counted: White Women
and Politics in Antebellum Virginia* (Chapel Hill: University of North Carolina Press, 1998);
"Lucy Barbour, Henry Clay, and Nineteenth-Century Virginia Politics," *Virginia Cavalcade*

a young woman author, Holcombe was no anomaly. In fact Nathaniel Hawthorne complained that "America is now wholly given over to a damned mob of scribbling women." Elizabeth Moss has studied five southern women who were best-selling authors during this time period: Caroline Gilman (1794–1888), Caroline Hentz (1800–1856), Maria Mc-Intosh (1803–1878), Mary Virginia Terhune (1830–1922), and Augusta Jane Evans (1835–1909). Nina Baym has analyzed the work of women writers in the nineteenth century who wrote fiction as well as that of women who wrote history. Holcombe combined history and fiction in her writing. According to Baym, many women authors used "dialogue and dialect" and "rhetorical and oratorical strategies whose terminology we have forgotten and which we no longer have the skill to recognize." Allusion to "literary figures" was another common feature.[13] All these techniques are certainly found in Holcombe's writing.

Although Holcombe adheres to the ethos of other women authors of the 1850s, *The Free Flag of Cuba* does not fit into the genre of women's writings that Baym has characterized as "woman's fiction." There is no defining plot wherein a woman proves herself against adverse circumstances put in her way by evil or stupid men. The evil and stupid men in this story are not the protagonists' guardians but the evil tyrant in Cuba and the stupid president of the United States who refuses to aid the captured Americans. No female character needs to grow more independent by resisting male authority. Neither does Holcombe's novel fit Moss's definition of southern domestic fiction as nineteenth-century literature "written exclusively by women for women."[14] Holcombe does not write exclusively for women.

---

41 (Autumn 1992): 72–83. Lucy Pickens would become involved in fund-raising in later years when she worked to memorialize the Confederacy.

13. Hawthorne quoted in Mary Kelley, *Private Woman, Public Stage: Literary Domesticity in Nineteenth-Century America* (New York: Oxford University Press, 1984), 345. Moss, *Domestic Novelists in the Old South*; Nina Baym, *Woman's Fiction: A Guide to Novels by and about Women in America, 1820–1870* (Ithaca, N.Y.: Cornell University Press, 1973), xvi–xvii, and *American Women Writers and the Work of History, 1790–1860* (New Brunswick, N.J.: Rutgers University Press, 1995). See also Carol S. Manning, ed., *The Female Tradition in Southern Literature* (Urbana: University of Illinois Press, 1993), and Susan K. Harris, *Nineteenth-Century American Women's Novels: Interpretative Strategies* (New York: Cambridge University Press, 1990).

14. Moss, *Domestic Novelists in the Old South*, 3.

Baym considers what she terms "woman's fiction" feminist because "the novels advocated an individualism that had not traditionally been a woman's option."[15] Holcombe likewise gives her females individuality that male authors of the time did not. Although her females have romantic appeal, Holcombe also gives them intellectual capability. She allows her female protagonists to voice strong political opinions without losing, indeed while adding to, their charm.

Holcombe is like other rediscovered nineteenth-century women authors in that she used her writing to engage in national debates of the time. Among the many women writers who were published in mid-nineteenth century, however, few were southern belles—that is, well off, unmarried women. Nevertheless, Holcombe was determined to give voice to her political concerns and to sway public policy on an international concern. At the same time, she did not want change in the domestic status quo. Similar to other women writers of the time, Holcombe introduces the idea of women's suffrage only to reject it. Opposition to women's suffrage was strong in the South, where the right to vote was commensurate with manhood and white supremacy. Holcombe was also very satisfied with the system of slavery, and hers was one of many southern novels written in response to *Uncle Tom's Cabin* (1851) which was very popular in the North at the time.[16]

Historian Mary Kelley states that women writers at this time secretly wanted to be creators of culture but still preferred to tell themselves and others that they were simply private domestic women.[17] Holcombe's use of a pseudonym could have meant that she felt a ladylike reluctance to enter the field of writing openly, but men as well as women, including career authors, used pseudonyms, as well as "claims of writing for the good of humanity." Most likely she thought a pseudonym would attract male readership at a time when the readership of novels in the United States was primarily other women.[18]

Jane Tompkins has found that southern domestic novelists "have de-

15. Baym, *Woman's Fiction,* xx.

16. Paula Baker, "The Domestication of Politics: Women and American Political Society, 1780–1920," *American Historical Review* 89 (June 1984): 643.

17. Mary Kelley, *Private Woman, Public Stage,* 184.

18. Susan Coultrap-McQuin, *Doing Literary Business: American Women Writers in the Nineteenth Century* (Chapel Hill: University of North Carolina Press, 1990), xii.

signs upon their audiences, in the sense of wanting to make people think and act in a particular way," and Holcombe is no exception.[19] She wanted to effect a change in the official U.S. policy of neutrality with regard to Spain's dominion over Cuba to one of active engagement in pursuit of freedom for the island. At the very least, she wanted the U.S. government to come to the aid of men captured in an invasion. Her avowed purpose in writing her novel was to vindicate the 1851 expedition to Cuba by Narciso López, to broadcast to the world that the expedition was a noble cause and that the men who were executed in Cuba were martyred heroes. Filibustering invasions were not uncommon in this age of imperialism. Derived from a term for English buccaneers who preyed upon Spanish ships in the 1600s, the word *filibuster* was originally derogatory (as the character Mabel exclaims, "Don't say Fillibusters! Call them by their proper name—Patriots! Liberators!"). Filibustering had enthusiasts among women as well as men. Literary critic Amy Kaplan has dismissed the general assumption that territorial conquest was a male activity that women opposed. She argues to the contrary that many women were very supportive of American imperialism at the time and that "the rhetorics of Manifest Destiny and domesticity share a vocabulary that turns imperial conquest into spiritual regeneration."[20] That vocabulary is clearly evident in Holcombe's novel.

Lucy Holcombe was representative of Young America, a movement of intellectuals, journalists, and businessmen within the Democratic Party who idealistically supported U.S. imperialism in the 1840s and 1850s. In her concluding chapter Holcombe writes, "Young America has made the attempt [to free Cuba], and though unsuccessful, yet, like a true knight, he stands ready at any moment to resume arms in a cause so worthy his chivalrous devotion." The movement took its name from an essay by Ralph Waldo Emerson (who was not involved), in which he called for "Young America" to lead the world. According to historian Edward

---

19. Jane Tompkins, *Sensational Designs: The Cultural Work of American Fiction 1790–1860* (New York: Oxford University Press, 1985), xi.

20. Amy Kaplan, "Manifest Domesticity," in *American Literature* 70, no. 3 (September 1998),: 588. See also Lynnea Magnuson, "In the Service of Columbia: Gendered Politics and Manifest Destiny Expansion" (Ph.D. diss., University of Illinois at Urbana-Champaign, 2000), and Brady Harrison, "Losers in the Isthmus: Central America in American Literature" (Ph.D. diss., University of Illinois at Urbana-Champaign, 1994).

Widmer, Young America started with the idealism of spreading freedom and democracy but ended in "a host of ugly threats toward neighboring countries." A contemporary of Holcombe's, New England abolitionist Lydia Maria Childs, opposed filibustering and later wrote that the popular discussions of national honor were "all pretense—too flimsy to disguise our eagerness to grab at the possessions of Cuba."[21]

Annexation of Cuba would have meant an addition of one or more slave states, yet filibusters had ardent champions in the North as well as in the South. Newspapers throughout the country endorsed their exploits, and communities nationwide held supporting rallies and raised money for the expeditions. Moses Beach of the New York *Sun* and woman journalist and lobbyist Jane M. Cazneau, a New York native, used the press for propaganda on behalf of Cuban annexation. John L. O'Sullivan, New York City editor of the *United States Magazine and Democratic Review*, was a strong advocate of filibustering. O'Sullivan, who had coined the phrase "Manifest Destiny" in 1845, was indicted in 1850 for his support of López.[22] Others felt torn between admiration and condemnation. Jefferson Davis (who would later become president of the Confederacy) helped thwart filibustering when he served as U.S. secretary of war, but personally he approved of the practice. And army officer William Tecumseh Sherman (who would later help defeat the Confederacy through his famous "march to the sea") opposed filibustering but wrote to his brother in 1851 that he sometimes found himself hoping the filibusters would succeed.[23]

Because the López expeditions had failed, and the victors usually write

21. Harrison, "The Young Americans," 80; Edward L. Widmer, *Young America: The Flowering of Democracy in New York City* (New York: Oxford University Press, 1999), 24; Edward P. Crapol, "Lydia Maria Child: Abolitionist Critic of American Foreign Policy," in *Women and American Foreign Policy: Lobbyists, Critics, and Insiders,* ed. Edward P Crapol (New York: Greenwood, 1987), 15.

22. After a mistrial, all charges against O'Sullivan were dropped. Chaffin, *Fatal Glory,* 195. Cazneau, who also had "Texas credentials," had actively supported the annexation of Texas, all of Mexico, and Cuba. Robert E. May, "'Plenipotentiary in Petticoats': Jane M. Cazneau and American Foreign Policy in the Mid-Nineteenth Century," in Crapol, *Women and American Foreign,* 19–44.

23. Tom Chaffin, "'Sons of Washington': Narciso López, Filibustering, and U.S. Nationalism, 1848–1851," *Journal of the Early Republic* 15 (Spring 1995): 79–108; May, "Young American Males and Filibustering," 871, 876.

the history, Holcombe was an early revisionist; her major theme was the righteousness of the López filibuster, "a glorious, a holy mission!" Narciso López was born in Venezuela in 1797, the son of a wealthy planter. Before becoming involved in filibusters, he filled a number of political and military positions in Spain and then in Cuba, where he married into a prominent Cuban family. When hard economic times hurt his iron and steel operations, he blamed the Spanish authorities. He tried to organize a coup in July of 1848 but was discovered and fled to the United States. From there he organized three unsuccessful attempts to overthrow the Spanish government in Cuba. The first attempt was in July 1849; the U.S. government prevented this expedition from departing from Round Island, off the coast of Mississippi. The second attempt was in April and May of 1850, when the filibusters took the Cuban town of Cárdenas but were forced to flee by Spanish reinforcements. In the final attempt, which took place in August 1851 and is the primary focus of Holcombe's novel, López and many of his men were captured. About 135 men were sent to prison at Ceuta in Africa. Fifty were executed by firing squad in Cuba shortly after their capture. Several weeks later, on September 1, 1851, López was executed by garrote, slow strangulation with an iron collar. Some of the men managed to get back to the United States; those who were captured but not executed were released in 1852, after the U.S. paid damages to Spain.[24]

Throughout her novel, Holcombe uses the "Free Flag of Cuba" as a symbol of independence and republicanism. In his filibusters Narciso López hoisted a flag which, curiously enough, was to become the modern Cuban flag.[25] With blue stripes in the background and a single star against a red backdrop, the flag is similar to the Texas Lone Star flag, a remembrance of Texas' history of revolution and annexation. If Holcombe had titled her novel "The Free Flag over Cuba," it might have suggested the U.S. flag flying over Cuba, implying an annexationist point of view. But Holcombe adamantly champions Cuban independence throughout her book. When Uncle Louis Clifton argues, "I stand on the Monroe doctrine, sir. I hold—a proclamation should be issued—the

24. Chaffin, *Fatal Glory*, xix–xx, 216–18.
25. Hugh Thomas, *Cuba: The Pursuit of Freedom* (New York: Harper & Row, 1971), 217; Chaffin, *Fatal Glory*, 119.

navy sent to blockade the ports—take Cuba forthwith, sir, and annex her to the United States," the idealistic hero Ralph Dudley replies excitedly, "The Cubans are not to be *taken* like so many *slaves!* Let *their* wishes at least be consulted. Cuba is for liberation, not conquest." Yet the young Texas woman Lucy Holcombe knew very well how her own Lone Star State declared independence in 1836 and voted in favor of annexation to the United States in 1845. Filibusters had helped to settle the Mexican territory of Tejas and, to Holcombe and the Anglo settlers, though not to the Mexican inhabitants, filibustering was a proud tradition in Texas history.[26]

Scholars disagree over whether López was for Cuban annexation or independence. López never specified what he expected after independence, but much of his financial support came from U.S. annexation committees. Organized throughout the country, these committees sold bonds to raise money for the filibusters. At least once, López told his men that they had come "to free a people," which could mean independence or annexation. One of the broadsides advertising the mission, however, stated that the expedition was "to add another glorious star to the banner which already waves, to the admiration of the whole world, over 'The land of the Free and the home of the Brave.'" Holcombe's fictionalized López mentions that the enemy, Spain, does not want Cuba to "shine amid the stars of the Columbian flag," that is, become a state in the United States.[27]

Holcombe's expressed hope was the establishment of a Cuban republic; to that effect, she used *republic* or *republicanism* twenty-seven times in this novel. Although her ostensive rationale for writing her novel was to advocate freedom for oppressed people, her cause of freedom was not

26. For a popular account of the Texas filibustering tradition, see William C. Davis, *Three Roads to the Alamo: The Lives and Fortunes of David Crockett, James Bowie, and William Barret Travis* (New York: Harper Collins, 1998).

27. Chaffin, "Sons of Washington," 89, 101–02. Rafael de la Cova finds that, before Herminio Portell-Vilá's biography of López (*Narciso López y su época*) was published, scholars regarded López as an annexationist. According to de la Cova, Portell-Vilá thought López was simply using the annexationists to help him to gain independence; however, he argues, Portell-Vilá overlooked López's desire to become an American citizen. Also, his second in command, Ambrosio Gonzales, made frequent public calls for the annexation of Cuba. Antonio Rafael de la Cova, "Ambrosio José Gonzales: A Cuban Confederate Colonel" (Ph.D. diss., West Virginia University, 1994), 7–8.

meant for the 436,000 enslaved in Cuba; in fact, one of the fears of the white South was the "Africanization of Cuba," the possibility that Spain would yield to pressure from England to free the Cuban slaves. In exhorting the need for republicanism in Cuba, Holcombe's character López laments that Spain meant to cast upon Cuba "the undying stain of African equality." In response Ralph Dudley, the main male protagonist, is aghast. "General," he says, "you dream; think you they would make them allies? Arm the dark race against their own?" Holcombe advocated freedom only for the 418,000 white people of Cuba, whom she perceived as slaves to Spanish tyranny. Like other white southerners of her time, Holcombe did not see the irony of her position, that the tyranny of the Spanish over Cubans was less oppressive than that of southern whites over slaves.[28]

The U.S. government had a history of ambivalence about Cuban annexation and independence. According to historian Louis A. Perez, the United States government did not favor independence for the racially mixed Cubans, and race played a role in the opposition of John Quincy Adams as early as 1823.[29] Holcombe lived in a culture caught between racial prejudice toward the native populations of color in Central and South America and prejudice toward the Spanish deriving from the "Black Legend," stories of the Spaniards' harsh treatment of those natives. In exhorting her readers to support the expedition, Holcombe presents images of Cuba calculated to stir the emotions: Cuba as the beautiful "gem of the Antilles," as an "unhappy Island Queen," and as a young white girl being possessed (raped?) by dark Spaniards: "With false promises on their lips," the narrator tells us, "they encircled in their dark, treacherous arms the fairest child of the southern waters. Once possessed, the deadly grasp of avarice and oppression crushed and marred her glorious loveliness." Such portrayals of the Spaniards as brutes grew more

28. Foner, *A History of Cuba,* vol. 2, Chapter 6. Slaveholders in the U.S. and Cuba were also fearful because France had emancipated slaves in the French Caribbean colonies in 1848. Furthermore, many whites feared the precedent set by the slave rebellion in Haiti led by Toussaint-Louverture, which succeeded in overthrowing the white establishment. Free blacks in Cuba numbered about 143,000. Chaffin, "Sons of Washington," 90.

29. Louis A. Perez, Jr., *The War of 1898: The United States and Cuba in History and Historiography* (Chapel Hill: University of North Carolina Press, 1998),13, 16.

harsh and more commonplace in U.S. media and public opinion between the 1850s and the time of the Spanish-American War in 1898.

In the early nineteenth century the Black Legend was combined with a "republican" ideology that asserted that the peoples of Spanish America, if released from the oppression of Spanish imperialism, would realize their innate capabilities much as the American colonists had done. Americans such as Holcombe believed that white Spanish Americans were better endowed with these capabilities than the natives of color. Holcombe refers to the native-born white people of Cuba as Creoles. Cuban Creoles were Roman Catholic, and Holcombe, though Presbyterian herself, uses Catholic protagonists and Catholic imagery in the novel. "I will ever kneel to the Mother of mercy to watch over and protect you," Genevieve Clifton tells her fiancé Ralph Dudley before he goes away to fight for Cuba. Although part of the Black Legend was aimed against Spanish Catholics, Holcombe was not prejudiced against Catholics and even used some Catholic icons in her personal devotions. In the early settlement of Texas, Mexico required immigrants to accept the Catholic faith, which many did pro forma. Holcombe's positive presentation of Catholicism was intended to give readers a favorable impression of the Catholic people of Cuba.[30]

Holcombe tied the revolution in Cuba philosophically and historically to the American Revolution, and patriotic fervor of the day often included honoring the U.S. Constitution. Protagonist Ralph Dudley cites the Constitution in his criticism of presidential denunciations of filibustering. Dudley quotes his friend Walker, calling the president's position "an outrage to the personal rights guaranteed an American citizen by our Constitution, and a disgrace to the spirit of the age in which we live. It assumes an authority over body and soul, which would well become the

30. Lucy's father, Beverly L. Holcombe, "headed the most prominent Presbyterian family" in their community. Randolph B. Campbell, *A Southern Community in Crisis: Harrison County, Texas, 1850–1880* (Austin: Texas State Historical Association), 103. Holcombe later became Episcopalian when she married Francis W. Pickens. When the novel was written, anti-Catholic sentiment ran high within the Whig party and was a predominant factor in the Know-Nothing Party. President Millard Fillmore, a Whig and the future unsuccessful Know-Nothing candidate in 1856, is not a respected character in the novel. Holcombe's disdain for Know-Nothings was typical among southerners.

Czar, but is highly disgraceful to republicanism."[31] Republicanism and revolutionary fervor are so prevalent in this novel that George Washington and Lafayette function almost as characters themselves. Lucy Holcombe's grandfather Philemon Holcombe, Jr., served with Lafayette, and he gave his son, Lucy's father, the middle name Lafayette.[32]

Holcombe explicitly compared her female characters with women of the American Revolution. "What would our revolutionary mothers say to the American women who seek to stay an arm uplifted in such a cause?" Dudley asks Genevieve in response to her protests of his plans to join the filibuster. Holcombe's message for her women readers was that they must be willing to sacrifice their loved ones for a just and honorable cause. Women of the Confederacy would come to accept this sentiment by the time of the Civil War. As one mother wrote in 1861, "I now offer you, a beardless boy of 17 summers,—not with grief, but thanking God that I have a son to offer."[33]

Holcombe's polemics also foreshadow other ideas that would become prevalent in the South during the Civil War. In discussions of presidential authority, Holcombe clearly states what will become the Confederate view, and her criticism of President Millard Fillmore ("The President is the servant of the sovereign people, not their arbiter") presages many white southerners' feelings about Abraham Lincoln ten years later. Expressing a sentiment others would echo in later years with regard to Confederate soldiers, Dudley says of the American soldiers on the Cuban

31. According to Baym, it was common for women writers at that time to regard the Constitution as "a sacred document," *Woman's Fiction*, xxxiii. Dudley's "friend" could be Samuel Walker, a planter and filibuster patron, or possibly William Walker, who successfully invaded Nicaragua in 1855 and set himself up as dictator. Ousted by neighboring republics in 1857, he tried again in 1860, but when he landed in Honduras, he was captured, court-martialed, and executed.

32. J. Walker Holcombe, "Lucy Holcombe Legacy Lives in Washington, D. C.," *Harrison County Historical Herald*, 7, in the Lucy Holcombe Collection at the Harrison County Historical Society, Old Courthouse, Marshall, Texas.

33. Quoted in Drew Gilpin Faust, *Mothers of Invention: Women of the Slaveholding South in the American Civil War* (Chapel Hill: University of North Carolina Press, 1996),14. On rhetoric from the American Revolution, see Linda K. Kerber, *Women of the Republic: Intellect and Ideology in Revolutionary America* (Chapel Hill: University of North Carolina Press, 1980).

expedition, "Now our men, while they make the best fighters in the world, are certainly the worst soldiers." That is, "Each one is determined on achieving the battle after his own fashion by his individual valor. No man is willing to see the most dangerous post assigned to another; *he* has the best right to die in a good cause." Holcombe's male protagonists fill a need for brave heroes in this story that harbingers the need for "manly" and brave men to fight for the Confederacy. Six years later young men with this set of ethics would be marching off for honor and glory in the Civil War. During that war Lucy Holcombe Pickens would present a flag that she designed (featuring the Star of Texas) to a legion named after her, the Holcombe Legion, commanded by Col. P. F. Stevens, superintendent of the Citadel Military School in Charleston. The men of the Holcombe Legion would have as their motto, "It is for the brave to die, but not to surrender."[34]

At the time she wrote the novel, however, Holcombe was clearly not interested in stirring bad feelings between North and South. Similar to other southern writers who believed it was "woman's duty to ensure sectional harmony," she includes a close friendship between her female protagonists, the Yankee Mabel Royal and the southern Genevieve Clifton.[35] Holcombe does not accept the stereotyped differences between northerners and southerners. Both female characters are intellectually inclined. Both are beautiful and sought after by honorable men. Both consider men superior—or rather wish they would behave that way. Holcombe went to school in the North, had friends in the North, and knew that most northerners were not the abolitionists so resented in the southern press. Her portrayal of a good-hearted, charming Yankee, one who loves the South and endorses southern values, answered critics of the peculiar institution. Just as she uses the Mississippi River as a metaphor to connect the North and the South, "that generous river, knowing neither north nor south, but alike kissing the frozen banks of the snow-hill states, and the sunny shore of the flower-dowered south," Holcombe uses the friendship between Genevieve and Mabel to show that the two sections should stay on friendly terms.

34. According to family legend, Holcombe financed this regiment with some of the jewels given to her by Czar Alexander II. Personal files of Mrs. Chas. A. Beehn, Marshall, Texas, Holcombe Collection.

35. Moss, *Domestic Novelists in the Old South*, 27.

Holcombe mentions both historical and fictional filibusters in the story. At one point, before the expedition members depart for New Orleans to embark on their adventure, they gather at a dinner party at the Clifton plantation on the banks of the Mississippi River in Louisiana. The narrator asks the reader to pause and observe the assembled group of filibusters, "rich with humanity's noblest attributes." It appears that Holcombe, whose family was friends with many of the filibusters, was present at such a gathering because the narrator observes, "But once again, even in fiction, will we mingle in this gallant circle." Included in this group are General Narciso López, General Pragay (which Holcombe spells "Pragi"), Colonel Downman, Colonel Haynes, Captain Gotay, Victor Ken, and Colonel William L. Crittenden, a significant figure in the expedition and in Holcombe's personal life. Crittenden, who, like so many of the filibuster volunteers, had served in the Mexican War, was a clerk in the New Orleans customhouse before taking on a military command with López. Crittenden recruited volunteers in the South and Midwest by offering Cuban sugar plantations as well as cash bonuses.[36] Also among this gathering is General John A. Quitman, to whom Holcombe dedicates the book with elaborate poetical flourish. Quitman, a brigadier general and hero of the Mexican War, was the governor of Mississippi and an ardent supporter of filibusters. In the novel, López asks Quitman to cocommand the expedition, but Quitman refuses, explaining that he does not think the people of Cuba are active enough in their revolt and that the timing is not right, both of which Holcombe knew to be true as of the time of her writing. After the death of López, Quitman did indeed take charge of Cuban filibustering endeavors. In this novel the character Quitman affirms the honorable intentions of Narciso López and declares him to be chivalrous and patriotic.[37]

36. According to the family history, William Logan Crittenden and Lucy Holcombe were engaged. Crittenden (1823–1851) had served in the military occupation of Texas in 1845–46. George W. Cullum, *Biographical Register of the Officers and Graduates of the U.S. Military Academy at West Point, N.Y.*, 3rd ed., rev. (Boston: Houghton Mifflin, 1891); Richard Tansey, "Southern Expansionism: Urban Interests in the Cuban Filibusters," *Plantation Society* 1, no. 2 (June 1979): 233.

37. According to Robert May, López offered Quitman command of this filibuster expedition and rulership over a Cuban republic. Quitman wrote to an associate that López promised one million dollars and an army of four thousand. Although Quitman did not join this

According to Tom Chaffin, foremost authority on the López filibusters, the expedition of August 1851—the final one as it turned out—was
to consist of three regiments (nine companies), but just over four hundred men actually set sail with López. López anticipated that Cubans
would fill in the necessary ranks. Holcombe does not include the number
of volunteers; neither does she discuss how the expedition embarked earlier than planned. Crittenden, who worked in the customhouse and was
privy to inside information, notified López that the federal government
was planning to impound their vessel, the *Pampero*. López had time to
embark before this occurred, but the rush meant that he could not wait
for all his recruits. Crittenden was supposed to have commanded the
Kentucky regiment, six hundred well-trained and disciplined soldiers
from Kentucky and Indiana, but they had not yet arrived. López decided
they could come later as reinforcements. Crittenden, however, would not
be left behind; within two days he enrolled 114 youths from the streets of
New Orleans and signed them on as the First Regiment of Artillery.
When the *Pampero* sailed out of New Orleans on its way to Key West for
repairs, an enthusiastic crowd of supporters saluted and waved. Among
the throng was Lucy Holcombe, wishing the best for her beau, William
Crittenden.[38]

López's early departure meant that his second in command and chief
interpreter (López spoke little English), Ambrosio José Gonzales, was not
on board the *Pampero*. Suffering from a severe fever, probably a symp-
tom of malaria, Gonzales thought he had time to recuperate before the
departure, which was scheduled for the fall. López had advised Gonzales
that he would pick him up in Jacksonville, Mississippi, along with other

---

expedition, he was a major advocate and put others in touch with López. Quitman was
indicted in June 1850 for disregarding the Neutrality Act by working so closely with López.
Quitman would head filibustering preparations against Cuba between 1852 and 1855, but
his planīed expedition never embarked. Robert E. May, *John A. Quitman: Old South Cru-
sader* (Baton Rouge: Louisiana State University Press, 1985), 238, 270–95. John Pragay, López's second in command, was from Hungary. Holcombe often mentions the Hungarian
exiles along with Irish patriots fighting elsewhere for liberty, and the story of the expedition
includes several Hungarian officers. In addition to the United States, Cuba, Ireland, and
Hungary, volunteers also came from Germany, Denmark, Poland, England, and Venezuela.
Language barriers caused problems for military organization. Chaffin, "Sons of Washington," 92. Chaffin's *Fatal Glory* does not discuss Haynes, Gotay, nor Ken.

    38. De la Cova, "Ambrosio José Gonzales," 200, 210.

recruits and the weapons and artillery that Gonzales had stored from the previous failed ventures. But López did not return for Gonzales, the others, and the weapons. When the *Pampero* departed Key West on August 11, 1851, López headed for Cuba, ninety miles away, rather than going to Mississippi, about a thousand miles' round trip. His new plan was to come back for Gonzales after disembarking in Cuba. Gonzales later wrote that López changed plans because he believed newspaper stories fabricated by the Spanish government that Cuba was in the midst of widespread insurrection and did not want to "miss the opportunity of marching in triumph into Havana." In the meantime, Gonzales was still recruiting volunteers when he heard the news that López and many of the men had been captured.[39]

The filibusters won the first skirmishes, but the hoped-for Cuban uprising never occurred. Crittenden's band was separated from the main group when López left them to guard supplies. They were split up again in an ensuing battle. Crittenden and about fifty of his men were then captured as they tried to escape in four small boats. These fifty were summarily tried and executed by firing squad. In describing the scene, Holcombe echoes an oral tradition that sprang up upon Crittenden's death, that he had defiantly refused to be blindfolded or to bow down; she writes, "Thank heaven, the noble form of Crittenden, the gallant Kentuckian, bowed not even in death, and his glorious lips gave to history the immortal words: 'An American kneels but to his God.'" Even the most ardent opponents of filibusters considered such bravery admirable. "I have forgiven the crime & delusion of the invaders for the immeasurable courage & uncomplaining spirit in which they all to a man met their death," wrote one.[40]

Crittenden wrote in a last-minute letter to his uncle, U.S. Attorney General John J. Crittenden: "In a few minutes some fifty of us will be shot. We came here with López. You will do me the justice to believe that my motives were good. I was deceived by López. He, as well as the public press, assured me that the island was in a state of prosperous revolution.

39. Ibid., 193, 203, 211. The López character in Holcombe's novel claims he "master[ed] the uncouth language of the Saxon," but this is at best a great exaggeration of his knowledge of English.

40. Samuel Francis Du Pont to Charles Henry Davis, Sept. 10, 1851, quoted in May, "Young American Males and Filibustering," 860–61.

I am commanded to finish writing at once. I will die like a man."[41] Quite likely Holcombe never saw this letter. Although Crittenden's final letter finds deception on the part of López, Holcombe does not. As leader of the filibustering expedition to Cuba, the character of General Narciso López is crucial to Holcombe's assertion that he was an honorable man and the expedition was an honorable venture. Although some claim that López was an excessive gambler and licentious womanizer, Holcombe's character López is a Christlike figure, doing good to his enemies, as he does, for example, when he takes care of the wounded Spanish soldiers whom the Spaniards had left to die (which the real López in fact did).[42] Like Christ, López is misunderstood by the populace and betrayed by a friend. Holcombe calls López worthy, esteemed by his associates, marked with honor and probity. She tells the reader that he hates tyranny and oppression and loves right and truth. During the battles in Cuba, Holcombe places the brave López, careless of danger, in the midst of the fiercest fighting. Even his horse is noble: "the gallant charger" has a "noble carriage and indomitable spirit."

One of Holcombe's villains is Captain-General José Guiterrez de la Concha, a historical character whom Holcombe treats fictitiously. Concha, the captain-general and governor of Cuba, "he of gory fame," is "Cuba's dark oppressor." His eyes glitter "with the cold flashing light of the assassin's steel." He is declared to have no generosity, no pity, no mercy. His cruel villainy is another reason to support invasion. Because only heroes are brave, Concha is described with "a coward's face."

Another villain, "small, cowering, and insignificant," is the fictional Hidalgo Gonzales, a trusted advisor to López but actually a spy for Concha. Holcombe gives this Gonzales the responsibility for the disastrous timing of the expedition. He purposefully urges haste by portraying the Cuban people as ready, willing, and able to assist López and growing impatient with the delays; yet Hidalgo knows all along that supporters in Cuba are already in jail because of correspondence he himself confiscated. Why does Holcombe use the fictional name Hidalgo Gonzales when López actually had an Ambrosio José Gonzales as his right-hand

41. Chaffin, *Fatal Glory*, 215.
42. Herminio Portell-Vilá, *Narciso López y su época* (Habana: Cultural, 1930–1958), 1:59, quoted in de la Cova, "Ambrosio José Gonzales," 30; Chaffin, *Fatal Glory*, 208.

man? We do not know. According to Gonzales biographer Rafael de la Cova, "Gonzales never wavered in supporting López." Ambrosio Gonzales later wrote that the Spanish authorities in Cuba deliberately fed misinformation to the newspapers and to Spanish emissaries "to precipitate the departure of the too confiding López, and cause him to land where he could be most speedily annihilated." Indeed, spies and infiltrators plagued the filibusters, who needed secrecy for their illegal activities but also needed publicity for raising money. Holcombe's novel includes these misinformation tactics, as well as the interception of letters and the incarceration of potential rebels. Holcombe needed a traitor to show that blame did not rest upon López.[43]

Also opposed to filibustering is President Millard Fillmore, a Whig from New York who, as Vice President, succeeded to the presidency upon the death of Zachary Taylor. His presidential proclamation of April 25, 1850, denounced filibusters and proclaimed the government's refusal to rescue any Americans caught while invading another country.[44] The

43. Ambrosio Gonzales was in favor of Cuban annexation. A member of the Havana Club, he was a leading organizer and part of several invading forces against Cuba. De la Cova, "Ambrosio José Gonzales," 190, 212. After this final expedition, President Fillmore issued an arrest warrant for Gonzales, but Gonzales was never brought to trial because he proved that he had been very ill. A year later, Gonzales wrote a pamphlet entitled "Manifesto on Cuban Affair Addressed to the People of the United States." Gonzales married into the aristocratic Elliott family of South Carolina in 1856 and served in the Confederacy. He named his second son after his friend Narciso López. Narciso Gonzales would go on to found the newspaper *The State* in Columbia, South Carolina. Lewis Pinckney Jones, *Stormy Petrel: N. G. Gonzales and His State* (Columbia: University of South Carolina Press, 1973). Chaffin mentions another Hidalgo in Mexico: "With the conspicuous exception of Mexico's Father Hidalgo, most mainland liberators were aristocrats who had only grudgingly embraced independence." Chaffin, *Fatal Glory,* 220. It is possible that Holcombe disapproved of this Hidalgo; just as likely, it was simply a fictional name. We do not believe Holcombe knew that the name Hidalgo derives from *hijo de algo,* son of someone, and implies minor nobility of pure breeding rather than mixed race.

44. Although Holcombe scorned Fillmore, she clearly wanted bipartisan support for López. In a cozy room in the protagonist's home were three busts, George Washington, Andrew Jackson (a Democrat), and Henry Clay (a Whig). Lucy Holcombe's sister Anna had written Henry Clay in 1846 from her school in Pennsylvania; in the midst of sectional turmoil, she implored him to "save the country." Greer, "Leaves from a Family Album," 45. When historian Richard Tansey used local newspapers to ascertain party membership of the López annexation committees, he identified 99 out of 153 committeemen: 69 Democrats and 30 Whigs. "Secession sentiment among Democrats and anti-Fillmore animus among

American consul in Havana, Allen Ferdinand Owen, who was in the position of enforcing this proclamation, offered no interference with Concha's execution of Crittenden and his men. As narrator, Holcombe asks
for charity toward Owen: "Owen—who has been held up to public scorn,
as an officer wanting in national spirit and pride; a man destitute of the
commonest emotions of humanity." She portrays Owen as simply a cowardly gentleman who followed the president's orders; he had an "unmanly tameness."

Proving manliness was one of the reasons men volunteered to fight
in Cuba, and the press manipulated this idea to foment rioting after the
execution of Crittenden, his men, and López. Protests occurred throughout the country, but rioting in New Orleans drove out Spanish residents
and businessmen to the economic gain of the Americans remaining.
Newspapers played an incendiary role. One paper used the symbolic removal of manhood to provoke anger, falsely reporting that "One of the
waiters [at a Havana barroom] showed to everybody as a proof of the
glorious act he had performed, the testicles of one of the victims, which
he had cut."[45] Manliness and gender roles are interlocking themes
throughout this novel.

Elizabeth Moss states in her study of women authors of this period that
life experiences "were critical to the formation of their intensely political
literary vision."[46] The themes of *The Free Flag of Cuba* are part and parcel
of Holcombe's cultural and political vision, and the novel certainly re-
flects her life and experiences. Lucy Petway Holcombe was born June 11,
1832, in LaGrange, Tennessee, into wealth and privilege, the second of
five children of Beverly Lafayette Holcombe and Eugenia Dorothea
Vaughn Hunt Holcombe. The family moved from Tennessee in the late
1840s after a loan signed by Lucy's father for a friend in LaGrange went

Whigs produced a temporary coalition between these traditional rivals," he explains. Tansey,
"Southern Expansionism," 238.

45. (New Orleans) *Louisiana Courier*, August 21 and September 1, 1851, quoted in
Tansey, "Southern Expansionism," 241, n. 42. Fear of spies also contributed to the rioting.
Supporters thought that the Spanish businessmen in New Orleans had informed the Spanish
government and would continue to do so against planned future expeditions. Tansey,
"Southern Expansionism," 229.

46. Moss, *Domestic Novelists in the Old South,* 8.

bad. With this need for a fresh start, the family moved to Marshall, Texas, not far from Louisiana, the setting of this novel. When the friend's finances recovered, he repaid Holcombe, who then built a new home in Marshall, a large brick house adorned with Greek Revival columns. In the exaggerated style typical of newspaper reporting of the time, a story on the Pickens family reported that in Texas Lucy "reigned as the most beautiful woman in the State" and added that "intellectually she had no superiors."[47]

Lucy's mother kept a diary between 1830 and 1866 with sporadic entries, not one of which mentions her daughter's literary efforts. One entry discusses education for women, a topic addressed in Lucy's novel. Mrs. Holcombe wrote on January 18, 1840, that she wished for her daughters to be "carefully educated" and "thoroughly informed" and that a "good education will make them independent."[48] Lucy and her sister Anna attended the local LaGrange Female Academy in Tennessee and then went to the Moravian Institute in Bethlehem, Pennsylvania. Holcombe's two female protagonists are friends from that school. Mrs. Holcombe wrote of a visit to the school and of how Mr. Holcombe was highly regarded by Lucy's schoolmates: "He is handsome and noble, princely in his gifts to the school girls and the servants. All admire 'the lordly southerner.'"[49]

Mrs. Holcombe took her daughters on various trips, including a visit to the Tennessee legislature.[50] One of the rumors regarding Lucy, the "Rose of Texas," was that as a guest of the family of Governor John Quitman of Mississippi, Lucy so captivated the state legislators that many left the assembly to accompany her on her journey home to Texas.[51] In the fall of 1850, Mrs. Holcombe and her daughters visited New Orleans. At this time sectional conflict was ascendant, as various measures known as the Compromise of 1850 were working their way through Congress.[52]

47. Bull, "Lucy Pickens: First Lady of the South Carolina Confederacy," 6; Columbia (South Carolina) *State,* January 31, 1910, 6.

48. Eugenia Dorothea Hunt-Holcombe, diary, January 18, 1840, Historical Museum Archives, Marshall, Texas, Harrison County. These diary entries are also found in Greer, "Leaves from a Family Album."

49. Hunt-Holcombe, diary, December 1, 1848.

50. Ibid., January 1850.

51. *Dallas Morning News,* May 19, 1929, 3.

52. For information on the Compromise of 1850, see James M. McPherson, *Battle Cry of Freedom: The Civil War Era* (New York: Oxford University Press, 1988), 70–77.

Narciso López and his men had just recently been indicted for a failed filibustering attempt against Cuba the previous May, and López was heartily cheered as a hero in New Orleans. Mrs. Holcombe's diary does not mention López.

Just as Lucy Holcombe uses her novel to extol education for women, she concurs with other ideas of her mother's. Her mother wrote about male character flaws and thought that women's role included suffering. These sentiments are echoed in the novel by Mrs. Clifton, Genevieve's mother. "Her woman's heart told her how rare a thing real happiness is to her sex," the narrator tells us of Mrs. Clifton. Holcombe and her mother were very close, a pattern between mothers and daughters found in families throughout the South, and Lucy's happiness as an adult was tied to a relationship with her mother, her "dearest and best friend," rather than with her husband. "Col. Pickens is only a husband, not a mother," she wrote to her sister. "As God is my judge no one steps into my heart before you or beside you—you are my first and dearest love," she wrote to her mother.[53]

Mrs. Holcombe worried in her diary about Anna's relationship with her fiancé, Elkanah Greer, "We all like him," she wrote. "He is so gentlemanly, respectful to me and is fond of Lucy who with her father admires him greatly. . . but I am so much afraid that she has formed too high an estimate of mans character and be disappointed, expecting more than poor frail mortals can accomplish."[54] Lucy, however, approved of her sister's choice. Greer had served in the Mexican War under Jefferson Davis and in the future was to become an active member of the Knights of the Golden Circle, a secret organization that supported filibustering in Mexico. In January 1860 Greer sent a letter to other leaders of the organization requesting immediate assistance before the government could interfere. "In Texas, there is organized already, two regiments of K's.G.C., who are ready to go forward in the good work," he wrote. "Had we the necessary means, the Texas regiments would move immediately, and take possession of the States of Tamaulipas, Nueva Leon, Coahuila, and Chi-

---

53. Lucy to Anna, undated, in Greer, "Leaves from a Family Album," 22; Lucy to Eugenia Dorothea Holcombe, July 22, 1858, FWP Papers, SCL. Orville Vernon Burton discusses such family relations in *In My Father's House*, 123–36.

54. Hunt-Holcombe, diary, October 1850; Greer, "Leaves from a Family Album," 49.

huahua, and of them organize a Government, thereby forming, or establishing a nucleus around which our valiant Knights would soon rally."[55]

No diary entry confirms that Lucy Holcombe was in love with and
fiancée to Lieutenant William Crittenden of Kentucky, but the written
family history asserts that Lucy wrote *The Free Flag of Cuba* in her grief
after Crittenden was captured and killed in Havana. In 1974 Jack Greer,
great-grandnephew of Lucy Holcombe Pickens, wrote, "While still quite
young she wrote a book, The Free Flag of Cuba, or the Martyrdom of
López, under the nom de plume of H. M. Hardeman [*sic*]." Greer declared that the story was "based on fact," but he was incorrect in ascribing
leadership of the expedition to General Quitman of Mississippi. Greer
attributes Lucy's motivation for writing the novel at least in part to her
love for Crittenden: "As it happened, in this expedition Lucy Holcombe's
fiancé, Lt. Crittenden, was killed. The book was written during the period
of her grief."[56] Historian John Edmunds concurs with Greer. "Earlier in
her life she had known love," he says, "but her beau, Lieutenant Crittenden, was executed after being captured in August 1851, while participat-
ing with General Narciso López in an expedition to Cuba."[57]

Three years later Lucy Holcombe met her future husband, Francis W.
Pickens, at White Sulphur Springs, Virginia. Lucy was almost twenty-six
years old when she married the fifty-three-year-old Pickens at the Holcombe home. Lucy's mother wrote on April 26, 1858, "My precious darling Lucy . . . is married and nearly broken my poor heart."[58] Pickens had
been widowed twice and had five living daughters; four daughters from
his first marriage were close to Lucy's age, and some of them did not like
their father's infatuation with the beautiful Lucy Holcombe. The youngest of the daughters, eleven-year-old Jennie from Pickens' second marriage, would live with Lucy and Francis. Reasons that have been suggested
for Holcombe's marrying Pickens include "her grief for Crittenden."[59] In

55. Greer, "Leaves from a Family Album," 34–35.

56. Ibid., 51.

57. Edmunds, *Francis W. Pickens,* 137–38. Marli Weiner asserts that Lucy "loved a Lieutenant Crittenden, an American captured and executed while part of an expedition in Cuba,
and wrote a romantic booklet advocating Cuban liberation, *The Free Flag of Cuba; or, the
Martyrdom of López* (1855), apparently with him in mind." *American National Biography,* 473.

58. Hunt-Holcombe, diary, April 26, 1858, 17; Greer, "Leaves from a Family Album," 28.

59. Bull, "Lucy Pickens," 8. James Henry Rice, Jr., suggests that Lucy married Pickens

letters to her mother, Lucy wrote that she married Pickens so that he would pay off her father's debts.[60] Edmunds writes that "Pickens had made tantalizing promises that were in line with her ambitious nature," and Holcombe's novel speculates about ambition in women. Edmunds also points out that, at the age of twenty-six, she was "fast entering the frightening age bracket of the spinster."[61] And Pickens was wealthy. In the U.S. Census of 1860, Pickens reported owning $45,000 worth of real estate in addition to a personal estate valued at $244,206 in Edgefield, South Carolina; he also owned plantations in Alabama and Mississippi and more than three hundred slaves.[62]

The newly married couple left the country one month later, as Pickens was appointed minister to Russia. After shopping in New York and meeting Queen Victoria in England and Napoleon III in France, they arrived at St. Petersburg July 6, 1858, and met Czar Alexander on July 18, 1858.[63] Their daughter and only child, Eugenia (named after Lucy's mother and brother, but referred to all her life as Douschka, a nickname given to her by her godmother, the Czarina), was born in the royal palace on March 14, 1859. Lucy loved her daughter, but before her daughter's birth, Lucy had written her sister about how much her heart was set on having a son: "No human being could imagine my sore disappointment in a girl."[64] Even so strong a personality as Lucy Holcombe Pickens adopted, or adapted to, the pervasive belief in male supremacy prevalent in the patriarchal South.

Lucy's letters from Russia show an abhorrence of Russian serfdom but

because she had used up all her romantic feelings with her engagement to Crittenden. *Glories of the Carolina Coast* (Columbia, S.C.: R. L. Bryan, 1936), 118. Friends in Marshall stated that she said she would never love another and that if she married it would be for position. Personal files of Mrs. Chas. A. Beehn, Holcombe Collection.

60. Lucy Pickens to Mrs. Beverly Holcombe, n.d., and December 2, 1859, Pickens-Dugas Papers, SHC.

61. Edmunds, *Francis W. Pickens*, 139.

62. Burton, *In My Father's House*, 48.

63. Edmunds, *Francis W. Pickens*, 140.

64. Lucy Pickens to Anna Greer, January 9, 1859, FWP Papers, SCL. Holcombe's brother's middle name was Eugene. "Douschka" was born eight months after Lucy's initial meeting with the Czar, so it is unlikely that Douschka was the Czar's daughter, as some have speculated. For more on southern patriarchy, see Burton, *In My Father's House*, especially 99–103, 135.

do not decry American slavery. The same pattern can be seen in her novel, which condemns Spanish tyranny against Cuban whites but fails to acknowledge the horrors of slavery in either Cuba or the United States. It seems Holcombe could accept oppression as long as it was racial.

The Pickenses left Russia in 1860 when Pickens received word that the Union was in crisis and that he might be the "moderate" South Carolina needed. Back in Columbia, Pickens was elected governor and presided over secession. An asset to Pickens, Lucy was adept at political maneuvering and enjoyed being the Governor's wife. When his term was up, the former governor and Mrs. Pickens moved to their Edgefield, South Carolina, home in December 1862. After Francis died in January 1869, Lucy continued her work on causes.[65] Just as Holcombe wrote *The Free Flag of Cuba* to memorialize the men who died on the expedition, some twenty years later she would help create other memorials. The Daughters of the American Revolution named their Washington, D.C., chapter the "Lucy Holcombe Chapter."[66] In 1866 she was appointed second Vice Regent of Mount Vernon Ladies' Association for the state of South Carolina, although she did not become active until ten years later. She founded the Maxcy Gregg Chapter of the United Daughters of the Confederacy and in her last years organized a fund drive to place a monument to the Confederate dead in Edgefield's town square. Her efforts to memorialize the Confederacy, like her efforts to memorialize the López expedition, show how Holcombe sought to influence a wider audience in perpetuating her image of the South. Lucy Holcombe Pickens died on August 8, 1899.[67]

When Holcombe finished writing *The Free Flag of Cuba* (the preface is dated September 19, 1854), she needed to find a publisher if she were to reach a wide audience. This proved difficult. Wanting the novel to stand on its own merits rather than upon her friendships, Holcombe used her pseudonym when writing friends about this work. In a January 1855 let-

65. Years later, an overstated newspaper account of the Pickens family reported that Lucy remained influential in politics. Columbia (South Carolina) *State*, January 31, 1910, 6 ff.

66. J. Walker Holcombe, "Lucy Holcombe Legacy Lives in Washington, D.C.," *Harrison County Historical Herald*, 7. Undated clipping from Holcombe Collection.

67. Southern domestic novelist Augusta Jane Evans, also worked on fund-raising for Confederate monuments. Moss, *Domestic Novelists in the Old South*, 219. Lucy Holcombe Pickens' obituary is in the Columbia *State*, August 9, 1899.

ter to John A. Quitman, she wrote as Henrietta M. Hardimann. "The publisher to whom I sent the manuscript gave a complimentary report of its literary character," she told him, "praising its style and grace, but refused to issue it for this reason. He said its principles were dangerous—its fillibustering tendency rendered it infamable, and he had conscientious scruples which prevented him from giving to the American public a work which contained such elements of agitation."[68]

When another friend of Holcombe's, Judge Henry Spofford, wrote to her from New Orleans on June 19, 1855, in response to her request for an evaluation, he seemed to agree with the publisher. Again, apparently she had not told him she was the author, but it seems he was wise to her ruse:

> I have read "The Free Flag of Cuba," and discovered that H. M. Hardimann is a woman. I think she is a blonde, of a delicate, ethereal beauty, who receives so much deserved praise herself, that she sometimes bestows praise upon others who don't quite deserve it.[69]
>
> I promised to give you my real opinion of the book, at a time when the suspicion never crossed my mind that it might be a task of some delicacy.

Spofford knew Holcombe's temperament well enough to worry that his criticism may cause her to "toss her head" and "stamp her foot." His critique includes an appreciation of her writing style, her "union of grace and vigor" and her clever use of dialect, but he did not approve of the subject matter. "The subject is unfortunate if you will give me leave to say so. The Cuban business is too recent and too real a thing for a work of fiction; the book is quite too imaginative for a history." He disliked her making heroes of the men who filibustered: "They had bravery in profusion; but mere bravery does not make a hero. . . . The men who followed López were, for the most part, of desperate or shattered fortunes. With many of them the hope of gain was stronger than the love of glory; and with most, the love of glory was as strong as any sympathy for

68. Henrietta M. Hardimann to John A. Quitman, January 1855, papers of John A. Quitman, Mississippi Department of Archives, Jackson, Mississippi.

69. Though Lucy's hair often appears darker in portraits, she was described at one time as having "titian hair said to resemble a woof of sunbeams spinning out like a flower at the ends"; no doubt Spofford teasingly refers to Holcombe as the "blonde" author of *The Free Flag of Cuba.*

oppressed Cubans."[70] Holcombe, however, saw glory in their bravery and wanted to use her eloquence to persuade her readers.

Lucy Holcombe's novel fits into the nationalistic spirit of the age, addressing issues of freedom and independence. But of course, this history is also a romance. Like Sir Walter Scott, Holcombe includes references to knights and chivalry, and the male protagonists leave home to perform heroic deeds and earn honor and fame.[71] The principal love story is between Genevieve Clifton, who opposes the filibuster, and the "master of her destiny," Ralph Dudley. Love also blooms for Eugene de France, Genevieve's friend and neighbor in Louisiana, who falls in love with Genevieve's best friend from school, the fire-eating Mabel Royal, a fervent advocate of manly honor; Mabel fans the flames that eventually consume her lover.[72] Her happiness would come only "When Cuba is free!" Using a common literary device among authors in the mid-1800s, Holcombe defines two of the main characters, one of each of these couples (Ralph and Mabel), as orphans. Orphans did not have parental obligations to circumscribe their actions, and an orphan had the initial automatic sympathy of the Victorian reader.

The male and female characters reflect the standards of the day for a wealthy young southern woman. Ladies getting dressed may keep a gentleman waiting, but not too long. After dinner, ladies exit the dining table to "seek the drawing-room," where they wait for the men to join them. Traits of a desirable man include wit and conversational ability. Were good looks essential in romances of the 1850s? Good looks are as important in Holcombe's story as they are in Harlequin Romances of today, but we might be surprised at what is crucial in these descriptions. Holcombe does not describe clothing. Neither is age important. Only two characters are noted for their height: Ralph Dudley is over six feet tall, and the evil Hidalgo is "small." Holcombe may describe hair, whether

70. Henry Spofford to Lucy Holcombe, June 19, 1855, Pickens Papers, Perkins Library, Duke University. Spofford was a judge in New Orleans.

71. One participant in the earlier López expedition in May 1850 wrote that he had engaged "in the most extraordinary piece of Knight-errantry on record—at least since the days of a certain *Spanish gentleman* dubbed *Don Quixote.*" O.D.D.O., "The History of the Late Expedition to Cuba" (New Orleans: Job Office of the *Daily Delta,* 1850), 1.

72. Eugene is probably named for Holcombe's mother and brother, just as her daughter would later be named for them.

curly or wavy and maybe its color. Eyes are important, as they reveal
character. Foreheads are important because of the racial implications in
the then-popular study of phrenology. And in describing the women protagonists, Holcombe stresses their whiteness.

Historians have dealt at length with the concept of the Southern Lady.
Image was of utmost the importance to antebellum southern belles. The
ideal southern lady was "gracious, fragile, and deferential to the men
upon whose protection she depended." The younger version, the ideal
Southern Belle, like Lucy Holcombe, was to be beautiful, flirtatious, and
wealthy, as well as deferential to men.[73] Genevieve Clifton is slight and
fragile, with a "willowy grace." She has dark curly hair, delicate features,
and a full and round forehead. The "extreme whiteness" of her skin (ex-
cept for "the rare beauty of the temple-veins") would be less appealing
today. Her eyes are dark blue. Her eyelids are almond-shaped and droopy
(as were Holcombe's), fringed with heavy black lashes. In temperament
she is calm, spiritual, timid, and clinging. Her expressions are gentle and
womanly. Genevieve's friend, Mabel Royal, has blue eyes, and her auburn
hair (the color of Lucy's) is neither curly nor straight but "lies in rippling
waves on a forehead so high, so white and broad." The beautiful Mabel
is more honest than coy in assessing her own attractiveness. "It would be
an affectation to say I thought myself ugly," she says. "Others, of fastidious taste, have decided the question of beauty in my favor. . . . Admiration is a pleasant thing after all, if we would only be candid about it."
Holcombe, whose beauty was legendary, must have approved of Mabel's
forthright manner. Mabel also declares that men are just as vain as
women about their looks.

73. Anne Firor Scott, *The Southern Lady: From Pedestal to Politics, 1830–1930* (Chicago:
University of Chicago Press, 1970); Elizabeth Fox-Genovese, *Within the Plantation Household: Black and White Women of the Old South* (Chapel Hill: University of North Carolina
Press, 1988), 109; Carol Bleser and Frederick Heath, "The Clays of Alabama: The Impact of
the Civil War on a Southern Marriage," in *In Joy and In Sorrow: Women, Family, and Marriage in the Victorian South,* ed. Carol Blesser (New York: Oxford University Press, 1991),
135. Despite the importance of physical appearance, the education of the Southern belle had
a lofty goal, "the development of the girl into a lady, healthy in person, refined in feeling,
pure in morals, & humble in religion." Christie Anne Farnham, *The Education of the Southern Belle: Higher Education and Student Socialization in the Antebellum South* (New York:
New York University Press, 1994), 120, 127–28. See also Catherine Clinton, *The Plantation
Mistress: Woman's World in the Old South* (New York: Pantheon Books, 1982).

The leading man, wealthy orphan Ralph Dudley, has a regal brow, dark brown hair, large hazel eyes, a Grecian nose, and a firm square chin. Eugene de France is "foreign-looking" with black eyes, full red lips, and heavy clustering curls. In Holcombe's time, an author might have included such a description to suggest some exotic African American heritage, but considering his close association with the white aristocracy, it seems unlikely that this was Holcombe's intention.[74]

Although not a protagonist, hero William Crittenden flirts with Mabel, presenting to her, as the most beautiful woman in the world, a rose named "Fillibuster." The love of Holcombe's life, Crittenden is "the noble Kentuckian," ideal in appearance, charm, and honor:

> The face thrown back, and thus exposed to view, must have been in early youth very beautiful; for the free careless grace of childhood still lingered on the bold brow of the man, though passion had pressed its pallor on his cheek. The lines around the mouth denoted thought, even care; and the smile of the lip, though sweet, was uncertain. It was a frank and generous face; one that is still fondly remembered by the many friends who mourn the undaunted hero's death. His large fearless eyes, with their half tender, half defiant charm, rested musingly, sometimes on the animated group before him, sometimes on a large carnation-hued rose, which he held in his hand.

Holcombe's novel clearly delineates white male and female domains, and the judgments of the narrator gauge what constitutes "femininity" and "masculinity." She addresses male and female roles on two distinct but interdependent levels. One level is the gendered roles that men and women play in the political arena; the other is romantic notions of how men and women relate to each other. The white females are thoroughly feminine, the males oh, so manly and honor bound. In manly fashion the men go off to war in Cuba; with feminine passivity the women miss them while awaiting at home. The African American Scipio also goes off to see action, but Holcombe does not see this as manliness, steeped as she is in the confounding link between racial and gender thinking.

According to literary scholar Richard Yarborough, at the time of this

---

74. See Joel Williamson, "How Black Was Rhett Butler?" in *The Evolution of Southern Culture*, ed. Numan V. Bartley (Athens: University of Georgia Press, 1988).

novel, masculinity, including physical attractiveness, was defined by the white culture exclusively "in white Western European terms." Yarborough lists nobility, intelligence, strength, articulateness, loyalty, virtue, rationality, courage, self-control, courtliness, and honesty as typical male virtues.[75] Holcombe's formulaic white male characters display many of these traits, in addition to their patriotism and masculine determination to uphold justice against all odds and against public opinion. Holcombe's slave men are also patriotic and willing to fight for what they believe, but her elite white world view does not credit them with being manly. According to this view, one of the defining characteristics of the white male is individualism, a man's freedom to use his own judgment, which by definition excluded enslaved men. The system of slavery demanded that "docility and abject obedience" take precedence over "manly independence and self-direction" in black males.[76] Yarborough finds that many nineteenth-century African American spokespersons responded to this indignity by frequently using the term "manly" to describe the worth and fitness of black males.

The novel depicts a distinctly white concept of masculinity, the ideal of the southern gentleman. Such a gentleman "had honor and integrity, indifference to money questions and business, a decorous concern for the amenities of life and a high sense of social responsibility."[77] Holcombe's white male protagonists are just so, and these are the very qualities that lead them to seek justice for Cuba in the novel. In short, Holcombe defines seeking justice for Cuba as the manly thing to do. Her pseudonym, H. M. Hardimann, is surely a play on "Hardy Man." At one point Ralph

75. Richard Yarborough, "Race, Violence, and Manhood: The Masculine Ideal in Frederick Douglass's 'The Heroic Slave,'" in Jones and Donaldson, *Haunted Bodies*, 161–62.

76. Bertram Wyatt-Brown, "The Mask of Obedience: Male Slave Psychology in the Old South," in Jones and Donaldson, *Haunted Bodies*, 24.

77. Sheldon Hackney, "The South as a Counterculture," *American Scholar* 42, no. 2 (Spring 1973): 24. According to Hackney, southerners believed that Yankees lacked these virtues. For more on masculinity, see Kristin L. Hoganson, *Fighting for American Manhood: How Gender Politics Provoked the Spanish-American and Philippine-American Wars* (New Haven: Yale University Press, 1998); Michael Kimmel, *Manhood in America: A Cultural History* (New York: Free Press, 1996); Gail Bederman, *Manliness and Civilization: A Cultural History of Gender and Race in the United States, 1880–1917* (Chicago: University of Chicago Press, 1996); E. Anthony Rotundo, *American Manhood: Transformations in Masculinity from the Revolution to the Modern Era* (New York: Basic Books, 1993).

Dudley laments, "My fate is a hard one, but I will bear it with at least a show of hardy manliness." The novel is an explicit endorsement of what is required of the true manly man. Her heroic male figures enter the fray on the side of a courageous defense of a just cause.

As Ralph Dudley plans his role in the expedition to Cuba, his fiancée, the ultrafeminine Genevieve Clifton, begs him to forgo the expedition. Dudley interprets her entreaties as an attempt to make him forsake his honor, potentially setting up a dichotomy of honor as a gender issue, with males for honor and justice and females against it. Dudley accuses her of trying "to cast a stigma on [his] honor as a man." Dudley's masculinity means that honor must not be thwarted, "least of all by a woman." As much as Genevieve tries to dissuade Ralph, she does concede privately that Ralph "would think it unmanly to yield principle to love."

Scholars believe that honor in the sense that Ralph uses the term was a white male concept in the 1850s. (A woman's "honor" referred specifically to sexual purity.)[78] Holcombe's heroes put masculine honor above other considerations of family and love. Yet Holcombe uses two female characters to illustrate how women should also uphold this concept of honor. One is the beloved protagonist, Mabel Royal, who supports man's quest for greatness and aligns herself on the side of Cuban independence. Mabel declares that she would despise a man if her love "stayed him from glory and honor." Mabel exemplifies for Holcombe an ideal woman who nevertheless has fervent opinions and a willingness to share them, thereby showing the reader that it is perfectly acceptable for a woman to be an advocate of honor and justice. The other is Oralize, an aristocratic Cuban woman. When offered her father's life in exchange for information, Oralize declines, affirming that her father would not want his life if it meant "his child's dishonor." For this she is beheaded on the spot in Captain-General Concha's office, where her blood seeps into the expensive carpet. (Concha has her head placed into a box to be delivered to her

78. See Bertram Wyatt-Brown, *Southern Honor: Ethics and Behavior in the Old South* (New York: Oxford University Press, 1982), especially 50–55 and 225 ff. See also Kenneth S. Greenberg, *Honor and Slavery* (Princeton: Princeton University Press, 1996); Dickson D. Bruce, *Violence and Culture in the Antebellum South* (Austin: University of Texas Press, 1979); Edward L. Ayers, *Vengeance and Justice: Crime and Punishment in the Nineteenth-Century American South* (New York: Oxford University Press, 1964); Burton *In My Father's House*, 90–95.

father in prison.) Oralize and Mabel, neither of whom are native southerners, show strong patriotic feelings. These two women, and not the
southern belle, Genevieve, put honor above selfish needs such as their
lives or the lives of fathers, husbands, or betrothed. These women play a
role in moving patriotism and honor from the male province into both
male and female arenas. The author herself would write to her father
from Charleston in 1861, "I am where duty and honor demand me, and
whatever dangers surround me, I will be with God's help true to my
name and blood."[79]

Honor is of little consequence to Genevieve Clifton, the earnest anti-
filibuster. Genevieve's opinions are well reasoned; she does not think the
rewards are worth the risks. When her friend Eugene enthusiastically
talks of the glory of the quest, she reminds him that "The glory is imaginary, the danger and disgrace real." When Ralph calls the expedition a
glorious dream of freedom and a waking to liberty, Genevieve points out
that he could awake in prison. When Ralph calls into question her patriotism, Genevieve reminds him that Cuba is not her country. "A patriot
loves his own country, and respects her laws," she asserts. Ralph dismisses
her out of hand, calling her arguments laughable and her sentiments "ungenerous." The more she pierces his illusions, the more angry Ralph be-
comes. He has no respect for the conviction of her conscience. The
narrator also dismisses Genevieve's arguments, intruding into the story
to offer this excuse for Genevieve's lack of honor: "She was a woman, and
this expedition was bringing danger to her lover." Genevieve's arguments
are coherent and convincing, but they do not convince Dudley, and the
narrator is sure that they will not convince the reader. Holcombe was
clearly on the side of the filibusters, but the arguments presented by Genevieve may have been thoughts that she herself struggled with. Nevertheless, her arguments do not prevail. Neither do tears and begging.
Masculinity has to be stronger than that.

As the fictional male protagonists pursue honor and glory in the expedition to Cuba, they often refer to "fame" as worth striving for. Fame is
patriotic and hallowed. In the context of this novel, fame is the goal of a
manly man. Ralph Dudley and Eugene de France seek fame in Cuba;

---

79. Lucy Pickens to Beverly Lafayette Holcombe, January 1, 1861, Pickens-Dugas Papers, SHC.

Mabel Royal declares that her lover must seek fame. Holcombe's view of fame implies more than noble triumph in a just cause. Fame means the glory of remembrance, having descendants who will continue to bestow honor into the future. In the antebellum South, fame or glory on the battlefield was a clear path to elite status in society. White males also felt a need to prove to themselves that they deserved their high place in the social strata; triumph in battle, or fame, prove their worthiness.[80] Women, however, did not seek fame for themselves. New York author Susan Warner (*The Wide, Wide World*, 1851) recorded in her journal, August 2, 1851, "Nay, fame never was a woman's Paradise, yet." At another time Warner wrote to a friend, "Mere personal fame seems to me a very empty thing to work for." As Kelley points out, when women writers did achieve fame, they were often "uncomfortable in the world beyond the home. At best they felt ambivalent, at worst that they simply did not belong there."[81]

Women's social status was not contingent on fame but dependent on their fathers and husbands. The fame heralded in this novel comes from zealous citizenship as defined by service in action, which excludes women. But the female good citizen, the patriotic woman, such as Mabel, will support her man's role in life, even sending her lover or son off to war. The mother and sisters of Eugene de France are not examples of the good female citizens; they beg Eugene as the only male member of the family to stay home. He listens to feminine persuasion and stays behind, and he is thoroughly ashamed that he allowed family obligations to supersede his duties as a man. He had yielded to feminine tears, and the women seemed to hold the power in the family. But given another opportunity to join, Eugene does so. Women may urge, but men must resist the entreaty if it goes against manly judgment of duty and honor. Portraying these women as interfering with their men's mission in life, Holcombe shows that a woman should use her influence to uphold patriotic fervor and help men fulfill duty bravely.

Fox-Genovese has found that "nineteenth-century American literature

---

80. For a discussion of the role of the military as an entry for white males into the elite, see Burton, *In My Father's House*, 95–99.

81. Kelley, *Private Woman, Public Stage*, 28–29. Nina Baym, *Woman's Fiction*, Chapter 6, discusses Susan Warner in depth.

severely limited the ambitions that women could attribute to themselves or even fictional characters." To the contrary, Moss finds that southern women writers show "an alternative standard for feminine behavior" and that upper-class women in their novels can "participate in contemporary political discourse while remaining within the bounds of accepted feminine behavior."[82] Stephanie McCurry, in her discussion of gender in pro-slavery discourse, allowed that, although there was some room within their boundaries, for instance that women were intelligent and that they were responsible for "upholding southern civilization," for the most part "there was also a clear and common sense of what constituted women's proper 'sphere,' or, at least, what constituted a transgression of it."[83] Although Holcombe's female characters fall into a standard gendered formula, within these prescribed roles Holcombe presents charming, beautiful women interested in political debate. Her development of Mabel Royal explores a wider range of acceptable feminine behavior, thus expanding the picture of the ideal lady, or the cult of true womanhood, into one that Holcombe could accept.[84] One of the points Holcombe addresses is whether an interest in politics meant that a woman was not feminine. Both Genevieve and Mabel are well read and interested in politics. Genevieve worries, "Are you not afraid of being called strong-minded?" But Holcombe defends political reading matter.[85] Holcombe herself wanted to play a role in policy decisions. At the same time, she was demure in defending her manuscript against a critique by a publisher; she wrote that he gave too much credit "to a romance which has only the power of a woman's pen." In her letter to Quitman, she wrote

82. Elizabeth Fox-Genovese, "Days of Judgment, Days of Wrath: The Civil War and the Religious Imagination of Women Writers," in *Religion and the American Civil War*, ed. Randall M. Miller, Harry S. Stout, Charles Reagan Wilson (New York: Oxford University Press, 1998), 238; Moss, *Domestic Novelists in the Old South,* 18.

83. Stephanie McCurry, *Masters of Small Worlds: Yeoman Households, Gender Relations, and the Political Culture of the Antebellum South Carolina Low Country* (New York: Oxford University Press, 1995), 215.

84. Barbara Welter, "The Cult of True Womanhood, 1820–1860," *American Quarterly* 18, no. 2 (Summer 1966), 151–74.

85. On women and the political press in the antebellum period, see Ronald Zboray and Mary S. Zboray, "Whig Women, Politics, and Culture in the Campaign of 1840," *Journal of the Early Republic* 17 (Summer 1997): 277–315, and their "Political News and Female Readership," *Journalism History* 22 (1996): 2–14. Both articles focus on New England.

that women were "morally superior," but only as equal intellectually as men allow.[86] Her novel, however, clearly shows women as equal intellectually to the men. Knitting together her high regard for female intellect, feminine influence, republican ideology, and political romanticism, Holcombe affirms that a woman has the same right to an opinion as a man does without upsetting the natural order of male supremacy.

Various discussions among the characters revolve around the patriarchal view of male superiority. Discussions on ambition, education, and the ideal mate endorse a wholehearted acceptance of male superiority. When questioned about being ambitious, Mabel denies the accusation, saying she prefers a humbler course of action. Even though she has a restless spirit and longs for adventure, she declares that she prefers assisting her man in his true duties rather than taking them on herself. Elizabeth Varon has found that southern women with strong political feelings and "a desire to be heard" were obliged to reconcile these feelings with "a commitment to the traditional gender order, in which women deferred to the leadership of men."[87]

An arena where a woman could excel is education. Genevieve believes that men dislike learned women, which Mabel emphatically denies. The two characters had met at school, and the narrator intrudes to disabuse readers of the notion that women cannot be friends, saying such friendship is often, but mistakenly, a subject of ridicule.[88] The two women have a lengthy discussion of education and the relationship between science and art. A gendered assumption underlies Mabel's love of beauty over science and her acceptance of a woman's power to influence society without being an active participant. Sounding very much like Lucy Holcombe Pickens, Mabel describes how a woman should use education to "exert on society a great and good influence. Woman has great power, if she would realize and accept it." Her power, of course, was one of influence not action.[89]

86. Henrietta H. Hardimann to John A. Quitman, January 1855. Quitman Papers.

87. Varon, *We Mean to Be Counted,* 9.

88. The idea that women could not form real and deep friendships is a theme in other literature also. See Caroll Smith-Rosenberg, "The Female World of Love and Ritual: Relations between Women in Nineteenth-Century America," *Signs* 1 (Autumn 1975), 1–29.

89. See, for example, Kathryn Kish Sklar, *Catharine Beecher: A Study in American Domesticity* (New Haven: Yale University Press, 1973).

If a woman is exceptional, all the more necessary is an exceptional husband. Genevieve worries over Mabel's love for Eugene because it is obvious that he has less strength of character, less passion, and less intellect than Mabel. Freethinking Mabel concurs with the conservative Genevieve that a woman's mate should be superior. Mabel admits that Eugene is less than her ideal love, who should be able to "awe [her] by his superiority."

The concept of femininity in the novel allows women to have spirituality and to pursue pastimes such as music, singing, and needlework, although Mabel rebels against the latter. Femininity implies small stature, which suggests powerlessness and the need to be protected.[90] Before meeting Mabel, Eugene jokes about the large size of Yankee women and the awkwardness a man would feel in loving a woman who was as big as a man. But as Mabel is small, Holcombe debunks the notion that Yankee women are not as womanly or feminine as Southern women.

One of the attributes ascribed to women in this novel, important to the definition of femininity, is their childlike innocence (until they become mothers). Women cry with childish anger or lay their head upon an arm like a child. Tears were an important symbol of the childlike nature of women, and women in this novel do cry and sob passionately and unrestrainedly. When Mabel's sorrow is so great that she is unable to shed tears, Mrs. Clifton encourages her to do so. Every woman in the book cries, as does almost every slave, male and female. And what is the white man's reaction to womanly tears? Silence, uncertainty, guilt. Upon López's death, several men "turned away to hide the honest tear that fell." The gallant López cries over the complete fiasco of his mission only in the depths of his being, "such tears as come not to the eyes, but lie hot and burning around an aching heart."[91]

If tears indicate a childlike innocence, so does blushing. Blushing is considered a feminine reaction for white women, and Mabel and Genevieve blush often. Mildness and amiability are womanly virtues, and the novel includes a philosophic discussion of whether it is better to be amia-

90. See Patricia Yaeger, "Beyond the Hummingbird: Southern Women Writers and the Southern Gargantua," in Jones and Donaldson, *Haunted Bodies*, 291.

91. On manly emotions, see Jan Ellen Lewis, *The Pursuit of Happiness: Family and Values in Jefferson's Virginia* (New York: Cambridge University Press, 1983).

ble by nature or through self-control. The amiable and mild Genevieve disagrees with the exuberant Mabel over this issue, proclaiming that resisting temptation to temper is a much higher level of achievement than not feeling temper at all.

Another gender role assigned to women is a capacity to endure suffering. Like Holcombe and her own mother, the wise Mrs. Clifton feels that happiness is rare for women. Genevieve also feels that suffering is the lot of women, and even Mabel thinks that suffering has a purpose in making women more "earnest." Suffering goes along with the image of motherhood. A strong stereotype of the 1850s was the Victorian image of "Mother," and this novel buys wholeheartedly into that image.[92] Genevieve's mother is the wise teacher, faithful guardian, and loving encourager. The narrator tells us that the devotion Mrs. Clifton feels for her daughter can be understood only by mothers. The orphan Mabel says, "If I had ever known a mother, who would have guided and controlled me by her love, I am sure I would have been so much better and happier." Mothers had the job of imparting to their sons the culture's patriarchal ideals. The narrator asserts, "It is conceded that early education has much to do with a man's future course. Then the mother, though she cannot herself struggle in active life, yet in the mind of her son she can lay the foundation of that strength which may, in after years, hold the storm of strife obedient to his will. The mother may implant in her boy that love for right and truth which will fill the man with lofty aspirations for good." In this light we can understand why Lucy Pickens would later be distressed at not having a son.

It was generally assumed in the nineteenth century that women would find "the realization of their hopes and dreams in marriage and domesticity."[93] This is certainly the expectation for the female protagonists of Holcombe's novel. The men had other occupations after soldiering; they were planters. Women were helpful but not essential to them in that role. For all the claims that a man needs the love of a woman to encourage his better self, to mold him into a better man, the characters of the story

92. Anne C. Rose, *Victorian America and the Civil War* (New York: Cambridge University Press, 1992); Carroll Smith-Rosenberg, *Disorderly Conduct: Visions of Gender in Victorian America* (New York: Oxford University Press, 1985); Burton, *In My Father's House*, 123–24, 142–44.

93. Elizabeth Fox-Genovese, "Days of Judgment," 232.

reinforce the idea that a man needs more than a woman to make his life complete. Genevieve is disappointed that she does not fulfill her loved one's need for adventure; Mabel is delighted in a man whose heart yearns for something more in life. The two friends disagree over the purpose of love. Genevieve feels that true love would keep a man at home. Mabel answers that her love is stronger and less selfish, more "womanly" by the standards of the day.

The Free Flag of Cuba is a story of love between white males and females, but it also shows the love between male slaves and their white masters and the fraternity between white men. Other scholars have found this sort of devotion in literary works to be homoerotic.[94] Although the love between the male and female characters is a major aspect of the novel, the protagonist Ralph Dudley is clearly more devoted to Narciso López than to Genevieve. He leaves Genevieve for long periods of time and is willing, almost eager, to die for López. She, on the other hand, loses her will to live when she thinks he is not returning safely from Cuba. She is literally on her deathbed when Ralph returns. Mabel, whose love, Eugene, does die in Cuba, is not left a single woman. Holcombe herself may have wanted to die after Crittenden's death, but she forged for herself a marriage and a new life.

As one might expect of the future "Queen of the Confederacy," Holcombe held the wealthy white view of slavery as a positive good. Her white protagonists would have found it hard to believe that a decade later some slaves would join the Union army and fight against their former masters or that slaves on the home front would sabotage Confederate efforts or inform Union forces about troop location and supplies. Holcombe may well have modeled her loyal slaves on the image of her own Lucindy, her long-time personal slave. Holcombe's descendants would also remember a faithful slave in their family history, where a page and a portrait are devoted to "Uncle Ned Hood and Wife (Holcombe slaves)." They wrote that Uncle Ned worked for them "until he was 100 years old."

94. Caroline Gebhard, "Reconstructing Southern Manhood: Race, Sentimentality, and Camp in the Plantation Myth" in Jones and Donaldson, *Haunted Bodies*, 133; Dana D. Nelson, *National Manhood: Capitalist Citizenship and the Imagined Fraternity of White Men* (Durham: Duke University Press, 1998).

Lucy's father purchased Ned Hood in Tennessee, and Hood, who worked as a butler, accompanied them to Texas. Lucy seems to have been fond of the Holcombe slaves and in her letters asked that her love be passed on to them, "especially Aunt Vivey and Uncle Neelus and Bee and Caroline."[95]

Although the enslaved people in Lucy Holcombe's real life had families of their own, her novel tells us absolutely nothing about African American families. Marmion, Scipio, and Emily, the three slave characters, have no families; all their emotional ties are with the white families and with each other. Emily's "greatest pride and delight" was not in offspring of her own but in Genevieve's hair, the opportunity "to twine the long shining curls over her dusky fingers." This is typical of women authors at this time, who, according to literary scholar Minrose C. Gwin, did not see African Americans "as individuals with selves commensurate to their own."[96] Holcombe is also less forthcoming in her physical descriptions of the slave characters. Marmion is old with white hair. Scipio is always the "negro boy"; it is not immediately apparent that this "boy" is actually a man about the same age as Ralph Dudley. Emily's physical description states only that she is a mulatto. By including a person of mixed heritage, Holcombe is, probably inadvertently, acknowledging interracial sex. Susan Tracy has noted that southern literature was "noticeably silent about planter sexuality," and especially so about miscegenation.[97] Holcombe shortchanges the physical descriptions of the

95. Greer, "Leaves from a Family Album," 13–14; Douschka Pickens (by Lucy Holcombe Pickens) to Theodore Holcombe, November 30, 1859, FWP Papers, SCL. Contrary to this example, Steven Stowe finds that the white elite seldom mentioned black people in their correspondence. Stowe, *Intimacy and Power*, xvi.

96. Minrose C. Gwin, *Black and White Women of the Old South: The Peculiar Sisterhood in American Literature* (Knoxville: University of Tennessee Press, 1985), 5.

97. Susan J. Tracy, *In the Master's Eye: Representations of Women, Blacks, and Poor Whites in Antebellum Southern Literature* (Amherst: University of Massachusetts Press, 1995), 18, 72. Tracy also points out that William Wells Brown, the first African American novelist, centered *Clotel: or, The President's Daughter* on concubinage and miscegenation on the plantation (143). Miscegenation was a common aspect of slavery. See Burton *In My Father's House*, 185–89; Clinton, *The Plantation Mistress*, 90–92, 187–88, 223–31; Jacqueline Jones, *Labor of Love, Labor of Sorrow* (New York: Basic Books, 1985), 11–43; Deborah Gray White, *Ar'n't I a Woman? Female Slaves in the Plantation South* (New York: Norton, 1985; reprint,1987), 27–61, 68–78, 146–48, 152; Elizabeth Fox-Genovese, *Within the Plantation Household*, 271, 294–99.

slaves because her cultural assumption is that they do not really matter as individuals.

This novel, like many southern plantation novels and domestic fiction, involves a defense of the slave system.[98] In her description of the slave quarters, Holcombe writes, "Ah! how I wish some honest, but misjudging north-born friends we have, could or would take the trouble to see the many neat and comfortable settlements on the beautiful plantations of the south. . . . There the clean whitewashed cabins, with their red chimneys, the clinging vines, the flourishing truck patch, were so cheerful, you could hardly connect cruelty or oppression with those who called it home." On one level, Holcombe was simply portraying the life she lived without giving much analysis to the injustice of the system. On another level, Holcombe was reacting to a national bestseller criticizing slavery, *Uncle Tom's Cabin*. Published serially in 1851–52, this deeply moving novel became a powerful weapon in the propaganda war against slavery. Wanting to neutralize the antislavery feelings Stowe stirred up, many southern writers, including Lucy Holcombe, answered with proslavery pieces. Caroline Lee Hentz's *The Planter's Northern Bride* is perhaps the best-known example. Although Holcombe is explicit that her motivation in writing the book is to vindicate López and the expedition, the images the novel also presents of loving kindness between master and slave are undoubtedly a response to *Uncle Tom's Cabin*. There is no auction block here, no Simon Legree, no Eliza intent on escape. Whereas Stowe's book is full of chains, handcuffs, and threats of whippings, Holcombe's novel portrays no violent control over slave behavior. Furthermore, her slave characters are all house slaves. As Scipio declares, "I knows quality; I not raised at de quarter." In Holcombe's world the field hands who lived in the slave quarters were different from the slaves in the Big House, who were considered part of the planter family.[99] Throughout the novel, the slaves show nothing but undying affection, concern, friendship, and love for their masters. Historians have pulverized this antebellum white myth.[100]

98. Southern domestic novelists "developed a compelling, if not altogether convincing, defense of slavery in terms of southern culture that reflected their perceptions of southern society and women's place within it." Moss, *Domestic Novelists in the Old South*, 10.

99. Eugene D. Genovese, "'Our Family, White and Black': Family and Household in the Southern Slaveholders' World View," in Bleser, *In Joy and In Sorrow*, 69–87.

100. The literature on slavery is huge. For example, see Burton, *In My Father's House;*

Literary critics also have used the southern texts themselves to punc-
ture the plantation ideal. Scott Romine writes of how critics have been
obliged to handle the plantation myth ever since the publication of William Taylor's *Cavalier and Yankee* in 1961. Among other issues covered
in his analysis of society and culture, North and South, Taylor explored
the literary icons of the aristocratic "cavalier" and the commoner yeoman
in John Pendleton Kennedy's *Horse-Shoe Robinson*. Surprising to the audience of that day, the yeoman, and not the gentleman planter, is actually
the effective figure in the story; it is the yeoman whose virtuosity and
resourcefulness carries the day. Romine applies this trope to African
American characters in some of the plantation novels of the day, "a figure
of resistance virtually absent from proslavery rhetoric." Slave characters
could exert "a tenacious pressure against the narratives that presumed to
contain him."[101] Holcombe's slave characters absolutely exert that pressure. Holcombe's racist stereotypes do not rob the slave characters of
their intelligence, pragmatism, wit, and ingenuity. The slaves in the story
actually have more depth than the whites, and the approach that Scipio
brings to problem-solving saves the life of Ralph Dudley on more than
one occasion. The quick-witted Scipio, separated in the fighting in Cuba
and unable to speak Spanish, has the wherewithal to feign dumbness and
thus travels around Cuba unsuspected. He proceeds to find the critically
wounded Dudley just as the villain is about to murder him. Scipio saves

---

Herbert G. Gutman, *The Black Family in Slavery and Freedom, 1750–1925* (New York: Pantheon, 1976); Eugene D. Genovese, *Roll, Jordan, Roll: The World the Slaves Made* (New York:
Pantheon, 1974); John W. Blassingame, *The Slave Community* (New York: Oxford University
Press, 1972); Charles Joyner, *Down By the Riverside: A South Carolina Slave Community* (Urbana: University of Illinois Press, 1984); Peter Kolchin, *American Slavery: 1619–1877* (New
York: Hill & Wang, 1994). Although now a little dated, the best historiographical studies of
slavery are Peter J. Parish, *Slavery: History and Historians* (New York: Harper & Row, 1989),
and Charles B. Dew, "The Slavery Experience," in *Interpreting Southern History: Historiographical Essays in Honor of Sanford W. Higginbotham*, ed. John B. Boles and Evelyn Thomas
Nolen (Baton Rouge: Louisiana State University Press, 1987) 120–61. The standard textbook
on African American history is John Hope Franklin and Alfred A. Moss, *From Slavery to
Freedom: A History of Negro Americans*, 8th ed. (New York: Knopf, 2000).

101. Scott Romine, *The Narrative Forms of Southern Community* (Baton Rouge: Louisi-
ana State University Press, 1999), 66–67; William R. Taylor, *Cavalier and Yankee: The Old
South and American National Character* (New York: George Braziller, 1961; reprint, New
York: Harper & Row, 1969), 193–99. John Pendleton Kennedy, *Horse-Shoe Robinson*, ed.
Ernest E. Leisy (1835; reprint, New York: American Book Co. 1937).

Dudley's life by sneaking up and killing the villain from behind. Dudley's white male code of honor would not have allowed killing someone from behind. Dudley's honor would also have prevented Scipio's next move: knowing they would need money to make their escape from Cuba, Scipio takes the man's money. "Marse Ralph . . . He'd starve an' die 'fore he'd tech dis money, but Scip ain't got no turn fur honer," he reasons. Honor does not allow for such practicality even in dire jeopardy, but Scipio provides the lifesaving remedy. When Ralph later accuses him of theft, Scipio replies that he had never robbed a living person, to which the narrator adds, "which, as far as we know, was true."

The story told today would present a worldview in stark contrast to Holcombe's. A modern movie might portray the brave protagonist Ralph Dudley as a pompous caricature of a hero, a "Dudley Do-Right" who needs to be rescued by his helper, Scipio, played by an African American comic who is actually the smarter character and ultimately the real hero. The standard role of the trusted sidekick is often that of a servant, as Sancho Panza is to Don Quixote, but not of a slave. Most southern authors at this time presented slave characters as "ignorant, improvident, lazy, and playful."[102]

Holcombe depends upon stereotypes to describe the slave characters. Critics today disparage the use of stereotypes, but nineteenth-century readers appreciated them. Stereotypes were popular and allowed authors to present cultural information quickly and easily; they were "the telegraphic expression of complex clusters of value."[103] Holcombe's Emily behaves like a Mammy stereotype, always fretting over her white charge. Scipio provides the comic relief in this melodrama, and the white audience within the novel enjoys laughing at his mischief. Holcombe uses written dialect for the slave characters, but never for the southern drawl of the white characters. The reader is also supposed to find humor in Scipio's mutterings and grumbling and his use of malapropisms, such as when he says, "Not my place to revulge; I feels honerated to say dis much, business of 'portance from the President." *Uncle Tom* uses the same stereotypes and humor, but Stowe adds a level of subtlety that Holcombe lacks. Stowe's readers are aware that the slave trickster's antics serve a practical purpose, such as delaying the wicked slave trader.

102. Tracy, *In the Master's Eye*, 152.
103. Tompkins, *Sensational Designs*, xvi.

Holcombe plays up incident after incident of treacly slave devotion to whites. Emily, passionately devoted to Genevieve, sobs distressingly when Genevieve mourns the fate of the filibustering expedition. Scipio speaks on several occasions of dying if anything should happen to his beloved Ralph. He says, for example, "Ef Marse Ralph die, de game is up wid dis chile, sure, 'cause dare ain't no place in dis worl' gwine to hold poor Scip den; he gwine to foller arter Marse Ralph, 'fore God he is." Maybe feelings of devotion are common for a kind owner, but Scipio also feels "half love, half duty" for Ralph's friend, Eugene de France, even though, the narrator tells us, "Eugene was not his master—a tie that cannot be appreciated by one unaccustomed to slavery." In Cuba Scipio recognizes the dead Eugene among the prisoners and somehow, ably, obtains his body. How he manages to do that Holcombe does not "revulge."

Holcombe characterizes slaves as honest and trustworthy, with integrity above reproach. Her Marmion is an equivalent of Stowe's Uncle Tom. In modern popular culture "Uncle Tom" has come to mean an accommodationist, servile slave, but Stowe's Tom is a strong character with immense dignity, obedient only up to the point of his own personal integrity. Both Stowe's Tom and Holcombe's Marmion are faithful and wise in matters financial as well as personal. No slave in the novel is untrustworthy, but Marmion has financial acumen as well as integrity. Ralph Dudley entrusts the elderly Marmion with all his finances and with overseeing the plantation while he is away.

To make the point that slaves prefer slavery, Holcombe sets up scenes where slaves refuse freedom. When Ralph offers Marmion freedom as a reward for long faithful service, the venerable old man is passionate in his response: "Don't 'sult dis grey head in yo' own dead father's house!" Loyalty takes precedence over freedom for Scipio also. Scipio, with many opportunities for easy escape, thinks only of how he might help Ralph survive the ordeal in Cuba. Scipio also makes the point later in the novel when he follows Ralph on a boat trip to California, "When I git to Calforny I free is you; den you see which sticks closes to you, white folk ur Scipio."[104]

104. Actually, the fugitive slave law of 1850 allowed owners to go after slaves even if they were in free territories. The question ultimately went to the Supreme Court, where Chief Justice Roger Taney ruled in the Dred Scott decision of 1857 that Congress had no right to exclude slavery from any territory, North or South.

Near the end of the novel, Ralph Dudley travels to California to seek another fortune because of his debts. Debt, a constant problem in the agrarian South, where cotton prices fluctuated precipitously, could create an exigency for selling slaves, a major theme in *Uncle Tom's Cabin*.[105] Given that one of her purposes is to show slavery in a good light, it is surprising that Holcombe also brings up debt and the possibility of selling slaves. Holcombe's father had several bouts with debt problems, and she wanted to show that even if people think selling slaves is necessary, another way can always be found. With debts he could not repay after the failed filibuster, the headstrong Ralph thinks he has no other recourse than to sell the family home, including his slaves. His slave Marmion persuades him to reconsider. Just as a good woman could influence a man for the better, so could a virtuous slave. Holcombe does not grasp the despair inherent in even the possibility of being sold. She sees only the loss of honor for the Dudley family, an argument effectively presented by Marmion. We see Marmion as wise enough to plead his case, not from a slave point of view, but from the white perspective most likely to affect Dudley. Holcombe, however, seems entirely blind to the idea that slaves had a point of view apart from whites. Holcombe also refuses to treat the debt situation realistically. Instead, with details outside the domain of this novel, Dudley strikes it rich in California, presumably in the gold rush. Like other American authors, Holcombe uses the West—the frontier—as the quintessential opportunity for personal and financial fulfillment. Dudley returns from California to save his ancestral home and slaves and marry the lovely Genevieve.[106]

Holcombe portrays slaves as similar to female characters in their childlike emotions and tendency to put more importance on human relationships than politics. Like women, slaves are able to cry, Scipio "with piteous lamentations." She gives her slave characters intuitive natures. In sync with feminine intuition, slaves see the true nature of things. This intuition gives them a certain perspicacity regarding "the bad guys." Holcombe's upper-class white males, being honorable men—trustworthy

105. See also Burton, *In My Father's House,* 162, 174–80, 189.
106. By 1853 the gold yield in California may have been as high as $65,000,000. The people who struck it rich, however, were mostly tradesmen who provided services to the prospectors.

and therefore trusting—lack such discernment. Holcombe's slaves, on
the other hand, though also trustworthy, are able to recognize who is a
traitor ("Can't fool Scip. . . . He ain't fit company fur a decent colored
boy, no how") and who is honest and reliable ("He is a gentleman every
inch, an' will do to trus'; wish I could say de same of all your frens").

Trust was essential in the Cuban expedition because secrecy was an
important aspect of the invasion. Therefore readers must be assured that
they can trust López as well. Holcombe leaves that indispensable judgment to Scipio to impart: "Ung Marmion may talk 'bout Ginel Washinton and 'Fayette, I don't know 'bout dem, 'cause I nuver recollects um,
but I'se 'pletely satisfied no braver man ever bin born dan dat same Cuby
gineral whut you bin trying so hard to die fur." To affirm the good purpose of the expedition, Scipio opines, "We nuver ment a bit uf harm;
we come fur good, to try and make 'spectable 'mericans of dese people,
like us."

Holcombe's novel shows some complexity regarding free blacks.
Scipio remarks that Boston is "a mighty bad free-nigger country" (only
slaves use this racial epithet in the novel), and he is concerned about California having a mix of free blacks and whites. Yet the free José is very
helpful to Scipio in Cuba. José, a fisherman whom Scipio happened to
have known in New Orleans, offers a safe haven for Scipio in Cuba. According to Scipio, "He's a good-hearted feller fur a free nigger, an' he'll
be mighty apt to 'trive a way to git us safe dare."

"Dare" (there) was home, the plantations in Louisiana, where the
women were waiting in agony to hear about the expedition. Home was
the United States, where the majority of the people were uncaring about
the expedition at best, an attitude that Holcombe aspired to modify.

For all her posturing, Lucy Holcombe could not change the outcome
of the expedition. But given this genre of historical romance, her novel
must have a happy ending. We see the happy marriage of Genevieve and
Ralph, a rapprochement of anti- and pro-filibustering characters. We see
the happy marriage of Mabel with Captain Stuart Raymond, a wedding of
North and South. But we see no reconciliation regarding Cuba. Holcombe
describes the coffin of López, where "The flag of the American republic,
and the free flag of Cuba, were shrouded and crossed above the chieftain's
head." This scene foreshadows a photograph staged during the Spanish-
American War, a tableau featuring Union and Confederate veterans shak-

ing hands in front of a blonde, curly-haired little girl with a crown reading
"Cuba," her wrists adorned with chains broken asunder. Behind the scene
is the Cuban flag in the middle of two draped American flags: A reconciled
North and South freeing "Little Cuba."[107] Holcombe's novel suggests this
late nineteenth-century phenomenon when north and south will choose
war with Spain and white reconciliation in the United States over racial
justice. In the 1850s the United States was not prepared to acquire Cuba
through invasion, and Cubans were not ready to accept López and his
wealthy white cabal as liberators. During the 1870s and certainly by 1895,
the movement against Spain was led by native Cubans such as José Martí
and focused on independence rather than annexation. Also, for the first
time, the movement reflected the racial composition of Cuban society.[108]

Holcombe wrote *The Free Flag of Cuba* in 1854 as a celebration of filibustering and the southern way of life, but her cause célèbre had been in
reality a failure. Her real-life heroes Crittenden and López were dead, and
Cuban independence would have to wait. Yet like many white southerners,
Holcombe felt a great need for myth and clearly believed that the story she
told was a heroic one. But we as readers note the contradictions. Holcombe
wanted to show the expedition as an honorable endeavor for freedom; we
see it as an illegal invasion for personal and political gain. Although most of
the filibusters were mercenaries out for their own glory and pocketbooks,
Holcombe portrayed them as heroes. She saw its failure as the work of a
traitor; we see it fail because of poor organization and timing. Holcombe
presented her male characters as superior to women, but we see her female
characters as more dynamic and intelligent. She portrayed noble white men
of honor, but we see their stupidity and vanity. Holcombe created aristo-

107. The tableau described is by Capt. Fritz Guerin. It is featured (courtesy of the Library of Congress) on the jacket of Nina Silber, *The Romance of Reunion: Northerners and
the South, 1865–1900* (Chapel Hill: University of North Carolina Press, 1993).

108. Cuba won freedom from Spain in the Treaty of Paris in 1898 after the Spanish-
American War, during which former Confederates fought alongside Union soldiers in Cuba.
The Treaty of Paris included the Platt Amendment, which granted the U.S. special privileges
in Cuba. That amendment, subsequent interventions by the U.S. in Cuban affairs, and
Cuban communism have kept the relationship between the United States and Cuba a trou-
bled one. Gerald Eugene Poyo, "Cuban Émigré Communities in the United States and the
Independence of Their Homeland, 1852–1895" (Ph.D. diss., University of Florida, 1983).
See also the work of Louis A. Pérez, Jr., especially *The War of 1898: The United States and
Cuba in History and Historiography* (Chapel Hill : University of North Carolina Press, 1998).

cratic fictional characters in the tradition of the cult of chivalry, extolling southern males as men of honor, generous, loving, gentle, and noble, but we cannot help noticing that the male planter aristocrats, weak and ineffectual, are less than admirable figures. In contrast is the ingenuity and intelligence of Scipio, who is insightful into character and able against incredible odds to rescue his white master, and of Marmion, who has a better grasp of financial responsibilities and plantation management than does the inept Ralph Dudley. Even as Holcombe tried to fit the slave characters into stereotypes, the characters themselves belied the myth of white superiority. Holcombe presented devoted and loyal slave companions, but we know these clever and capable slaves posed more of a threat to the white social order than she would ever be willing to admit.

The Free Flag of Cuba heralds a later literature that followed the Civil War. Authors such as Thomas Nelson Page who celebrated the "Cult of the Lost Cause" greatly influenced the direction that literary and historical interpretations would take in their portrayals of the Old South.[109] The Confederacy lost the war on the battlefield, but it won in the literature that glorified the Old South afterwards, such as in Margaret Mitchell's 1936 novel, *Gone with the Wind.* As young Lucy Holcombe's novel illustrates, the South understood the need for mythmaking prior to 1865. Despite the nobility of character of Holcombe's white southern male heroes, we cannot imagine them winning a war against Yankees, or even against their own clever slaves. We can only note the irony that in the years before the Civil War, literature such as *The Free Flag of Cuba* portrays southern aristocrats standing for a noble "lost cause."

The 1854 edition of *The Free Flag of Cuba* was a rather poorly edited book by modern standards. We present it here with a minimal amount of editorial intrusion. We have corrected obvious printer errors, and to prevent confusion for the reader, we have made some changes to punctuation at the end of quotations in accordance with modern printing conventions. We have corrected certain inconsistencies in dialect passages but have en-

---

109. Moss, *Domestic Novelists in the Old South*; Anne Goodwyn Jones, *Tomorrow Is Another Day* (Baton Rouge: Louisiana State University Press, 1981). Michael Kreyling traces the myth of the lost cause forward to the present in *Inventing Southern Literature* (Jackson: University Press of Mississippi, 1998).

deavored to maintain the flavor of Holcombe's representation of dialect as much as possible. We corrected inconsistencies in the spelling and punctuation of many contractions (for example, *ain't* was often printed with an apostrophe in the original and often without one, so we added the apostrophe where needed for consistency), but if variant spellings suggested different pronunciations, we did not make any changes (thus the reader will find both *ain't* and *ain* in this edition of the novel, for example). If the 1854 edition consistently did not use an apostrophe for a given dialect spelling, we did not add one (the *ain* variation of *ain't*, for example, never has an apostrophe in the original, so we did not add one). We did not correct any spellings (such as *fillibuster*) that were used consistently in the 1854 edition. We made the capitalization of *de France* consistent (in the original it was occasionally printed "De France"), but generally we corrected only a few unambiguous errors in the original's very irregular and inconsistent capitalization. Although the capitalization in the original often seems arbitrary, it also seems clearly intentional in many cases, so rather than imposing modern standards of capitalization throughout or subjectively correcting some inconsistencies and not others, we felt we would best serve the author and future scholars by leaving the inconsistent capitalization essentially intact.

THE

FREE FLAG OF CUBA;

OR,

The Martyrdom of Lopez

A TALE OF THE LIBERATING EXPEDITION OF 1851

My ashes as the Phoenix, will bring forth
A bird that shall revenge upon you all.
Shakspeare.

Oh, beauteous land! So long laid low,
So long the grave of thine own children's hopes,
When there is but required a single blow
To break the chain.
Byron.

BY H. M. HARDIMANN.

NEW YORK:
DE WITT & DAVENPORT, PUBLISHERS.
160 & 162 NASSAU STREET

Facsimile of original title page

TO

GENERAL JOHN A. QUITMAN,

THE HERO AND PATRIOT,

THE CHAMPION OF ALL RIGHTS SAVE THOSE CLAIMED BY TYRANTS

THE FRIEND OF ALL LAWS SAVE THOSE OF OPPRESSION,

NOT FOR ANY INTEREST HE MAY FEEL IN ITS PERUSAL BUT AS

A Tribute of Earnest Admiration,

THE FREE FLAG OF CUBA

IS DEDICATED.

H. M. HARDIMANN.

PREFACE

THE MEAGRE ACCOUNTS we have of the deeds and sufferings of the brave soldiers, who died in 1851 for Cuba's freedom, leave impressions on our minds wholly inadequate to the realities of those scenes. These dry historical records, like the drums that accompanied the last address of the patriot, serve to drown the cries of woe that would otherwise rend the ear. Distance, too, dims the sight of cruelty and injustice, and our spirit of vengeance is not thoroughly roused. But could we follow those ill-fated men in every step of their bold march; could we hear their words through the burning day, and read their thoughts, as they lay at night on the bosom of the betrayed isle; could we place our ear, as it were, on the breast and listen to the very heart-throbs of each of those noble spirits; could we witness the insolence of the haughty foe in his triumph, not of valor, but of numbers and advantages; could we see the champions of freedom mercilessly slaughtered by the unions of tyranny, then would our indignation burst all bounds, and America would, with one voice, call aloud for vengeance! It is the object of the succeeding pages in some measure to supply this vivid picture; to pay a tribute to the memory of those who died in that noble cause; to do justice to the pure motives of their deeds, which are condemned more for their want of success than for the want of virtue in themselves; and to depict the occurrences of those hours of which there can be no record left. And it is impossible that these can be exaggerated. We know not the worst, but from what we do know we must infer that in the undescribed intervals which exist between the landing of the forces and the fatal termination of the enterprise, there occurred heroic deeds and sufferings, which must for ever lie like jewels in the bottom of a darkened valley from which no historic light will ever chase the shadows away. But we have dreamed of those scenes and we will endeavor, though with an unpracticed hand, to share our dream. We will hold the lunar light of fiction over those hidden diamonds, that they too may be faintly seen; while those facts, of which there are true records, loom up like mountains in the sunlight. But amidst all, my greatest wish is that so much heroism, and suffering, and blood, may not at least be uselessly expended; and this, and every other record of them may freely be given to the flames, if from the ashes "shall arise a bird which shall avenge them all."

September 1, 1854

CHAPTER I

"The past but lives in words."

LET THE EYES THAT ARE to follow me through the romance rest with kind indulgence on its pages. I do not write to see a book in print, and call it mine—Ah! no. I would not put forth my hand to call the brightest flower of fame; for it would be worthless to me, since there is not one who would smile and call it beautiful, because it lay upon my brow. I am utterly alone. The only kindred blood I ever knew, stains the green shore of Cuba, and now my own heart clings with a sad, passionate fondness, to that fatally loved isle, which has robbed me of all that made life beautiful.

If, when the bitter waters of memory and sorrow are stirred, I speak with such harshness as 'twere "better not to know," let the happy pause ere they condemn, let the sad of heart muse on their own suffering, and judge me kindly.

My characters are not, then, all fictitious; some of them have, or have had, living originals in the actual world. Then, dear reader, as I sit in memory's silent chamber, as one by one I take from the imaged wall those pictures which I strive to paint on the mental canvas of your mind, throw thou the warm light of sympathy around them; let their colors glow in the generous interest the fair and brave ever feel for the nobly unfortunate.

The subject which I have chosen is one not only of interest, but of importance. I, in common with my countrymen, the freemen of America, feel a deep and growing sympathy for the oppressed abroad, and more especially the unhappy people under our own immediate cognizance, for whom Lopez and his followers so heroically died. I am glad to pay a tribute, however slight, to the memory of him whose character presents the admirable union of modern enlightenment and olden chivalry, whose life was one long struggling sigh for freedom, whose martyrdom was a sublime vindication of his great faith and sincerity.

The name of Lopez is destined to stand first on the pages of Cuban history, when Cuba has, by a victorious struggle, made herself worthy of his death.

By the greatness of his love, the earnestness of his faith, the bitterness of his death, he won the first and holiest place in the heart of the republic which will arise and call him father.

The character of General Lopez has suffered much injustice. He did not succeed; and men judge him by the result of his enterprise. This is most unjust, for there are few aware of the dark treachery which surrounded on every side his effort to relieve from despotism the country he loved. It is true, like all generous natures, he trusted too much. Honest himself, relying confidently on the integrity of others, he knew no trait so dark as suspicion. Spies paid by the government of Cuba wore the garb of patriotism, and stood in the secret councils of the liberalists, bearing every plan to their dark employers. Thus the officials become aware of those who were most actively concerned in the revolution, and while General Lopez expected them to receive him with gladness, to meet him with ammunition and provisions, they were either confined in heavy dungeons, or sleeping by the assassin's dagger.

The small-hearted, illiberal policy of a misguided administration has thrown around the character and effort of Lopez, an unjust misconception and ungenerous prejudice. Yet every man, after divesting himself of this influence, if he has the elements of candor and honesty implanted in his own heart, cannot fail to recognise with intense admiration the beautiful and good which display themselves in every act of the illustrious Cuban's political life.

The wondrous constancy of that devotion which gave his fond death-words to Cuba, the holy strength of his patriotism, the sublime faith and trust which no disappointment could shake, *must* touch every generous heart.

His was not the struggle of a day; it commenced at an early period of his life, was unyielding and superior to circumstances, striving and hoping with that stern power of endurance of which truth is ever capable when combating with error. He *could* not know despair, he hurled it from him with a giant's power; turning with cold forgetfulness from past adversity, still aspiring, still pursuing with the ceaseless energy of conscious right his glorious scheme for Cuba's liberation.

Then, disrobed of all prejudice, I place him before my reader, standing on the evidence of his own life—a patriot, pure in heart and honest in purpose, a noble champion for Cuba's liberty and humanity's rights.

CHAPTER II

IN A SPACIOUS ROOM, with brilliant lights and luxurious furniture, sat two men in earnest conversation. They were very unlike, the American and Cuban General.[1] The face of the one was calm, almost stern, with clear searching eyes of patriotism's "true blue." The stiff military mustache gave the curved upper lip of his haughty mouth an expression still more determined. The voice was quick as a staccato strain in music, decided as one accustomed to command and be obeyed. As you looked on him you felt that he was a man, who with a knowledge of right would stand before a world's opposition as a strong marble pillar in a raging storm, never swerving, never yielding, unbending and defiant.

The other was dark, with the passionate splendor of a southern clime; his face, although open and generous, had an air of sturdy resolve and perseverance. His eyes flashed with patriotic enthusiasm as he paused in the statement he had been giving of that enterprise which now occupied his whole attention. He listened anxiously as the American replied—

"It seems, indeed, that the present juncture calls for your immediate action. But are you sure that the Creole forces on the island are organized and ready to co-operate with you on your landing?"

"Their organization is as far completed as the necessary secresy will permit. I do not fear to trust them. They would not sacrifice my gallant little army by any weak indecision.

"But, General, the Americans with whom I am associated, are most anxious to put themselves under your direction and control. Their confidence in your valor and skill will inspire them with a stronger hope and trust. Many of them have fought under you in other days, and will will-

1. The American general is John Quitman, to whom the novel is dedicated; the Cuban is López.

ingly obey your orders, and be entirely guided by your judgment. I have come then, once more, to offer you that position, whose acceptance will give Cuba powerful aid. It will give dignity to the expedition even in the eyes of the prejudiced; and, with its supporters, it will place its success beyond a doubt."

There was a hushed silence in the room. The Cuban's face was eager with intense interest, as if a nation's destiny depended on the answer. *Who can say!* The steadfast eyes of the American General looked earnestly forward as though they were searching into futurity. At length he said—

"General Lopez, you well know my sympathy with your hopes, my respect and hearty approval of your cause—a cause justifiable in the spirit, intent, and conscience of its supporters. I thank both you and my own countrymen for this mark of trust, even while I decline the responsible position you offer me. I rely not less on your good faith and ability than on the courage and fidelity of your men. But I greatly doubt the expediency of the expedition at this present time. That the Cubans desire a change of government I do not deny. You have certainly strong proof to that effect. But are they now prepared to make a struggle in behalf of their liberty? To rise, that you may assist them to unfasten their yoke? Have you force enough to inspire them with confidence of success? For they will dread the fearful consequences of a failure; and they well know, in case of defeat, the garrote will be their fate. Then, again, should they flock unanimously around you without arms, they could render but little assistance. You should be strong enough, independent of their aid, to make your first battles decisive; for the men you take with you must necessarily do most of the fighting. The Creoles are not, as you know, a warlike people. Forbidden the use of arms, they are mostly ignorant of the ordinary management of a gun. Our own men, accustomed as they are from early boyhood to the free use of firearms, require the severest drilling and discipline. You should have, instead of five hundred, five thousand men, well trained and equipped; sufficient means to maintain the government which you establish until it is able to stand on its own strength. The military adage, 'discretion is the better part of valor,' is peculiarly applicable. In providing for a failure you avert it."

"Very true," answered Lopez; "but, General, I dare not wait longer. My men are impatient for action. They have been thwarted and delayed, until their hopes and trust are well nigh gone. Besides, it is no scheme of conquest. We do not go to *rouse* the natives to rebellion, but to *aid* them in driving from their land the dark oppressors who encumber its soil. I have the assurance of a people weary of their bondage, whose chains have long been festering on them; and who, from this attempt, can fear no consequences more grievous than the daily burden they have so long borne without resistance. I have this surety, beside their expressed promises and their actions already begun, that they will fly to the standard of freedom as soon as it is raised."

"I do not feel the confidence which you perhaps are right in placing *in* the firmness of the Creoles; therefore, in taking the direction of the Patriot forces, I should be acting contrary to my judgment and conviction of propriety. This I cannot do. It is not a love of inactive ease," continued the veteran soldier, "neither is it a regard for personal interest or safety that restrains me, but I cannot lead men where there is not a prospect of overcoming danger with hardy courage and skill. You land with five hundred men. Your first battle may be victorious, but your numbers, in all probability, much diminished, while those of the enemy will be hourly increased by the addition of fresh troops. Your band, Spartan though it be, can effect but little against the immense force that will be brought to bear upon it; for the whole strength of the Spanish army is, as you well know, concentrated on the island. Yet I would not discourage you. God grant your success may prove my fears groundless!"

"Your reasons," said the Cuban, thoughtfully, "may be just and true; but I am urged by convictions equally strong, though opposite, to proceed. If, in the singleness of my zeal, I am rash—if, in the greatness of my hopes, I am blind to the scruples of your superior judgment, it is, that I cannot put from me the reliance I have on the sturdy strength of my American allies, or the unshaken confidence I repose in the powerful support which will be given me by the natives of Cuba. If I fail, I shall have the honest knowledge, that I dared for good. This will, in a measure, compensate me for any misfortune to myself, which may follow my effort in behalf of my country's liberty. Yet hope is very strong in my breast. My aim is a high and glorious one—the elevation of a degraded people. The proclamation of the President is—"[2]

2. In April 1851, President Millard Fillmore issued a neutrality proclamation, which forbade filibustering and declared that the U.S. government would not intervene to save Americans captured in any such endeavor.

"A mere piece of coquetry with Spain," interrupted the American, with a lurking smile, "intended to open her friendly ear to any proposals which may hereafter be made relative to the purchase of Cuba, which Mr. Fillmore is doubtless anxious to secure for the glory of his administration. This severity is but seeming. Yet the proclamation is not only arbitrary, but most unwise. The President of the United States cannot, with propriety, by any act of his own, estop himself from claiming the right to protect the life of an American citizen under *all* circumstances; *he has no right to will away the lives of freemen.* If, through his mistaken policy, he deems them erring, they are still the sons of Washington, and their error is on the generous side of freedom. It is his duty, and should be his pride, to shield and protect American interest. It is not his province to wantonly assign away to a foreign power the lives and liberties of men by whose sufferance he holds his position of limited—*not absolute*—power. He is not their master, nor are they his slaves, to be thus delivered up at pleasure to the mercy of a despotic oppressor. The President is the servant of the sovereign people, not their arbiter. This assumption of absolute control—this taking on himself the right to withdraw a government's protection from her free-born sons, is unlawful and most derogatory to the patriotic dignity of the man who stands in that position once held by the 'immortal lover of the people.' It is an unnatural mother who forsakes her child, and permits him to be harshly dealt with by a stranger. A common sense of justice scorns the sophistry which admits that America can, with any show of consistency, condemn her children because they seek to extend the very principles which are the life-breath of her own existence—the very principles which she from their infancy instills into their minds, inculcates in their hearts, as the surest foundation of moral and political good. If, with this before her, she could bring herself to censure the advocacy of the fundamental doctrines of her own nationality—it should have been with the loving-kindness of a mother, and not with the violence of a despot. It was not *her* place to cast reproach and indignity upon them. These men are no cowards to be menaced with arms—no children to be frightened into a servile obedience! The proclamation was disgraceful! The President has laid down—given away his right to interfere in their behalf. It was wrong, sir—all wrong, injudicious, and uncalled for."—The general brought his hand down in the most emphatic manner upon the table by which he sat.

"Its consequences," said General Lopez, "may indeed be deplorable, for if we are unfortunate, which God forbid, Spain will be emboldened to treat with the utmost rigor the Americans who fall into her hands."

"It is true, the President has evinced an unpardonable want of forethought—has given up his right to interfere in their behalf; yet I believe him to have the honest heart of a free man, and he will in case of emergency be true to his trust. He cannot with consistency stand between them and the tyrannic cruelty of Spain; but the consistency of an administration is a little thing to sacrifice for the preservation of American life and Republican honor. Spain will not dare to use harshness—save, sir, at the peril of her national existence."

There was silence for a moment. Lopez looked on the brave proud face before him, and said—

"General! I have much to thank you for the unfailing kindness which you have shown me as a man, the generous sympathy you have manifested in the cause which I represent. Your interest in behalf of my unhappy country is plainly without the stain of self, for what more can you ask of fortune or fame than that which you already possess! I daily feel the loss Cuba will sustain in your absence from this struggle. If you were but identified with the hopes of Cuba's friends! if you would but accept this commandancy, which I cannot, through regard for your scruples, urge upon you ———"

"Ah! sir, you have nothing to thank me for. I did but give you that hand whose fellowship shall never be withheld from those whom I conceive to be truly good, whatever censure may ensue. I am as honest in my good feeling for yourself, as in the deep abiding interest I cherish for the enslaved land whose just rights you are seeking to establish at such fearful hazard. This act, by which you risk your life for the honor and liberty of a people, I can but admire. An act which in its motive, its daring, and its intended results, is of the most chivalrous and patriotic character; an act whose performance is but the natural duty you owe to Cuba. It is a laudable undertaking, and I trust that you may remove the restraint and gloom of tyranny from that beautiful island, that you may live to see commerce, agriculture, and education, flourish even as in my own glorious country—the proudest nation the world ever saw. This, sir, would, I know, compensate you for past misfortune, and all which you may yet incur. Then—bring your Creole forces to stand firm beside the American

allies—put arms into the hands of the people who pine for freedom—
lead them to battle against the enslavers—and God help you!"

The Cuban grasped the cordial hand of the bold, honest American
hero. There were no further words between them, yet he felt that, whatever his fate, *Cuba would not be without a friend.*

CHAPTER III

"She was like
A dream of poetry, that may not be
Written or told—exceeding beautiful."

WILLIS.

"I'll do whate'er thou wilt, I will be silent:
But O! a reined tongue, and bursting heart,
Are hard at once to bear."

BAILLIE.

"I have such eagerness of hope
To benefit my kind."

LANDON.

IT IS NOT, I KNOW, the fashion to describe your heroine; her personal
charms, if she have any (beauty being rather at discount in the literary
world), must appear stealthily,—now and then; but I have a strong fancy
for seeing or reading of a beautiful woman, and trusting to find a sympa-
thetic taste in my reader, I will at once say how much more than beautiful
was Genevieve Clifton, as she stood at evening's hushed hour, within the
recess of a deep window, in one of those splendid houses found on the
southern coast.

The dark curls thrown back revealed a face at once passionate and
spiritual; a calm delicious moon light face, with features of that pure delicate cast, whose tranquil repose saddens the heart with a vague fear of
future clouds. The full round forehead, relieved of its hanging shade, was
rather low, with a gentle womanly expression, which you admired more
than its extreme whiteness, or even the rare beauty of the temple-veins,
blue with Louisiana's oldest and richest blood.

The arched brows and keenly cut nostril gave an idea of pride, which was contradicted in the cheering smile of the small red mouth, whose lips unclosed with reluctant grace, as if jealous of exposing the white pearl gems within.

But the rarest charm of this sweet face lay in the eyes, of that deep dark blue the summer sky wears before a storm. Over them the almond-shaped lids drooped as if wearied by the heavy black lashes which fringed them, and rested on a cheek where the rose seldom came.

The form was round, but slight even to fragility, with that appealing willowy grace seen only in women of the south.

Now, there was an anxious shadow on the brow of this young girl, as she stood with her eyes fixed sadly on the dark waters of turbulent Mississippi. How true it is, that though we willingly acknowledge the superiority of intellect over beauty, though we admit it to be a higher gift, one more worthy of homage, yet there certainly is a spell in unconscious loveliness that immediately reaches the heart, a mystic fascination in the perfect harmony of beauty, which rouses every deep sympathy, and draws you towards its possessor with an influence nothing else can exercise.

So it was with Genevieve. You loved her at once, for the promise of "inner beauty" which her face gave, a promise of spirit-loneliness which made you turn again and again to look on her, that you might assure yourself it was no picture-dream of your own imagination, but a living reality of nature's highest perfection—a true and beautiful woman.

The last gorgeous sunbeam was gone, but Genevieve lingered, evidently watching, for she stepped suddenly on the terrace, and looked eagerly down the long avenue of magnolias; then, sighing, she threw her arm across the balustrade, and, with impatient weariness, her head fell on her small white hands—for 'twas but the rustling evening wind that parted the fragrant orange-boughs, bringing the mellow tones of the negro's evening song.

Twilight, with its purple shadows, veiled the earth, and now that her eyes were hid, the stars came timidly forth.

Time glides on evening's starry wing. The moon's pale trembling beams fell around her, but still the maiden watched. But eager steps are heard, and she turns to greet the lover of her youth, and the master of her destiny—Ralph Dudley.

"Ralph, I thought you would never come; I have watched till my heart ached with its own loneliness, and yet you lingered until now."

The eyes raised so reproachfully to his own were unheeded. He did not answer for a moment, but raised her hand caressingly to his lips, and drew her in the lighted room.

"The night air is too damp, Genevieve; your curls are heavy with the dew."

"I did not think of my curls; they are not so heavy as my heart."

"See," he answered, holding a letter, "I have brought something to cheer you."

She broke the seal, and scanned its contents rapidly:—"Mabel, dear Mabel! She is coming, Ralph; now, by to-morrow's boat. I am so glad," and she laughed happily.

"Ah! Genevieve, laugh always. I tell you I can't stand a woman's sad face; I feel like shooting myself, and sending for 'my friend, the under-taker,' if it would only make her smile."

"Don't be so heroic, Ralph; let me tell you about Mabel. I know you will like her."

"I dare say I shall think her a very nice little Yankee, whom my Gene-vieve's enthusiasm has idealized into 'an angel and a dream.'"

"No," she said decidedly, "you will think her the rarest, loveliest woman you ever knew. You have too much good taste not to admire Mabel. If you call *me* beautiful, what will you say of *her?* For she is the very perfection of the highest order of beauty."

"Genevieve, the enthusiasm of one woman for the beauty of another, is laughable to me; for, in most instances, it is the affectation of an amia-bility they seldom possess."

"It is an amiability one gentleman can't even assume towards another, so, not being able to appreciate it yourselves, you do not give us the jus-tice of its sincerity."

"Nay, my honey-flower, don't frown; I did not mean a doubt of *your* love for Miss Royal. Heaven knows I ought to be convinced, if constant dwelling on the theme would do it."

"Love her! Ralph, if you had never loved anything *else,* you would love *her.* She is so unlike every one; such a delightful contradiction in both character and person. She is not a regular harmonious beauty, yet at school, when the painting class was ordered to prepare each one an ideal head of loveliness for the exhibition, it was so laughable—six of them painted Mabel's face, which certainly is in defiance of all rule as regards color.

"You know, she has auburn hair; such hair as Bulwer meant his heroine to have, when he said, 'her curls looked as though they caught the sunbeams, and kept them prisoners.'[3]

"But Mabel's does not curl, and it is not straight; it lies in rippling waves on a forehead so high, so white and broad. Then her eyebrows are darker and not at all arched, but straight and a little heavy, for they meet on her small Grecian nose. Mr. Shultz used to say it was that which gave so much character to her face. But the strangest thing is, that the lashes are very long and perfectly black.

"Then think, Ralph, of the smallest, haughtiest mouth in the world; and a chin so perfect, that the world has never seen one like it, only in Powers's 'Greek Slave.'[4]

"Now, when I tell you her eyes are a pale uncertain blue, you will not think them divinely beautiful, as they really are!"

"No, for I love rich glowing eyes, like—"

"Hush, Ralph; Mabel's are diamond eyes, not only in brilliancy, but in color; they dazzle with the clearness of their light till she speaks, till she feels; then the iris dilates, it expands, and you are bewildered with the strange dark beauty of those glorious eyes.

"Then the inexpressible charm of her love-drawing manner. You must see and know that, to feel its power. Her whole being is the very essence of fascination."

"I will acknowledge her a divinity at once, Genevieve," he laughed; then added more seriously, "I am really glad she is coming *now*, for she may, I hope, in some measure, cause you to forget my absence."

"Your absence! When do you go, Ralph?"

"To-morrow."

3. Edward George Earle Bulwer-Lytton (1803–1873), British politician, poet, and critic, chiefly remembered as a prolific novelist. Among his detailed historical novels are *The Last Days of Pompeii*, 3 vol. (1834), and *Harold, the Last of the Saxon Kings* (1848).

4. This sculpture by Hiram Powers in 1843 caused quite a sensation. It is a white marble statue of a nude girl chained after being captured by the Turks.

The child-like abandon of joy that had made her face so lovely, vanished, as she burst into tears. Ralph, man-like, frowned, but looked terribly guilty and miserable.

"Don't be unhappy, Genevieve," a little impatiently.

"How can I help it, when I think of the future—that future which is to take you from me; that night without a coming dawn, for I cannot hope you will return! And if you are lost, how could I bear to live?"

The head was raised, and the blue eyes looking on him, she said—

"Ralph, dear Ralph, don't go."

Ralph Dudley ran his fingers quickly through his hair, as men do when they are half moved, half vexed, and threw himself on the silken sofa with a hopeless sigh.

He had met the same gentle entreaty again and again with such strong conclusive reasoning, that he had hoped it was hushed; for it was very hard at best to leave her—his tenderly loved Genevieve.

So he sat silent, not knowing what more to say. But he was very uncomfortable, as most lovers would have been under the circumstances, for he felt her tears were reproaches to him. So he drew her to his bosom, and prayed her not to grieve him by her sorrow.

"You do not know what it is you ask, my Genevieve; you require me not only to forfeit my sworn word, to cast a stigma on my honor as a man, but to become a recreant and a deserter."

"No, no; it is only to forsake a wild visionary scheme for an unattainable result; to give *me* that love you lavish on a people wholly unworthy of it. The Cubans are not worthy of freedom—they are not true to themselves; how can you expect them to be true to you, even though you peril so much for their good?"

"But they *will* be true to the noble principle that now spires them." Ah! you little know the intense desire for liberty that fills the breast of this people, so long and cruelly oppressed! Our gallant little army have but to raise in their strong arms the standard of Cuba's free colors, and they will gladly flock to its support. No more will Moro's dark walls echo with the cries of spirits pining for the light of heaven and the right of thought; no longer shall the tyrant crush the growing power of that beautiful isle.[5] Cuba *must—Cuba will be free.*"

5. On a cliff overlooking the Caribbean, Moro Castle in Havana contained a large dungeon.

"Ralph, your words are those of an enthusiast. We cannot always have what we would. How can you hope, with your little band, to contend with an established government, to defeat the power of Spain?"

"Genevieve, your words are those of a woman or child. Think you so little of American prowess that five hundred of our strong, brave men, with the addition of the armed natives, would fail to snatch from the poor crumbling power of Spain that bright child of the waves, and place her a brilliant jewel 'mid the clustering stars of liberty?

"Poor Cuba! she is burning, she is pining for the dear light of freedom. Her children send to us from every quarter, and shall the cry of the oppressed reach the American and find him cold and dumb?

"God forbid that freemen should scorn the wail of the weak!

"Should the fear of what a selfish world might say restrain a man, when his own conviction of right urges him to the contest?

"Should that law, which has *no right* to shackle the individual actions of a man, stay the arm already raised to strike in a cause so good and just!"

He paused, musingly.

"Ralph—a patriot loves his own country, and respects her laws. Will, then, a true-hearted American involve his country in trouble because of a miserable, cowardly race, who are not quite determined if they will say yes or no to the daring band of adven——"

"Don't talk of what you don't understand, Genevieve. It is useless to reason against arguments that any school-boy might laugh at. Above all, don't quote from that contemptible, office-lauding, power-serving paper (pointing to a weekly edition of the —— lying on the table), from which you get your ungenerous sentiments. If you want truth, you will find it in the fearless king of the press—the *Delta*—that paper which has enough moral and political honesty to have and express its own opinions; that paper which does not wait to know public feeling, in order to cringe to it, but defends the cause of justice and right, independent of popular applause—having a strength and integrity of character men are forced to respect."[6]

"Ralph, you are very unjust to me. The *Delta*, with all its sincerity,

6. The New Orleans *Delta* supported the filibuster in Cuba, as did the *United States Magazine and Democratic Review* in New York and the New York *Sun*.

could not influence me when my own conscience tells me you are wrong. Besides, you have no right to complain of *me* when your President has expressed his disapprobation in such severe terms. Denounced as a plunderer and robber, it is laughable to hear you complain because I venture to call you an enthusiast. I cannot feel very proud of knowing you to be the associate and follower of the rebel, the robber, the pirate—Lopez."

An angry crimson flushed Dudley's face, and his haughty eyes looked anything but love when he said:—

"I had rather you had died than uttered words so unworthy the lips of a woman; for in *her* pitying breast the brave and unfortunate have ever before found sympathy.

"Confine, I pray, your censure to me, but do not seek to throw reproach on the man whose purity the good have never doubted.

"The honest sword-taught hand of Quitman would hardly grasp the fingers of a robber; his stern, true lip would, methinks, scorn to call the rebel and pirate *friend!* What will you do with your hero-worship for this great man, when I tell you that so much confidence had the *pirates* in his sympathy, that they offered him the first command; and that though he declined the position, yet he has manifested his earnest and generous sympathy for the enterprise, and bids them God speed in their good work. He acknowledges the uprightness of their motives and intentions, and has given such instructions and advice to Lopez as will be of great benefit to him in case of his success, which, I fear, our skilful American general doubts."

"Ralph, I would say General Quitman acted as he always does, rightly and for his country's good. He knows she will need his strong faithful arm in the very war these *patriotic* men will bring on her."

"How absurd a woman is when she attempts to reason! I think he has himself said that the freedom of Cuba would secure, not only her own happiness, but the future safety and prosperity of America. Thus opening a door through which her free institutions may pass to the southern continent, strengthening the power of our own government, and doing infinite service in the cause of humanity by shedding the ennobling light of freedom on the now degraded children of tyranny.

"General Quitman is not the only man in high position who feels an interest in the cause of Lopez, and a hope for his success; but generosity is a more common virtue than moral courage. There are others who cordially sympathize with the sentiments *he* openly avows, but they dare not acknowledge that sympathy.

"They have political aims to accomplish, personal advantages to gain which they imagine, justly perhaps, would be greatly injured by any *public* support, any positive encouragement given the noble exile. There are few men who can entirely divest themselves of selfish considerations, who can boldly throw aside public opinion, that tyrant of petty minds, when it conflicts with their own conviction of honor and justice; feeling the heaven of a quiet conscience to be a happiness far above that uncertain power the shadowy splendor which gratified political ambition gives him who has bartered honesty and truth for the poor applause of meaner souls. Purity of heart is the substance of true greatness. This is what gives strength to the influence of the hero-statesman. The Roman sternness of his patriotic virtue has never yet faltered between principle and interest; for he has yet to hesitate, either in word or action, when the question of right and wrong comes before him for decision. Genevieve, I do not think I am a worshipper of Heroes, and I am certain I have no servile admiration for men of high estate, but I do respect that power which makes, which takes position.

"By position I do not mean office; that is no longer the reward of merit, but the mere accident of party trickery and policy.

"I mean that station which *he* holds, who has by the stainless purity of his political career, by the honest sincerity and integrity of every purpose, enveloped himself in the confidence of a people whom he has faithfully served. Ah! this is *real* fame. This reward is worth a life of toil!"

"Ralph, in the enthusiasm of your subject you have quite forgotten my offence and your own anger, of neither of which I will remind you; though I must by some means break the thread of your thoughts. For the next step will take you into Mexico, and I will have to listen for the fiftieth time to a description of battles, whose glory is so fully impressed on my imagination, that you have only to mention Monterey, and I actually fancy I hear the booming guns, and see the starry flag in its floating triumph.

"But I can easily understand the devotion of a soldier for his general.

"If the mere hearing of heroic bearing and intrepid courage has so great an effect on the world at home, how strong must be its influence on those who witness and share its deeds!"

"Would to heaven I had a prospect of fighting the coming battles under his command!" said Dudley, moodily pursuing his own thoughts.

"Why does he refuse the offer of the Cuban General and his associates?"

"I do not certainly know his reasons. Though there are many good ones he might have, the strongest I think is, that while he heartily approves of the object, his military prudence is not satisfied by the organization of the expedition.

"The want of system and discipline he would soon correct, but he thinks we are too weak to inspire the natives with that trust and confidence which are necessary to secure success. He thinks, knowing as they do that the main strength of the Spanish army is concentrated around them, they will not rely on a force so small as that of Lopez. He fears they will falter, and American blood and life be uselessly spilled."

"Then, Ralph, why will you go?"

"Because I have an honest difference of opinion. I think Lopez knows his people better than Quitman could. He is all-confident of success, and faith is very catching when your own inclinations lean towards it.

"The Patriots have been again and again assured by prominent and influential men of the island, that if they will only make that stand which they are unable to do alone, deprived as they are of arms, and watched in every movement by spies, the Creoles will, to a man, rally to their support.

"Lopez has the strongest evidence, the most satisfactory proof, that the Cubans earnestly desire a change of government. The peril is imminent to them and to us should the expedition fail, which I do not fear, for the cause is just. We have but to land, and our numbers will be swelled to a formidable army; ammunition and arms will be provided the insurgents; one strong greeting from our guns will overthrow the tyrant, and a republican government will be established which will look to America as its model.

"Whatever the vicissitudes of my after life, Genevieve, it will be a happiness to look on Cuba as she enjoys the comfort of a happy, and pride of a great nation; and think that I, in advocating her cause, did some service to the divinest of all principles, that of human rights."

Genevieve only sighed, she had very little sympathy with any rights but her own at that moment. These sentiments would have been truly admirable in Miss Brown's lover, but "circumstances alter cases," as every woman knows.

"What we most want," continued Dudley, not heeding the want of sympathy in his listener, "is an American commander. General Lopez, with all his ability and courage, will, I fear, have trouble in instituting that order now most requisite among men so unaccustomed to restraint as those with whom he is associated.

"He has before commanded those who were taught from their birth to fear and obey.

"Now our men, while they make the best fighters in the world, are certainly the worst soldiers. Each one is determined on achieving the battle after his own fashion by his individual valor. No man is willing to see the most dangerous post assigned to another; *he* has the best right to die in a good cause.

"Had we not had in the Mexican war the ablest and most powerful generals in the world those accustomed to this peculiarity of our men, we should have had detachments of tens in every direction, each party bent on carrying the victorious banner into 'the halls of Montezuma'; for American volunteers have very little idea of subordination."

"So I think, Ralph, from the regard these men pay the proclamation of their President."

Dudley bit his lips to keep back the harsh, indignant retort, which would have been uttered to any one but her, to whom he said kindly—

"Genevieve, don't say anything you may hereafter regret. What you say of these men has equal reference to myself, for I am identified with them, their fate is mine. Do not let me leave you, perhaps for ever, with reproach upon your lips."

"Oh, Ralph," she answered passionately, "do not leave *me* for *them!* I do not care for Cuba, it will be nothing to me whether they are right or wrong if you but stay. Give up this fearful enterprise, it is not yet too late, and surely happiness may be found in the dear valley of the Mississippi."

Ah, Ralph Dudley, pause yet longer as you gaze in those deep pure eyes, linger in the sweet light of their pleading beauty—for a moment more, and your own words have clouded them with tears.

"Genevieve, be it to triumph or to death, I have pledged myself to Cuba and her Champion. I have stood beside Lopez, and looked over towards the beautiful bound land of his love. I have laid my hand upon his sword as I swore to strike with him, and God alone can stay my arm. Genevieve, you have called it a dream, but is it not a glorious one when a people dream of freedom and wake to liberty?"

"But what will it be, Ralph, to dream of freedom, and wake to chains still darker, still heavier?"

"But that must not, that will not be. Think, Genevieve," and his eyes burned with the fire of an honest enthusiasm, "think what it would be to live the La Fayette of Cuba, to be loved by her future generations as one who gave his fortune, and ventured his life to vindicate her trampled rights; and then, dearest, when I have become a man of deeds, when we have achieved a noble triumph in a good cause, I will feel more worthy of your love. The red rose of the warrior shall be thrown aside for the sweet orange flowers that are to grace the fairest brow in all the south. Fame, next dearest word to Genevieve, dearer because of Genevieve!"

"Nay, Ralph, think you I would love you more because the world had called you great, or because circumstances had caused men to acknowledge that superiority I already know you to possess! The world's applause is nothing if you yourself feel the greatness of one you love. Were you President of our grand Republic, I should not be more assured than I now am, of your capability to fill that office with dignity and honor; if you were Emperor of the world, I could not be more fully impressed with your lordly perfection. Heart-worship, Ralph, does not depend on the voice or will of the people, neither on the force of arms: it is a homage which once given cannot be recalled, but clings around its hero, softening in the mellow rays of prosperity, brightening in the night of adversity. The idol may fall—but the green moss covers the withered oak."

From the blue eyes raised with tearful fondness to his own beamed a woman's heart, and the light of the southern star paled in their lustre.

Dudley turned away in silent perplexed thought.

"Genevieve, you would not have me break my oath?"

"The wrong here, Ralph, is in the oath taken, not in the oath broken."

"Oath broken!" he repeated. "Gods! it cannot be. My destiny was cast under a stormy star, and I must boldly follow its course. Ere the summer-flowers have faded, may fate bring the freedom of Cuba! God forgive me if I pray for the freedom of death, if, living, I shall not see the glory of her redemption. I will call on your name, my beloved," he continued tenderly, "the sweet name of Genevieve, and you will pray the saints it may not be in vain."

Genevieve did not answer, and the dark curls fell kindly over the pale face, hiding its silent wretchedness.

"Will my guardian-angel withdraw her sweet protection, and must my life and cause fall without one sustaining prayer?"

The little hand trembled in his own, and she said, half passionately, half sorrowfully—

"You know I will ever kneel to the Mother of mercy to watch over and protect you for whom I would gladly die, but I can ask nothing for Cuba, that Spanish beauty whom you love more than Genevieve, for it is for her that you leave me miserable. You are smiling, Ralph, you are going to say I am childish and selfish. I know I have not sufficient generosity to sacrifice my own happiness for the imaginary good of others. I could not love you more if you freed the whole world—and if you should fall!"

The sweet eyes closed wearily as if to shut out the darkness of that hour.

"We will not despair, my beautiful; cowards alone dread the future. We will trust it for joy until it brings sorrow.

"Come, the moon is sinking, and we have not given the Virgin her evening hymn."

He brought the guitar, and stood beside her as she swept its rich chords with unconscious grace.

Ah! how much of beauty has earth! But more beautiful than all its created beauty is music, because the most spiritual. In the simple negro refrain, in the revelling Bacchanalian air, as in the full rushing tones of the impassioned oratorio, there is a veiled spirit of heaven, a something unexpressed, a vision of immortality.

Genevieve sang as few sing, "from the lip to the heart." In the clear thrilling notes of her glorious soprano all the spirituality of her nature found vent.

That longing, pleading voice, like the lark, soared higher, higher, till the entranced listener almost feared it would mingle with the music of heaven. This voice of which I write is not one of imagination. I have in other days heard its tones in real life, and they linger in memory now.

The contralto which mingled with Genevieve's soprano seemed its low distant echo, it was so full, so rich, so trembling with the mellow dreamy spirit of the grand old masters of song.

But now to-night, the song-bird was weary. It was struggling to rise, but an invisible influence pressed it nearer earth; its wings were laden with the dew of tears which it strove in vain to shake off.

There was the story of a heart's keen sorrow in every tone, and her very soul sang in wailing passionate accents—

> "Thou who hast looked on death
> Aid us when death is near,
> Whisper of heaven to faith,
> Mother, sweet Mother, hear!"

The young voice was striving to break from the cloud of sorrow, and lay its earthly grief and passion at the feet of the ever listening Mother of mercy.

Beautiful religion, which brings the suffering daughter of mortality so near the divine woman, the holy and sympathizing Mother of Christ.

The music ceased, and Ralph rose to greet the lady who entered.

CHAPTER IV

WHILE HE IS SEATED beside her, near the same deep window in whose recess we first saw Genevieve, while she is sadly, lovingly warbling to the music of her white fingers, the old Castilian ballads he had taught her, we will turn from the softened miniature of the daughter to the portrait of the mother, for they were very like—the mother and her child.

Mrs. Clifton had in her youth possessed that imperious beauty that gives so much dignity to middle age. She was always calm, always composed, reasoning where Genevieve felt; passing by emotion to look to its future results.

The fair curls that had twenty years ago veiled the cheek of Colonel Clifton's haughty bride, time and care had shaded into brown, and they were worn in simple braids. The eyes, though very black, were mild and thoughtful; the passion which once burned in them had been quenched in sorrow, and its memory lay in gentle lines on a brow too broad and high for feminine beauty.

She had a kind and feeling heart, that sure foundation for gentle manners; but the love of all things earthly, save that which lived in her child, she had long since buried in the grave of her husband.

Her devotion to Genevieve was mingled with an anxious fear, with which a mother only can sympathize.

Her child was an only one, and a daughter, and her woman's heart told her how rare a thing real happiness is to her sex. How she feared for this child! How she joyed over the days that passed, and left no cloud on her brow! But she knew it could not always be thus. Earth has sorrows which she must give the best and purest of her children. As the path of life winds through years it grows more shaded; there is sunshine, but not the generous, sparkling sunshine of youth; it comes cautiously, glancingly, growing fainter, like the memory of childhood's happiness.

The heart-flowers that spring up in early youth, its trust, its bright imagination, its hope and faith, lose their wild brilliancy, their seductive fragrance, and sadly, gradually fade. They are repulsed by the world, and the beautiful strangers shrink back to their spirit home!—sometimes haughtily, sometimes sadly. The latter visit us again in the violet virtues that peep from some characters; the former, like all flowers too much shaded and neglected, lose their rich colors, and grow cold and white. Then comes the winter of the heart. No fire! no warmth! no comfort!

Weep, then, for the warm, gorgeous, purple-hued enthusiasm of youth, but in vain, for it has vanished with the past, and returns no more. Flowers may again blossom over that heart, but it will be when the green earth covers it; and yet there is hope—a hope of happiness. For how many fold the mantle of life calmly over an aching heart, and wear it smilingly, looking forward beyond the coming night of death, to a day more bright, more beautiful than even "the pictured heaven of young imagination."

Mrs. Clifton's life had been very sorrowful, and when she wandered far back into the desolate past, when "old fears clothed with reality flitted around her, old hopes bathed in tears came mockingly before her," she said wearily: "If she might die, God would take to himself the pure heart in which lay no withered flower of passion; no broken faith; no wasted trust or dying hope." She knew that she would mourn her,—this fair young girl, this beautiful sparkle on her "goblet of life,"—but God was so merciful, his love so sure and unchangeable, while what the earthly future might bring this griefless heart, was yet unwritten.

Her manner towards Dudley was exceedingly kind, but it wanted that cordiality whose absence made the young man say impatiently to himself—"I wish she would tell me at once she don't like me."

But she did like him. There was no one in whom she felt so much interest. It was impossible to withstand the strange mixture of childish and courtly fascination which made his manner so winning.

Ralph was an orphan of gentle blood, and inherited an immense fortune, but Mrs. Clifton was not worldly. She knew that though brave, generous, and unselfish, he was passionate and wayward—impatient of the slightest control; rash and daring, he followed every fresh impulse, regardless of everything but his own honest conviction of its worth.

He must not be thwarted even by those he loved, least of all by a woman. *She* must look up to him in her love, silently forgiving, for he would never think to say "forgive."

Thus it was she shrank from giving him her child. She feared to trust the young heart with its deep love to the full control of his fiery, storm-freighted spirit.

Yet he was so trusting, so loving of truth, so credulous and good, even while he erred. Some spirits there are, whose very faults attach us; a certain royalty of transgression that defies blame, and even deserves our pitying love.

Such are seldom irreclaimable. The good within will at some time gain for itself an ascendency. The incense of a mother's prayer, a sister's love, will linger around, shieldingly, pleadingly, till the bad angel departs, and the native goodness and nobility of soul asserts itself in a better man.

Ralph Dudley was not a man whom Mrs. Clifton would willingly see Genevieve marry, and her scruples were not overcome by the passionate eloquence of the lover, but she knew that Genevieve returned his wild worship. The idol had been enshrined, and wreathed with the beautiful passion-flowers of the heart.

Genevieve was not one to love lightly or forget. Her heart was already given; and no will of hers could withdraw it.

The master-hand had swept the richest chord of life; neither time, nor change, nor death itself could hush its wild sweet music. For it is a beautiful philosophy which teaches how the great strength, the entireness of love lies in eternity—lives even in heaven.

But Genevieve had long since ceased her songs, and sat listening to Dudley's gay conversation with her mother, listening to his wit and anec- dote, his own peculiar laugh, which was very musical.

She wondered how he could be so careless, so joyous. She could not comprehend that to a daring spirit the excitement of coming danger is its intensest happiness.

"Genevieve," said Mrs. Clifton, "has Ralph told you he is going imme- diately to New Orleans?"

"Yes, mamma."

"I cannot think what urgent business could call you to the city. The gay season is over, and surely your interest in the commercial world would not tempt you to brave the danger of the epidemic? We must per- suade you to think better of it. Come, Genevieve, tell the knight his lady bids him stay."

"Nay, mother, I do not care to show you how unpersuadable Ralph is, or how little he would heed my bidding. If he will sacrifice himself, I sup- pose I must not complain."

The true meaning of her words lay in her reproachful eyes, which he well understood.

Mrs. Clifton continued to dissuade, but Ralph laughed, and declared, when he came back with those famous Persian roses that she had so often written to her florist about, his disobedience would be quite forgotten, and even Genevieve would forgive. "And," he added softly, "love me for the dangers I have passed."

"If you must go," said Mrs. Clifton, as she rose to leave the room, "I will send an order to Greenwood, for there are my poor geraniums to be replaced."

"Yes, madam," he said, taking her extended hand, "they shall have strict attention, though I cannot promise to bring them myself; since," he added smilingly, "I must make no promise to you I am not certain of performing. But the flowers shall come, and if I do not, you will let my memory live in them."

There was a sadness in his voice, and Mrs. Clifton pressed his hand kindly, with many warm wishes for his safety.

"Genevieve, don't sit looking so like a madonna; come and say something to make me feel less sad."

"I thought you were very gay, Ralph. What has caused this sudden depression?"

"I don't know. It is not fear of the future; it is its uncertainty that saddens me. I was thinking if I should fall, what would be your destiny. Genevieve, I was wondering if you would marry."

She raised her head and laughed.

"Oh, Ralph! you *real* man, not thinking remorsefully of crushing my heart and darkening my life, but whether *you* would be forgotten. Ah! if you only knew, that you might now reproach me. Ralph," the voice was so fond, the white hand lay so clingingly, so tenderly in his, "do not let us speculate on impossibilities; I have sometimes wished you might feel a doubt of my love; but you are very secure—for, you know, in seeking after perfection, I found you. What more could I ask? If I should meet one more noble, more really good and true, I would acknowledge his superiority. But—" she shook her head lovingly.

"Angel Genevieve, how little I deserve such love! If the Virgin would but make me better—God knows, I cannot do it myself." He rose impatiently. "Come on the terrace, love. The moon goes down so slowly, she waits to kiss you good night! See how lovingly she throws her beams around you! How beautiful you are! Does it make you very happy to be so lovely, Genevieve?"

"Yes, Ralph—*very* happy; because it brings me love. And yet, I shall not care for it now, since I cannot, like the fair ladies of old, 'bind my lover to my sweet will by a silken tress.'" And she wound the long curl round her snowy finger.

Ah! how the eyes pleaded that looked in his!

The radiant form stood tempting him to forget the stormy path he had chosen. His brave heart beat passionately to throw itself at her feet, to give up all for her it so much loved. But the love of the patriot was stronger than that of the man, and he was firm.

"Nay, lady-love, these silken threads shall not bind an unworthy knight, when conscience and duty call, but they shall be a pledge to bring a fond and absent lover to his mistress's feet."

Before she was aware, a glittering dirk severed the curl, and it lay near that fearless heart that loved honor and right alone more than Genevieve.

She raised her eyes hastily, and oh! the wild, imploring grief of that sorrowful glance. She strove to speak, but the words sobbed themselves away in passionate tears. Now, for the first time, she believed he would actually go. She had heard him speak with fervid brilliancy of his campaign in Mexico, she knew his daring nature loved the perils of war; but to leave her—to join this dangerous, mysterious enterprise, in the very face of *that terrible proclamation!* It was worse than rebellion; it was downright traitorism to his country and—*to her.* She was a woman, and this expedition was bringing danger to her lover; therefore, we can excuse thoughts in her which we, dear reader, thou and I, have scarcely the courtesy to read—presuming, as I do, that we both love "honor, truth, and justice," wherever it is found—whether it be in the memory of our own revolutionary heroes, the Irish patriots, the Hungarian exiles, or the noble little band which the martyred hero Lopez led from our bright shore.

Poor Genevieve! It was very hard—she had never thought he would really go. She would, even at the last moment, win him from his determination. Now, she felt that she stood—perhaps for the last time in life—beside him. The words of love, the tender cheerfulness with which he strove to assure her, only brought more abundant tears. Would she ever hear those sweet words again? Might not her heart pine in the long coming years for the tones of that dear voice, and in vain?

"Ralph, Ralph! why must you go? Would you kill me, cruel Ralph!" and the poor young head laid itself, like a wearied child, on his strong arm.

He knew it was useless to reason, so he put the curls from her bowed face, and said—

"Genevieve, you would make but a poor soldier's bride. What would our revolutionary mothers say to the American woman who seeks to stay an arm uplifted in such a cause? Think you the heart of your country could safely trust in you?"

"Hush, Ralph!" the blood rushed over her pale face. "I would give you to my country—my brave, righteous country, who has the first right to her sons; I would myself gird on your sword, and bid you Good speed! But," she exclaimed passionately, "what is Cuba to me that I should give her the light of my destiny, the sun of my happiness—that she should take the great hope, the bright dream of my young life, and leave me desolate?"

What could he do but fold her in his arms, and curse himself for bringing those bitter tears?

"Ralph, let me call mama—listen to her." Poor girl! she had an instinctive trust in her mother's power to persuade.

"No, no," he said, very quickly; "I will write her before leaving; for, Genevieve, I *must* go. I had rather die than grieve you; but God knows I have no choice now."

"Ralph—it is so hard to bear sorrow alone."

"Alone! Do I not suffer with you?"

"I think you feel a good deal, Ralph; but you don't suffer."

She knew, if his heart had broken, he would not have felt the bitter, hopeless pain that filled her bosom. She sat silent, and he painted to her the future—the brilliant future of a bold, hopeful heart, unchilled by disappointment, unclouded by regret.

"Now, Genevieve, sweet honey-flower, look on me. Tell me, with your smiles, that you will hope and trust. Tell me, beautiful, beloved!" he took both her hands and looked fondly on the still white face, "tell me that you will love me always, even in death—if death should come."

The blue heaven-light faded from her eyes; they darkened, till the blackness of night stood in their voiceless agony.

"Love you, Ralph!" the sweetness of all music floated in that passion-toned voice. "God forgive me this love—Holy Mary shield its idolatry! Oh, Ralph! how much better you know I love you, than I can tell you!"

"Then, Genevieve, lift that dear head; there is nothing to fear. Liberty and Cuba! How my heart bounds with the words! Ere the autumn leaves have come, I will be with you, love, and our theme shall be joy—not only our joy, but the joy of a people. Smile, Genevieve—I cannot leave you thus. My path would be dark without the memory of that sweet sunshine."

Poor Genevieve, she did smile—a smile that struggled through tears. She even asked the many lip-questions which woman finds when the heart is too weary or full to speak. Her grief was unavailing, since it only pained, but could not keep him. Gentle heart! *that* was the hushing power.

The chill night-wind murmured the moon a low lullaby, as she darkened in the waves of the broad river; all light was passing from earth when Ralph Dudley left Genevieve with life's first sorrow on her heart.

CHAPTER V

ELLAWARRE, THE BEAUTIFUL plantation of Mrs. Clifton, lay on the fertile coast of the grand old Mississippi; that generous river, knowing neither north nor south, but alike kissing the frozen banks of the snow-hill states, and the sunny shore of the flower-dowered south.

The house was of modern structure, and really southern in all its conveniences. A wide hall, large spacious rooms, deep floor-reaching windows, and, above all, the low vine-shaded verandas.[7]

The grounds around it were very beautiful. Exquisite taste had planned the shaded walks winding to the river, giving you coquetish views of its mighty waves. It was sometimes called "the paradise of flowers," for these many-hued divinities smiled in such luxurious profusion on the wide green lawn. The trees that formed the avenue, and stood back of the house, were unrivalled.

There was the noble old oak, with its ever-living leaves, spreading its benevolent arms to the shade-loving children of its clime. The haughty magnolia, "the pride of the south," stood in graceful but unbending beauty, her emerald leaves crowned with snow-white blossoms. Ah! where is her equal!

Further back from the river, near the house, were thick clusters of orange trees; some laden with rich golden fruit, hiding, like young sunbeams, 'mid the dark green leaves; others, heavy with perfume-breathing flowers,—those mystic, fateful flowers, ever mingling with the bridal-veil, blending their incense with lovers' vows; silent witnesses of pledges, which make the joy or woe of hearts even more pure and beautiful than their own rare but fading loveliness. Off in the distance, where the young sugar-cane waved in verdant beauty, stood the negro houses, or, in southern parlance, "The Quarter." Ah! how I wish some honest, but misjudging north-born friends we have, could or would take the trouble to see the many neat and comfortable settlements on the beautiful plantations of the south.

7. Holcombe's home in Marshall, Texas, also had floor-to-ceiling windows, lavish flower gardens, and abundant trees.

Mrs. Clifton's, it must be acknowledged, was a model; many are not so good, others better.

There the clean whitewashed cabins, with their red chimneys, the clinging vines, the flourishing truck patch, were so cheerful, you could hardly connect cruelty or oppression with those who called it home.[8]

Apart, was the overseer's house, remarkable for nothing but its comfortable look and the great swing in the yard, where the father tossed the laughing children after the day's work was over, while his wife sat sewing on the cool pleasant porch.

It was the morning of Ralph's departure: the sun was shining broadly in the room when Genevieve awoke; she lay listening to the gay birds chirping and whistling as they drank the young morning's health in dew; she longed to send them away, she wanted to be very still and think; she was striving to recall the troubled scene of the past night, when the door opened, and a young mulatto girl entered, bearing a breakfast tray.

"Hi! Miss Genevieve," she said, placing it on a small table, "ain't you never goin' to get up? Mistis done up and eat breakfus a long time ago; she and ung Jefferson down in de shrubbery cutting roses for de flowerpots. I reckon she 'spects company, from de way aunt Betty and Gustus cleanin' and fixin' all over de house. Mistis sent down word for nobody to wake you, let you sleep jes' long as you want to.

"But, Miss Genevieve, you ain't eatin' none of dat breakfus! an' your face look red like you got a fever; now jis try one dese figs, right sweet and fresh off de trees; dey mighty good and coolin' for fever, cause I hear Dr. Carter tell mistis so hiself, dat time when she did not want aunt Dilsey to have um, 'cause she was fraid dey make her sick."

"No, no! Emily, I don't want anything; please take it away, and dress me."

"No, I ain't goin' to take dis waiter down jis as it cum. Now drink dis coffee, Miss Genevieve, it good for your strength. Lem me put your chair close to de winder, so you ken get de air while I am dressin' your hair."

Genevieve submitted herself to Emily's hands, whose greatest pride and delight was to twine the long shining curls over her dusky fingers.

"Emily," said her mistress, "put up my curls—braid my hair. I shall never wear curls any more; no, never!"

8. A truck patch is a vegetable garden.

"Comb out them curls! Oh! no, Miss Genevieve, I can't do it."

"Yes, Emily, you must. They are heavy; they make my head ache."

"Never did hear talk of sich a thing. I don't know what Marse Ralph will say—Scipio tell me more an once, dese very curls is his marse heart-strings.' Marster Ralph got so mad he never knowed what to do, when dat Spanish gentman, what used to send you boquets in New Orleans, talked 'bout givin' a kingdom for one of um."

"Colonel Dudley has gone away for a long time, Emily."

"Oh! is he, Miss Genevieve?" said the mulatto, perceiving, with all the quickness of her sensitive race, the delicate sentiment lying in the ordered braids. "Well," she added, passing her hand lovingly over the rippling waves, "I never did 'spect to comb out them curls."

The toilet was over, and Emily stood looking at the graceful form in its loose white dress, and the small head, with the soft sunny braids around it.

"They *is* pretty, but dey don't look nothin' t'all like de curls, no how"; and she gave a sigh to her lost treasures.

"Did some one knock? See who it is, Emily."

"Wait a minit; I fixin' de flowers for your hair. Mistis don't think you is drest widout um. Now,—" she placed them before Genevieve, and went to the door.

"What you want, Gus?"

"Mistis sen me for tell Miss Genevieve if she done wid dat letter what she sent her for read, please give it to me; she want it."

"You must be 'stracted, boy! Miss Genevieve ain't had no letter dis day. Who mistis sen it by?"

"She give it to me, but Daddy Dennis keep on quarrelin' 'bout de peas ain't shelled fur dinner, so I giv' it tur William."

"You foolin' wid dem peas when you ben sen anywhar; you go right straight and git dat letter," said the nipperish Miss Emily, pushing him towards the steps; "you better now."

"Wait, Miss Genevieve, till dat boy come back wid de letter, fore you go down in de library. Mistis dare, and I does hate fur her to know what a set of little niggers she is got. Lord knows dey 'nuff to make any body 'stracted. Here he now; you better come runnin'; whidn't you bring dis letter 'fore now?"

"Cause I forget it."

"You always forgettin'; go along down, sir; you got no more bisnis up here."

Emily gave the letter to Genevieve, who broke its seal, and glanced impatiently over its contents. She was evidently disappointed. The truth was, Genevieve expected the letter was from Dudley, telling her of his determination to stay. So much does woman hope in her love; so much does she trust to her influence over the one beloved.

"Only a note from Uncle Louis! Emily, why did you not say note? You knew it was not a letter,"—rather crossly.

"Hi! Miss Genevieve! T'warnt my fault. Gustus said letter."

"Take it to mamma. So kind in uncle Louis," she continued, musingly. "He says he will bring my Arabian, my beautiful Sea-foam. But I shan't care to ride now. There is no one to ride with me but Eugene, and he"— she laughed at her own thoughts,—"shall ride with Mabel. It is such a comfort to think of having her with me; though I hope she won't find out how much I love Ralph, for she *will* laugh, and I could not bear that, even from Mabel. Ah!" she sighed, "how happy I was yesterday! Mamma says 'suffering makes one charitable.' How kind I will be now I suffer so much."

Poor child! how well it is we cannot read the future.

"But I must go to mamma," and she ran down to the room where her mother sat writing.

CHAPTER VI

"Mamma, kiss me, and say how glad you are, for Mabel Royal is coming at last." She gave Mrs. Clifton the letter.

"Yes, my love; she writes beautifully, and I am very glad she is coming. We must try and make her happy."

"Oh! she makes herself and every one about her happy; that is the charm of her society. Mamma, I will send a note to Eugene de France. I am impatient to see how astonished he will be to find Mabel really so lovely; he thinks love exaggerated my description."

"Very well, my daughter; ring for Gustus."

Genevieve rang the bell, and the note was quickly written.

"Now, Gustus, hurry; do you hear?"

"Yes, marm; Gus go in no time."

"Genevieve, come here, my love."

She went, and sat on the footstool at her mother's feet, and noticed, for the first time, the troubled look which her face wore.

"I have had a letter from Colonel Dudley," Genevieve sighed.

"What do you think, mamma?"

"That he has acted very wrongly—very unwisely, even selfishly."

"Oh, no! it is uncertain and dangerous, but very daring and noble, mamma."

"Very disgraceful!"

"It is very generous in Ralph to involve his fortune and risk his life to assist an unhappy people! It does not matter what you or I may think, mamma; *he* believes it right and just, and you know, when once convinced, how firm he is—"

"How obstinate! Strange he could love you and enlist in—"

"Oh, mamma!" she hastily interrupted, "I know he *does* love me; loves me *dearly. No one could convince me that he did not.* But Ralph would think it unmanly to yield principle to love; to be guided in a matter of conscience, even by a woman whom he adored. I should, too. He is very unselfish—very noble. He did perfectly right. I am sure I think so, mamma." But she covered her face to hide the betraying tears.

"It is certainly very wrong in Colonel Dudley to—"

"Don't blame him, mother, you *must* not,—it makes me miserable; besides, you can scold him when he comes back."

"He writes, he had last night a message from General Lopez, the 'liberating army,' as he styles his associates, will not sail as soon as he expected, so he returns on Wednesday, bringing Captain Raymond with him."

"Coming back! not going!"—it was all she had heard. "Ralph and Mabel both! Oh, I am so glad! Now, mamma, I will go and arrange Mabel's room, just as she will like it," and she went smiling.

"Now, Emily, put the windows up, and bring the flowers. I shall make the vases up, and arrange the books myself."

"Miss Genevieve, who is dis Miss Babel?"

"Not Babel, Emily! *Mabel.* She is the young lady who was at school with me, and is coming to pay us a visit. So I want everything very nice.

No—let that picture hang; don't take it down; it will remind her of Bethlehem. The dear old church, the sister's house, and the beautiful Lehigh—"[9]

"I don't know what make Miss Genevieve set so much by dat ole gray picter; heap better lem me bring one dem fine 'talian drawin's in here, for Miss Mabel look at. Dis room too dark for my use! I'll jes' put de curtin' up, so we can see if anybody comes. Hi! who dat 'long wid Gustus? B'leve in my soul 'tis Mr. de France! Do, pray, Miss Genevieve, don't go down in that white wrapper! 'tain't fit. Put on your seben flounces!"

"Pshaw! it's only Eugene. I don't mind him. Besides, he wouldn't know if I had on velvet or calico. But don't look so distressed, Emily; I promise to dress for dinner!" And she went to meet the handsome, foreign-looking youth, who entered the hall with the air of one very much at home—throwing his hat aside with all the appearance of extreme ill humor.

"Ah, Eugene! I am so glad to see you," said Genevieve, cordially.

"You need not be; I am as unamiable as possible today."

"But you won't be when I tell you; so sit down and listen to me."

He was very handsome as he sat listening. The languid, mellow light of the black eyes, the rich, clear complexion, the full, red lips, and heavy clustering curls, gave the face that glowing sunset beauty, so inexpressibly charming in the Creoles of Louisiana. Now, the brow was slightly contracted and the full, round voice was complaining.

"If you expect company, and wish me to be entertaining and agreeable, I might as well go home. Nothing could have brought me away but a summons from you; and I repent obeying that, for I can be of no service to you in my present humor."

"What has vexed you?" said she, in a sympathizing tone.

"I wish you would not use that word. People are not *vexed* when they are miserable and unhappy."

"*You* unhappy! Don't be angry, Eugene, I can't help laughing, it is so absurd."

The troubled expression did not leave his face, and for a moment he was silent.

9. Lucy Holcombe attended school at the Moravian Institute in Bethlehem, Pennsylvania, on the Lehigh River.

"Genevieve, I have heard of persons pining to be loved; I wish there was no one in the world to care for me; that I was one all alone—the happiness of no one depending on me, and I, independent of the world."

"Oh, Eugene! how ungrateful! Think of your devoted parents—your beautiful sisters. You surely did not mean anything so unkind."

"Yes, I did. I am too old to be in leading-strings. What is the use of being a man if the youngest member of your family is to control your actions? I would like, for once, the luxury of doing what I pleased, without interference."

"How unreasonable! You know—"

"Don't tell me anything I already know. What is the use—I hate lectures even from you, Genevieve."

"Well, I cannot compliment you on your politeness. Don't sit pulling my flowers to pieces, but tell me at once what troubles you."

"No; I shall not tell you anything. I wish to heaven I had gone with Colonel Dudley, as a man would have done. Who but a coward would yield to tears when brave men beckoned him to follow to a generous strife?"

The hot flush of shame and anger burned on his cheek. Genevieve now understood it all—how the entreaties of his adoring family had prevented this only son from joining the daring expedition of Lopez.

There was a deeper interest at her heart, as she looked on the regretful face of this dear companion of her childish life.

"Eugene," her hand was laid softly on his arm, "don't let that make you unhappy; it was noble to yield your own inclination to your mother's love. You will never repent it, Eugene."

The young Creole turned away impatiently.

"I *do* repent it! I detest myself for my weakness. I tell you, Genevieve, it is nothing to have your conduct approved by others, unless you yourself are convinced of its propriety, and satisfied with its justness. Colonel Dudley says—"

"Eugene," she interrupted, "did he persuade you to go? It was very wicked—very unlike him!"

"Persuade me!" indignantly; "I am not quite a child. I don't see anything, however, so wicked, in striving to enlist sympathy in behalf of an oppressed country."

"I do; in engaging in an enterprise full of danger and—"

"Glory!" enthusiastically added Eugene.

"The glory is imaginary, the danger and disgrace real."

"Disgrace! I never knew a woman who could be just and generous where her love was interested!"

"Unkind Eugene! I wish Cuba would sink into the waves for ever!" she cried, with childish anger.

"Don't cry, Genevieve; I could never see the beauty which poets find in woman's tears! I thought you were above scenes."

"I can feel."

"For yourself, you have just said how noble it was to sacrifice your feelings for the happiness of another. Think, now, of the generosity which forgets self in the good of a whole people! Is not this patriotism—the highest order of patriotism?"

"But Cuba has no claim on you—none whatever."

"The strongest of all claims, that which a suffering people has on its prosperous neighbors."

"Don't say any more, Eugene, for I shall always think just as I do now, and still try and influence Ralph not to go, even if he does get angry," she added, in a lower voice.

"Not to go," he repeated; "he has already gone."

"No; mamma had a letter. Something went wrong, and the expedition does not sail—perhaps for two weeks. He is coming home on Wednesday with General Lopez and Stuart Raymond. Who is Stuart Raymond, Eugene?"

The young man's face had brightened, and his fine eyes were lighted with a sudden determination. Everything was decided, when he answered:—

"Ah! he is one of the few men whose friendship is an honor! Brave and bold, if truth vanished from all else earthly, you would find it in his bosom."

"You are always so enthusiastic. Why could you not say, 'he is a very clever fellow?'"

"Because men are, generally, willing to do each other justice."

"I know you mean to say women are not; but, Eugene, it is not at all creditable in a man to sneer at our sex. Brave men never do; it is only the mean, who are themselves deficient in good. The better a man is, the more he loves and respects women."

"Heavens! what have I said? Nothing in the world; yet one would think I had written fifty satires. However, a passion is excusable in you, and all other women who have pretty eyes."

"Oh!" laughed Genevieve, "that reminds me, Mabel is coming at last, Eugene."

"Don't bore me with that girl, don't; I am tired of hearing of her."

"Never mind, she is going to pay me a long visit. I hope we may keep her always—eh, Eugene?"

"You may keep her as long as you please; I am going away for the rest of the summer."

"How provoking and disagreeable you can be! You won't go after you have seen her, for you will love her."

"Love a red, bouncing Yankee girl!" he laughed scornfully.

"She is far more lovely than any southern girl you ever saw."

"I hate Yankee girls," persisted Eugene.

"Why? It is a very silly prejudice."

"They have such large hands and feet! They ought to stay up north, where they are put like sunflowers at the back of the garden. It is bad policy in them to come south, among our lilies and roses."

"Nonsense! what does that matter? besides, I could not begin to wear her gloves or slippers," and she held her pretty delicate hand before him.

"Matter! a great deal; think of a man swearing to love through life, while his eyes rested on a white satin slipper; No. 6,—and then fancy him ordering her wedding-ring to fit his own finger.—Pshaw!"

Genevieve laughed: "Well, Mabel shan't run off with you. I won't have you married by force—sacrificed to friendship."

"Miss Genevieve," said Gustus, making his appearance at the door, "Marse Louis done cum, he say de boat most here too; you ken see de smoke out de chimleys, ef you look down todes de river."

"Come, Eugene," she exclaimed, starting up all expectation, "come!"

"No."

"Stay then"; so she ran out to her uncle Louis, "dear uncle Louis," the kindest, best-hearted old bachelor that ever lived.

"Ah! pretty one," he said, kissing the glowing cheek of his niece, "there is Sea-foam as fine and gaily as if the ugly nail had never pierced her foot."

"You are so good, my darling uncle, but see, the boat is landing; you wait for mamma."

There was much real happiness in the tearful but joyous meeting of the two young girls. It is, I know, a subject of ridicule, but I believe that ofttimes the strongest friendship of a woman's life is formed at school. It was so in this case; they had a memory apart from the world—the memory of calm and happy years, spent in the quiet and excellent Moravian Institute, on the beautiful laurel-covered banks of the romantic Lehigh.

Mrs. Clifton received the orphan friend of her daughter with all a mother's tenderness.

Uncle Louis was charmed. Her cordial manner and unrestrained delight were so different from the stiff northern shake of the hand he had expected. So Mabel established herself at once, as the reality of Genevieve's oft repeated description.

Charming, is not the word to describe her manner; that applies only to the present. It is "fascination," for that has a kind of enchantment that lives even in absence. When I say she was free and careless, both in manner and conversation, I do not by any means intend the bold and dashing style, so much affected by our modern belles; everything about her was delicate and refined. Besides, there was a forgetfulness of self, a charity for others, an interest in the happiness of those around her, which you rarely see in a beautiful woman, who is accustomed to homage and admiration as her right. She did and said many things at which others would have hesitated—but the wrong was in them, not in her. "To the pure all things are pure." Again, the ancients said, "The gods give the impulse, man the motive." Mabel followed the impulses of a warm true heart, with guileless innocence, never pausing to think if you or I would approve, but strong in the consciousness of good. There was a child-like trust, a generous, open confidence, which gave her character an inimitable charm—a charm far more touching, more lasting than beauty.

CHAPTER VII

"Oh! for a tongue to curse the slave,
Whose treason, like a deadly blight,
Comes o'er the councils of the brave,
To blast them in their hour of might."
MOORE.

NOW WE WILL TURN TO Dudley, as he walked slowly down the long avenue which led to the river. Now that he had left Genevieve, he felt a sense
of relief. He loved her with the tenderness we love children, the strength
we love woman; he loved her "not as men *do* love, but as they can"; still
his was not a heart which the holiest spell of woman could entirely fill.
There was a voice within, calling for the great things of life, which she
could not answer. Now that he had broken the silver chains that strove
fondly to bind him; now that he had resolutely thrown himself to fate,
there was nothing to stand between him and the flashing light of his patriotic ambition. On reaching the bank of the river, where a small boat
was moored, he waked Scipio, the negro boy, who was his constant atten-
dant, and their light oars dipped quickly across the rushing waters.

"Mighty dark night, certain; moon done gone down, too; but 'tain't
fus time, Marse Ralph an' me fly like lightnin' bugs 'long here."

Scipio sprang lightly on the shore, and fastened the boat.

"Hi! 'tain bit of light in de hall; you jes' take yo' time, Marse Ralph; I
run on an' see what de niggers is 'bout."

He hastened forward, and left his young master, the last of a noble
name, standing with his eyes fixed sadly on the large old mansion before
him, whose grey walls were partly hid by magnificent oaks, looming up
in the darkness like sturdy sentinels; keeping a quiet protecting watch
over the thousand gorgeous flowers and shrubs, which made the beauty
of the young planter's home.

Cool waters poured their refreshing showers into gleaming marble basins; the low-voiced night-bird sang to the sweet-falling accompaniment;
the south breeze sighed among the dewy flowers of the dark-leaved or-

ange, but nature's charms won no thought from the heart that was wandering far into the future.

Dudley walked moodily up the shell-paved walk, and entered the hall where Scipio's eager face waited.

"Somebody here, Marse Ralph."

"Who, sir?"

"Same one whut cum up wid you an' Mr. Segur bufore.[10] Got name jes' like sum dem Spanishers we kill in Mexico." (Scipio had accompanied his master in the campaign, to which honor he never lost an opportunity of referring.) "Settin' up in yo' own room, smokin' jes' like he feel hiself at home; Marse Ralph, better let dem Spanisher 'lone," he continued, as Dudley sprang up the oak steps which led to the room containing his guest. "Dey not gwine do us no good, no how."

As the door opens, and stream of light falls on him, we will for a moment regard the gallant young hero of our story.

More than six feet he stood; straight, agile, and stalwart. Nature seemed to have sent her model soldier in his form. There was a look so regal on his brow, one might dream it had worn a heavier crown than the chaplet of dark brown hair that encircled above it. It was not the brilliancy of the large hazel eyes which first attracted you; they did not dazzle—the spirit did not beam out; it drew you down into their mellow depths, where the heart sparkled joyously, like a child playing in sunshine. The brows were slight and graceful, but wanting in that strength which marks a man's face with determination. The Grecian nose was sternly cut, like that of a statue; and the force and power of the face centred in the firm square chin. His nether lip was in profile haughty, but there was a tender beauty in its smile, inexpressibly sweet. The hand which threw aside the Spanish cap, as he advanced to meet the stranger, told its own story of high birth, it was so small and white; but the grasp was nevertheless cordial which closed over the dark fingers of Gonzales, whom Dudley thus addressed:—

"You are unexpected, but not the less welcome, Gonzales. I trust you have fared hospitably, in spite of my absence."

"Right sumptuously, noble Dudley; but one scarce thinks on personal comforts in these stirring times. The expedition, however, is delayed; I

10. Laurent Sigur, editor of the New Orleans *Delta* and staunch supporter of López.

came to bring you its movements,"—he laid a sealed package on the table by which they sat.

The young man smiled as he recognised the delicate Spanish characters.

"Ha! you come from the General himself! God keep him!" He rang a small silver bell, which Scipio answered.

"Order the cloth laid in the dining-hall, and come to me."

The visitor, Hidalgo Gonzales, as Ralph had called him, looked from the open window on the dim star-lighted prospect, while his host read with eager interest the coming movements of those generous but ill-fated patriots.

How different they were, the occupants of that room. Gonzales was both a Spaniard and traitor; though born in Spain, he had lived for years in the pay of the official authority in Cuba. After amassing a large fortune he sought the luxurious city of New Orleans, as his home. He had early espoused the Cuban cause, and was in the full confidence of its supporters, who relied greatly on his zeal and trust-worthiness.

But, alas for Cuba! No holy fire burned in those small down-looking eyes; and the low brow retreated, as if to hide its want of beauty in the blackness of the straight over-hanging hair; the rest of the face did not lack comeliness, but the figure was small, cowering, and insignificant; and that sweetness, which we are told lies in the most subtle poisons, floated in that voice which was to pour the deadly venom of its traitor tones in the bleeding wounds of the unhappy Island Queen.

Wailing land of beauty! the serpent which thou hadst nurtured on thy generous bosom, was yet to stab thy burning, breaking heart. Scipio's summons came; Dudley laid the papers carefully by, and the two young men proceeded to the room where the cloth was laid, the wine set on. They seated themselves at the table; but Hidalgo was silent, and glanced uneasily at the honest black face peering over its master's shoulder.

"Shade the lamp, Scipio, and leave the room," all of which the boy did with a very bad grace.

"Can't fool Scip," he soliloquized, seating himself at a distance from the door as an outer guard. "I see him look at Marse Ralph, make him sen' me out, like I kers to hear enny of his gibberish talk. He ain't fit company fur a decent colored boy, no how. Dun know what Marse Ralph make so much of him fur. I jes' natrally hates dem Spanish fellers, 'cause

I seen too much on um in Mexico. Give our boys lots trouble. Dem battles! My soul! diden we pour down de shot, an' gib um siczars! I bet dem Mexicers 'members Scip."

While Scipio reviews with great complacency his former encounters, we will return to the room in which sat the patriot and traitor.

"Now," said Ralph, filling the Spaniard's glass, "tell me, Hidalgo, whence came this glorious news. The Cubans in arms—the flag of the new republic already raised—these many cheering letters from men so long known as staunch loyalists! God is surely with us! But how came they to the hand of the noble exile?"

"Secreted about my person, I was in imminent danger of being seized; but fortune favored, and I arrived in safety with the good tidings. Concha is in despair; his trusty officers are deserting, and he has nothing to hope from the people.[11] This is the tide in Cuban affairs, which will bear the patriot ships to her redemption."

"You have seen the general, and told him this?"

"Aye; all this, and much more. I brought letters from the very officers of the Captain-General's household, swearing their allegiance. I have told him how eagerly the people watch his coming as the worshippers do that of the sun; how hopefully they stand ready to throw their wrongs at his feet, their cause in his hands, to follow him to victory or death."

"What says Segur to this?"

"Ha! you will think both Lopez and his friends have turned cowards when I tell you he it is who counsels this delay. Yet I myself brought his dispatches from the revolutionists, telling him the Cubans are weary of waiting, and begin to question if the promised succor will ever come. That they are inefficient and wholly unprepared to sustain a revolution within themselves; that they have, depending on foreign aid, more than once pronounced, that assistance did not come, and they were speedily put down, being powerless before the superior arms and numbers of the troops. With sullen sorrow they have seen the best and strongest of their partisans condemned to brutal death. They are growing hopeless from bitter disappointment. Lopez swore to come, but he has apparently abandoned them. If their American friends refuse to aid them, then are they

---

11. Captain-General José de la Concha, despotic ruler of Cuba. Concha was appointed because his predecessor was too lax in opposing López. Chaffin, *Fatal Glory,* 190.

lost. This is the purport of their appeal to Segur, on whose sympathy they entirely rely. And yet, in my presence, he said: 'General, it is for you to decide, yet let us remember it is useless to go unless prepared for any emergency; delay is far better than failure.' Lopez urged the impatience of his men, the difficulty with which he controlled them. Segur answered, with his lordly tones, 'Disband them, sir; there are five hundred others ready at any moment to take their places.'"

"It is all very true," said Dudley; "for it is useless to give Cuba our lives, unless they purchase her liberty. We should be better organized; and by waiting, our men may be disciplined, and our supplies doubled. In the mean time, the natives will bravely sustain their cause, knowing we are at hand to succor."

"Think you," replied Gonzales, "they have forgotten the fate of the Round Islanders?[12] Is it likely to inspire them with faith? Do they not know that more than one American vessel hovers in the southern sea, guarding the island—assisting her Majesty to hold the galling chains around the bleeding neck of that unhappy land who would fain follow her example, and accept the generous aid of foreign liberalists, in this struggle to throw off the heavy yoke of a crown? The Cubans are well aware of the hazardous position in which their friends are placed. Denounced as outlaws, guarded as robbers, how know they you have not again been arrested—cut off from all supplies—starving in the very face of the officials? How think you they can, after so many disappointments, trust a people whose government vies with Spain in crushing their rising, struggling hearts?"

A deadly crimson flushed the American's face, and the Spaniard smiled as he watched the fierce young spirit writhe under his words.

"Oh, my country!" exclaimed Dudley, pacing the floor mournfully; "have I lived to blush for thy small-hearted, selfish policy—thy shameful inconsistency! Proclaimed and threatened as pirates, thus has she cast from her those who would die to avenge *her* wrongs—men whose blood has stained the starred banner in its hour of victory—these, she has in-

12. In August 1849, about six hundred men gathered on Round Island, off the coast of Mississippi, awaiting arms before shipping off to invade Cuba. The navy blockaded the island, preventing any reinforcements and arms from coming in. By October all the would-be filibusters had left the island aboard naval ships and returned home. Chaffin, *Fatal Glory*, 64–71.

sulted and branded with reproach. Yes," he added, bitterly, "her forbear-
ance is reserved for foreign powers, but denied the children of her bosom,
whose error, as she is pleased to call it, consists in loving too fondly the
great and beautiful principles of her own national character. You are
right, Hidalgo, we must hasten to strike while our own arms are free."

Dudley sat silent and gloomy. He felt that keen sense of injustice so
galling to a man of conscious integrity. He loved his country, and had
resolutely dashed from his heart the bitter, complaining thoughts which
the words of the wily Spaniard awoke in his breast. The recollection of
the unjust, disgraceful detention of the Round Islanders, the cold-
blooded cruelty of the late proclamation rushed hastily over him. How
dared the man who had sworn before God to protect the rights of American citizens, thus defy the Constitution and outrage their liberties? How
dared this chance President assume a royal power, and wantonly deliver
freemen to the dark despot of Spain, perhaps to an ignominious death?

They had nothing to rely on but their own strong arms, and Cuba's
only hope was in them.

"I do not know precisely," he said, pausing before Hidalgo, "what the
general intends doing; whatever his course, we may rest assured it is that
which he deems best. Segur, that admirable patriot, to whose generous
sympathy and undaunted support the Cuban cause is so greatly indebted,
will counsel him aright."

"If, after the letters I have brought him from the patriots, the strong,
undoubted proof he possesses of their urgent need of assistance, he does
not encourage immediate departure, I shall think I have perilled my liberty and life most uselessly."

"No, no, Hidalgo, do not regret any service rendered so good a cause.
General Lopez writes me, you will return with minute instructions to the
revolutionists, and a promise of our speedy coming. He says, however, at
this present time, we would not reach Cuba, so strict is the watch which
is kept over the gulf by the American men-of-war."

"You will accompany me to-morrow?"

"Yes."

"Then, I pray you use any influence you may have with the general
and his friends, for they are blind to Cuba's interest when they thus delay.
Now or never."

"Haste certainly seems to be imperative. It is true we are few, but Lopez writes with enthusiastic confidence of success."

"Ah! but every hour that finds you on American soil lessens the hope of the Creoles and endangers our success. So remember—but when comes the boat?"

"At early dawn. You are weary, and have but a few hours to rest. Scipio," the boy had long since entered unperceived, "conduct Senor Gonzales to his room."

Dudley remained gazing from the window on outer darkness. The momentary depression that came with the tidings of their delayed departure, had left his fitful spirit;—they *would* go. He knew Lopez and his men too well to imagine they would falter. There was no gloom on the brow from which the wind raised the dark chaplet of hair, and his large eyes were brilliant with gorgeous visions of success. There was no spirit of revelation near, to draw the veil of futurity and unfold its coming scenes; no hand to paint shudderingly in burning colors on the curtain of night, the fearful picture of American degradation; the piercing cry of unavenged freemen was yet sleeping with the power of the tyrant.

The glorious future of Cuba! His heart bounded with the thought—he walked slowly down the room, and paused before the full-length portrait of our own gallant La Fayette. He looked with wistful earnestness on the still but speaking features. The frank honest eyes beamed down, down, into the heart of the brave young liberator, filling it with a secret encouragement, a strange solemn hope and joy. The lips, so firm in their beautiful patriotism, seemed to whisper, "Go—follow in my footsteps," and his hand lay meaningly on that trusty sword, which so promptly came to the aid of our own oppressed country. He turned with silent reverence to the form of Washington, as he stood on the canvas, in his full military uniform. Could he ask a nobler cause than that which involved the same great principle for which he had fought? The great heroes of a struggle nearly resembling the one to which he looked forward, were on either side, as if to inspire him. A holy zeal filled his breast, he felt as if *their* spirits listened approvingly from the hovering world around, as, in that picture-haunted room, his heart filled with the chivalry of the past, strengthened with hope for the future, he solemnly renewed his allegiance to Cuba and her cause.

Midnight had long since passed, and Scipio came urging his master to retire. "Marse Ralph, ef you goin' way in de mornin', you better be gittin' sum sleep dan standin' dare zamenin' de same ole picters we bin seen ever sence we wus boys. Ginel Washinton and Ginel 'Fayette ain't had nobody set wid um dese las' twenty-five years."

"Scipio, tell Marmion to come to me."

"Hi, Marse Ralph! he done gone to his house long time ago; it mose day. I don't see what you wants wid 'nother sort er wine to-night, Marse Ralph,"—(Marmion was the butler,)—"but ef you does, I'll jes' go; I boun' I knows de way to dat cellar."

"Go and send Marmion to me, sir; and you get ready to leave to-morrow."

"Dat's right," muttered the boy, proceeding on his errand, "nuver lef poor Scip, Marse Ralph, 'cause nobody gwine stan' by you like dis nigger, whut got no 'pendance but his master. Ef he die, Scip die—ef he live, Scip live too, bless de Lord." Scipio succeeded in rousing the butler, and starting the old man in rather brisker measure than he was accustomed to towards the house.

"Scip, what dat Spanisher come fur?"

"Not my place to revulge; I feels honerated to say dis much, business of 'portance from the President."

"Hope he isn't sent for Marse Ralph to fight no more wars fur him; 'cause dis family, what ain't got but one in it, dun 'nuff fur dey country. Marse Ralph got two gret uncles dead in de 'mortal 'Merican resolution; an' his granfather, when he 'manded under Ginel Washington, got shots 'nuff to kill a commun man. Den his own father, my blessed ole marster, sarve his time under Ginel Jackson. Menny is de time I bin cleanin' dere firearms, while dey set 'round de table drinkin' wine an' jokin' like real born blood gentlemuns, as dey wus. Dem wus fine ole days when de Eng-lishers turned pale an' run, same is Injuns, ef you look 'Merican at um."

"Yo' talk 'minds me of Mexico, uncle Marmion, do *we* neber had no wine. Lord knows we wus glad 'nuff to git water. 'Twas always curus to me how Marse Ralph live through it!"

"De Dudleys is hard to kill, dey is born fur solgers!"

"Mus be dat way, 'cause nobody could live and went through what me and Marse Ralph did. You see, uncle Marmion, you nuver bin in a furrin' lan' sick an' got no money, nur frens, when you got plenty of bofe at home—me an' Marse Ralph is; an' 'tain much glory in it nuther, sir."

"No, Scip, I nuver is; please God when I lef 'Merica lem me step up to heaben. But you say," he added, in a lower tone, "you ain't got no notion what dat Spanish man cum for?"

"I feels oblergated to say nothin' 'tall 'bout it. But," added the body-guard mysteriously, "I'll 'mark dis much fur yo' satisfaction, bein' it's you, uncle Marmion; de President is in Orlens, waitin' fur Marse Ralph to make 'rangements 'bout de marter." He shook his head cautiously, and opened the door, which Marmion entered alone.

"Marmion," said Ralph kindly to the white-headed servant of his father, "it is an odd time to call you, but I shall leave very early to-morrow. I wish you as usual to take charge of affairs, and keep everything straight until I return; which may be in a few days, or, perhaps, not for a long time. If anything should occur, and I do not come at all, take this yourself, remember," he laid his hand on a small cabinet of beautiful workmanship, "to Mrs. Clifton. I leave the key with you, Marmion, for I know, as you were faithful to my father, so you will be to his son."

"God bless you, Marse Ralph,—las' words my blessed marster say to me, wus, 'Marmion, 'member, nuver lef my motherless boy.' Poor nigger coulden talk, he takes dat boy up in dese ole arms, an' dem streamin' eyes look up to de heavenly father—dat 'nuff—de ole solger die in peace. Now dis grey head proud an willin' enny day for lay down under de groun for dat same boy what ole Marmion done raze up fur be a solger and a gen-tleman like his father wus 'fore him." He shook the honest tears from his eyes. Dudley was much moved. His recollections ran back through the spent years of his orphaned life; his childhood, over which Marmion had great control. He remembered how he had taught him to sit on a horse, and to excel in all his boyish sports, how he was never tired to taking him before the portraits of his father and Jackson, telling him all the while, with his simple but touching enthusiasm, wondrous stories of their war-like deeds; how when he showed him the great sword that lay beside the well preserved uniform, he laughed to see the little hands try to thrust its shining blade, and said, with a famous smile of complacent pride, "You gwine be jes' like yo' brave father, thang de Lord, and dat sword is yourn when you gits a big grown up man." He remembered Marmion's grief when his guardian sent him to college, and how he persisted in his yearly visits, watching over with untiring devotion, even to the present, the child of his adored master. All this, and much more came to his heart, when he said, "Marmion, I believe you are the best and truest friend I have ever known. I wish there was something I could do for you—if you would only have your freedom."

"Marse Ralph!" exclaimed the old negro, passionately, "don't 'sult dis grey head in yo' own dead father's house!"

Ralph smiled. "Marmion, you know I could not mean to hurt you."

"No, no, Marse Ralph, you ment it fur good, but you oughter knowed better. I furgits it dis time, and all Marmion 'quires is, fur you to hold yo'self like my marster's son, and 'member you bars dat name Ginel Jackson was proud to call his fren' in de camp, an' in de gret house at Washinton too. But it 'pears to me," he continued, looking inquiringly at his master, "dem Mexicans is mighty comical folk ef dey ain't satisfied wid de flogging you and Ginel Taylor dun giv' um. Dey oughter had Ginel Jackson holt of um; I reckon dey nuver would want to fight agin, time he made Britishers of um; lopt um a' roun' de tree wid de trace chains. I boun he never had his work to do over, 'specially ef my marster's rigimentals wus on de fele. Marse Ralph, you gwine 'way now, and dare is one thing I does 'quest of you, don't s'pose yo'self to de enemy's fire onnecessary, 'memberin' es you doe you is le las' Dudley—ef de balls cums thick don't be shame to dodge um, sir, 'cause 'twas de i'mortal ginel hisself whut said—'Never mind de hed movin', boys, ef de foot stan' still.'"

"Marmion!" exclaimed his master, smiling, "you must be dreaming; who the d——l has been talking of war?"

"Nobody, sir; Scipio revulged de 'fair of de President waiting in New Orleans fur your 'rival, and I 'vined de res."

Ralph laughed heartily. "So, you have been listening to one of Scipio's infernal yarns."

"Marse Ralph, ef de President wants to stop on his way up, jes' lem me know, 'cause I mus prepar things to give him a 'ception. You can jes' sen' Scip back, ef you please, sir."

"Hang the President! it is very probable I shall return myself in a few days, unless I am wanted elsewhere; if I do, Stuart Raymond will accompany me. You remember him, Marmion?"

"Dat I does; he is a gentleman every inch, an' will do to trus'; wish I could say de same of all your frens. Marse Ralph, mind whut you 'bout, an' don't 'gage in nothin' harum-scarum, 'cause t'ain everybody got a name an' fortune to los, and you mighty don't ker."

"I shall be wonderfully cautious, Marmion," he said with a smile, "and try and keep the name and fortune both unhurt. I will leave a letter on the table, which you will send to Ellawarre to-morrow. Now, you may go."

"God bless you, Marse Ralph, Lord a'mighty bless my marster's chile." The dark ebon fingers closed over the hand they had led from childhood to manhood's estate, and the dark fine form, with its wrinkled brow and snow-white head, slowly left the room.

Colonel Dudley sat down, and wrote Mrs. Clifton; telling her, for the first time, of his connexion with Lopez. When the letter was finished, the morning light was coming in, and he threw himself on his couch to sleep, as we do when youth is in its first promise, and hope is making its own future.

CHAPTER VIII

MABEL HAD BEEN LONG enough at Ellawarre to charm the whole house-hold by her unaffected gaiety and good-humor. She was so curious, so amused and interested in everything relating to southern life. Eugene, reader, was ever by her side, explaining with gentleness and patience, truly remarkable in him, all that excited her wonder and astonishment; laughing with her at her own ignorance; riding, walking, singing with her; arranging her favorite flowers; neglecting everything for her smile; show-ing by a thousand little things, how deeply the "Yankee girl" had touched his heart. Genevieve was too wise to say anything; but tried, with wom-anly tact, to convince him by her silence that she had quite forgotten his wonderful aversion, so soon overcome.

Ralph had returned with Stuart Raymond, and the circle at Ellawarre acknowledged them a great addition. The one was so gay, so joy-loving; the other, so calm and entertaining. Mabel said she wondered how they could be such friends. The two men were so different, that she compared them to sunshine and twilight.

When Genevieve, with confidential curiosity, asked Mabel what she thought of Ralph, she said:

"Think of him as Glaucus.[13] No, not the Greek either. To whom shall I compare him? Ah! Essex—that is better.[14] Bold, brave Essex! the rash, daring spirit, whom royalty itself could not tame or subdue. Lordly and superb, he is a man to whom any woman might be proud to lose her heart. Inasmuch as you are happy, Honey-flower, I am by grace of necessity content with your choice. Yet, while I admire Colonel Dudley, I cannot help seeing that he is—"

"Never mind finding fault with Ralph, Mabel. I would not have him changed in any one respect. I should be happy with him, even in unhappiness. Do you understand that?"

"No, not exactly; though I suppose you mean to express a wonderful degree of satisfied love. I do not anticipate unhappiness, for you are the very one to love him. Now, *I* should not mind the shadows that come entirely too often to his magnificent brow. I would resent his imperiousness fifty times a day. You subdue it by your gentleness. You are so loving—so good."

"No, no, Mabel! If I am by nature milder than you, I do not deserve any praise for it. I have seen you control both feeling and temper by an effort of your queenly will. That was a nobler goodness than the mere exercise of a passive amiability, in which there is no positive evil to be overcome. Triumph over temptation, resistance of evil, is, I think, one of the highest virtues we can exercise."

"Yes, my love; but you are the pure unalloyed gold. I am the precious metal with any amount of dross. I fear it will take the hot fire of misfortune to make me the earnest woman that I feel I ought to be. If I had ever known a mother, who would have guided and controlled me by her love, I am sure I would have been so much better and happier."

"Mabel, I always thought you the happiest person in the world."

"Oh! yes," she answered quickly, "I believe I am always cheerful, even gay. But there is no one to care particularly if I am happy or not. My friends love me—but there are others dearer to them. Strangers are polite, and call me beautiful and fascinating, as long as I please and interest

13. Name of several figures in Greek mythology, one of whom was a sea divinity. Originally a fisherman, he ate a magical herb and leaped into the sea, where he was changed into a god.

14. English soldier and courtier famous for his relationship with Queen Elizabeth I (reigned 1558–1603).

them. But there is no one from whom I have the right to claim affection. I am doubly an orphan, and have no home-ties; those ties which can alone bind happiness permanently. Sometimes I am very lonely, and envy the poorest beggar-girl who can lay her head upon a mother's bosom. My aunt, you know, is only my uncle's widow, and has children enough of her own to care for. She is, however, very kind in her way, and likes to have me with her; I gratify her ambition, which is the laudable one of chaperoning a beauty and belle. My guardian is a nice old man, but bores me with accounts of my fortune, and reasons why, as an heiress, I should make what he calls a splendid match."

"Mabel, how strange it is to hear you acknowledge yourself 'a beauty and belle.'"

"Yes," she laughed, "but it would be an affectation to say I thought myself ugly. Others, of fastidious taste, have decided the question of beauty in my favor. I admit the sincerity of their decision, even while I differ with them. I do not think I am beautiful, for I like a dark style of loveliness; but I am very glad other people do. Admiration is a pleasant thing after all, if we would only be candid about it. Is it not, Honey-flower?"

"I don't know. It is very wrong to like admiration too much."

"Oh! of course. That means, you must not care for more than you receive—must not covet that which is given to your pretty neighbor with the dark curls. Men make a terrible fuss about the vanity of women, but I never saw a handsome man yet who was not ridiculously vain of his beauty."

"Ralph! Mabel," said Genevieve, reproachfully.

"Ralph," repeated Mabel, with a wicked smile, "is an understood exception."

"How do you like Eugene, Mabel?" asked Genevieve, abruptly.

"Oh! very well."

"Only very well, when he is so devoted to you? Do you not love him a little?" She looked earnestly at her friend.

Mabel tried, with a laugh, to frighten back the blush that dyed her cheek. But it stayed to crimson her neck and arms.

"Nonsense! You don't expect me to love every handsome man who admires me."

"You are always strange, Mabel. I hardly know what to expect. Well, Stuart Raymond comes next."

"Stuart Raymond!" repeated Mabel, thoughtfully. "Genevieve, I dare say I get the sentiment from some novel; for they generally have a mysterious character who exerts a mysterious influence over some one else. But it is nevertheless true, that I feel as though this man, this Stuart Raymond, was intimately connected with my future life. His eyes draw me, with a strange fascination, to look into them. Sometimes I feel as if my own destiny was linked with that of the strong spirit that looks from them. But I know it is not," she murmured in a lower voice, with a quiet smile.

"He has beautiful eyes," said Genevieve.

"Very beautiful, royal purple eyes—colored like the dark leaf of the pansy. He is not really handsome; but then his features are fine, and full of character, with such dignity of expression."

"I think him too cold and calm."

"Yes; until his interest is awakened. Then how his face lights up with enthusiasm!"

"When he speaks of Cuba, for instance."

"His face could never be handsome to me, while his lips dwelt on the fancied wrongs of that troublesome island, who does not deserve half the fuss they make over her."

"Fancied wrongs!" exclaimed Mabel, indignantly. "Genevieve, it is fearful to say that. In all the world there does not exist such cruel despotism as that exercised over these unhappy people."

"I do not care for the Cubans," persisted Genevieve; "and I think it very wrong in America's citizens to defy her laws, and violate her President's express command."

"Defy her laws!" said Mabel, scornfully; "that is the usual false charge brought against these noble men, and is very unjust. America has no law which takes from her people the liberty of going to any country they please. Neither is there anything in the laws of nations to prohibit them. The friends of Cuban independence seek to introduce no new feature in national laws, to disturb no diplomatic friendship. Their aspirations are honorable and just, and whoever seeks to crush them, ignores the work of Washington."

"I don't know anything about 'the laws of nations.' When did you learn them, Mabel?"

"I know very little myself," she answered, pleasantly; "but I like to understand what others talk of; and as I was ignorant on this subject, I read all that I could."

"Are you not afraid of being called strong-minded?"

"Oh, no!" she laughed. "It is not knowledge that makes women strong-minded, but the want of it, or rather the affectation of it."

"But, Mabel, men dislike learned women so."

"No, my love; that is an erroneous idea. Besides, you confound pedantry with a well balanced and cultivated mind. A woman with liberal information, one who comprehends, fully and correctly, the principles and propriety, not only of the intellectual but *social* world, may exert on society a great and good influence. Woman has great power, if she would realize and accept it. It is conceded that early education has much to do with a man's future course. Then the mother, though she cannot herself struggle in active life, yet in the mind of her son she can lay the foundation of that strength which may, in after years, hold the storm of strife obedient to his will. The mother may implant in her boy that love for right and truth which will fill the man with lofty aspirations for good. It is woman, after all, who crowns the hero. His best reward is—her smile. 'For this a world was bartered, and the loser counted himself richer than Caesar.'"

"Mabel, I do not wonder Stuart Raymond stops to listen when you speak. You advance his own ideas."

"No," she answered, shortly; "I am not indebted to him. Yet we do agree singularly. But, Genevieve, what was the conclusion? I heard Colonel Dudley persuading your mother to accompany them to New Orleans, and remain at ———, or somewhere over the lake, while the Pampero is gone."[15]

"Yes, we will go. Uncle Louis says the sea breeze will keep our spirits up. General Lopez went up yesterday to the estate above, where he has strong friends. To-morrow he and his staff dine here. In the evening we take the boat for the city. But there is the dressing-bell; and the gentlemen are coming from their ride. Let us make our toilet."

15. The ship López took on the expedition. He left New Orleans on August 4.

CHAPTER IX

"Nay! my love must soar upward,
Like the eagle pierce the clouds.
The wings of his great mind
Borne by a lofty energy, must catch the rays
Of Fame's imperial sun:
Must, like a star, with brilliant eyes,
Look down on meaner things.
Then will I crown him with my smile,
And he shall fondly swear
It is Elysium—lightly bought."

THERE WAS AN ANIMATED discussion around the dinner-table, when Mabel, who was late, entered, and took her seat opposite Stuart Raymond, and beside Eugene. "We were just wanting you," said Genevieve; "I was supposing Fortune stood in benevolent waiting, and we were to ask and receive a boon. What would you ask, Mabel?"

"Rest," she said, almost solemnly.

"Rest! You are as unsatisfactory as Captain Raymond. He wanted 'truth,' Colonel Dudley 'success'; uncle Louis was more reasonable—'a wife,' and Eugene, what do you suppose he asked? Look on his eager, heroic face, and guess what boon he prayed the bounteous lady to give him? Nothing less than 'Fame!' the noble bride of statesmen, of warriors, and kings! Is he not over-bold to bend his boy brow at such a shrine!"

Mabel turned her rich glowing eyes upon him, and said, "It is a right brave shrine at which you kneel. One whose wild deep worship has filled the greatest souls. I warmly encourage your devotions. Only be loyal, and your reward will come. Wear the crown, even though its bright roses be red with hero blood. Let it grace your brow, and tell of the triumph of a strong heart in the well-fought battle of life. See," she folded her white hand, "I am ready to clap you applause."

"Miss Royal," laughed Dudley, "beware how you encourage that '*incautious young man*' to his destruction."

"It is very safe for a woman to talk as Mabel does," said Genevieve, "she does not have to prove the heroism of her words by deeds."

Stuart Raymond looked with a quiet smile on the downcast eyes of the young girl, while he said, "Would Miss Royal send her lover to win this brave crown? Would not the sands of the passing hour be wet with tears?"

Mabel raised her eyes, gleaming like the brilliant fire-flies of a summer night. "My lover must have a prouder idol than even my peerless self. He must strike for honor and for fame. Not for the praise of men, that is poor and empty, passing away; neither for my smile, which, even though it enveloped him like light, could not fill a heart truly great. He must be honest and true; having, as his best reward, the assurance that he has rendered some service to virtue and human good."

"Miss Royal is ambitious."

"No," she replied very quickly. "I am not ambitious. What has woman to do with ambition? Hers is an humbler, but, for her, a holier and better sphere of action. But," the smile on her lip was so beautiful, "for the man I loved, I should be *very* ambitious. The more I loved him, the more gladly would I welcome the fair goddess of Fame as my rival. I would even submit to be—*almost*—neglected for her sweet sake. But—for her alone," she added with a laugh. A soft winning laugh had Mabel Royal.

"Mabel," said Mr. Clifton, smiling, "I think, from your own concessions, you *are* ambitious. Not for yourself exactly, as your position in society does not allow you to exercise it; but it amounts, after all, to the same thing."

"Hush, uncle Louis! don't put on your thinking-cap now, to make me contradict myself. Remember my inconsistencies, and, in kindness, don't quote me on myself. Why don't you look gratified, as if I had said something very grand?"

"Perhaps," said Captain Raymond, "Miss Royal would change the position of her sex—would give woman the right to throw herself into the whirlpool of politics, and wrestle with the plebeian democracy; to place herself at the head of a gallant regiment, and shout with her silver-toned voice, the cry of victory."

She looked at him an instant, and her face flushed, though she said quietly, "No, I think woman's position is right, just as it is. It is a happy and honorable one. But I cannot help it, that my spirit is restless, and sometimes longs for activity. I regret and condemn the growing strong-mindedness of my sex. Yet, I think, if man was truer to his duties, woman would not seek to assist him in his legitimate sphere."[16]

Stuart Raymond bowed over his glass, with a submissive smile.

"Mabel, my love," said Mrs. Clifton, "I have some pleasant information for you. General Lopez and his staff dine with us to-morrow, and we accompany them as far as the city. Now, your anxiety to see the heroic general will be gratified."

"Well," cried Mr. Clifton, with a quizzical smile, "who would have thought to hear my cautious, conservative sister, avow not only her sympathy for the Fillibusters, but her actual intention to join them!"

"My sympathy," replied the lady gravely, "is with its supporters, not the expedition."

"But," resumed Mr. Clifton, "the Fillibusters are—"

"Uncle Louis," interrupted Mabel, "don't say Fillibusters! Call them by their proper name,—'Patriots!' 'Liberators!' Though you do come nearer doing that than our kingly President. Colonel Dudley," she continued, turning to Ralph, "what do you think of the proclamation, proclaiming you a pirate?"

"I think, to use the words of my friend Walker, 'It is an outrage to the personal rights guaranteed an American citizen by our Constitution, and a disgrace to the spirit of the age in which we live. It assumes an authority over body and soul, which would well become the Czar, but is highly disgraceful to Republicanism.'"[17]

"Don't look so fierce, Ralph," said Eugene, when Dudley had finished his spirited quotation. "You only want a belted sword and black feather, to represent the pirate complete."

"Colonel Dudley! your friend Walker has a gallant spirit. Don't forget your promise to present him. Does he not meet you in New Orleans?" inquired Mabel.

"Yes; but don't be after bewitching him with your bright eyes, Mabel—having him transfer his allegiance from a republican to a royal mistress."

16. Manly virtue is part of a gendered system; men must do their part if women are to do theirs.
17. See introduction, pp. 9–13, on Republicanism.

"Nay, Colonel Dudley," she laughed, "though non-commissioned, you know I am the best recruiter you have. 'Liberator' is a sure passport to my favor; and I only smile on the disaffected to draw them into ranks."

Beautiful, bewitching Mabel! how she blushed at the pretty speech Ralph made; after which, they drained their glasses to Cuba's fair advocate.

"Mabel," began uncle Louis, "you are a very wicked girl—very—and—"

"Don't let him find fault with me, Mrs. Clifton," she interrupted.

"Find fault with you, Mabel!" the lady repeated, with a smile; "there is the trouble. No one can do that; even though we acknowledge your fault, you charm away the very blame that might correct it. Yours is a beautiful spirit, my love—a strange mixture of pride and tenderness."

The beautiful eyes of the young girl filled with tears; and Mrs. Clifton hastily asked Captain Raymond if he admired the Cuban general as much as his officers usually did. Let me here pause to ask why it is that words of kindness publicly spoken are, for the most part, regarded as flattery. Sarcasm, too often received as wit, brings applause, or passes at least without remark; when a gentle word, or any show of good feeling, is immediately construed as affectation. This is an injustice society has too long labored under. Let us be more true to our kindly impulses, which conventionality has certainly no right to cloak. But we have kept Captain Raymond waiting to say:

"I do not know, madam, what proportion my admiration bears to that of others, but it is very great. General Lopez is certainly worthy of the highest esteem his friends can feel for him. His whole life has been marked with honor and probity. Before his renunciation of his government, he was a favorite with its queen. Wealth, power, and the highest distinction were within his grasp. Why, then, did he renounce this government? Because his noble heart had an innate tendency to liberal institutions, and hatred to tyranny and oppression; because, in his intercourse with the people of Cuba, he discovered a spirit of opposition to the existing government, and a disposition among them to follow the example of our country in achieving their independence. Next, his untiring energy and perseverance in a cause, the justice of which, he is convinced, must command respect. Thwarted as he is on every side, in his effort for freedom, yet he will not know despair. Though he has made a gallant but

unsuccessful attempt to land a force on Cuba's shore, yet is his good purpose unshaken.[18] This brave, self-reliant spirit points to a future, whose
victory will cover with oblivion every disappointment of the past. By the
strong power of an indomitable will, he sustains himself; resolute and
calm, still pursuing, with unyielding hope, the goal of his just and noble
ambition; trusting that the achievement of his good purpose will garland
the victorious brow with a patriot's fame, and put the happy song of freedom into the mouth of that people, for whom he is willing to venture so
much. Ah, madam! does not such virtue justly claim our praise?"

"He is very noble," sighed Mrs. Clifton.

"Captain Raymond," said Genevieve, "look to Mabel, if you want
sympathy. Her enthusiasm rises to the highest point at the very mention
of your general's name."

Stuart Raymond turned to meet, for an instant, the eager, listening
eyes fixed on his face.

"Do you, then," he said, with a kind of tenderness in his voice, "feel
hope for the noble exile? Would you sorrow if he met misfortune?"

"Oh, yes!" she answered earnestly. "I hope it is not strong-minded, for
I *do* feel the deepest sympathy for the cause which Lopez and his followers so generously espouse. I am interested in the entire expedition—in
every one concerned in it—from the seamen who man the Pampero, to
the noble general himself. I will pray most devoutly for a glorious success."

"And if we fail?"

"It is better to meet dark disappointments than never to know great
hopes."

"Mabel," cried Mr. Clifton, from the other end of the table, "listen
to me now. Suppose me to be your *lover*—though only for a moment,
remember—would you send *me* off fillibustering over the Mexican sea?"

"I would send you to assist in liberating an oppressed and unhappy
people."

18. López had previously invaded Cuba in May 1850, fought with Spanish soldiers, and
won the town of Cárdenas. Upon hearing that Spanish reinforcements were on their way,
he abandoned the expedition and returned to the U.S., where he was arrested for violating
U.S. neutrality laws. Released on bail, he became a celebrity in many circles, especially in
New Orleans.

"Oh! perhaps that *is* a better way to express it. But what if I had con-scientious scruples?"

"I would try and overcome them, and any other obstacles which pre-vented you from doing good."

"After Cuba was freed, I might repose at leisure on a coffee plantation; eh, Mabel!"

"No," she answered shortly, indignant at the insinuation. "You should go wherever right was to be asserted, or good effected. Perhaps to Hun-gary or Spain, even to—"

"Well! when the whole world had been fillibustered into republi-canism—"

"Then—we would, after giving thanks, examine minutely, and if there was the shadow of a chain around the neck of 'the man in the moon,' we would immediately fit out an expedition for his relief."

"You are a right royal girl, Mabel; but I should not much like being at the mercy of such a lady-love."

"No," she laughed; "I sometimes feel very sorry for the poor fellow I am to marry. If he only knew the life that *is* before him, I am sure he would join this expedition, or hang himself at once."

Mabel colored, in spite of herself, as she looked up and found the large "royal purple eyes" of Stuart Raymond fixed sadly on her face. She sprang impatiently from the table; for at that moment Mrs. Clifton gave the sig-nal for the ladies to seek the drawing-room.

When the gentlemen joined them, Mabel was leaning from the win-dow, looking towards the river, whose bright waves gleamed in the star-light.

Eugene hastily crossed the room, and stood by her. Long and earnestly they talked of the future. When the gentlemen rose to leave, Mabel un-folded a tiny flag, not larger than the hand which had covered it, and said—

"I have wrought the banner you so much wanted. How beautiful," she continued, admiringly, "are the colors that mingle in the free flag of Cuba! How noble are the spirits who support its claims! But it was a strange fancy of yours, Eugene, to have those blue eyes looking from the star."

"My heart will be so strong," he answered; "Miss Mabel's dear eyes keeping guard over it."

"Ah! Eugene, you *are* brave; you *must* be strong. When Cuba is free, *then* think of Mabel."

CHAPTER X

"I know not why
I love this youth; and I have heard you say,
Love's reason's without reasons."

THE GREEN ROOM OF Ellawarre was the favorite retreat of its guests when summer grew warm. It had such an air of coolness, such an expression of freshness, as Eugene once said—"The highly-polished floors seemed to send you along with scarce a conscious effort on your part, though all the while you had a vision of a fall and a laugh. This was the reason, perhaps, you would seat yourself with a secret, triumphant glee on the light cane chair, or fall negligently on the velvet-cushioned lounge, to admire the graceful flowing of the gossamer curtains." On the marble mantel were two curious old vases, in which the crimson flowers of the pomegranate, the fragrant honeysuckle, jasmine, and roses rested on wild-looking sprigs of oak. A box of rare shells, a bust of Washington, one of Jackson and Clay, were all the ornaments of this room, in which Mabel and Genevieve sat on the morning of which I write. Genevieve's white fingers were busy weaving gold beads with purple threads, that mysterious, fairy-looking employment which ladies so much love. Mabel sat with her drawing implements before her, but it was evident her thoughts were not with the languid movements of her pencil. She drew awhile in silence; then impatiently pushing the table aside, she threw herself on the lounge, and said, "I wish it was not so warm; I would like to have a canter on Seafoam, a real race with the wind. I feel wonderfully adventurous just now; would not object to a fall, provided a robin came to my rescue, and I made a lover by it."

"Mabel, I wonder you don't sew; I don't think I ever saw you engaged in that womanly occupation."

"No, Honey-flower, and you never will; I could not sew if I wished, and I would not if I could. There are people enough in the world for that, without my being a martyr to a mistaken sense of industry. I have had numberless lectures from my aunt on the subject, but she has not convinced me that the world would be either wiser or happier for my stitching. It would interfere greatly with my own comfort, and I don't see why I should do anything I don't like, as long as I can avoid it."

"But, Mabel dear, suppose you should marry, and be unfortunate, and not have any one to sew for you?"

"Well, yes; I am glad you mentioned it; that decides me. I will marry a tailor, and he can do the sewing for the family."

"Nonsense, Mabel; you might embroider; there is sentiment in that."

"No, no, Genevieve, not a bit of it; when you are in the mysteries of tangled silk, broken needles, and aching eyes. I love a beautiful effect, but I have no fancy for a thorough knowledge of causes. Don't you remember how our beloved preceptor, Herr Schultz (our 'beau ideal' of a gentleman and a Christian) used to scold me, because I would not study astronomy; I now congratulate myself I did not. It is delightful to me, in this age of wisdom, to look up to the stars in utter ignorance of that knowledge which has reduced them to a science, to read the lessons written by the gods on their calm, eternal faces, without a vision of figures and distances to bring me again to earth. For this reason I detest botany; to think of dissecting a lovely flower to define the philosophy of its mechanism. I object to reducing the beautiful to science; wait till you read my treatise on the subject."

"But, Mabel, science is in itself beauty."

"Ah! but its beauties are too deeply hidden for me to discover; who cares for that beauty which requires an effort to be appreciated! Why must the eye grow dim, the cheek wax pale with midnight researches after that with which our actual world is teeming? The creation itself is one deathless dream of joy. Why cannot we clasp it just as God has given it, with its ten thousand whispers of bliss, and be satisfied? Why must we toil to make for ourselves other charms, ere we have enjoyed those already given?"

"Mabel, the wise tell us—"

"Never mind, Honey-flower, what 'the wise' tell us; they are no wiser than ourselves, only we think so. Wisdom is a mere playing allowed men to amuse them. Love is the grand principle of life. Does not the *Bible* teach us that? for it is love alone we can take with us to another world; there he who has loved most will be greatest, not he who has known most. Loving the created; seeking to do good to humanity; thus shall we be sanctified to the Creator. Now change the subject, Genevieve, for this brings us to Fillibusterism, and your heart is already sick with that.

> "'Her lover, her brave lover,
> Will seek the stormy main,
> And his lady love is weeping,
> He may not come again.'"

"Hush, Mabel! What are you talking of this morning? Love is an unusual theme for you."

> "'Has the maiden forgotten her early song,
> Has she listened to love's soft lay!'"

"Yes," Genevieve listened and believed. "I have drunk a new and strange draught from the goblet of life, and I am intoxicated with its delicious influence."

Genevieve threw aside the golden beads, and looked suddenly on the reclining form, and its face half supported by the tiny hand.

"Eugene!" she cried.

The brilliant crimson of the cheek, the sweet beseeching smile of the haughty lip answered, "Eugene!"

She was kneeling by the low couch, nestling on the bosom of the beloved.

"Fie, Genevieve; you give a poor welcome to my pretty secret; your tears will stain the orange flowers and bridal favors which necessarily throng your brain."

"Mabel, Mabel, it is a fearful thing to love," she sobbed. An impatient shadow darkened the radiant brow, but Mabel answered quickly—

"No, no, Genevieve; it is a glad, a glorious thing to love. The soul is so strong with life; the fulness, the entireness of its delight. Hope goes dashing in rushing waves of joy on the white-breasted sands of future years, decking them with happy thoughts, like rosy shells in childhood's lap— like pearl gems on its unshadowed brow. It is a golden gate through which we enter a world of happiness. Ah! beautiful gate, beautiful world, bewildering dream!"

"Mabel, Mabel! may not the dream fade—will it not pass away?"

"Never, never! It is greater than life; it is divinity, Genevieve; mortality has no power over it—death is but its purifier—the drop of materialism is consumed—the nobler part of our being lives in heaven—heaven is God, and God is love."

"Dear Mabel, love brings sadness, oftentimes great pain, and much sorrow."

"No; that is romance; its birthright is joy; it is man who gives this heaven-born child sorrow for its earthly portion. Love is bright till we ourselves cloud its beam with distrust or neglect, then 'tis only obscured—it cannot die. Now, Honey-flower, kiss me and tell me, you are happy in my happiness."

"Oh, Mabel, beloved! you know it was once the dearest wish of my heart that you should love Eugene; but now, since I have grown older, and can better judge, I fear," she raised her eyes to the brilliant face bending over her, "he is not worthy of you; you are so high, so noble, so beautiful, Mabel—like a star. *Your* husband should have strength of character, power of intellect to counsel and direct your own fitful, passionate nature, Mabel. Eugene is your intellectual inferior; yours must, necessarily, be the master spirit, and that will not be good for every-day domestic happiness. He is noble, good, and true; but yet," she sighed, and resumed, "he loves the beautiful of life not for itself, but for the effect it has on *him*—not because it leads him to higher and better things, but because it gives him pleasure. His is the intellect of passion, yours of spirit—one the glowing sunset which night follows, the other, moonlight calm and holy when it brightens into day. I do not mean to speak lightly of Eugene, my friend, my brother; I do not love him less, but you—oh! so much more, your spirit so bright, so glorious—the freest thing of earth, will not bear patiently even the silken chains of love. Oh, Mabel! had I the hand of fate, how gladly I would hold back all shadow from your life. Love is not for you; put it away, Mabel. It is necessary to fill up the measure of my being; yours is in itself complete. Why should you love, oh, Mabel!— why?"

"Because it is the crown-jewel of our humanity, and I would wear it. Angels smile to see it gleam in purity on the brow of mortality. Though I have ridiculed the divine passion with all my power, yet deep in my heart I felt the capability of a mighty love; I was only defiant till the conqueror came; now I am just waking into life—just tasting its joy. I should die, now, if I ceased to love. Do not look on me with such mournful forebodings, Genevieve; I tell you, the future has not one single shadow; do not you cloud it with your sadness; Eugene is not—now, Honey-flower, you know I am always candid with you—well, then, Eugene is not my *ideal* lover; not the man whom I thought I would love. He, you know, was tall and good-looking, with cold, quiet manner, and large command-ing eyes—a perfect prince of knowledge, at whose feet I was to sit with timid wonder and love; who was to guide me with his mightier will, and with an affection only shown to myself, he was to charm me by his ten-derness, and awe me by his superiority. No imagination could convert Eugene into this redoubtable character; and I am myself shocked at my own inconsistency. That Eugene has faults, it would be useless to deny; they are certainly self-evident; I have more than once turned impatiently from the contemplation of his character, and said, thou art not the strong, brave master of my destiny; I *will not* love thee; I close and make fast every door of my heart, and sit resolute in its stern silence. But when he comes, with the magic charm upon his lips, the portals unclose like receding waves, and he enters like a conqueror and a king. With royal grace he stands in the deep secret chamber of my soul; and as his dark, glorious eyes beam with mocking tenderness, he whispers, '*Thou art mine!*' my treacherous heart fervently responds, amen. I know he is not great to the world, but he is greater than all the world to me. I could no more live without his love than without air, than flowers can without light. It does not matter if he be cold or fond, harsh or gentle, my truest happiness will be, nearness to him; my love is not the effect of grateful vanity, or gratitude for kindness shown me; it does not depend on *him;* it is self-existent. I should love him if he never cared for me; but I know he *does* love me, and with that knowledge my heart is sorrow-proof; life can bring nothing but joy. Now, Genevieve, are you satisfied? If you could look within my bosom, you would be more than content; you would think the spirit of the elements had chosen my heart as a prison-house for its rainbows, it is so full of glittering visions of light and beauty. Come, Genevieve," she continued, kissing the sweet face hushed on her bosom, "you are a poor confidant; not one word of love or sympathy."

"All love, Mabel; but I don't believe I can sympathize with you; some-how, the old feeling comes over me that I used to have at school; I know it is very foolish; but the memory comes of the time when, after reading 'Undine' in its grand original, we sat in the clear moonlight, on the green island, you had bathed your head in the cool Lehigh, and twined many white water-lilies, sparkling with crystal drops, in your hair; don't you remember Mr. Shultz stopped you, and called you his water-spirit, his bright Undine, and bade you beware of mortal love? Do you remember?"[19]

"Yes," murmured Mabel.

"But hush with superstition, we are not romantic young ladies. Come! I am going to commence life in earnest; I shall begin by going to get aunt Patty to teach me how to make a plum-pudding. Eugene is rather French than English; but I don't believe it is in the nature of any man to refuse one of aunt Patty's puddings. Mabel, there is one thing I meant to tell you. How happy Mrs. de France will be, for now you will persuade Eugene not to join General Lopez. He will give up Cuba for you."

Mabel raised herself till she sat upright; a haughty smile kissed every feature of her beautiful face.

"Never!" she exclaimed, "never! I would despise him if my love, my beauty, or my tears, could win him from principle, from a cause so good, so noble. I will not come to his heart, to crush its most generous impulse; my love would be a curse, a weakness, if it stayed him from glory and honor.

> "'Lives of great men all remind us,
> We can make our lives sublime.'

"And what life is more sublime than one given to a nation struggling for the principles of moral and political freedom? Think you, when I see General Lopez, the brave, self-sacrificing patriot, waiting with anxious hope to welcome the chivalrous spirits gathering around him—think you, I could bear to watch others flock with generous haste to his support, while *my* love, my dearer self, reposed in sluggish ease? If he had scruples, I would be silent; I would not have him act against his conscience; but he is honest and sincere in his knightly desire to free the beauteous child of the old sea-king, and I would not be true either to him or myself if I strove to detain him."

"How can you say you love him, and avow your willingness to see him

19. Undine is a mythical nymph inhabiting water.

enlist in an expedition so fraught with danger and hazard? Mabel, this is strange love."

"It is *strong* love, Genevieve. You are more selfish than I; you would not have Ralph go, because the separation gives you pain. It is my very love which makes me proud to give Eugene to the noble work."

"Mabel, listen! Something whispers me you are giving more than you are aware of—your whole happiness. And what will you receive in return? perhaps a broken heart."

"Hope stands sentinel in my breast to banish fear. I trust so much in the God of my faith, the all-powerful helper of the brave old Puritans—He who held in His almighty hand the white sails of the lone 'Mayflower,' He who steered that frail bark into a haven of rest, is still strong to protect the true of heart and purpose. It is a glorious, a holy mission! Freely do I make the venture. Not in the records of past history can you find a band of men so unselfishly courageous; they are the very embodiment of chivalry, and what true woman will deny them praise? They go to Cuba, not to conquer the Spaniard, in order to rob the natives; not for her slaves, not for her lands, nor her wealth—but for her liberty. In after years, when the song of freedom shall echo along her prosperous shore, when she has made herself a name among nations, when, with glowing hearts, we read the history of her victorious struggle, with what fond delight I will turn to the noble patriot by my side, and say,—*thou, too, wert there!* What is the momentary pain of a weak girl, compared to the happiness of a whole nation? We should live for the greatest amount of good to our race, Genevieve; in that we will find most happiness. But, darling, your eyes are heavy with rebellious tears; come, and let me find the rosewater for them, then you will rest till dinner, for we must be very beautiful to-day; our heroes must have pleasant thoughts, while absent, of their last day at Ellawarre."

CHAPTER XI

"Valor sits on every side,
And radiant beauty shines on all."

SOME HOURS LATER, the guests of Mrs. Clifton were assembled in her drawing-room, waiting the announcement of dinner. The ladies have not yet entered: then, let us pause, and look on an assembly rich with humanity's noblest attributes. But once again, even in fiction, will we mingle in this gallant circle. Alas! its links were soon broken, never more to be united. More than one heart, then beating full and strong, now lies crushed underneath a tyrant's heel. Some wander in distant lands, and others live with saddened lives, wearing, in their breasts, the sickness of hope deferred. First, was our own hero, Ralph Dudley, whose rich, peculiar laugh, was of itself enough to fill the room with music and mirth. The wit that sparkled on his lip was so bright, so genuine, it found an echo in the saddest heart. Around him, in earnest, hopeful conversation, clustered the gallant officers of General Lopez's chivalrous army—General Pragi, Colonel Downman, Colonel Haynes, Captains Gotay and Raymond, with others not less fearless, not less manly and true. Near the centre of the room, before a table on which lay an open map of Cuba, sat Victor Ken—the brave Creole, whose fate was a mockery to his name.[20] Eugene was beside him, talking in very decided tones. The question of dispute was, perhaps, the point of landing, for they now and then appealed to the towns upon the shore of the "Palm Tree Isle."

Opposite, with one arm resting on the table, the hand thus supporting his head, sat the noble Kentuckian—William Crittenden.[21] The face thrown back, and thus exposed to view, must have been in early youth very beautiful; for the free careless grace of childhood still lingered on the bold brow of the man, though passion had pressed its pallor on his cheek. The lines around the mouth denoted thought, even care; and the smile

---

20. See introduction, pp. 15–16, regarding these men.

21. William Logan Crittenden (1823–1851) may have been the love of Holcombe's life. See introduction, pp. 15, 23–24.

of the lip, though sweet, was uncertain. It was a frank and generous face; one that is still fondly remembered by the many friends who mourn the undaunted hero's death. His large fearless eyes, with their half tender, half defiant charm, rested musingly, sometimes on the animated group before him, sometimes on a large carnation-hued rose, which he held in his hand.

In a distant part of the room, near the low-reaching window, stood General Narciso Lopez—the spirit of the scheme for Cuban independence. His was a face, which, seen among thousands, would have fixed your attention. A face once seen, never forgotten. The beauty of the noble head was of the highest order, and, in the face, contended the stern strength of a mighty mind, and the glowing softness of a brave spirit, alive with every warm and generous impulse. To the broad full-veined brow, with its royal look of power, nature had given an "inherent aristocracy"; it seemed so fit a temple for the holy visions, which, alas! placed on it a martyr's diadem. The glorious falcon eyes, darker than a starless night, yet burning with all the fire of a southern sun, how they drew you with mystic influence to trust the great heart which beamed in their depths. If you turned from their shining lustre, the stern melancholy of the large but firmly cut mouth, again attracted you to that most remarkable face. The black moustache, worn short and thick, was slightly mingled with grey, and the frost of care had also touched the dark silken beard which curled around his chin. What most struck you in his presence, was a strength of endurance. He had suffered, but was still strong in an undaunted will. There was an intense exaltation of enthusiasm which you could feel, but not define. You intuitively recognised a nature unfit to contend with petty artifices. He looked what he was, the noble spirit of honesty, truth, and honor. He came to you in all the majesty of old romance—a hero, from those brave days when success lay not in a cunning brain and false tongue, but in a good cause, a true heart, a strong arm, and trusty sword. The short, richly 'broidered mantle, which the heavy tassels scarcely held around his broad shoulders, the jewelled handle of the small sword just visible, the flowing black hair, and listening attitude of the princely head, brought you visions of the grand old Italian pictures artists so much love. This was the man who left upon the records of this age

"A name that cannot die,
While freemen live!"

He stood with folded arms listening to the quick, earnest tones of that proud son of America, whose very name is the embodiment of man's highest virtue. That man, whose intrinsic worth, whether it be in council or in war, is far above the "worthlessness of common praise."[22] He who has never hesitated to throw aside every feeling of self, every thought of interest, and stand with unyielding firmness on the great platform of truth and integrity—he who has trodden the dangerous path of political life, surrounded as it is with the glittering hues of ambition, yet keeping in his brave heart the pure principles of patriotism untarnished. Forsaking with calm indifference, party for principles, office for conscience; thus presenting in his noble character a high model by which American youth may mould its own future destiny, with honor to itself and glory to its country. This man, with a moral excellence, rare indeed in our age of self, had extended his generous hand to clasp in friendship the unfortunate and exiled patriot beside him.

The American held in his hand a late number of the "Delta," to which their attention had been directed. The face, usually so cold in its imperial calmness, glowed with the fire of excitement; but the flashing of his eye was steadied into a clear pointed beam, as the warlike covering of his lip quivered, and he spoke—"I tell you, General Lopez, it must be certainty, not hope, that takes you to Cuba. Defeat will bring entire destruction, not only to yourself, but also to the brave men who go to share your danger and fight for your cause. Your friends may be over zealous, your enemies more treacherous than you imagine. Doubt, for a moment, the truth of these accounts of the revolution. Suppose after landing with your band of men, wretchedly armed as they are, you find the island quiet, and twenty thousand troops, armed to the teeth, brought to face you! What then would be your position? What the fate of your five hundred men with their miserable muskets? Death, sir—instant death! All the courage in the world could not save them." The General shook his head. He did not like the idea of American blood being rashly spilled.

"I cannot doubt these statements," answered Lopez, with a quiet smile

22. Quitman.

of satisfaction. "They are too well authenticated by private information from men on whose honor and sincerity I rely, as on my own—men to whose truth I trust my own life, and those which, God knows, are dearer. We have been much delayed; and I have with difficulty restrained their impatience until this auspicious moment. Now it would seem folly and weakness to hesitate longer. I am perfectly confident the insurgent natives will give us a warm welcome, and, O God! the glory of the battles which shall free Cuba!" A smile of ineffable beauty lay on his lip, and a mighty hope beamed in his falcon eye.

The American looked for a moment on the speaker, then said, with a kind and earnest voice, "The God of battle be with you! I heartily trust Cuba will prove herself worthy of such devotion."

The doors were thrown open, and Mrs. Clifton entered, leaning on her brother's arm, followed by Genevieve and Mabel. She greeted her guest with that courteous kindness of manner by which a hostess may dispel any embarrassment a stranger feels. Genevieve had caught much of her mother's ease, and went gracefully through the presentation. Eugene joined her, and they followed Mrs. Clifton to where the two Generals stood, who, however, advanced to meet them. Ralph drew Mabel's hand through his arm, and they lingered with the group of officers around them. Mabel! royal Mabel! how enchanting she was with her brilliant beauty. How glorious with her fresh sparkling enthusiasm! and, oh, so winning in the child-like warmth of her natural unstudied manner. She had a real heart-smile for each one of Cuba's brave lovers. Her joyous delight and admiration were so genuine, so unaffected, Dudley himself caught its spirit; and began imagining those "fine fellows of his acquaintance," heroes—positive heroes. He laughed as she half led him to General Lopez; and he just did mention her name, when her white hand was laid in the exile's, and she said, earnestly, "General Lopez, I am glad—I am proud to know you."

The Cuban smiled kindly on the eager young face, with its wondrous beauty; but ere he could reply, she had turned to pay her smiling homage to her own distinguished countryman.

"Miss Royal!" cried Colonel Crittenden, hastily approaching her, "is it possible! I little thought to meet you here."

"Don't forget in your astonishment to say, how delighted you are, Colonel Crittenden."

"My looks are saying that," he answered, with a smile. "But your presence relieves me of a serious dilemma. See!" He held the magnificent rose of which we have spoken, before her. "I know but little of flowers in general, but this has a history. Will you listen, lady?" He paused to catch the gracious smile, and continued. "Last winter, while Dudley and I were in New Orleans, a celebrated florist was making a grand parade over a species of the rose he had just received, which, however, was without a name. Dudley purchased the plat at an immense price, and called it—like a gallant fellow—'the Fillibuster.' This morning there was a single flower upon its stem, which he plucked for the general,"—glancing towards the American—"who gave it to me, with instructions to present it to the most beautiful woman in the city. I can go further. I offer it to the most beautiful woman in the world." He laid the rose, with its fresh dewy loveliness, in her hand.

"Colonel Crittenden," she cried, her face crimson with a vivid blush, "if you fight half so boldly as you flatter, Cuba may congratulate herself on having such a champion. But," her eyes were filled with mocking smiles, "believe me Venus prized the golden apple not half so much as I this rose, this superb Fillibuster. Come, tell me, is my brow worthy of its splendid beauty?" With a merry laugh she placed it in the sparkling waves of her golden hair. "Do not mind saying, its beauty pales in the radiance of my own. I shall not be the least vain. I only like compliments artistically, for their grace of execution or expression, not any reference they have to myself. But when this flower has faded, Colonel Crittenden, I will treasure it as a sacred thing, and in after years let me point to it with pride, and say, the same hand which gave me this, raised the *Free flag of Cuba* to float from Moro's heights.'"

A smile, bright as a glancing sunbeam, lit the Kentuckian's face, but we lose his low reply in the announcement of dinner. Mrs. Clifton paused, but the American general had already drawn the arm of Genevieve through his own, and General Lopez led his hostess from the room. Dudley and Eugene came quickly towards Mabel, but she laid her hand on Colonel Crittenden's arm, and they laughed at the gentleman's discomfiture.

"Dinner parties are stupid," every one exclaims, and so they are, usually; but the one at Ellawarre was certainly a contradiction to this received opinion. The hour was rapidly approaching for the arrival of the New

Orleans boat, and gaiety did not wait on ceremony. Hope and mirth, smiles and repartee sparkled with champagne, even Mr. Clifton grew patriotic, and toasted the Liberators.

"Victory has already begun," cried Mabel; "uncle Louis has at last surrendered!"

"Not so fast, my little girl! I only mean—"

"Mr. Clifton, you are surely not hostile to Cuban independence!" interrupted Colonel Crittenden.

"No, sir—certainly not, sir; but I would achieve it in a different manner. I stand on the Monroe doctrine, sir. I hold—a proclamation should be issued—the navy sent to blockade the ports—take Cuba forthwith, sir, and annex her to the United States—"

"But, sir," said Dudley quickly, "the Cubans are not to be *taken* like so many *slaves!* Let *their* wishes at least be consulted. Cuba is for liberation, not conquest."

"All right, sir. I have no arguments for the subject; just as Cuba pleases. Her condition could not be worse."

"Boat's in sight, Marse Ralph!" announced Scipio, from the door, where he stood waiting, hat in hand.

The party were rising, when a clear, full voice from the head of the table cried—"Officers of the liberating party: I fill to your success—a success which shall build on the fair Island of Cuba an eternal monument to the divine rights of humanity, which will plant in the bosom of that genial soil the young tree of liberty, whose growth will be the mighty fulfilment of a people's hope; may the God of Washington and La Fayette, those twin spirits of the American Revolution—the guardian spirits of universal liberty, shield your banner from defeat. I drink to your triumph in this glorious enterprise—glorious, even though it fail."

The gallant American was warmly responded to, and a moment after the banquet-hall was deserted. The ladies were soon in travelling costume, and the whole party awaiting the landing of the "queenly Magnolia." Her warm-hearted but eccentric captain hurried them aboard. General Lopez was the last to leave the shore. He lingered with grateful emotion, perhaps with a sad foreboding of ill, for he was leaving the veteran soldier whose judicious counsel might have saved him, had he listened to the man who had bravely and resolutely recognised the justness of his cause, and purity of his motives, who had shown him generous kindness and sympathy, through all the long and weary days of his exile.

The first link of the circle was broken. They parted to meet—no more. The lover of Cuba, and her faithful friend—the hero of Mexican battles. At an early hour the next day they reached New Orleans, and Mr. Clifton, with his party, took the boat just leaving for the watering-place on the lake, where they were to remain for several weeks. This was Saturday, August 1st, 1851.

CHAPTER XII

THE CAPTAIN-GENERAL of Cuba, he of gory fame, was alone in his splendid apartment. Slowly with a clouded brow, he paced the floor, pausing now and then before the deep open window, through which came the cool breeze of the summer night, bearing on its noiseless wing the fragrant breath of a thousand flowers.[23]

The features were not really so harsh as imagination would likely make them. The face would have been handsome, but for its dark, forbidding expression. The eyes were large and brilliant, but they glittered with the cold flashing light of the assassin's steel. It was a coward's face—hard and compressed. No generous smile had ever relaxed its gloom, no pity had ever moved, no mercy had ever softened the relentless heart of Cuba's dark oppressor. There was a footstep in the room. The Spaniard turned hastily—

"Ha! Hidalgo! make fast the door, and come near me, for there are traitors around me whom fear alone restrains from desertion. We will not give them the power to betray."

"It is late, your Excellency, but—"

"I have been waiting your coming for hours," interrupted Concha, impatiently; "how goes your work?"

23. The chapters in the 1854 edition are numbered incorrectly, with this chapter identified as a second "Chapter XI" and all subsequent chapters misnumbered accordingly. We have therefore corrected the numbering of this chapter and those that follow.

"Bravely," answered the other, laying a package before him. "These are the last communications that will be sent. The Pampero sails on the second—"

"Let them come, the pirate dogs, we are ready for them. You delivered the letters from the *patriots*—*our* letters—right well written they were, coming as they did from the pen of Her Gracious Majesty's most loyal subject, eh, Hidalgo?"

"Yes, your excellency!"

"You told the traitor, Lopez, how the Creoles were praying for his coming, but you did not add—in dungeons."

"No, Senor!"

"You told him how the rebels were hourly gaining strength—the troops deserting—the *tyrant* trembling with fear in the very bosom of his household, surrounded by treason and hate. You told him all this! 'Twas well concocted, by my soul! ha! ha! ha! Let them come. Now we will to business." He broke the massive seals and spread the letters before him. His face grew dark and threatening as he read fresh proof of the terrible disaffection reigning throughout the *"ever-faithful"* island, as he found the just cause Lopez had for relying on the support of the wealthy and influential subjects of his royal mistress. *He* knew it was no "mad scheme." *He* knew the bloody deeds by which he was to make the world regard it as such. *He* knew that all the power of his despotic cruelty must be actively exercised to prevent this *vision* of freedom speedily becoming a reality. Letter after letter, brought by Hidalgo for the Creole patriots, he had destroyed, having the men to whom they were addressed, put to death; himself dictating answers calculated in every way to mislead the unfortunate but heroic General. He looked on the long list which he had hastily made; base and inhuman as he was, he shuddered. "This man Lopez is not so daring as men take him," he said, looking thoughtfully at his companion; "one less bold than he would venture at such bidding as these rebels give him. Treason is rife upon the island. By our Lady, 'tis a bold stream of blood which must wash away the influence of this dangerous foe to the crown of Spain."

"Yes," replied Hidalgo, with a dark smile, "he is well beloved by the people. There is a story abroad that he once, in the power of favoritism, stood between royal displeasure and your excellency. It is said by men who know thee not, that thou wilt show mercy to thy benefactor."

"Thou liest, slave!" cried Concha, glaring fiercely on the cold mocking face of the traitor. "*General* Lopez is no more; this rebel should die a thousand deaths had I the power to give them. Let him come! they will see what mercy I show. I will offer him rank, life and the restoration of all he has lost, in case he recant his *error* before the people. Then shall he die."

"So I said, your excellency; but their coming will no longer be delayed. The Pampero sails on the coming week, and they land at—"

"Puerto Principe," said the Captain-General, pointing to the letters beside him.

"Nay, your excellency, at Murillo."

"How is that effected?"

"Easily. We have *our* men on board who will *accidentally* steer towards this port. Besides, it will matter but little with them, they are so confident of meeting rebels at any point."

"Yes," said Concha, with a grim smile, "let them land where they will, I am prepared to give death to every man in their ranks. Even at Puerto Principe they would find no welcome, for that rebellion is already quelled—the strongest of my troops watch the movements of the treacherous Creoles at that point; and these," he laid his hand on the fatal papers, "taken from their ranks, will fill them with dismay, and crush effectually any intention to rise which may linger in their timid hearts. The stratagem has worked well; the plans of the traitor have fallen into *my* hands; his rebel accomplices into dungeons, or have met *that* mercy which we will show these pirates; making their fate a terror to all future attempts to revolutionize this island. Now let them come!" he threw himself back and resumed, "these men here mentioned, who are the wealthiest of the Creole population, must, ere to-morrow's sun goes down, be imprisoned or shot. Four of my own officers! Holy Mary! but the royal service is one of blood! Go now, Hidalgo, and bid the officers of the guard come quickly to me."

The traitor obeyed; and the man of blood, with moody brow and folded arms, was again alone, musing fiercely on the day which should bring death to his own benefactor and poor Cuba's daring champion, Narciso Lopez.

CHAPTER XIII

THE CRESCENT CITY—the gorgeous flower-crowned bride of the lordly Mississippi—the beloved at whose feet he pours in rushing waves of commerce the gathered wealth of the Union—slept.[24] The air-set diamonds of the sky glowed with quiet beauty, and the young moon timidly looked love on the fair clime of the south.

Along the deserted street, with rapid steps walked a form, which we recognise as Colonel Dudley. Street after street he traversed, until, reaching the upper portion, formerly known as La Fayette, he paused before the small but beautiful French cottage, occupied by General Lopez during his exile. It was literally embosomed in flowers. Shrubs of every variety grew in unusual luxuriance, as though the gentle children of nature strove, with unpretending incense, to cheer the lonely heart of the noble stranger. Cool fountains here and there sprang joyously up, and fell with laughing ripples in gleaming marble basins.

Dudley gave a low, peculiar whistle. A slave quickly appeared, and, conducting him in, pointed to a door opening from the hall. He knocked softly. A rich, musical voice bade him enter, and the next moment he was warmly greeted by the Cuban General and his principal associates.

A perilous, death-bringing enterprise was before them, but they sat talking joyously, hopefully, of coming days, the glory of battle, the honor of success, the happy day when Cuba would be free. With a good cause, stout hearts, and steady arms, what cared they for dangers, that would have tremblingly stayed common men—men less chivalrous and brave.

Lopez mingled but little in the conversation, which flowed unrestrainedly around him. Yet when he *did* speak, it was to cheer them with his own great hope—to point them to a glorious future.

He sat among the flower of his little army; those brave men who loved him—those *who love his memory now*—with the same gentle yet martial bearing which never left him, even in the dark, hopeless days of his after life. There certainly was a strong, irresistible fascination in the character

24. Crescent City is a nickname for New Orleans.

of this noble and unfortunate man, which commanded not only the confidence and respect, but the devotion of those with whom he associated. His influence was great wherever he chose to exercise it. Over the bold and young, whom he peculiarly loved, it was unbounded; he seemed, in their unclouded hopes, their unembittered spirits, to live over the fierce freshness of his own youth. His was a powerful and active mind, one which would have made, had fortune favored, *the glory of a nation.* His earnest and unselfish zeal awakened an interest even in those who looked coldly on his cause; his steadfast love touched even the prejudiced; and with his noble supporters—poor Cuba's generous friends—its charm remains indescribable.

I know men cold and stern, whose hearts thrill at the mention of his name—whose voices soften with its syllables. It may be that memory, that jealous friend of the lost, takes them back to those bright days when they shared the high resolves and passionate aspirations of his great heart. Perhaps to this very hour of which I write, when the fond lovers of Cuba were dreaming the glorious dream of her redemption. Ah! there were choice spirits in that little circle! One with dark, lustrous eyes, and never-failing sparkling wit, whose laugh was echoed again and again ere they rose to seek the vessel that waited to bear them to the fair but fatal isle.

A few hours more, Lopez and his men were cradled on the blue waters of the southern gulf, steering for the land to which they were hoping to give the boon of freedom.

CHAPTER XIV

"Oh! heaven, he cried, my bleeding country save!
Is there no hand on high to shield the brave?
Yet though destruction sweeps these lonely plains,
Rise! fellow-men! our country yet remains!
By that dread name we wave the sword on high,
And swear for her to live! with her to die!"
                                              CAMPBELL.

HUNDREDS OF YEARS have passed since Cuba, the Island Queen, smiled in the gorgeous splendor of her beauty on the dazzled and enraptured

Spaniards. Filled with wonder and delight, they stood amazed at the wondrous beauty of the ocean-born goddess.

With false promises on their lips, they encircled in their dark, treacherous arms the fairest child of the southern waters. Once possessed, the
deadly grasp of avarice and oppression crushed and marred her glorious
loveliness, sending from her torn bosom a piteous and continued cry for
mercy and relief. No ear heeded the sweet, complaining voice; no breast
heaved with compassion for her wrongs; she wept over her bitter suffering in agonized endurance, for there was no arm to screen or save. Poor
Cuba! long has she mourned, but not always in vain, for her deliverer has
come; he who is to commence the work of her final disenthralment, to
break the first link in the chain of her moral and political servitude—
stands on her shore.

The liberating army had landed—that hour for which Lopez had so
long hoped and struggled, towards which he had bent every energy and
purpose of his life, had come. He stood upon Cuba's shore, with a band
of brave men, whose stout arms were raised to strike for her freedom.

Lopez and his men! Ah! how sacred to Cuba's children must those
words for ever be! The army disembarked at Murillo, and was there di-
vided into two portions; General Lopez taking two hundred and fifty
men, and leaving the remainder under Colonel Crittenden's command,
with orders to follow him to Los Pozas as quickly as transportation for
the stores could be provided.[25] Captains Raymond and de France were
left at Murillo, being in Crittenden's company, while Colonel Dudley
proceeded with Lopez to the interior.

The sun was just breaking into radiant beams on the young morning's
brow, when the main body of the army commenced its march. The men
were weary enough of the tropical warmth, however, before they reached
Los Pozas, which was not until two o'clock. They found, with surprise,
the town entirely deserted. Here let me explain that this was done by
order of the Captain-General, who was, as the reader has seen, com-
mander-in-chief of the expedition, as far as ordering and preparing for
its movements constitute that office. He had by a crafty cunning, which
in some measure supplies the want of intellect in his race, accomplished
his fiendish purpose, which was not by any means to prevent the expedi-

25. Among these provisions were ammunition and maps of the Cuban interior.

tion but to encourage it, to get it in his power, in order to make its fate a terror to all future attempts at revolution or liberation. Thus by a train of stratagems, of which Gonzales was the principal instrument, he had so far succeeded in his infamous design, for the Liberators were at the feet of the enchained Lady, the fair child of the old sea-king, and the fiery dragons, her dark and brutal oppressors, had closed around them. The town had been evacuated by express command of the Captain-General, so well he knew the mighty influence with Lopez possessed with the people; so much did he fear for his power even at the mouth of the cannon.

The army remained in quiet possession of Los Pozas; Lopez expecting, with great impatience, the arrival of Crittenden's command, for he had despatched a messenger ordering them to abandon everything and join him, as he was every moment expecting battle. But alas! that order was not obeyed.[26]

On the morning of the 13th the sunlight came burningly down on the little army as it stood in battle-array, bravely awaiting the troops who approached from the direction of the sea shore. General Lopez, in his brilliant uniform, dashed down the thin ranks on his bold black charger, encouraging them by expressing his unbounded and fearless reliance on their valor and firmness.

"See," he cried, "the troops are advancing; deprived of our comrades, we are but a handful before their numbers. Keep your faces to the sea-shore—your strong arms shall cut down the dark line of slaves which thus divides the liberating army. My gallant men, you fight against fearful odds—but remember it is—"

"For freedom, for Cuba, and Lopez!" shouted the Patriots with intense enthusiasm. "Look," continued the clear cheering voice, "look beyond the battle-field before you, in whose dust the hated colors of the tyrant flag shall lie low. Already are we welcomed by Crittenden and his companies; onward we bear the glorious, triumphant flag—the free flag of Cuba, around which her tyrant-trodden sons will joyfully flock. The

---

26. According to historian Tom Chaffin, Crittenden questioned the wisdom of leaving all their provisions. Moreover, they were already camped for the night, so he planned to go the next day. The next day, however, a battle ensued. Winning the skirmish, Crittenden and some of his men pursued Enna's army into the forest, while Capt. J. A. Kelly stayed with the provisions. Then Enna turned the tables with a much bigger force, cutting Crittenden off from Kelly. Kelly and his men later found their way back to López. *Fatal Glory,* 207–8.

beautiful child of the sea will put off her tears; radiant in smiles, she opens her grateful arms to receive the valiant good who have redeemed her from ignoble bonds. Let us battle bravely to the death-hour for a victory over which future generations shall rejoice; a victory that will found a republic, who will rise in power and call Columbia sister."

A long, loud huzza rent the air. The troops rapidly approached—they were on the very edge of the town. With firm and steady arms, every man at his post, the Liberators stood with breathless impatience. Lopez rode rapidly along the line—pausing before the standard-bearer, he seized the free flag of Cuba, and with a glad, proud smile, waved it high above him.

"Charge!" rang his clarion voice; "charge for Cuba and her liberty." Onward rushed the intrepid soldiers, sending with unerring aim their deadly greeting to the enemy. Hotly the death-shower poured on the Spanish troops, who faltered and swayed back with great confusion. They retreated a short distance, and the regular battle commenced. Fiercely the combat raged, the officers shouted to their men, exerting and encouraging them to stand firm to their arms, to show themselves worthy of their glorious mission. Hardly they pressed on the ranks of the enemy, throwing the wildest destruction in their midst. For hours they kept up the deadly play of booming balls; and the contest continued with deadly energy. Victory hovered over the field of carnage, poising her brilliant winds in mid air over the battling hosts. The crown of Spain, and the free flag of Cuba, were struggling for ascendancy.

"Long time in even scale the battle hung." With the Spaniards it could not be a decisive action, but to the Americans a defeat would have been at once fatal. With ceaseless din the battle raged. Regardless of the destructive fire of the troops, the Liberators advanced with characteristic intrepidity closer upon them. With determination, with certain aim, the "noble few" pressed into the very midst of the foe, who at length gave way, and retreated with great confusion and disorder. The Patriot army rushed forward with a wild eager shout, but General Pragi, the brave Hungarian, himself bleeding profusely from a mortal wound, seeing the dead and dying lie thick around him, knowing they could ill afford to lose their men, hoping every moment for succor from Crittenden, raised himself, and with a firm voice cried, "Halt!" The main body of the army fell back, but Colonel Dudley shouted to his men, and dashed on in pursuit, closely followed by Downman. Encouraged by the bold heroism of their leaders, the soldiers rushed with hot haste and deadly fire upon the retreating Spaniards. General Enna perceiving that he was but partially pursued, instantly rallied, and quickly turned upon the advance detachment of the liberating army. Then fell Downman, a brave American, a generous patriot, who was worthy the life of a freeman, the glorious death of a liberator.

"Happy man! so to have lived, so to have died." Pierced by a deadly ball, he reeled in his saddle, and his weapons fell heavily to the ground; with a strong effort raising his arms, he clapped the morning sunshine with his stiffening hands, and cried: "Charge, onward! death to tyranny!—Cuba—liberty—I die!" He sank into the arms of his men, and was borne from the field. Colonel Dudley paused an instant beside his fainting friend and brother officer; then, maddened with fury and grief, heedless of the galling fire that streamed from the enemy, he bounded onward into the very face of what seemed certain death. His faithful men, with rash enthusiasm, followed up his impetuous charge.

> "Destruction thinned his gallant band,
> As beating waves sweep off the sand."

Still they grappled with undaunted courage in the unequal contest. But lo! the black charger flew with lightning speed across the bloody field, and the stern voice of Lopez shouted, "Back! retreat." The heroic Liberators slowly retired, keeping up an incessant fire on the column of the foe. But the order came when Dudley was surrounded by a small advanced detachment of the enemy. With a mad chorus of bullets singing a wild death-song around him, he sat on his reeking steed, like a young war-god, proudly, fearlessly defying the host of slaves that encompassed him about. Erect in the manly perfection of his bold beauty, he kept them at bay with the long broadsword his strong arm bravely wielded—his fierce spirit revelled in the wild excitement of his daring, dangerous position. They were nearing on him—a fresh body rapidly approached—when, raising himself upright in his stirrups, with a passionate cry of "victory," he dashed his rowels deep into the gallant charger, and rushed boldly through their midst, leaving a heavy death-stroke from his sword on more than one falling trooper. On his "winged courser" his dark hair floating back in waving triumph, he sped to where his General stood, and hastily dismounting, threw his bloody weapon down.

"'Twas bravely done!" said his commander, with an animated smile; "the danger was rashly incurred but boldly defeated." The Patriots speedily formed in line and awaited a second attack from the enemy. Seeing no manifestation of a renewal of hostilities on the part of the Spanish General, Lopez ordered the men to attend to the wounded and dead, not only of his own army, but those of the Spanish, who showed no intention of returning for their disabled comrades.[27]

In the battle of Los Pozas, the combat between *nine* and *two* hundred men, the Spaniards lost two hundred, the liberators thirty.[28] What would have been the fate of the expedition had Lopez landed with five thousand well armed, properly disciplined soldiers!

The day was fast declining, but Lopez, restless with anxious fear, sent a division of his little army to learn the movements of Colonel Crittenden. It was late. The weary soldiers calmly slept, the sentinels guarded the town, and Lopez with his officers kept watch around the flag so dear to them, whose folds fluttered with soft music in the night-wind, whose gay colors streamed proudly in the caressing beams of Cuba's pleasant moonlight.

"Ha! no tidings?"

"No," said Colonel Dudley, under whose command the company had been sent out. "A large body of troops lay between us, and I knew it would be useless to attempt to cut through them without a greater loss than we can well sustain. Despairing of affording Colonel Crittenden any relief, we hastened to return."[29]

"You did right, sir. Dispose of your men with what comfort you can. We march at early dawn."

Lopez threw himself against the flag-staff, and slept.

27. According to Chaffin, this is true. *Fatal Glory,* 208–9.

28. These figures seem to be correct. Chaffin also remarks upon the total lack of discipline on the part of the filibusters. López also lost experienced officers in Downman, Oberto, and Pragay (which Holcombe spells "Pragi"), who are identified in the introduction. According to Chaffin, Oberto and Pragay, having received nonmortal wounds, each committed suicide so they would not be a burden to the expedition. *Fatal Glory,* 208–9.

29. Cut off from Kelly and the provisions, Crittenden and his men tried to get to López but could not get past the Spaniards. They decided their best hope was retreat. At Murillo, where they had landed, they put off in four boats, heading for Key West. They were captured by the Spanish two days later; taken to Havana on August 16, they were executed that same day. Chaffin, *Fatal Glory,* 214–15.

When the faint morning light glimmered over them, the army was in active preparation for their immediate departure. Tempest—the noble and faithful war-horse of the Cuban General, stood ready caparisoned, waiting impatiently his master's coming, but the General lingered in consultation with the remaining officers of his staff. A hum of voices arrested their attention, and they turned to see, coming rapidly towards them, a body of men, wearing the liberating uniform, and bearing in their front the free colors of Cuba. Captain Raymond came hastily towards the General, who advanced to meet him, expressing much joy at his arrival, eagerly inquiring for Crittenden.

"I was certain he had joined you," answered the officer, "until questioned by the sentry as to the cause of his delay. He left on the morning of the 13th, yesterday, taking eighty of the best men belonging to our company. I waited his return until a late hour; he did not come; the volunteers grew impatient and insubordinate. Imagining he had reached Los Pozas, I followed with the remainder of the company."

"It was well."

"But, General, if you approve I will return; he may be hardly pressed, and in imminent need of succor."

"Nay," replied Lopez. "Holy Mary defend our brave comrades from harm; but that would be a useless kindness; only throwing you into danger, without a possibility of relieving them. Two companies have I already sent, but no tidings did they bring. The troops surround us on almost every side; the Spanish General only waits the full light of day to open his artillery on our ranks. It is then evident that we can no longer hold our present position. The army is already under marching orders; we will hasten to the mountains, where a large body of Creole patriots are awaiting us with anxious hope. There will we remain until reinforced by the Cubans and our expected American friends whom the Pampero will quickly bring.[30] That it grieves me thus to leave my gallant officer and his little band you cannot doubt"; his large, generous eyes rested, with a moment's sadness, on his listeners. "That every drop of blood lost from my army, brings me pain, you surely know; but mine is a stern duty, and I must resolutely perform it, pursuing our present advantage, regardless of any feeling, however strong, which seeks to detain me. Captain Raymond,"

30. López had sent the *Pampero* back to the U.S. for more soldiers and equipment.

he added, turning away, "you will see to your company; we march in twenty minutes."

CHAPTER XV

"A virtuous deed should never be delayed.
The impulse comes from heaven, and he who strives
A moment to repress it, disobeys
The God within his mind."

DAME'S SETHONA.

"Renown that would not quit thee, tho' reproved,
Nor leave thee pendant on a politician's smile."

A SHORT DISTANCE from Havana, just far enough to be called *out of the city*, stood a handsome residence; its white walls gleaming through the thick foliage of the surrounding trees. In an apartment luxuriant with eastern comfort, sat Owen, the American Consul; Owen—the man who has been so severely censured, so harshly denounced throughout the Union.[31] Owen—who has been held up to public scorn, as an officer wanting in national spirit and pride; a man destitute of the commonest emotions of humanity. There was nothing to indicate this in the quiet-looking person, who half reclined with indolent ease, fanning the hot breath of the summer morning from his face, which was remarkable for nothing unless its unoffending appearance, generally. Altogether, Mr. Owen had the appearance of a comfortable, good-natured gentleman, rather indifferent and undecided. Now, however, his face had a perplexed air,—"What am I to do" was plainly written on his countenance. He looked up quickly, as if glad of any diversion from his own thoughts, when a slave approached to announce a gentleman, who walked impatiently past him, and by the Consul. The unceremonious intruder was flushed with haste, and his large black eyes were restless with excite-

31. Allen Ferdinand Owen, U.S. consul to Cuba, whose office was in Havana.

ment.[32] He declined the chair which was courteously offered him, and said hastily—

"No, you have no time to lose. You must come with me instantly."

"Where? For what?"

"To Havana. Crittenden and his men are condemned to death."

"I am sorry, sir," said the Consul, uneasily, "very sorry; but what am *I* to do?"

"Do!" repeated his companion, "that is plain enough, when you remember that you are the only American on the island who can exercise the least authority. All their hopes of life hang on your immediate action."

"It is a bad case, then, for it is entirely beyond my power to aid them. It grieves me; but, really—"

"Great God, Mr. Owen!" exclaimed the other, passionately, "will you sit in supine ease, and know that your countrymen are in the clutches of the insolent tyrant? Will you, without an effort to prevent, allow fifty brave *freemen* to be shot, like dogs upon a common?"

"What am I to do?" again exclaimed the Consul, in an irritable tone. "I have no power to interfere."

"Assume it, Sir," the speaker's eyes flashed, and his lips quivered with emotion. "Take all the power of a Republic on yourself, claim these men, enter a protest, defy them to proceed—seize the flag of freedom, and threaten them with its vengeance. Call in the men-of-war who hover around; they will gladly support you in your remonstrance. Take the President and his cabinet on your shoulders, and talk boldly of blockading. Only rouse your spirit, and do something. Why, sir, a strong volley of hearty oaths would delay these cravens. You cannot free them, perhaps, but you may save their lives; for upon your protest they will be kept prisoners, and the right to punish be a question upon which the two governments will hereafter negotiate."

Mr. Owen drew a long breath, and fanned himself energetically. "I cannot transcend instructions. These men were duly warned; they have brought this upon themselves. I cannot commit the President in the face of his own proclamation."

---

32. The intruder, we later learn, is John S. Thrasher, a journalist and member of a group of businessmen in Cuba who advocated U.S. annexation of the island.

"Commit the President!" repeated the advocate scornfully. "You are not a full minister, and your official acts are not binding on the government; still, being the only representative of the nation, if, after your remonstrance, they proceed to execute these men, it will be a palpable indignity to our flag, and one for which instant reparation will be demanded. Do not, sir," he continued earnestly, "let the love of office trammel the natural prompting of humanity, which you must feel for men who claim the same national mother as yourself. Even though the State department reprove, the great voice of the American public will strongly support you; fifty noble freemen will own you their deliverer, and, better than all, your own heart will reward you with the consciousness of having performed a just and virtuous action. Do not hesitate; time flies, and every moment of indecision brings them nearer death."

"It is hard, sir. I assure you I sympathize, but without instructions I can do nothing. I have no authority to interfere; I must adhere to the duties of my office."

"The strict performance of those requirements incident upon your position, is certainly commendable; but as the stars pale in the radiance of the sun, so the lesser virtues give way before the nobler. Even if you have no positive official right to demand these men, you have that authority which God himself has given every man to exercise in behalf of humanity. Enter," he continued, with growing impatience, "your protest, which will at least occasion delay, and Mr. Fillmore will thank you for the step by which you saved his and your own countrymen. If, sir, by your weak indecision they are lost—God forgive you both."

The face of the Consul flushed, and he said angrily, "I have nothing to do with the conscience of the President; my own is clear. He has placed me in office, and it is evidently my duty to support his measures. He has seen fit to outlaw them, and withdraw the protection of their government; therefore I can have nothing to say in the matter. I wash my hands of all accountability."

The dark eyes of his listener beamed down on the man of office, and his voice was cold with scorn.

"You then, deliberately, without a single struggle for release or delay, give these Americans up to their gory fate—"

"I may perhaps visit them, though it will do them no good. I will go to—"

"The devil!" muttered the indignant man, who abruptly left the room, and hastened to Havana to bestow every kindness on the unhappy captives.

This was he who dared to hold the pen of truth, even in Cuba, drawing its silver lines in the very shadow of the despot's wing. Who, by his sympathy with the patriots, brought on himself imprisonment, and a sentence more fearful than death. This was the man for whose release the guardian goddess of liberty bent a suppliant knee before the Spanish throne, while the monarchical world looked in laughing wonder on the tableau of republican humility and royal condescension. This man was the determined advocate of liberty, who, a few weeks since, was arrested in *"the glorious land of freedom,"* because the authorities *suspected* him of the same crime for which Congress sent him to Spain—the crime of entertaining hope and sympathy for the oppressed.

Mr. Owen found a republic ungrateful, Mr. Thrasher's fast and conditional release certainly testify to its inconsistency. Imprisoned by a tyrant—threatened for the same offence in the United States—in the name of heaven, where *is* he to find freedom of action and thought? Who will wonder if he *did* long for the existence of a government of power where man will not only be free himself, *but* free to act for the freedom of others?[33]

Mr. Owen has just cause for complaint; and the administration which he served certainly made a direct admission of its own inefficiency in his removal. Owen was weak, and destitute of that native spirit which no American has a right to be without. He deserved censure, but not from the government, for he erred as a man, not as an officer; consequently, Mr. Fillmore's dismissal was a singular and, doubtless, unexpected reward. Had Mr. Owen been true to the higher dictates of his nature, had he stood squarely on the side of his countrymen, his recall from office would have brought him no disgrace; for honor from the hands of the American people would have waited his acceptance. Mr. Owen is not by any means a bad man. Because he was wanting in one virtue—moral courage—it does not follow he is without any. We blame him for being without force of character, for an unmanly tameness, for quietly submit-

33. Thrasher was arrested in Cuba in October 1851 and released in 1852. Chaffin, *Fatal Glory*, 145, 243 n. 16.

ting to what he knew to be a national and human wrong, because that submission was necessary to the support of the power which had placed him in office. If Mr. Owen merits the odium cast upon him, what are we to think of the administration whose policy he carried out? Had the infamous proclamation, so fatal to Crittenden and his gallant company, never existed, Mr. Owen's conduct would doubtless have been altogether different.

It has been said the Consul was sacrificed; one would imagine the President might have been satisfied with the sacrifices which his power had already made. However that may be, Mr. Owen, who is much "sinned against," may, with truth, affirm that "republics are ungrateful."

CHAPTER XVI

"Oh! if there be on this earthly sphere
A boon, an offering heaven holds dear,
'Tis the last libation liberty draws
From the heart that bleeds and breaks in her cause."

CRITTENDEN AND HIS murdered men!

I have written a sentence that will bring the warm, hot blood of indignation to every American brow. It needs no comment from my pen, even though it had the power to portray, with vivid distinctness, the horror of that scene.

On the 16th of August, the fifty patriots captured by the Spanish steamer, were brought from the vessel which had been their prison to the place of execution. With heavy clanking chains on their free-born limbs, these noble sons of the eagle came forth to die.

In the glad, bright morning sun, firm and resolute they stood, living monuments of the most exalted philanthropy. They had listened to the cry of the oppressed, not coldly, selfishly turning away, till a more propitious or convenient time, but following the uncalculating generosity of a warm, heaven-given impulse, they went forth strong in the same knightly, chivalrous spirit that actuated the valiant Crusaders, leading them against the infidels, inciting them to deeds which have lived through the lapse of time, and made their memory glorious.

Love of their holy religion took the Saxons from their homes, sending them across the blue waters of the far Mediterranean. Is not the principle of liberty in reality the religion of our people? Who can separate them? Does the one rest on the other? For these holy and beautiful principles the American expeditionists fought, though they had no positive bearing on themselves. There is a something selfish in the purest local patriotism; our country is ours, and its welfare and prosperity are intimately connected with our own happiness. But to possess an abstract love of truth and good, unconnected with self, having reference only to the benefit and improvement of mankind, is an attribute of the highest moral heroism; this heroism, allied with strong, unflinching courage, makes such men as composed Crittenden's gallant band.

Oh, my countrymen, why then do we wait for future generations to give that homage to our martyred brothers they so entirely deserve? Why shall we strive to justify our weak, unpitying government, who sat in its luxurious capital with a frozen heart, looking calmly—I had almost said approvingly—on the terrible massacre of its children?

Ah! Crittenden, thy brave, proud heart is cold; its life-breath, drawn by Spanish arms, has not in all the broad land of thy birth found an avenger; the death-agonies of thy men live in the boastful memory of slaves, yet the fire of retribution slumbers. Ye, who sat in power; ye, whom these very men sent to wear the dignity of high office, to watch over and guard what was dearer than life—their liberties and rights; ye, who swore to protect the children of Washington, can ye in the lonely stillness of midnight hour, when the heart, spiritualized by a sacred silence, recognises that truth and justice it must not wear in high places; can ye fold the mantle of slumber around you, and repose undisturbed by conscience? Comes there not a vision of the lover of his people, of one pure and holy, with the fadeless laurel of a nation's love upon his brow; one whose great heart would have ceased to throb in defence of the lowliest American life; comes not this face all sorrowful, haunting your dreams with reproach? As it sadly passes by, does not another stand with flashing eyes brimful of haughty disdain, demanding the murdered children of his country, pointing with voiceless scorn to the first stain upon that flag, which for eight years he held untarnished in his bold lion grasp? Does he listen very patiently, this eternal hero, to the poor sophistry of party policy with which ye strive to shut out the wild death-shriek of the slaughtered brave?

Ah! yours is a rich reward. What care ye for the averted faces of good men, the tears of the weeping mother and wife, the wailing of the bereft sister, or the passionate grief of the boy for his sire?

Have ye not the priceless approbation of the peerless Isabella, the august Queen of mighty Spain? Have not her loyal minions sung your praises in the burning ears of crushed and broken hearts, in a southern city, whose proudest boast is—the defeat of a crown! Does she not encouragingly say—well done, thou patient ally; thou hast borne much, thou shalt yet bear more; how much more, God only knows.

But again I turn to that scene that has thrilled so many hearts with mingled feelings of pity and horror, admiration and shame. A scene without a parallel in a world's history.

The mock trial was over—the trial without a council was ended. The hurried words of love and high resolve were written. The soft emotion which came with the recollection of his last home; the holy memories of the beautiful and loved, that bowed for an instant the soldier's head in sorrow, ere his fate, were hushed back. Each felt 'twas *his* to show the world how a freeman would die. Forsaken by their country, scorned by her representative, delivered to an unrighteous and brutal death, denied the common justice, the defense accorded the most abject criminals; under the burning sun of Cuba and the flaunting flag of Spain; alone, in the midst of dark, jeering, hating, and hated slaves, these proud, brave men stood to die. If emotion had darkened their brows, they remembered they were Americans; and those daring, generous spirits loved the honor of that name too well to falter.

The platoon of troops was drawn up, and the stern, unshrinking eyes of the patriots glanced proudly over the multitude. If their cheeks were pale, not a lip trembled; they were as calm and firm as though their "feet stood not upon their graves"; every man was sublime in that courage which triumphs over the darkness of death and the bitterness of despair.

The Spanish officers approached; with brutal compulsion they forced them to kneel. God! how my blood burns to write it! Americans prostrate before the power of a crown! Thank heaven, the noble form of Crittenden, the gallant Kentuckian, bowed not even in death, and his glorious lips gave to history the immortal words:

"An American kneels but to his God."

Bound with the same chains that confined Crittenden was a proud young form, who smiled to hear the haughty words of his colonel, and strove to stand beside him, but one stroke from the sword of the minion officer, and Eugene fell, too faint and weak to rise.

Above the deep thunder of the drum the death-signal is given. They wheel, they aim, they fire, and Cuba's fate is sealed. The rich, hot blood of the patriots dyes her soil, and consecrates her for ever. She receives the baptismal drops of freedom, *and she will be saved.* There is a seal upon her, be it of vengeance or of love; it is one that cannot be broken, and it rests upon her brow.

The eagle of Columbia shrieks hoarsely for vengeance over her slaughtered sons, *and she shall not shriek in vain.* The people are tired of charity which lives not at home, not where our *own* citizens are concerned, but exists only in our relations with a nation who is continually heaping insults on our forgiving government. Let our rulers pause. It is a fearful thing when true and honest men can no longer respect the administrating power; it is a fearful thing to make the law a yoke, a band of iron to keep down a sense of wrong, to crush every high and generous impulse. A deep sympathy is awakened in behalf of the unhappy and oppressed Cubans; the memory of our own murdered brave kindles the fire of indignation that is glowing in great and good hearts; its flames may be suppressed, but they cannot be quenched; they leap higher, still higher; they burst, they rage on the tyrant-trodden shore of the "Antilles Gem"; the dross is consumed, the gold is refined; Lopez is vindicated; Crittenden is avenged, and *Cuba is free!*

CHAPTER XVII

I WOULD NOT, even had I the power, dwell on the barbarous, the inhuman and revolting scene, which succeeded the slaughter of the patriots.

It has, alas for the wrung and tortured hearts mourning the loved and lost, been too faithfully portrayed by abler pens than mine.

When the terrible day was closing, when its bloodstained hours were darkening into night, in a poor fisherman's hut, just beyond the city, on a rude bier lay Eugene, the young heir of the proud house of de France; and beside the rough coffin sat our old friend, Scipio (Africanus). The same kind and generous friend, who had risked everything to befriend the unfortunate Patriots, assisted Scipio to procure the body; and the poor desolate negro watched, in heart-broken grief, over all that remained of "poor Marse Eugene."

Like the marble triumph of some sculptor's skill, he lay in the silent majesty of death. Hard, indeed, must have been the heart that could have looked unmoved on the still death-beauty of the form. The gory stains had been removed, and he lay calm and serene; as though life had sighed itself away upon his mother's breast. The sunset glow had faded from his face, but death had given a mild dignity before unknown. The large thick curls, lay like loving shadows about the youthful brow, on which the light of fame had fallen so heavily. The dreamy lids closed tightly, naturally over the eyes, as if they had veiled them in slumber, and there was yet no pallor on his cheek,—it had that passionate paleness dreams sometimes bring. The young lip still retained its haughty curve, and the death-struggle that hushed his warm heart, was marked in its look of marble-cold defiance.

Scipio had, on landing, been separated from his master, and being unable to speak either French or Spanish, he assumed to be dumb, and thus found his way to Havana unsuspected, where, meeting the fisherman, José, a free negro, whom he had known at New Orleans, he accepted an asylum with the kind-hearted man, and assisted him in his daily occupation. Poor fellow! it was hard work to sustain his speechless character, and conceal from all, save José, the gnawing anxiety that filled his faithful breast, concerning the uncertain fate of his master, and "de rest uv our boys." He had recognised Eugene among the prisoners, and never rested until he obtained the precious body, which lay in the humble dwelling of José.

Never was there a more sincere mourner than Scipio. He would stand beside the dead patriot, take his cold hand, and look with child-like love

on the white motionless face; then throw himself on the hard ground-
floor with piteous lamentations.

Thus he lay, when he heard the voice of a woman, speaking in the
gliding music of the Spanish tongue. On looking up, he saw a tall, delicate
girl, talking earnestly with the fisherman. A white dress was gathered low
off her beautiful shoulders, fastened at her breast by a rich girdle of gold
and purple silk. Her large, lustrous eyes were sad, even pitying, shedding
a holy, Madonna expression on a pale, weary-looking young face, whose
high birth was stamped on its small, finely-cut features. Long braids of
raven hair coiled around an exquisite Grecian head, and over it was
thrown in thick hanging folds, the graceful mantilla of Spain. José was
evidently speaking of the occupants of the room, for he inclined his head
more than once towards them. The poor fellow's face grew uneasy, he
drew nearer to the corpse, and glanced suspiciously at the maiden. At last
he asked José gruffly, "What he was talking' 'bout?"

"Never mind, boy, don't be 'feard, I ain't tellin' no tales on you. I jes'
tellin' Miss Oralize, 'bout your poor young master dare. She nuver brings
nobody no harm; 'sides, she is much 'merican herself, 'cause, though she
is a Morentez' daughter, she lived heap uf her life in de New-Nited
States."

"Yes," said the sweet voice in English, though its accent was foreign,
"you may trust me. My mother was a Louisiana Creole, and I love all
Americans. I wish I could do something to help you, Scipio."

"Lord bless you, young mistis, you can't do poor Scipio no good, 'less
you find marster, and bring Marse Eugene back to life. Oh, Lord! ef we
had all stayed at home an' let dese furrin' folks 'lone, like we oughter
done, we would all bin livin' now. Poor Miss Mabel, she'll break her heart
an' go ravin' 'stracted, I know she will. Oh, Lord! jes' have mercy, an' lem
see Marse Ralph one time more, 'cause we nuver ment a bit uf harm; we
come fur good, to try and make 'spectable 'mericans of dese people, like
us. But do we nuver done it, Lord knows, 'tain't our fault, 'cause dese
Spanishers is 'satefuler 'an Mexicuns."

"Scipio, is Miss Mabel his sister?" asked Oralize, pointing to the dead.

"No, Mam, better 'an dat; but she'll nuver see him no more now."

"Does she live in Louisiana?"

"No, Mam, me an' my marster, that's Colonel Dudley, an' Marse Eugene du, but Miss Mabel, dey say, come frum a mighty bad free-nigger

country, close to Bostown. But she loved Marse Eugene, jes' as good as ef she growd up 'mung de sugar-cane."

His listener was so silent and attentive, it encouraged Scipio to talk; so he relieved his honest heart by giving a full history of Colonel Dudley, Eugene, Genevieve, and poor Miss Mabel, for whom he seemed to suffer greatly. When he had concluded, Oralize asked, "When they would bury the American?"

"After dark," answered José. "Nobody to do it but me an' dat boy. We done dug de grave in de darkest part de orange grove, out by de house here."

Oralize looked once more on the calm sleeper, and slowly left the lowly roof.

"If dere's an angel out of heaven, it's her," began José. "You see, my wife 'longed to her mother 'fore she was married, and nused dat chile. Well, she nuver forgits ole Alvez. But she's good to rich an' poor, dat she is."

José smoked in silence, and Scipio moaned over his dead. At last the old man said, "Don't keep grievin' so, boy; folks 'bleeged to die. Young marster gone straight heaven, 'cause he wus a brave man; ef he wan't, he nuver would a cum to fight all dese solgers, I know."

"'Tain't no use in talking', 'cause human nater isn't goin' to 'stand everything. Lord knows, I thought I had 'nuff trials in Mexico, wid all dem battles, 'twasn't nothin' to dis. Poor Marse Eugene gone, an' maybe my own marster dead too, 'cause I don't b'leve dis would happened ef he'd bin here, for he's 'nuff to sker a lion, when dare is any fightin' to do."

"Put your trus' in de Lord, boy, he'll nuver forsake you."

"Don't talk 'ligion to me, José; it put me in mind uv home, an' I can't stan' it. 'Tain't no pleasure to think uv them ole days now. Oh, Marse Eugene! we little know'd then what we wus cumin' to."

José smoked on, and Scipio watched, with an aching heart, the slowly sinking sun.

A light step came past the window, and paused at the door. José rose quickly, just in time to meet Oralize, who softly entered the room. In one hand she bore a small portfolio, the other was filled with rare and beautiful flowers, which she placed with gentle care around the soldier's form. On the young hero's brow she placed a chaplet of ivy, woven with laurel, whose dark green leaves mingled with his night-black curls.

As she stooped over him, her eyes fell on a white roll, sprinkled with blood. She drew it forth, and shook from its folds Mabel's little flag.

"Sweet eyes," she murmured, and hid it in the braids of her hair, 'neath the concealing mantle. Then, seating herself low beside the bier, she drew, with rapid grace, the semblance of the brave youth, whose death and history had created so deep an interest in her own suffering heart.

The task was finished. There it lay, that haughty, boyish face, with its glory-wreath around it. The lady paused, and looked more closely on the dead; then, she mingled on the proud curve of the defiant image-lip, an expression of future hope, of passionate love and remembrance. Gently she severed from the many, one dark curl, and laid it on the picture face in a small casket. Again she bent over the sacred dead; actuated by that holy refinement of sympathy a woman alone can feel, she took the cluster of delicate white jasmine resting by the cold cheek, and added its fragrance to the precious treasures she had generously garnered for one whose agony and grief, she well knew, none could ever comfort. Then, with a trembling hand she wrote:

"Lady, we are strangers, but I have wept for you and your brave countrymen. I am standing where you would sacrifice your life to stand—beside the cold form of your murdered lover. I have tried to send you the death-beauty of his face, but in vain. There is a divinity hovering around the features which mortality cannot portray. My heart bleeds for your sorrow. As you mourn now, so I once mourned; but I have found rest.

"God bless you, sweet lady, and send his own angels to comfort you.

"ORALIZE."

Oralize pressed the tears from her eyes, and motioned Scipio to come to her. She placed the casket in his hands, and said:

"You will be very careful of this; it is for poor Miss Mabel."

"I'll die by um," was the laconic answer.

As he spoke, a muffled figure entered the room, placing a box on the floor, and departed without speaking.

José came forward to examine it, while Oralize said:

"It is only a coffin; you know his friends may, at some time, find an opportunity of removing him."

Scipio's grateful tears flowed, and he said:

"Lord bless you, Mistis, long is you live. Though de ain't nobody here to thank you but poor Scipio, you'll nuver be forgot at Marse Eugene's home."

It was growing late, and José said the body must be buried.

Scipio begged "jes' a little longer."

"You better do is I tell you, 'cause you don't know what time de solgers mought come sarchin' roun', an' if dey find him here, you'll be sorrier 'an you is now."

The boy reluctantly consented to put away the man to whom he was bound by a strange tie—half love, half duty; and yet Eugene was not his master—a tie that cannot be appreciated by one unaccustomed to slavery.

He and José went to make the necessary preparations, and Oralize was left alone in the spirit-haunted chamber. It was with no feeling of dread or superstition that the Cuban girl stood beside the lonely dead. Hers was indeed a watch of love. All the softness of her woman's nature was roused by Scipio's rude but touching story of the fond lovers—Eugene, the brave hero boy, and his fair Mabel.

She thought how he, the first-born, the only son of a noble house, had left his father's princely halls, radiant in unselfish hope, to stand among the daring few who came with their strength, to hurl defiance in the very face of tyranny and death. Glad and glorious in strength, pride, and power, he had come to conquer in the fight, to wave the victorious banner of a nation's independence over the blue mountains of Cuba. But, alas! a cruel fate bared his breast to the human blood-hounds of a crown.

Now his heart was still; its red life-stream stains the fair bosom of the beauteous land, mingling with the tears of her weary children.

"Life and love with him were past." But he had fallen fearlessly as any knight of olden time; for the tress of auburn hair that lay on his true heart was deluged with a martyr's blood. Oralize was sorely oppressed. The shadow of coming woe seemed hanging over her. She laid her warm fingers on the marble, death-kissed brow, and tears fell with bitter unrestrained anguish.

"So young," she murmured, "so loved, so brave and beautiful! Oh, Cuba, my country! all for thee!"

She took a small jet cross from her neck, and laid it on his cold breast, then, kneeling by the bier, chanted, in a low trembling voice, the hymn for the dying and dead. As she rose, they came and laid him in his close, narrow bed. José took the lid, and paused beside the coffin. It is a hard thing to cover, for ever, the image of ourselves.

Oralize, gentle Oralize, with tender reverence pressed her red lips on the unkissed cheek of the dead, and turned away, while they shut out from living grief the noble form of the young patriot. The two men bore him to the quiet, secret spot they had selected as his resting-place, followed by a single mourner, with a dimly burning light. Silently, they lowered the coffin, and threw upon his breast the rich soil of the country for which he died.

Oralize turned with sickening sense from the fragrance of the low-hanging orange flowers. Scattering them over the new-made mound, she murmured:

"They were to deck thy Mabel's brow. Alas! they wither on thy lonely grave."

When they returned to the deserted room, and Oralize had wrapt her mantle to depart, she said, with her kind voice:

"Scipio, you must try and keep a good heart and hope for the best. If you want a friend you must come to me, I will help you, poor boy, while I can." Scipio brushed the tears from his grateful eyes. "Lord bless you, young mistis," was all he could say.

"José, put down your hat; it is not well for you to be out at this hour. I do not fear, me they will not dare to harm."

The girl glided rapidly along the street, and reaching her father's mansion, sprang lightly up the marble steps, and softly sought her luxurious chamber.

"How still everything is! Zulime, where is my father? Has he not yet come?"

"Nay, Senorita, me have no tidings of him."

"I cannot rest. My heart is filled with sad thoughts as the storm-rocked sea with waves. I will while the hours with reading. Zulime, bring hither that volume. There, shade the lamp. I will take courage from the struggles of victorious America. They, too, were few, and hardly pressed. But hope is crushed by the sad news from the liberating army. Anxious fear comes in its stead. The future—oh! the future! What will it bring? Its dark mists gather around my soul, and something whispers—woe to Cuba. Oh! Lopez! my country's savior; God preserve thy sacred form; Holy Mary

smile on thy generous effort to shake off poor Cuba's chains! Hark! Zulime! what noise is that? Ah! my father comes; go, pray, tell him to come
quickly to me. I cannot be alone. He must cheer me with his firm reliance, my brave sire. Stay, Zulime! list! it is the tread of many. It cannot
be the Patriots come to seek a refuge. By the Virgin they shall have it,
though it cost me my heart." The door was flung rudely open, and two
officers of the palace entered the young girl's chamber. All the blood of
her haughty race rushed over her brow as she rose proudly before them.

"Back!" she exclaimed; "why come ye at this hour? What would ye
with a defenceless maiden?"

"We come," replied the foremost officer, "in the Queen's name, to
bear the daughter of a traitor to the tribunal of the crown."

"My father—oh! my father," she cried, looking helplessly around;
"where art thou in the hour of thy child's despair?"

"Thy voice, Senorita, is too low to reach Moro's dungeon."

"It cannot be," she cried, "you have touched with your death-giving
hands, the noble, the good Morentez! Oh! God, where is thy vengeance!"

"Come, follow us. But, ha!" he lifted the book that lay on the table;
"how has the lady beguiled her time since the burial of the outlaw!" He
laughed sneeringly, "a fit place for the daughter of a noble and once loyal
house."

"Watched in every movement, outraged and insulted. Oh! my country! how thy children are degraded. Outlaw! oh, it was a nobler office to
close that young patriot's eyes than to hold the crown of Spain. There are
souls which your bands may reach and hold, but they cannot crush the
vital spark—the hope for liberty. They will rise and conquer. It has been
done. This," her hand rested on the volume of American history, "this
tells how a few bold men threw the tyranny of a crown from their country's shore; how they cast it into the deep waters of the ocean, and rose
greater than the oppressor's power."

The Spaniard hurled it down and crushed its pages with his iron heel.

"Ha! traitress!" he cried, as his eyes fell on a small painting of General
Lopez, hanging above her; "how dare a subject of Spain cherish the image
of that pirate dog! Thus shall the garrote rid Her Majesty of the troublesome slave." He raised his sword and sashed its blade across the neck of
the picture.

"Oh! God, never! not that," she cried; "my life is nothing. There are none now to care for me. A people will mourn him, the fearless lover of his country."

"Hushed be thine accursed tongue! We will see if its boldness does not forsake thee, in the presence of the Captain-General. Now to the Palace. If one cry is uttered,—" he looked meaningly on his sword. The Senorita smiled scornfully, and waved her hand that they should proceed. Calmly and silently she followed through the dear familiar rooms of her father's house, leaving her home for ever, perhaps to die. It was a sad thought, but her lips were resolutely closed, and no sound told how the heart was swelling with grief and scorn.

Guarded by dark, pitiless faces, she was borne into the presence of Spain's bloody minion—Concha.

CHAPTER XVIII

ORALIZE WAS BUT a woman, and shrank timidly from the open door, turning to the officer, hoping at least to find a look of sympathy for her friendless condition. Vain hope! She advanced softly but firmly into the room, and stood with folded arms before the Captain-General, his cold stern eyes resting on her pale young face. There was a stillness in the room. Purity and innocence had before now hushed fiends into silence. Oralize raised her hand, and threw the folds of her mantle from her brow.

"Thou art bold, girl," pointing to the tiny flag waving in her hair, which she had until now forgotten; "art thou mad to bring that traitorous emblem into the council of Her Majesty's faithful? What mean those colors?" She pressed the small, beautifully wrought flag, to her lips, and said bravely—

"These are the bright colors which will wave over the free. It is the flag of the future Republic of Cuba."

"Ha! fair traitress! thou shalt tell us of this wonderful Republic. Whence springs its power?"

"From the goaded long-tried spirits of my countrymen; from the arms that will bring vengeance on the *murderers of the free.*"

"Thy words bring thee death, girl."

"But not too soon. Every flower in my path of life is crushed; its every source of happiness poisoned. You threw my brave lover to the deep sea, because his lips spoke the love he bore his island home. For the same crime my father pines in Moro's dungeon. I alone am left, whose life, alas! is useless to Cuba."

"By our Lady, thou art bold! Fear you not vengeance?"

"Nay—not the vengeance of slaves. That cannot reach the spirit."

"Come nearer, accursed rebel, and answer with truth, if thou wouldst have mercy. There were papers brought thy father from the traitor Lopez; tell me where they are secreted, that I may direct my officer in his search."

"Search would be useless; they are burned."

"Thou liest! base accomplice of rebel dogs!"

"Your gentle excellency has power to lay bare at any moment all a Cuban holds sacred. Send thy minion on his errand." Concha was silent for a moment.

"Thou knowest the contents of those papers. Speak! The just tribunal of thy queen demands it."

"Never," replied the firm, sweet voice of the Cuban girl. "Never shall word of mine betray the knightly brave, who loved my poor country, even in her degradation; who risked their lives to assert her rights."

"Bring hither the instrument of torture! Thou shalt be made to speak, haughty one."

The maiden's cheeks grew white with mortal fear. Her little hands she clasped over the poor beating heart, and bending forward, said in low, earnest tones—

"You may crush my limbs with torture, you may throw my body on the rack, but you cannot, you *cannot* bring one word to my lips. Thou art already drunk with generous blood; does it need a woman's agony to complete the unholy feast? I will not shrink; I do not ask your mercy. I can but die; yet I would save thy guilty soul from a darker crime; for by our holy mother, our blessed Virgin, *I will not betray.*"

I know not why he paused. Perhaps the pure, strong spirit looking so firmly from the beautiful eyes, touched his breast with one spark of human feeling, for he said, slowly—

"Think upon thy father, girl! Wouldst thou not save his life?"

"Not with his child's dishonor. Nay," she added, scornfully, "*no promise of life could tempt me; but think you a Cuban would trust thy* false lip! Too well thou doest the bloody work of her who has forgotten the mercy of a woman, and the dignity of a queen."

"Thou vile traitoress," he cried, springing with stormy rage to his feet; "thou stout rebel! thou shalt die! Here,—now—in our very presence— the block! the axe! slaves! Our insulted queen shall be avenged; let her faithful subjects bear witness."

There had been a movement among the officers, a few of whom were present, to retire; but his words stayed them. They stood in moody silence, with folded arms, for their blood grew chill at the fearful tragedy that was to damn the night with crime. More than one was touched by compassion, as he looked on the young girl, calmly watching the hasty preparations for her death. A heavy block was brought, and placed in the centre of the room, and a shining axe silently laid on it. Concha fixed his gleaming eyes on the prisoner, and asked, "Art thou ready?"

"Dare you do this thing?" she said.

"Peace! Art thou ready?"

"Ready to die? Oh, no! Bring hither a priest, in our Lady's name; grant me this."

"Nay; thy traitor soul shall go unshrived to hell. Come, bare thy proud neck for a felon's death."

"Thou must thyself be the executioner. Thou wilt not find a headsman there" (pointing to the guard); "they, at least, are human."

As she spoke, a low, thick, mis-shapen negro, of most revolting appearance, entered the room, and stood beside the block. She covered her face with her hands, and the low groan of a woman's agony thrilled the room.

"Thou canst save thyself. There was a list of names sent thy father by this man, whom the rebels and pirates call their General. Give me these, that I may arrest the traitors, and thou art free."

Oralize raised her head, and said with passionate scorn—

"Never! If I shrank, it was that I am a woman, and the thought of blood filled me with horror. I am proud to die thus, in the cause of my dear native land. Many stronger and braver have fallen, but not one more loving or devoted. Oh! sainted mother," she cried, clasping her hands, "look in tender pity on thy child! Sweet mother of our Holy Redeemer, pray thou my soul may rest in peace!" She approached the block, while he, the son of blood and crime, looked on. The officer beside her placed his cross in her hand, and said in a low voice—

"Senorita, would that I could save you! Is there a message I can bear?"

"Wilt thou?"

"By faith."

"Tell my father I died as the child of brave Morentez should—without fear. For this gentle pity," she laid the cross an instant on her lip, "I thank you. Farewell! It is sad to leave my earthly home without one kind adieu."

He raised the white hand to his lip, and turned sadly away. The Captain-General stood beside her.

She knelt her brow on its cold death-pillow, and murmured the same prayer she had repeated beside the bier of the murdered patriot.

"Girl! wilt thou die?" shrieked the hoarse voice of Concha, while his eyes glared with lurid light upon her. Oralize, beautiful Oralize! Oralize, heroic child of Cuba! brave young daughter of the summer isle!

She raised her lustrous eyes, trembling with the moonlight beauty of a southern clime, and answered—

"Bid him strike quickly."

The Spaniards turned aside as she laid down her high-born head. One instant—the axe severed the frail neck, and ringing on the block, told— all was over!

The warm rich blood of the young Cuban gurgled on the luxurious carpet, dabbling the feet of the Spanish General, as he stood gloating over the fair victim of his tyrannic cruelty. With his own hands he raised, by the long braid of black hair, the head yet warm, and oh! so beautiful.

"Bring hither a box," he cried. He laid it in, with the fatal flag waving over the white cheek.

"Ho, Lorenzo! bear this to the keeper of the castle, and bid him, in my name, deliver it to the traitor Morentez."

Every vestige of the bloody deed was removed. No sign remained to tell how the life-stream of the Cuban girl mingled with the strong blood of freemen, and cried to Heaven for vengeance.

Gentle Oralize! no strange but generous heart wept in moving pity over thy murdered form. Darkly, silently, it was cast into the sea,

"And the waves mourned over the early dead."

CHAPTER XIX

THREE DAYS THE Liberating Army continued marching, scarcely pausing for necessary repose. On the morning of the fourth, they reached the estates of the Cuban General, which had been confiscated on suspicion of his entertaining republican principles and aspirations. Here, in the cool, refreshing shade of the magnificent trees which covered the grounds, the weary soldiers rested. General Lopez, moved, perhaps, by memories that naturally arose in the sight of his former home, left his men, and rode slowly through the grand, silent woods of which he was once master. He had as yet found no patriots, though through all the march, he encouraged his soldiers with this certainty, that the patriots were awaiting them in the mountains. Yet he was, as has been asserted by every surviving soldier then in his army, treated not only with great kindness, but with every demonstration of devotion and love by the people.

"Where are they?" he murmured; "the Creoles, the patriots! Still further must I take my weary troops, to meet that succor which they so much require? Their spirits droop and faint, with hope unfulfilled; I must hasten onward to where the revolutionists rally."

He turned, and rode rapidly towards the encampment. On approaching it, he perceived that the Liberators were charged by a body of cavalry, moving in beautiful order and array down a sloping ground, which fronted the encampment. Lopez was on the mountain-side—an immense chasm separating him from his army. This he had avoided, on riding out, by a circuitous route. His elevated position commanded a full view of the forces, and he paused to watch their operations; seeing that his officers were at their posts, and every man stood with his trusty arm in deadly aim, coolly waiting the descent of the enemy. The betrayed son of Cuba stood on her purple heights, his eager eyes bent on the scene below.

The word was given; a strong volley of balls from the Liberators overthrew the Spanish dragoons with much confusion, bringing down more than one horse and rider. Again they fired, with great destruction to the chargers, who, seized with a panic, retreated rapidly.

"My brave men!" he murmured, with a proud smile of admiration.

But his face suddenly grew anxious, for, winding down the mountain to the right of the Patriot army came a body of infantry, a thousand strong. To the left of this army ran a deep stream, from whose bank a small hill arose. By reaching this, the quick eye of the General saw that his left flank and rear would be protected. His men, missing his cheering voice, stood in evident irresolution, and the fearful chasm yawned between them. Not a moment was to be lost. One thousand against two hundred! and the only possible advantage remained untaken. It was a bold leap; but the war-trained charger and his daring rider were equal to the emergency. He who never knew the weakness of hesitating fear, bounded impetuously forward, and the noble courser proudly bore his master among his cheering men. Lopez ordered them to form and march to the prominence, which they did with great rapidity. The Liberators stood eagerly waiting the signal for attack. Lopez rode along the ranks, bearing aloft the same flag which waved victoriously over the battle-field of Los Pozas. He seemed to have a fond pride in thus making himself the standard-bearer of his little army, in keeping, protectingly, in his own brave hands the beauteous flag under which they fought—the free flag of Cuba.

The enemy were assuming their position; Lopez still harangued his men; their hearts bounded with enthusiastic impatience; for his words rang with the glad music of hope as he pointed them to the future—the glorious future of Cuba. At that moment Captain Raymond hastily approached the General, followed by a Cuban boy, looking tired, and covered with dust. Lopez turned to hear the hurried words of the officer. The waiting men watched, with intense interest, the deadly paling of their commander's face, the slowly dimming of those brilliant eyes that drooped, as if in one moment years of misery had fallen with leaden weight upon them. Captain Raymond's voice was heard, urging him to speak, but his noble head rested on his gun, as if it would fain seek death from its friendly mouth. The generous heart of the exile bled for American wrong and shame, and for Cuba's loss.

"General! the troops advance; they are upon us!"

That bowed face was raised, looking in its beaming glory upon the waiting Patriots. A darker, fiercer light than that of beauty shone in those burning eyes, and from the voice which had a moment before filled their sinking hearts with hope, fell in piercing, dagger tones—the fate of Crittenden and his murdered men.

There was silence along the ranks. Oh, God! what a silence! A world of shame, misery, and bitter wrong filled those valiant hearts. They gazed with stupified horror on the flashing eyes of Raymond, the stern, white lips of Dudley, and on their General. He, too, was silent, but his eyes glowed with the fearful gloom of a mighty agony. Raising himself erect in his stirrups, his martial form quivering with passion, he cried:

"The brave blood of Crittenden, the heroic blood of America, stains the soil on which you stand! Shall it call in vain for vengeance?"

He waved his hand to still the hot, raging murmur.

"Soldiers! you have fought to free slaves; you will not bear yourselves less bravely now that the slave of slaves gloats on the butchered forms of freemen. Stand firmly to your arms, and trust the God of truth for victory," were the hurried words of Lopez, for the troops were close upon them.

God knows, they did stand firm; and braver men never fought than that Spartan band of patriots. Madly, fiercely, they stood, repulsing the slaves of a crown—the dark oppressors of the Island Queen. A natural thirst for vengeance, mingled with sympathy for enslaved humanity, and love of the holy principles for which they bled, urged them on in this vast, unequal conflict. What was this little band, of scarce two hundred men, before the well armed thousand of the tyrant? Ah! it was the resolution of men bent on right; it was the same great, animated love of justice and truth, the elevated hope, and unconquerable spirit which laid the noble Warren, the bold Montgomery, on the sacrificial altar of American freedom. On the sloping hill they stood—these earnest missionaries in liberty's sacred cause. The light of the sinking sun fell in brilliant rays on the overshadowing trees, forming a gorgeous canopy of green and gold above them. Unmoved, with unbroken ranks, they poured their deadly fire into the face of the Spaniards. Lopez, ever careless of danger, was where the balls raged thickest around them, shouting to his devoted men with that clear voice of wondrous music and power, which never failed to thrill their hearts with encouragement and hope. Planting and supporting the flag in full view of the enemy, he was thus exposed to their aim. Here it was he received the severe wound from which he afterwards suffered so much.

Seeing his general stagger, while a copious stream of blood flowed to his feet, Captain Raymond hastened to relieve him of the banner.

"Nay," cried the sweet imperious voice, "let me fall beneath its floating colors."

Raymond rushed to his post. Vehemently he urged his men to falter not. Falter! *never!*

The Liberators stood, keeping up an incessant hailstorm of balls upon the troops. With determined bravery, the Patriots poured their death-shower on the foe. Suddenly, unable longer to stand targets for American skill, the Spanish ranks fell back, and fled precipitately.

In this, the battle of Cafatel del Frias, the Liberators lost one man; the Spaniards, three hundred.[34] General Enna, second in command to General Concha, was killed. General Lopez was also severely wounded. After this signal victory, purchased with so little loss, the spirits and hopes of the brave little army rose to a strong enthusiasm. Loudly they cheered their gallant commander, "and he was cheered."[35] The names of Dudley, Raymond, and Haines rang amid loud huzzas. In the last glowing beams of the sun, with the glad, proud smile of triumph on every brow, the heroic victors clapped their hands to heaven, with the wildest enthusiasm of joy. Oh, fearful Cubans! where were ye then? Why rushed ye not to the battle-field, made glorious with the hero-blood of Lopez? Why swept ye not, in one hard-fought, nobly-won battle, the dark usurpers from your sun-kissed, wave-fondled isle?[36]

After so glorious an achievement, what had the Liberating army gained? What should they do? After attending to the last rites for the chivalrous soldier, who had fallen alone in the engagement, they were ordered to march, even though night was coming rapidly on. They pro-

34. Cafetal de Frías was a plantation once owned by López's in-laws. Chaffin finds that although the Spaniards were indeed routed and Enna killed, they did not suffer heavy casualties. *Fatal Glory*, 211–12.

35. The Americans were *not* enthusiastic after this victory. López tried to rally them to pursue the Spanish, but they were unwilling. "By then, the filibusters harbored no illusions about their deteriorating situation," says Chaffin. They knew they were outnumbered, and the Spanish knew where they were. *Fatal Glory*, 212.

36. An uprising in Puerto Príncipe had been put down before López left the U.S. Another revolt failed at Pinar del Río. López heard that another revolt was about to begin at San Cristóbal, which is where he headed. Chaffin, *Fatal Glory*, 210.

ceeded, hoping to meet the co-operation from the Creole patriots, which Lopez yet, with a singular and beautiful trust, confidently expected. But, alas! it was a vain hope. The rains commenced with great violence, drenching the army with pitiable discomfort, and rendering their guns utterly useless. Hungry and exhausted, suffering the most terrible privations, many of the soldiers sank down by the wayside, to be massacred as soon as found by the bloodthirsty troops. Four days after the last battle, that of Cafatel del Frias, they were, at an early hour, surprised by a large body of troops. Utterly destitute of any means of defence, there was no resource left but to fly. Here it was that the men were scattered in all directions. Soon after this, the so-called pardon was proclaimed.[37] Thirty of the Patriots resolutely remained with their suffering general, who continued his march, not being pursued to any distance. Four days longer they continued this toilsome, desperate move, destitute of every comfort for body or spirit.

They were dying—famishing before him, this small remnant of his brave army. General Lopez ordered a soldier to bring his bold charger, the daring "Tempest," of his march, into their midst, and dispatch him with his sword;—he must be sacrificed to their extreme necessity.[38] The man obeyed, and Lopez turned away. The gallant charger had bravely borne his master through all the weary march, and still preserved his noble carriage and indomitable spirit, astonishing the army by his extraordinary agility in climbing steeps, leaping precipices and chasms. They had a strange, yet natural attachment for the animal, and his ordered executioner stood irresolute. At last his sword (the only weapon, besides the one worn by Lopez, which they possessed) drooped, and he walked away. The general ordered another to stand in his place, but he, too, was unable to perform the deed. The third took his place, and raised his arm for the death-blow. The noble steed, with an instinctive intelligence, turned his great dilating eyes, glancing in their beseeching beauty on the man, who shook his head and stood back. "Is there not one," said Lopez, sternly, "to do his general's bidding? Do you, in this last hour,

37. The *indulto*, issued August 26, said that all filibusters who surrendered would not be executed. Chaffin, *Fatal Glory*, 213.

38. López did in fact kill his horse to feed his men, who had not eaten for four days by this time. When the horse meat was gone, they ate the insides of palm trees. Chaffin, *Fatal Glory*, 213.

refuse me obedience?" He drew his own sword, and approached. The war-horse, with a wild neigh, bounded towards him. "My bold Tempest! after all thy faithful service, must thy master's hand give thee death." Captain Raymond stepped hastily forward, and snatching the weapon, laid the gallant charger weltering in his blood at his master's feet.

CHAPTER XX

"Oh, break, my heart! poor bankrupt, break at once."

OUR PARTY HAD BEEN more than a week at ———, the delightful water-ing-place on the gulf, so much resorted to by the beauty and fashion of the southern states. They had spent long, anxious days in seeming gaiety, Genevieve and Mabel reigning jointly on the throne of love and beauty, and never were queens' hearts more filled with care.

Though Mabel bore her spirit bravely, and cheered Genevieve with a happy future, which her eloquence painted in hope's own colors, yet if in the dance, the promenade, or crowded saloon, her ear caught the uncer-tain fragment of a sentence on the absorbing topic of the day, her heart stood still with sudden fear, and her tongue refused to ask if "all was well."

To-night—this night whose fearful anguish cannot now be recalled without tears, the two girls had just returned from a sailing excursion, and were slowly, negligently preparing for the dance. Mabel was in the most unaccountable spirits. She had, as is natural, and often the case with a nature like hers, resolutely thrown every shadow away, and given herself up to an abandonment of mirth, that owed its existence to the saddest mental agitation. Perhaps it was an unconscious effort of the will to mock the storm that was gathering above her; it may be, the unseen angel of her destiny held to her lips the cup of life, and bade her drink now its every drop of joy, ere the gall of despair had for ever embittered its wa-ters. She laughed at Genevieve in her old childish way, and sang snatches of songs that Genevieve wondered she could think of without tears.

"I've seen heap uv geyrls in my life, but I nuver did see none like Miss

Mabel, she goes on so strange, jes' like she isn't got no feelin' for them that's 'way"; and Emily gave a mournful sigh to the memory of Scipio.

"Oh! Emily, you are sentimental to-night; well, don't get out of humor until you have finished my hair, for I am pretty sure the poet's head had never been in the hands of an angry dressing-maid, when he gave his idea of the worst of pains."

"No 'casion for dat, Miss Mabel; but I don't know what you want curls for to-night; you great deal better; let me make them wide braids, an' put um roun' your head, like a crown, 'cause every body says you looks heap de best so."

"No, I must have curls—wild, free curls—I can shake them from my face, and feel careless, like a child; besides, Monsieur Devone says, curls win his heart, and I shall attach that priceless jewel to my chatelaine to-night. You don't want me to have curls because Miss Genevieve has; but you know mine are much the prettier. See how long they are; 'way below my waist."

"But yourn is 'most red, an' Miss Genevieve's is black as a crow."

"Oh, that is a mere difference of taste and color. But I see"—she laughed—"I am to be all alone in my admiration of myself, for the present, at least."

"You know, Miss Mabel, I think you is de beautifulest thing on earth, after Miss Genevieve; but de Lord knows he robbed hisself uf a singin' angel when he sent her in dis troublesome worl'. But you all better hurry an' dress, 'cause de young gentlemen always makes a fuss, and frets mightily, when dey has to wait so long 'fore you is ready, tho' dey looks smilin', and says t'ain't no matter. Tell me what you goin' to put on, Miss Mabel; I done smoothed out your blue silk wid de white lace flounces; you hasn't worn it sence you bin here."

"No; give me my India muslin, with its graceful train and silver stars. *He* loved the dress," she murmured softly. "I remember when last I wore it, how fondly he said, 'Night, with her jeweled train, is not so glorious in beauty as *thou*, my Mabel.' '*My* Mabel!' Ah! beautiful words. When will they come again?"

"Emily, give me that ambrosia from the vase; fresh fragrant ambrosia," she continued, murmuring to herself, "whose green beauty the very gods have loved; it shall loop these wide hanging sleeves, and I will mingle with its spray-like sprigs the white star flowers of the jasmine; together they shall fasten the curls from my face. Now clasp my bracelets," and she held her white arm to the admiring mulatto.

"Come, Genevieve, don't stand looking from the east window; the star of your destiny is shining in the south."

"Or has faded for ever from our earth," was the sad reply.

"To rise on a nobler world than ours. But hush! do not talk thus sadly, Genevieve; do not seek to cloud my spirits; let me smile now, for I am soaring to-night, far above care; I am wedded to hope, immortal hope. See what a radiant bride I am," and she shook her starry robe.

"Mabel, beautiful Mabel, you are the lost pleiad, waiting for your mortal love." Her fond arms were thrown around the shining form.

"Miss Genevieve, mistis say ef you please to not keep de gentlemun waitin' no longer."

"We are coming," and they descended to join the brilliant throng of revellers.

Genevieve complained of a headache, and refused to dance. She sat by her mother's side, listening with careless courtesy to words of adulation that were forgotten with a smile; but her earnest eyes watched every movement of a dazzling form, whose very soul seemed floating to the music of the dance. I, too, stood amid the crowd, and gazed on that loveliness, upon whose shrine I long since laid the fondest worship of my heart. I, too, marked the fitful radiance of eyes whose strange passionate beauty haunts me now, filling my own with tears; for the loved, the peerless original of my Mabel, I shall, through all the weary years of my future life, see only in dreams; the kindly dreams with which the angel of sleep and the spirit of imagination gild with momentary happiness, the barren waste of my actual life.

Yet pause a moment before the unclouded beauty of her who was the inspiration of every high and nobler dream my life has known; her who first taught me the moral and mental excellence of my own sex. Sweet lady! though far removed from the fascination of thy actual presence, its charm, memory is faithful to keep. As the miser, in counting o'er his treasure, lingers more fondly on the one rare jewel of his wealth, so do I pause beside those hours which owed their wondrous beauty and delight to thee!

"Mabel," pleaded Genevieve, "don't dance again, your cheeks are crimson and your eyes *so* bright; mamma, she has a fever, I know she has.

Sit down, Mabel, I want to talk with you. Your curls really have melted Monsieur Devone's heart; he says you are—"

"Don't tell me what any one says. I am out of humor with compliments, because I have grown fastidious, or conscientious, perhaps, and can't return them. I know I am beautiful, divine, and all that; but I shall detest the first man that tells me so. Don't shake your head and look so wicked, uncle Louis. I am in earnest. Listen to that music, Genevieve; I am delirious with an irrepressible joy to-night. I won't sit here. I don't wish to talk; I shall make myself absurd and disagreeable if I do. You believe *that,* uncle Louis."

"Come, Genevieve, *one* Mazourka. Quick, or I shall dance with that standing collar and moustache coming across the room; then Uncle Louis will have to take that model lecture on propriety from his vest-pocket, where he always keeps it convenient, for my especial benefit. Come."

The beautiful Mazourka! In all the dancing world, there is nothing like it. The graceful springing step, harmonizing so well with the wild, glad music of the dance. The first steps have all the dreamy grace of the waltz, as though the feet lingered on roses; the second find the thorns, from which they bound defyingly.

Joyous dance! full of fascination—peculiar to a people whose very existence is a poetic spell.

The hour of midnight had passed, and the unusual bustle below gave notice that the New Orleans steamer had arrived. Mr. Clifton joined the throng of gentlemen, who hastened to get "the news from the city."

The room was well nigh deserted, and the hurried hum of voices repeated the fearful story of America's wrong, and her disgrace. There were muttered curses—passionate exclamations. One voice of hot, honest indignation, for a tyrant's triumph, and a Republic's shame. Low cries of anguish, the sound of weeping mingled with the wild music, now unheeded. The dancers paused. Genevieve sank, flushed and trembling, beside the cool window. Dread and apprehension brought the ready tears to her eyes, and she hid her face in her mother's bosom. Mabel, the shining, star-clad form, walked with firm but rapid steps, down the long room, steadily making her way through the crowd, which again thronged it, until she stood beside Mr. Clifton. Kind Uncle Louis—there was something very like moisture in his eye, as he looked on the white, motionless face, with its mild, questioning eyes. He could not himself speak;

he put a letter in her hand, and silently supported Mrs. Clifton and Gene-vieve, who were now standing anxiously by her. It was in a crowd of angry, gloomy faces, but Mabel with strange calmness broke the black seal, and read the last sad letter of her martyr lover. "God help me," she said, and glided softly, swiftly from the room.

"Don't follow her, Genevieve," said Mr. Clifton, keeping her hand in his, "you can do her no good. Eugene is dead." They bore the fainting form of Genevieve from the room, and all night watched beside her, lis-tening to the agonized raving of her delirium.

Mabel, with her poor, bleeding heart, how went the hours with her? Mrs. Clifton sent, again and again, but Emily said the door was fastened, and Miss Mabel would not answer. Ah! it was a night of sorrow to more than one heart. At early dawn, when Genevieve at last slept, Mrs. Clifton sought the chamber of the bereaved girl. Those who have themselves suf-fered, those who have felt the keen bitterness of a hopeless disappoint-ment, the heavy, leaden weight of a great sorrow, are silent before the sufferings of others, for they know so well how coldly the fondest words of sympathy fall on an aching heart. The young girl sat before an open window, watching the morning break over the calm waters of the quiet lake. Her festive robe was still around her, and its stars looked cold and pale in the chill, dim light. The white, haggard face, with large, tearless eyes, and the dark blue rings of sleepless agony, were so mournful: Mrs. Clifton sat down beside her, and wept in silence. At last she said, "Mabel, my poor, dear child! I am very sorry for you. Unhappy Mabel!"

"Miserable," she answered with a shudder, "very miserable and com-fortless. Last night I called myself the bride of hope. Poor, deserted bride!" She sat pulling the dead flowers from her long hair. "Genevieve may hope." She looked at Mrs. Clifton, as though she feared to be contra-dicted: "Yes, she may know hope, but I can feel nothing. My heart is hard and cold, like a rock; barren and desolate, like a desert. Everything is gone, shut out;—even despair. I wish I could go mad, insane, forget my-self. I wish I could die! Oh! that yesterday had never passed away!"

"Hush, Mabel, my darling, don't talk so. I cannot comfort you. Noth-ing earthly can reach your sorrow: but there is one, whose ear is ever open to the cry of the distressed, one who does not willingly afflict the children of men. Lay your heavy burden at his feet, and he will give you rest."

"Rest!" she said, with a desolate smile. "Never more, never more."

"Mabel, my poor Mabel, do not sit so cold and still. Mabel, 'Jesus wept.'"

"I have no tears; they are frozen. The ice of sorrow presses hard on my soul. Last night, when my heart was bursting with its grief, I prayed that it might break at once. I sought the lonely chapel on the shore, and threw myself before the 'Mother of Mercy'; I implored her to stand between me and my bitter despair. Cold! cold! cold! There was no answer in my breast. The storm of passion raged fiercely on. I could have dashed the calm and silent marble into atoms, so frenzied was my agony. I stood by the sighing waves, and cried to the Everlasting God of my fathers—I stretched forth my arms to the Almighty God of my faith—but His face was hid from me, and the waters of grief overflowed my soul. The very stars shrank back, as I held out my supplicating hands. I laid my breast on the damp earth, and moaned for my terrible desolation. I longed to throw myself on the outgoing waves, that they might dash me on the lonely grave of my murdered love—my lost Eugene. Poor heart!" she said, covering her tearless face with her hands, "where is thy strength? Stricken heart! where is thy trust? Gone, all gone. The blackness of night is around me!"

"Mabel, you must lie down, my child, you want rest and quiet. Let Emily take your dress, and you drink this my love." She brought a cup she had prepared. "Don't put it away; you will sleep."

"And forget," she muttered, then eagerly drank its contents. The bright morning sun was in the room when Mrs. Clifton left her, and the motherless girl lay in a deep, oppressive slumber.

CHAPTER XXI

LOPEZ HAD REACHED the mountains, with the small remnant of his brave men. The beautiful blue mountains of Cuba, from whose shelter he had hoped so much, brought him, alas! no relief. Where now were the thousands who had sworn to meet him with ammunition and provisions, where nature herself had made for them a garrison? Alas! alas! gem of the

Antilles! where were they tyrant-wearied sons, that they stood not beside these devoted friends of thy soil? Ask them of the deep dungeons, whose cold, dark walls, shut out dying groans! Ask them of the lonely chaparral,—they tell no story of foully mangled bodies. The waves, that fondly kiss thy green shore, bring they no tidings of noble hearts, chilled in their embrace? No whisper how, in the dead of night, they drank the life-breath of the fiery youth, hushing him with their melodies to a dreamless sleep! Speak to the mourning wife, the sorrowing child; tell them, beneath thy heaving billows repose—the lost husband and father. On thy foam-white breast, let them fling the love-twined wreath, which should have decked a warrior's brow or soldier's grave. Unhappy land! thus bereft, how many hearts were beating for thy freedom? but they beat against chains. Bound in by the untiring vigilance of the tyrant, they were left with the will, but without the power to be free.

The Cubans had been for so long crushed by the most grinding despotism, morally and physically, they were easily intimidated and discouraged. They were well aware of the extraordinary activity with which our government sought to deprive them of all aid, and detain that succor to which they had eagerly, hopefully looked. This, the Spanish papers did not fail to proclaim in the most impressive manner, laboring to convince the heart-sick natives, of the inability of their friends, and the falseness of their own ardent hopes.

Lopez had, with an unfortunate caution, instructed the principal men favorable to the revolution with whom he was in confidential correspondence, to receive no communication as authentic, unless delivered by his own trusty messenger, who was, alas! the arch-traitor Hidalgo Gonzales.

No tidings from Lopez came. They saw daily the most powerful and influential of their numbers arrested, cast into prison, or openly put to death. Nothing was sacred; spies hovered around their very firesides, and the slightest suspicion drew on them the assassin's dagger. Thus depressed in spirit, without arms, ignorant of the intended movements of the patriot army, we can scarcely wonder that the Liberators found not a welcoming people, but one filled with fear and despair. It may be asked, why, after General Lopez had made a landing, the Creoles did not come to his support. *Many did go!* but all these causes of which I have spoken found them unprepared, and without concert. It was impossible for them to give that immediate support which Lopez *certainly* expected, and which they were most anxious to render. Before they could summon their leaders and concentrate, the tide had flowed out which would have washed the stain of slavery from that beautiful land. The American allies were scattered, and their General a prisoner.

Had the force of General Lopez been sufficiently strong, I mean in numbers, to maintain the position he occupied after the battle of Los Pozas; had he had the reinforcement he expected in the mountains, the result of the expedition would have been very different. Yet the train of circumstances, the dark treachery which effected its unfortunate failure, does not take away purity from the motive, or honesty from the purpose of the man who proved his sincerity by sacrificing his life in the cause he espoused.

Lopez had reached the mountains. In spite of his woeful disasters, he had hoped the Creoles would rally in the interior; he could not give them up; his noble heart clung to their ardent professions, and yearned to save them. But now, sadly the conviction forced itself upon him that all was lost. He stood with the thirty faithful patriots, surrounded by the still mountains, with none to help him. No, not one—and they must die. For days he had watched the terrible sufferings of his wounded, starving men, and his tortured heart bled with unutterable love and pity. Oh! who can think lightly of agony like this! Who can charge that martyr-heart with indifference! Lips unworthy to breathe his name! Cold cowards alone withhold all they can now give—simple justice. Noble hearts who would themselves suffer and dare, feel that sympathy the brave give the brave even in misfortune; these will honor the name, and sorrow over the fate of Cuba's illustrious hero. Now, hungry and exhausted, the men slept on the soft green turf of the betrayed isle. Lopez leaned wearily against the trunk of a large sheltering tree, and watched the bright stars fade from the sky, vanishing like his own holy visions. Heavy heart! how lonely were thy silent chambers, now the life-cheering hope was gone. A hand was laid on his shoulder, and he turned to Dudley's pale, haggard face.

"My poor boy! I thought you slept."

"Not while my General waked," replied the devoted officer. Lopez motioned that he should sit beside him, and said—

"I am weary—I am weary; repeat to me the Marco Bozzaris of your poet." The last thrilling line was uttered, and for a moment the silence of night was unbroken. Then he said with that earnest enunciation peculiar to him, "Would that God had given *me* such a fate. To *fall* on the battle-field, to spill my worthless blood for my country, to die with the shout of her freemen in my ear. For that which I believed to be her good, I gave up all, became a fugitive and exile, a pensioner on warm but foreign hearts. For this I staked, dared, and lost all. I have toiled, struggled, alas! lived in vain, for oh! Cuba, best beloved of my breaking heart! I must leave thee bound, ignobly bound in Spanish chains. Since I cannot live for thee, oh! mother of Christ, may my death not be in vain. Queen of the south! arise, put on the pride of strength, and avenge the generous blood already spilled. Dudley," he continued, and his eyes burned on his listener; "there is no coward at my heart; I do not fear death—even the terrible death I know they will give me. I rejoice that I have a life to lay down in a cause so glorious; I love Cuba but the more fondly since I must give her my life, but, my men," he turned to the sleeping forms; "stout, gallant hearts! is there no hope! must they, too, perish?" Dudley did not answer, he sat watching the troubled face of the speaker. "Ralph," he resumed earnestly; "there is but one thing that can be done. You must take these men and leave me." Dudley sprang before him with folded arms, and the large eyes in which the sunshine no longer played, looked the devotion his lips uttered.

"God curse me when I forsake you," he cried; "Oh! my General, turn not away!"

Lopez bowed his head with a bitter sigh, and was silent. How poor are words in such a moment! At length he laid his hand on the young officer's arm, and said—

"Listen to me. You may yet save yourself and the faithful remnant of my little army. You will doubtless be able to make terms with the government, and procure for them a safe return. If found with me, the shadow of my destiny will cover them, and they will surely die. Do not refuse my prayer. Take them, my last best friend, and go; it is all I can do for them, or for you."

"General! you do not know these men. They will *never* desert you. I will 'rouse them, that they may themselves decide."

"No—no, poor fellows, let them forget while they may; sleep, the momentary oblivion of the wretched, is the only luxury their hard fate has not taken. When the morning's sun comes, then—not now."

The hours of night moved on, and morning came. Again General Lopez urged Ralph to leave him; but in vain.

"Never!" said Dudley; "never! I have chosen to stand by you, and the fear of death cannot take me away; for," he added, with touching enthusiasm, "you came to me as the rare embodiment of all the high and noble dreams of my restless heart, pining for the good and true. Whatever the world had been to you, or you had been to the world, to me you were the perfection of all good. I pledged myself to Cuba and to you. However fond the ties of home, I left all to follow where you led. It was no passing enthusiasm, for this bitter reality finds my devotion but increased. I would gladly have stood beside you as a successful general and liberator; now, all I ask is to share your fate, however dark it may be. Nay, you shall not reject me," he cried, passionately, as Lopez strove to speak. "My sword will cleave my heart—its blood shall wash your feet ere I desert you."

Faint with excitement and fatigue, he sank beside the Cuban.

"My noble boy," he murmured; "this is, indeed, hard. Oh, God! that I should blight such a heart!" And he turned away from the wasted face of his officer.

Morning broke, with mocking cheerfulness, on the hope-reft men who stood for the last time around their beloved general. Beautiful, beyond all description, was the kingly form which rose to address them; no suffering could rob it of that dignity nature herself had given to command. He reasoned, entreated, and now he implored them to leave him. But they firmly, scornfully refused.

"Right, my staunch men," cried Dudley; "I did not reckon too strongly on your true hearts. 'The fortune of a general, however hard, should be shared by his soldiers.' You have bravely fought for Cuba, and bled for her liberty—now, you will not shrink from death in the sacred cause which claims Lopez as its martyr."

The dear, old enthusiasm of the past, beamed in the wan faces of the warriors. They dared not shout their truth; but the little band for a moment bent low before him whose faith they had never wronged by one unworthy doubt. The bitter cup overflowed. His head sank slowly on his breast, and the proud, brave spirit of Lopez wept such tears as come not to the eyes, but lie hot and burning around an aching heart. A moment—he raised his lofty brow, and the great, dauntless spirit sat lovingly in his eyes, as they rested on such loyalty as a crown has never boasted.

Who will say that human nature is wholly lost, while these hearts yet beat? In the dark, bitter hour of the Cuban's life, there came a light of joy. He would die, but not hopelessly; they would live to vindicate his memory and cause. Who can measure the love of that doomed man, for the few whom his terrible adversity found unchanged?

"My men," he cried; "my brave men, you who have loved me—have suffered with me—whose gallant hearts cling to my adverse fortune— words are too poor to thank you. Dear to me—oh, how dear!—is your faith and trust. It soothes, in this last hour, the many sorrows of my life. But in vain—in vain you plead. If you will not go, I must leave you. Yours are no common lives; they shall not be sacrificed now, when they will avail nothing. Remember your homes; there is a future for you. My country was my all, and I have lost her. Life has for me but one scene—the garrote. Even that I welcome," his face grew radiant; "for a vision comes that Cuba will avenge it. Unworthy of so much glory, yet I die for my country, and you will live to justify my memory by your fidelity to her. I die content, for I leave her not alone in her wronged loneliness. Bear a little longer with her, this mourning child of the ocean; she will yet rise to bless you as—a republic. Comrades!" his voice of music brought touchingly from his generous heart, these words, "tell my countrymen— those brothers so dear to me, I have never, even in my sorest hour of trial, reproached them with my misfortunes. I now know, how the dark power of Spain held the drawn sword above them; they would, but could not come to me. Betrayed and deserted as I am, there is no blush upon my cheek for a treacherous son of Cuba. Tell them how I struggled, hoped, and oh! how gladly I die for them. They will not regret my death—the poor atonement the tyrant exacts—because I dared to love them."

There was a fulness at his great heart. He paused, then holding his arms tightly across his breast, he cried:

"Oh, friends! freemen! favored of heaven! let not your generous sympathy for the oppressed die with this struggle for liberty. As you have been true to me, be you faithful to my country when I am no more. From this hour which the tyrant fondly dreams the hour of our despair, springs a bow of promise which shall arch over, and bind you in the brotherhood of a new order. Be the emblem of that order a lone star—the propitious star of hope. See!" he waved his hand brightly towards the rising sun, "as he comes to light the morn, so will come the great day when the radiant eyes of the 'goddess of liberty' shall smile peace and happiness on this isle of never-fading summer beauty. *The destiny of Cuba is freedom.*"

The sublime faith of patriotism cast a halo around the speaking head, as if the light of prophetic inspiration rested on his brow.

"Beloved in arms!" he cried, "once more on earth let me hear the liberating patriot's oath."

He stood for a moment with his sword pressed to those lips unstained by falsehood, then, in the solemn stillness of the lonely wood, his voice mingled, for the last time, in that vow which still lives, and has, I trust, thrilled every manly heart, whose eyes rest on this page.

When the patriots rose, the brave, bright spirit of the Revolution had passed from their midst, and they knew they must not follow.

More than one stout heart turned away to hide the honest tear that fell for his honored but unfortunate general.

"Come, boys," said Ralph, with a poor assumption of his usual hardihood; "it is a sad thing, God knows. The only friend now on whom we may rely with any certainty, is—the undertaker. We will, however, do the best for ourselves, and make all haste to reach ——— which is the nearest point."[39]

They commenced the weary march; but ere they arrived at their destination, Colonel Dudley was missing, and no man doubted that he had gone to share the fate of Lopez; and they were right.

CHAPTER XXII

WHEN RALPH RETURNED to him, General Lopez no longer remonstrated, neither did he express surprise. He knew so well the enthusiasm of that bold young heart, that his own sympathy with it made him now accept its homage. He could fully enter into the generosity of its devotion, for

39. Probably San Cristóbal.

Dudley "stood beside him as the spirit of his own youth." He knew there was to him a fierce gratification in thus linking his destiny with his own fallen fortune.

It had been long since they had tasted food, and the two men were weak and faint. General Lopez could with difficulty stand, the pain and fever from the severe wound in his shoulder were so great. At length they found a cavern in the mountain's side, which might protect them from the scorching sun. Here Dudley left the General resting on his hard rock-couch, his head pillowed on his unloaded gun, and went in search of food. All day long the Cuban lay in the fearful agony of mental and physical suffering, and night found him still alone. His feverish memory brought all the records of his stormy life before him. It dwelt on the victorious battles of the south, in which he had commanded with such éclat, the wealth, the power, the station, the prosperous days when his friends numbered thousands, all of which had been sacrificed for an adversity *which will yet be his highest fame.* Then alone, friendless, concealed in the bosom of the country he loved, with the price of blood upon his head! he almost questioned his own identity.

"Alone," he murmured. "No, General, not alone, but what is worse, under the circumstances, supperless; for even the wild fruits have failed us. If I could have gained the neighboring estate, whose owner is, I know, friendly, we should have feasted famously, but the troops were hovering around and I dared not risk it. But this cave is almost as hard as a prison; let me assist you out, the cool night-air will revive you." So they sat on the soft moss in the pleasant moonlight—Lopez and his one faithful friend.

"I am greatly relieved," said the General, "now that I can hope for the safety of my men. They have lain heavily on my breast. Gallant fellows! if I could have led them to success!" he paused, and then exclaimed with sudden feeling; "Oh! why from my boyhood has my heart lived in visions of freedom; why was all the good in my nature stirred to act for Cuba, if her liberty be but the dream of an enthusiast? God forgive me if I murmur; he alone knows how entirely Cuba's advancement and elevation have been my first hope, my last prayer."

"General, there lives no heart so base, to doubt the purity of your patriotism. Will you not prove it with your life? for the Spaniard will hardly spare you."

"God forbid! I meet my fate resolutely. Death in the cause of good is honor. Adverse fortune has caused this revolution to fail in its great aim, yet it will be productive of good. Others will stand in my place, and finish the work we have commenced. Ah! had our noble cause found favor in the American government; had she but exercised the charity and benevolence becoming a great nation towards a people striving to follow her bright example, Cuba would now be free."

"Yes," said Dudley, bitterly; "I had rather died than lived to scorn the cold selfish policy of America! To feel that my country is not only ungenerous, but unjust. America, walking the waters, hand in hand with Spain, protecting the crown of a despot, helping a tyrant crush spirits struggling to be free, sealing her unholy faith even with the blood of her children."

"We can but deplore that America, wrapt in her own greatness, had not that sympathy as a government, which she felt as a nation for a people groaning under the deadly oppression of tyranny. But no power can stay the light which shall shine on Cuba. A star has arisen that will not set in night. A glorious destiny was given it at its birth. Its guiding beams will lead great and good men to work out Cuba's predestined redemption. Spain herself, with trembling hate, sees the future freedom of this island. The dark heart rages with the thought, and she may yet, in the extremity of despair, throw upon the victim of her gloating tyranny, a more fearful indignity. Yes," his hands were clasped hardly, and the Cuban's face grew crimson; "rather than this silver-set gem which nature so much loves, should shine amid the stars of the Columbian flag, rather than she should stand in the self-sustaining life of her own republicanism, the Spaniard would cast upon her the undying stain of African equality. He would bid the Cuban clasp his slave as a brother, and together kneel before a crown whose pollution, fiends might blush to wear."

"Great God! General, you dream; think you they would make them allies? arm the dark race against their own?"

"None know so well as I, who have tasted the very dregs of its bitterness, the infamous policy of that nation whose whole history is shadowed with crime. There is no deed too dark for its hatred and revenge. I have spoken of what may be, of the dark hours that *may* come before the rising of Cuba's day-star—the dawn of her own emancipation. The hour of my own fate comes on; I feel that I sit for the last time with you, and my lips dwell with lingering love on this theme of my life. We will have but little companionship, my boy, in the dungeon of the Moro."

"General," said the American, breathing deeply, as though the suffocation of confinement was already on him; "it is a little thing to die—to give your life for the faith which you have professed, but the torture of a close dark dungeon—oh, God! why submit to that which is worse than death! Let us forget life in the free air of heaven, with the fresh beauty of nature around us. The sad, cold moon will not smile on our dying struggles, and the stars are no paid hirelings to shout the victory of the tyrant." He looked wistfully on his sword blade, flashing in the moonlight. "No— no, fiery heart! have you not yet learned to wait! Seek not to thwart fate. She will bring a fitter destiny to those who have thus far bravely breasted her waves. It is glorious to fall on the battle-field, but think you the noble blood of the heroic Crittenden, and his martyred men, will flow less brightly down the stream of time, because the hands which *had* been raised in the great cause of humanity, of justice, and truth, were manacled! There is a moral sublimity in their death, which will hallow it with fame. I have," he continued, "in my dark hours longed to live, for I feared the disastrous issue of this struggle might chill all hearts, who would have dared to succor Cuba. But 'twas a coward thought to doubt the final triumph of right. Ah! who could turn unheeding from thy plaining cry, thou star-queen of the southern waters! Chivalry will live again in that love which brave men will feel for thy beauty and thy wrongs."

The night wore on. To while away its weary hours, Lopez spoke of his early life. He said how from his earliest recollection he had loved Cuba with the strong peculiar love which men feel for their native land, that love which had made her his destiny. How he had lived in her loveliness till his heart was saturated with her being, and throbbed to the music of her song-birds and murmuring waters. Now, as an old soldier, after the vicissitudes of many battles, comes home to die, so he had come to breathe out life on the shrine of his boyhood's idolatry. Then he told of war-like scenes—when he had led men on to the contest amid the clash of arms, and roar of cannon; of the hour when his stern heart bounded to the trumpet's blast of victory, and swelled with the triumph of the brave again. How he scorned the rank and station in which he was but the slave of a crown, and longed for the life of the commonest soldier, who protected the rights of the free. How he grew impatient over the ancient records of haughty Greece, and mighty Rome, for their beauty dimmed beside the light of the Antilles gem. What they had been to the past, so might Cuba be to the present and future. Then he brought a pure vision from his boyhood, and spoke of his mother, the daughter of a sunny clime, with clear radiant eyes, who first taught him the beauty of human love. He passed his hand across his brow, and said, "In feverish sleep, when the cares and duties of life lay heavy on his breast, he snatched happiness from dreams, for an angel form stood by him, singing the hymns of his country, and he waked with re-invigorated strength, with the holy Ave Maria on his lip, she had taught him in the old days when he knelt beside her a happy, careless boy at the Virgin's shrine.

"She was herself so gentle," he continued; "she wondered why I left the flowing melody of our native tongue to master the uncouth language of the Saxon. Ah! it was a glad joy to speak in freedom's tongue. Then it was I felt the stain which blackened the land of my love. I felt there was a mighty glory in the great, strong north-men, who came down in their good ships to make on this western continent a new world where men might proudly live. I paused over the pages of America's heroic history, until my soul was filled with ardent longings to benefit my country and her people. These thoughts grew with my youthful strength, and my manhood had but one star, the same which rose in early boyhood, and pointed to Cuba's liberation. This fairest land was still beautiful, but to me it wore a saddened aspect, for 'the nobler part of existence,' the spirit, mourned over its bondage. I felt there was a band of disgrace on my brow—its weight grew insupportable. I could not 'bow in servile fear'; I dared to utter words and form schemes of good which made the tyrant tremble for his power, and they sent me an exile to a foreign shore. Then the light came shining upon me—the morning light of hope. On the loved, the generous soil of America my high resolves met sympathy, found supporters more brave and noble than those whose memories live in ancient knightly glories. My brothers, the sons of Cuba, were pining in degradation, praying for an arm to teach them to strike. With wild joy I sprang to their call. Oh! how I lived in visions of Cuba's renown! Free in government, free in conscience, and free in her natural rights, I thought to see her stand high among nations, in the greatness of her power. But it is not yet to be," he continued, sadly; "the dark power prevails for awhile. Spanish spies betrayed our cause, and the glory of Cuba lies in the future. She yet groans in her chains; but I thank God death finds me on no silken couch, but on the fair bosom of my life-long love; I will as calmly die as a warrior on the deck of his own proud ship, which he would but could not save. Let my blood mingle with the waves that dance around, and hold her in an eternal embrace. Holy Mary! may the blood spilled upon this soil nourish the young plant of liberty till 'neath its wide-spreading branches, the weary sons of despotism may repose in the happy security of freedom, and its leaves be sought for the healing of distant tyrant-wounded nations. Oh! how the visions of my youth come back; when my heart sprang eagerly to the future; its impulses made holy by a high resolve to benefit my suffering kind; to make its grand imaginings the actual foot-paths of my after life; to free Cuba, and live in her happiness, content to be the humblest of her children, or die, and be remembered. How earnestly I have striven to be worthy of her remembrance! to feel that the arms of my country would cling around my memory, as one who in life never faltered in his honesty and devotion to her advancement and elevation." Lopez paused, and groaned with bodily pain. The hot fever of hunger and exhaustion scorched his veins, and his wound bled afresh.

"General," said Dudley, "God knows you have won this reward, and it will yet be given you. But you are weary and worn. I will lay my cloak beside the stream; come and rest upon it, while I try my skill as a surgeon. Your wound has been too long neglected," and he drew his commander to the damp, hard bed he prepared. Gently, as a mother tends her suffering child, did the soldier do all in his power to alleviate the pain of his leader and friend. Silently he watched, as the wearied man slept, forgetful of his misery and his wrongs.

The hours of the night wore on. Dudley kept his guarding post by his General's side, busy with sad memories. He thought how the bold spirit of Lopez had fearlessly stepped forward and espoused the cause of his enslaved country. How the young, the valiant, the chivalrous had flocked around him, full of high dreams of the "New Republic," which was to rise up and call them blest. Betrayed and deserted, fighting against fearful odds, his followers had fallen into the hands of the tyrant, on the battle-field, or wandered, friendless, in a strange land. Keenly as he felt his own disappointment, there was a deeper sorrow in his heart as he looked on the unconscious Cuban, wounded in spirit, crushed and bleeding in body; the man whom he had loved as a friend, honored as a hero, and followed, even to death, lay helpless as a tired child beside him. He thought of him as he was, pure in heart, generous in action, and unflinching in courage. True to himself, to the impulses of an upright nature, it was not possible that he could be false to others.

The hours of the night wore on, and the chieftain waked not. Fated one! sleep on. The last lone-watched sleep thy stormy life will know. The fiend-hounds, even now, bay the rich blood slowly, sadly beating in thy heroic heart.

Softly rest thee, betrayed son of Cuba! thy destiny comes on. Far beyond earth soars thy fiery star—above it gleams a crown, such as martyrs wear. Slumber gently! it falls not yet upon thy brow, oh! thou champion of freedom.

CHAPTER XXIII

WHEN GENERAL LOPEZ awoke, it was with a very comfortless sensation; for the morning sky was overcast, and the rain fell in torrents upon them. Dudley sat by him, with that weary, haggard look, which comes when the body has been for a long while without sleep or food.

"You have watched well," said the General kindly. "Should you escape the blood-hounds of Spain, thus will you watch through the dark night of my poor country's despair; ever wakeful to her interest, awaiting with patience the dawn of hope in her political horizon. Then will you renew your devotion to me—in the strength and energy of your support to her."

"I have no wish but to die with you," was the hopeless answer, for every energy was exhausted.

"My brave Dudley! your life can better serve me than your death. My cup of life is well-nigh full—the death-drop is alone wanting to complete its measure. For Cuba, there is a great future—and you, my noble boy, must share it. The hope of her redemption *will not die* within my breast. Wear you this trust bravely, without despair, till the hour comes when you shall again face her foes. Hark!" His quick ear caught a distant sound, his eye rested on a line of troops coming slowly over the opposite mountain; he hastily unfastened the small, beautifully-wrought sword, which he constantly wore, to which a pleasant memory was attached, perhaps of a former victory, and, giving it to his young officer, said, "Dudley, I am famishing; bring me food, or I die. Go:—in that direction you will be safe from the enemy. God bless you, my boy,—true, even in the face of death. If death come between us—keep faithfully my memory and *my words.*" His voice, the clear, stern voice, that had sounded above the clash of arms, that had rung with fierce distinctness down the line of battle,— was mournful with suppressed emotion.

"Oh, God, General, this is terrible! I will have it, if I give my blood." He grasped the hand of his commander; he looked, unconsciously for the last time, on the noble face of the Cuban patriot,—of the hero and the martyr.

Those glorious falcon eyes—the softness of a grateful and generous love beamed in the splendor of their light, as they watched the retreating form. "The faithful friend of my exile," he murmured, "the devoted sharer of my adversity. I could not see him meet a fate like mine. My country! betrayed and forsaken—my men! scattered like autumn leaves—my friends! where are they?"—he smiled bitterly. "Gone, all gone! They come nearer; I hear the wild cry from my blood! I will go forth, and meet my fate." He walked with evident pain, but his step did not falter, until he stood underneath a large tree, the same under whose shelter he sat with Dudley. The ground, then occupied by his sleeping men, was now covered with Spanish soldiers. Haughty and erect he stood, with a mocking smile on his bold warrior face, calmly waiting his destiny.

The officer dismounted and approached him. "You are my prisoner," he said.

The chieftain bowed his head upon his breast. "Like a wild beast bayed," he murmured, and with a mournful smile, a smile full of bitterness and pain, he looked on the fierce blood-dogs, as they ran with eager, savage joy, toward their masters, him from whose hand they were accustomed to receive a reward for their success. A burning crimson tide welled over the marble paleness of the Cuban's wasted cheek, as he recognised in the cowering, shrinking form of his betrayer, the man he had once saved from the garrote. "Ha! Castaneda!" he cried, "ingrate, is it thou who hast sold my blood for gold? Unhappy man!"[40]

There was no exultation among the troops. In sullen silence they waited, while their officer himself assisted General Lopez to mount. No conqueror's train was ever more respectful than the guard who escorted the captive through that gloomy and memorable march.

CHAPTER XXIV

"What I did, I did in honor,
Led by th' impartial conduct of my soul."

"I have a thousand spirits in my breast,
To answer twenty thousand, such as you."

SHAKSPEARE.

"Still in his stern and self-collected mien,
A conqueror's more than captive's air is seen;
Though faint with wasting toil and stiffening wound,
But few that saw—so calmly gazed around;
The better warriors who beheld him near,
Insulted not the foe who taught them fear;
And the grim guards who to his durance led,
In silence eyed him with a secret dread."

BYRON.

WITHIN THE PALACE the Captain-General of Cuba sat, surrounded by his officers. With heavy, gloomy silence they looked towards the opening door, by which the Cuban General entered, attended by an armed guard. The eager eyes of Concha, as they fell upon his daring, dangerous prisoner, glared with lurid light, as a tiger's, when he springs upon his prey.

---

40. A Cuban peasant, José Antonio Castañeda, informed Spanish troops about López's location; he received ten thousand pesos for the information. Chaffin, *Fatal Glory*, 214. It is possible that Castañeda was one of López's Cuban supporters until this moment. We do not know what Holcombe is referring to with regard to López's having saved Castañeda from the garrote.

Lopez, the good and great, stood in their poor presence alone, yet undaunted. Pale he was, deadly pale, for bodily suffering and mental anguish had robbed him almost of life; but the strong, unconquered spirit looked proudly from his large burning eyes, for he was innocent of guilt. The wound upon his shoulder was too painful for the ordinary dress, and his martial form was shrouded in a rich dark mantle, whose folds were held by a hand so large, so powerful in its outlines, victory seemed written on its broad surface, as its natural right.

There was silence in the hall, as though they feared to speak, lest the fiery spirit before them should burst its bonds and escape their foul control. At last, Concha, in harsh grating tones, in which his insolent triumph was poorly concealed, thus addressed the patriot:—

"Narciso Lopez! thou art brought before us for the dark crime of treason. Thou hast lifted thyself from the feet of her most gracious majesty, and sown discord among her subjects. Thou hast openly abetted this rebellion; defied the power of thy queen, and emboldened the people of the island to throw off the royal authority. Thou hast encouraged discontent, and boldly incited civil confusion. Thou hast basely used thy influence to occasion discussion and revolt. For this offence thou must atone with thy life; royal justice demands thy death!" He paused, and the Spaniards watched closely the cold, changeless face of the prisoner, whose eyes were bent, mockingly, upon them. "But," he resumed, in a different tone, "our royal mistress is ever pleased to manifest grace and clemency. We would, then, be merciful to thee, traitor though thou art. Inasmuch as thou hast been the recipient of queenly favor and trust, we would fain save thee from the miserable fate of a felon." Again he paused, but the mocking eyes smiled on him, and he continued: "We would establish more firmly the power of the throne; we would quell for ever and entirely this pernicious desire for change, and crush at once these dangerous plotters against the crown. Thou canst most effectually do this thing, and on these terms thou mayest save thyself. The attempts at revolution have been fruitless. You have lost everything, and gained nothing but ignominy and disgrace. The very people for whom thou hast in thy blind error forfeited so much, will not do thee honor; at this very moment they shout over thy downfall. Then we offer thee pardon in case thou wilt renounce thine error, and make before the people a full recantation. This will arrest, without further effort on our part, any hope for a future revolution. Thy followers will return with thee to that natural allegiance they have so rashly forsaken. Thou shalt be restored to wealth, power, rank, and station, far greater than that which thou hast forfeited. Bend, then, the penitential knee before the tribunal of thy merciful mistress, our gracious queen."

A fiery flush of scorn and shame scorched the Cuban's pale cheek, and his haughty form quivered with disdain. "Ha!" he cried, "is it with this paltry snare thou wouldst tempt me? Thy words want truth; the Creoles have never deserted me; 'tis thy *hirelings* who proclaim a tyrant's triumph."

"Thy words are hot. I tell thee thou art offered mercy."

"What, dost thou not know me yet? Am I taken for a coward, that this base insult is thrown upon me? Have I not written my truth in blood upon this soil, and ye would that I proclaim my whole life a living lie? Nay, my death shall seal its earnestness. My Queen!" he continued, with bitter scorn. "I acknowledge no Queen. I have cast off the hated allegiance, and stand before you, defying all monarchs, save the high monarchy of heaven. Ye have pronounced me a traitor; that charge I deny, as barren of justice or truth. For my country's good, her advancement has been the sole endeavor of my life. The deeds for which I stand your prisoner, I thank God I have lived to perform. It is better death in a noble struggle for liberty, than life in chains and abject degradation. I do not ask your mercy—I throw it back with contempt upon your craven hearts. I scorn the mercy of a tyrant. Do not longer mock me with this trifling. Give me the clasp of the garrote; I know it awaits me, and that at least is true. Had I as many lives as the sky has stars, the sea waves, I would gladly lay them on freedom's altar. I am content with my fate; for *as I have lived, so I die, in the full, exalted faith of Cuba's final redemption.*"

The clear, mellow voice was hushed.

"Slave! dost thou glory in thy shame, and boast of thy treason? Dost thou dare to scorn the representative of royalty?"

"*Scorn!* Aye, it is too poor a word. I abhor, with all the power of hate, the ready minion of despotic cruelty and oppression—he who is without one impulse of humanity or gratitude. I once spared thy life; all I ask is, that the instruments of *war* may draw the life-current from my heart.[41] It

41. We know of no factual account of López's sparing Concha's life. However, when

is a pitiful revenge to take from thy benefactor the right he has to a soldier's death."

"Liar! slave!" shouted Concha; "thou shalt taste the very gall of a righteous vengeance."

"I do not fear thee," replied the Patriot General, proudly, "thou miserable slave-fiend of a demon crown! Thou canst not rob me of my high
reward—the remembrance of a people. Thou canst only give me the freedom of death, and even in death, *I scorn and defy thee!*"

His swarthy face purpled with rage and passion.

"Chain him!" shrieked the Spaniard; "thrice chain him and drag him
to the lowest, foulest dungeon!"

The noble Cuban calmly wrapped his mantle around him, and said:
"I am ready."

They laid no hands of violence upon him. Many present had known
and called him friend in prosperous days, and now they sat in silent admiration for the unbending majesty of his truth. Lopez slowly left the
hall, supported on either side by an officer; for he walked with great pain
and difficulty. When they reached the portals of the castle, the captive
turned, and, fixing his mild, fond eyes on the scene, drank in its loveliness
with passionate rapture.

"How beautiful!" he said, mournfully; "how beautiful is night!—the
last night I may ever behold. Ah! my spirit will pine for this blue sky,
these bright stars, the wavy sea, and this fresh untainted air. It is hard,"
murmured the warrior, as they closed the iron gates, and left him in the
silence of his dark and narrow cell, "it is hard even for thee, oh, Cuba!
beloved as thou art!"

Covered with heavy chains, he lay—this untamed child of the sun—
this fearless "apostle of liberty," his fierce spirit chafing, his impatient
heart beating against the hours that moved so wearily on, till they
brought the triumph of his martyrdom.

López was an officer in the Spanish army stationed in Spain, Concha served under him.
Chaffin, *Fatal Glory*, 216.

CHAPTER XXV

"'Tis come—his hour of martyrdom
In freedom's sacred cause is come;
And, though his life hath pass'd away
Like lightning on a stormy day,
Yet, shall his death-hour leave a track
Of glory, permanent and bright,
To which the brave of after-times—
The suffering brave—shall long look back
With proud regret—and by its light
Watch through the hours of slavery's night
For vengeance on the oppressor's crimes."
MOORE.

FRIDAY, SEPTEMBER 1ST, came the day appointed for the martyrdom of General Narciso Lopez, the friend and lover of his country.

The morning dawned dark and cheerless, for the sun hid his bright face with heavy clouds, and refused to look on a deed so foul.

At an early hour an immense crowd assembled, and waited in gloomy silence the coming of the captive. The whole space between the Punta fort and the Carcel was filled with troops, cavalry and infantry, who formed an immense square, in the midst of which was erected the scaffold, about twenty feet high, the top surrounded by a balcony, and in the centre of the platform was the garrote.

The troops were heavily armed, every cannon of the fort charged and pointed to the place of execution. The solemn voice of the tolling-bell announced the coming of Cuba's great champion, and the deep rolling drum sent its death-notes out on the morning air.

First, marched the strangely-dressed priest, bearing the black flag of death, after whom came a detachment of soldiers, and, in their midst, walked Cuba's brave son, whose crime had been to love her honor and to seek to advance her happiness. The procession moved slowly across the square, towards the scaffold. Far above the tinselled slaves towered his haughty form, clad in spotless white. A mantle of fine linen hung from his shoulders to the ground, in heavy folds. A white cap of the same material drew the raven curls from his face without concealing his features, and on his knightly hands he wore the base fetters of a tyrant's power. Ah! who that gazed upon it, can forget the noble presence of that illustrious victim! There was no sign of guilt, or fear, on his calm brow. He walked with the firm, stately step of triumph to the death-shrine, the sacrificial altar. The earnest power of an unconquered spirit beamed in his dark eyes—that quenchless energy, that love of right and truth, which had made him struggle to live a free man, gave to the doomed patriot the lofty bearing of a conqueror. They strove to hurry him forward, they were impatient to seal with his death-stroke the chains of Cuba,—but the chieftain's step was slow and measured. He had walked before that multitude in the pomp of wealth and station, but never so proudly as now. One officer, more brutal than the rest, raised his dishonored sword and struck the Cuban on his neck, saying, "the neck should bend before it broke." No flush of anger dyed his brow, no sound came from that lip of pride; he looked sorrowfully on the poor minion of a crown, and turned to mount the scaffold as a king would approach his throne.

He stood amid that dark assembly, gazing for a moment with changeless brow on the terrible instrument of death. A look of haughty defiance flitted across his face, as his eyes swept scornfully over the dense throng of negro and Spanish hirelings, ere they rested on the unhappy Creoles, whom the policy of Concha had removed as far as possible from the sound of the hero's words. Then his rich voice, clear as the blast of a silver trumpet ringing through the morning air, thus addressed them:— "Cubans! I have come here to die. To you I need not justify the act which has brought me to the scaffold. Your own hearts acquit me of the false charges with which they seek to blacken my memory, and rob me of my country's love. Whatever I have done, *Cuba's good* has been the great object of my life. I aspired to high things, to bless her with the free institutions of a Republic, to promote her happiness by establishing a government liberal in its political and religious principles. Though that effort has failed, the hope of it is not lost,—and I am content to meet my death if it brings the day of my country's redemption nearer; for the free flag of Cuba shall—"

He was rudely, angrily thrust aside, and the officer motioned the priest to approach. His hands were relieved of their heavy bonds, and he received the cross. *Then* his noble head *was* bowed over the blessed emblem of his faith, and the holy father slowly repeated the prayer for the dying. When he arose the executioner attempted to draw the white cap over his face, but he dashed it aside—"Nay," cried the stern imperious voice, "my death shall be a witness in the face of heaven against you. I am sinless before God and man of the charges which ye bring." With fearless dignity he sat in the chair of death. The cold iron serpent of despotism was coiling around his neck, when a sudden impulse fired his mighty heart; he sprang to his feet, and stood before the breathless multitude, a shining form of light. A glory, a splendor not of earth, beamed in the royal majesty of his beauty; his wild, dauntless spirit glowed on its brow-throne, and filled his eyes with eager flashing brilliancy. With yearning love the patriot stretched forth his arms, and forgetting all, he gazed fondly in the distance on the purple mountains and waving verdure of the Summer Isle—then, with a voice full of southern melody, saddened with eternal love, he cried, "Cuba,—*dear* Cuba!—*adieu!*" He sank back—his eyes closed with a proud smile upon the slaves,—and Lopez gave his life to Cuba, and his name to fame.

There was silence—even those whose hands reeked with the crime of his death, were awed by the bold heroism of the feared and hated foe of the tyrant. The cry for which Spanish gold had bartered, rose for a moment and died faintly away. But, hark!—there is a wail of agony! it echoes hoarsely through Cuban hearts; it is

> "A nation's funeral dirge for her patriot son."

Lopez! mighty-spirit! unrewarded in life, unforgotten in death, thou shalt yet be avenged. The divine principles for which thou gavest thyself a willing sacrifice, glow with quenchless fire in hearts who know no such word as fear,—when every conviction of right, every prompting of humanity, urges them *onward*. There are those whose patriotism is not bound by mountains or rivers, it rises superior to self, it spreads beyond the land of nativity, going, like a beam of light, to smile gladness on a country weeping in all the darkness of despotic degradation. Thy wondrous martyrdom kindles a sacred enthusiasm in the chivalrous and brave; the holy sympathy, the generous daring of La Fayette—of Kosciusko, thrill America's nobles sons.[42] Thy name, thy bright and honored

---

42. Thaddeus Kosciusko (Tadevush Kastsyushka) was a Polish general and statesman who served in the American Revolution with George Washington.

name, oh, thou lover of freedom, shall be their watch-word to victory. The day of Cuba's redemption comes surely on. Thy glorious spirit, radiant in the dazzling splendor of its immortal life, shall hail, with holy rapture, the glad shout which proclaims, "Thy work finished—thy country freed!"

CHAPTER XXVI

WHEN DUDLEY LEFT his commander, it was his intention to go immediately to the nearest estate, and at any risk procure food, for he felt that he would soon be unable to struggle longer against the terrible cravings of hunger and exhaustion. He wandered for some time in the dense wood, went miles as he thought, but no prospect of a house appeared. The desolation of the lonely wood was horrible to the man; in the delirium of his despair he shrieked aloud, but no answer came. The hot fever of pain, the burning agony of starvation raged in his veins; his sight grew dim, his blood felt like molten lead; he had strange visions of home and of death in a foreign land. He roused himself with a strong effort, and slowly groped his way back to the spot where he left his General.

"I will die with him," he muttered, but in vain he called; Lopez was then in Spanish custody, solacing his weary heart with the one comforting hope, that his brave officer had met a better, he knew he could not have a more miserable fate. "Gone—oh! God! I must die alone." Yet he did not realize all the wretchedness of his condition, for a torpor stole over him, and he fell unconscious on the earth. Thus he lay when the dark face of a Spaniard bent over him, and a sword flashed over his head. The brittle thread of life was quivering one moment—a wild fierce yell— the Spaniard *Hidalgo* lay dead, and Scipio knelt by his master.

"Aha! I got you, is I! I wus fas' 'nuff fur you dat time. 'Tends to be too. You thought you had my Marse Ralph, but you see I had you, ole feller. How you like dat now! you outlandish nigger; you ain't white folk, no how. Settin' up in Marse Ralph's house sassy, as if you real quality. I knows quality; I not raised at de quarter.[43] I know'd you want thar for no

---

43. Holcombe's white perspective separates slaves into a hierarchy of house slaves versus field hands, or those raised in the slave quarter. See introduction, p. 41.

good. I watched you out de corner ob my eye. I could'er chocked you every glass ev wine I gived you. I wus too well raised a nigger to distreat you Spanisher is you wus in my own master's house—but I done settled wid you now, you sateful cat; here looks 'nuff like a monkey to be a cat. Look you, Marse Ralph! wake up now, don't go to make out you dun dead, and Scipio cum too late. No, you ain't dead, you know you ain't. You nuver went to die, 'cause dat Spanisher was 'bout to kill you. I knows what'll bring you to. Whar's my bottle? dun lef' it at home. Good God! I ain't got no home. Wouldn't have one in dis place. No genteel nigger would stay here, no how. Umph! got de Spanisher's; lem me tase it, see ef it got pisen in it. Good brandy, 'fore God, 'tis. Fus thing good I ever know him to have; jes' take little, Marse Ralph, you knows good brandy well is me, an' it nuver wus in your heart to 'fuse it. Oh! yes, I thought twould bring you back to life. You's not ded; you heart beat too strong, Marse Ralph. You'll do. How is we goin' to git 'way frum here now. I wander ef Marse Ralph got any money!" Scipio proceeded to satisfy himself by searching. Dudley opened his eyes, and a faint smile flushed his pale cheek as he recognised the familiar face.

"Is that you, Scip? What the devil are you doing?"

"Umph! know it Marse Ralph, now; jes' like him. Nuthin' 'tall, sir; jes' seein' ef you had som' brandy fur giv' yerself. Might know'd you didn't, tho'. Well, nuthin' here. Dat's right, Marse Ralph, jes' shet yer eyes tell I get through wid dat Spanisher. I boun' he's got money! and money we's got to have; 'cause how is we to get out ev dis confounded country widout it? Now, ole feller, I'll see what you got. Sorter hate to put my han' on you, confern yer yaller life.[44] Umph! movin'—is you got notion comin' to? You mus' love to die, 'cause you knows I'll kill you agin, an' glad de chance. Playin' possum, is you? you please me now. I knows jes' what to do wid a possum. I puts yer tarnal head under de rail. Possum on, ole feller, tell I gits all de money you got. I mus' make hase too, 'cause ef Marse Ralph wake up he knock dis boy down, 'cause he always wus so curus' 'bout som' things. He'd starve an' die 'fore he'd tech dis money, but Scip ain't got no turn fur honer. He'll die 'fore he lef dis, shure," with a hearty chuckle he pocketed the well-filled purse.

"Scipio!" called his master's feeble voice, "what *are* you doing?"

44. Yellow meant racially mixed.

"Jes' payin' my las' 'specs to your poor fren', Marse Ralph; I mighty glad to see you settin' up. How far you reckon you ken walk, Marse Ralph; needn't 'quire, tho', cause you looks jes' like death. But don't look so faint-like Marse Ralph, 'cause I skerd to lef you long dat hateful feller eny how. He look too much like a cat, not to have nine lifes; consarn him, he jes' 'pears dead, 'cause I stannin' ober him. I glad 'twas me killed you 'stid of Marse Ralph, 'cause you ain't fit fur a white man to kill.

"Marse Ralph, is you 'feard to stay here by yo'self wid my Spanisher?" he said, bending over Dudley, "umph! Marse Ralph 'lapsed, wants more brandy; well, here 'tis, drink 'nuff dis time to do you some good, 'cause 'tain nothin' like it in sickness nur health nuther. Poor Marse Ralph! ef 'twas jes' Scip now, I woulden mind it, but it goes to my heart to see him dis way. My poor marster," he repeated, bending with tearful eyes over the still, haggard face, "I never did see nobody look so much like a corpse; well, one thing shore, ef Marse Ralph die, de game is up wid dis chile, sure, 'cause dare ain't no place in dis worl' gwine to hold poor Scip den; he gwine to foller arter Marse Ralph, 'fore God he is." Dudley slowly revived. "Marse Ralph, does you feel better?"

"Yes. Where have you been all this time, Scipio?"

"Lord bless you, Marse Ralph, don't ask me. You ain't in no perdicerment fur hear all de trials I is gone through. Mexico want nuthin' to em. Gineral Quitman and all his brigan would uv—"

"For God's sake stop, and tell me where I am, and what has happened." He drew his hand languidly across his brow, as does a waking dreamer.

"'Umph! Marse Ralph, you too hard fur me now. We ain't no whar— and everything done happen."

"The general, Scipio—have you seen him? Where is he?"

"I 'spect he in heaben 'fore now."

"What! my God! have they taken him?"

"Dat dey ain't—he take hisself, 'cause, sir, he jes' *met* um. I tell you, Marse Ralph, ung Marmion may talk 'bout Ginel Washinton and 'Fayette, I don't know 'bout dem, 'cause I nuver recollects um, but I'se 'pletely satisfied no braver man ever bin born dan dat same Cuby gineral whut you bin trying so hard to die fur. I ain't pertiklar 'bout bein' 'long de army ef you ain't dare, so de minit I catch sight uv de solgers, I clome a tree, and watched um when dey come to whar Gineral Lopez was standing, looking is scornful at um is a king. I tell you he jes' walked in dare face is bold is a lion. But, Marse Ralph, I don't know what I gwine do wid you, 'cause you can't begin to walk ten steps, an' ef I lef you here sum dem troops find you, an' den you gone fur shore, long is you can't lif dis sword whut I done 'mortalised. I foun' it on de road, an' I reckon one uv our solgers loss it. Marse Ralph, s'pose I lays you in dat cave dare, 'tell I come back."

"No," said Dudley, with shuddering recollection, "not there."

"Well, I mus' hurry back, 'cause I'll be mighty oneasy. Thang God I foun' you, now I means to stick to you. José an' Scip'll cum presently. You don't know José, Marse Ralph, 'cause he is one my own 'ticlar frens, but you see we couldn't begin to git to Havana widout him, 'cause he knows folks 'long here, an' is up to things in dis country. He's a good-hearted feller fur a free nigger, an' he'll be mighty apt to 'trive a way to git us safe dare, an' den, Marse Ralph, we mose home, thang God."

The night of September 1st, Ralph Dudley sat in the cottage of José, his face bowed in his hands, silently wrestling with his heavy sorrow, gazing with a kind of cold apathy on the pale dead visions which lay like withered leaves upon his heart.

Scipio stood, looking expectantly from the door.

"He comin', Marse Ralph, I jes' ken see him, but he comin' by hisself." A moment after José entered the room, and approached the Liberator.

"The body," said the wretched man, in an anxious voice, raising his haggard face.

"Ken git it, sir, by bribin', if we had de money, but you see, sir, we ain't got de money."

"I know'd dat," interrupted Scipio, "dare ain't a Spanisher in dis town, dat wouldn't be glad to sell his soul, ef he had one, fur two bits."

"S'pose 'tain't no use to think enny more 'bout it, Colonel Dudley," continued the fisherman, "'less you could think un some way to git de money."

"Money!" repeated his listener, in harsh, biting tones. "Oh, God! that I should want for it *now!*"

Scipio stood by, with his hand in his pocket, looking irresolutely on the troubled face of his master; at last he said, boldly:

"Marse Ralph, *I* got plenty of money. I len' you some ef you wants it, an' you ken pay me back when we gits home."

He displayed the long purse with its shining gold.

"Where did you get it, Scipio?" asked his master, rather sternly.

"I—ar—well—I jes' tell you, Marse Ralph. You see, sir, when Ginr'l Quitman was commanding us in Mexico, in one dem battles we wus in, I wus 'bout to kill a Spanish officer, what wus fool 'nuff to be fightin' wid Sant' Anna; but he beg so hard fur me to let him off dat time, I spard his life; he promus to send me somethin' when he got home; but I s'pose he furgot it; an' t'other day when I met him, I s'pec he felt 'shamed, 'cause he jes' pulled out dis an' giv' it to me."

"You rascal! I would stake my life you have been robbing some poor devil."

"'Fore God, Marse Ralph, I nuver rob a livin' man since I wus born," which, as far as we know, was true.

After the moon had gone down, when the earth was dark and still, they bore in silence from the hut, a coffin, and laid it in the little boat of the fisherman. In the frail wave-rocked bark, the illustrious hero was borne from the land he had so daringly loved. The hands which had borne aloft the free flag of Cuba, boldly dashing its bright folds in the face of tyranny, were crossed in quiet stillness on the cold, hushed heart. The clarion voice which pealed in words of hope down the line of the Liberating Army, had rung out its last tones of chivalrous tenderness, and floated like some holy spell in the wind-music of every zephyr that kissed the beautiful isle, for whose redemption he had striven with such resolute, untiring devotion; the martyr-crowned brow was pillowed on the heaving bosom of the waters, guarded by a single sentinel—the faithful sharer of his adversity. As a plaything for the tossing waves, the tiny bark reeled through the hours of the night. On the following morning the New Orleans vessel bore to America's shore—to a foreign land, the dead form of Cuba's heroic son. An exile in life, an exile even in the grave; thus will he slumber until the land of his love can receive him into her bosom—*as a republic.*

CHAPTER XXVII

"Your oaths are passed—look to it they be kept."

"Can that man be dead
Whose spiritual influence is upon his kind?
He lives in glory; and his speaking dust
Has more of life than half its speaking moulds."

THE SAD, QUIET AUTUMN moon sat on high, and her falling splendor lay in beams upon the earth. The sweet, twinkling things, which men call stars, clustered around the gracious empress of night, and bent their calm, mournful rays on an unfilled grave—a lonely grave, underneath a magnificent oak, on the bank of the great "father of waters." The room in which the Cuban traitor had sat with the Patriot, was hung with heavy folds of black. The portraits of Washington and La Fayette were draped with the crape of woe, and the group of men who stood around the coffin of Narciso Lopez wore the badge of mourning; a single silver star gleamed on the coffin, and its semblance shone on the breast of "the noble few,— the distressed good," who stood around their sacred dead, their brave, unfortunate General—honor's hero, Cuba's Patriot, and liberty's martyr. The flag of the American republic, and the free flag of Cuba, were shrouded and crossed above the chieftain's head. There was no funeral dirge, no martial music, no rolling drum or playing artillery—a solemn stillness reigned throughout the room. The moonbeams stole silently in, "like princes royal into a deserted palace," and the sighing wind made fairy-like music without. No careless eye looked on the holy bier; it was in the midst of those who had been true to him, and who were still constant to his cause. Raymond and Dudley raised the flags from their resting-place, and the warrior was borne by his own officers, slowly, slowly towards the open grave, 'neath the grand old oak. Sadly, silently, without a word, they laid the Patriot down to rest. The fierce struggles of his stormy life were past. Rejected by the country of his love—her for whom he died—cold, calm, and still the hero lay, in the bosom of a foreign land. The grave was surrounded—the short swords which the men wore were drawn, and their shining blades flashed in an arch above the lowered coffin. In deep, earnest tones the Liberating oath rose on the stillness of night, and the angels of justice and mercy bore it to the court of heaven.

"Comrades!" cried Stuart Raymond, "we have yet another vow to make; let it be registered over the grave of Lopez."

Again their voices mingled thus:

"By the eternal God of our fathers, and of our liberty—by the blood of Lopez and of Crittenden—by our love of truth and hope of heaven—we swear that the sole purpose and aim of our future lives shall be, to lay this sacred form of the Patriot martyr in the bosom of a republic—the republic of Cuba. Amen." It was recorded—*see that it be kept.*

They bent a moment over the grave of the exile; then the glittering star was hid, and they slowly departed.

The lonely mound was left to the solemn watch of night's imperial bride.

CHAPTER XXVIII

GENEVIEVE WAS FOR many days very ill. Delicate and fragile, the storm of sorrow had crushed her to the very floor of death, and they reluctantly told her wretched mother that she must enter in. Mabel roused herself from the lethargy of grief in which we left her, and watched with untiring care beside her suffering friend. There was no outward mark of grief—no words, no tears, but her face was stern and colorless, as if its features were cut in marble, and the large eyes looked weary and complaining. Hers was a spirit too generous and good to live very long in self. She sank for awhile under the desolating blow, but her earnest heart said, "Rise, Mabel, put on thy strength, thou art greater than despair; that is for the weak; thy sorrow *must* be borne; hide its wounds with calmness, that others may not weep." So she covered her heart strongly, that its inward wailing might not be heard, and was to those whom she loved, truly a comforter and friend in this hour of deep affliction. She soothed with her tender care and thoughtful attention the sick and weary hours of her unhappy friend. She tried to comfort Mrs. Clifton, and consoled "uncle

Louis," giving him hope, even against the physicians, that his darling might live.

Once she spoke for a long while with Mrs. Clifton, of her murdered lover. Then a fierce, passionate crimson burned on her cheek, and her eyes flashed through hot scorching tears. At last she said, "You do not mention him in my presence, you fear it will give me pain; I know you mean it kindly, but this silence grieves me. Do not banish his dear, familiar name from your lips. Sometimes it would be a relief, a happiness to hear it mentioned lovingly, as in the sweet old days that are gone. A place, a name, a flower, a song, these little things that bring back the absent and half-forgotten, will not remind me of *him*—will not call him to my heart; he is there always, for ever. It has but one great thought—Eugene! Though he has passed away to the beautiful heaven given the brave of heart and honest of purpose, yet he is living in a temple within my breast, whose foundation is my life. You shrink, too," she continued, "from even speaking of Cuba. Dear Mrs. Clifton, you do not know how my heart is henceforth for ever bound to her. Poor Cuba! so fallen; even the brave could not save her. I loved her for the wrongs she had suffered; now I love her for my own—those she has given me. To me she is a holy thing; this sepulchre of my buried love; this beautiful urn which holds the ashes of joy and withered flowers of hope."

The weary days went by. Chill September winds sang summer's dirge, and the pale autumn flowers stood mourners.

Tidings came of the overthrow of the Patriot party, and of the martyrdom of General Lopez, but not a word of Dudley. Nothing was heard of him, his name not appearing in the list of prisoners or among the wounded or killed. Poor Genevieve! her moments of consciousness were but few, and even then, the loving watchers almost grieved to see them come; for the sweet inquiring eyes would close with heavy tears. They had no hope to give her. The guests had left their pleasant summer retreat, and the sounds of mirth and laughter were hushed in the promenade, and in the spacious festal hall. Our party were very lonely, and wearied with their absence. They longed to be at Ellawarre; but Genevieve, its loveliest flower, was fading, sadly, slowly away.

It was evening. In a distant part of the room the physicians were conversing. For these most respectable persons will talk even when the question of life and death is pending. Around the bed of the sufferer hovered the pale face of Mabel, Mrs. Clifton, and "uncle Louis." Poor Emily sat at the window, trying to hush her sobs, which were very distressing. It was a moment of agonized interest. One of those in which the angels of life and death contend for mastery.

There was a step without the door. Mr. Clifton went hastily forward, and Mabel followed softly. The first words that met her ear were, "Ralph, you shall not go in; it would be her death to see you now." The next moment Mabel was silently clasping, with a sister's fondness, the out-stretched hand of Dudley.

"Let him go," she said, with her sweet, low voice; "joy never kills." The door opened, and the wasted but noble form was kneeling beside the beautiful, the beloved.

"Oh, thank God!" he murmured, "I am not too late."

Genevieve's eyes slowly unclosed. With a low cry, a smile of inexpressibly joy, she laid her hand upon his head. She was saved—her best physician had come.

A week after Colonel Dudley's arrival they returned to Ellawarre.

CHAPTER XXIX

WITH FOLDED ARMS the master of Dudley Hall paced the long verandah which surrounded his princely mansion. So changed was he, you scarcely recognised the gay hopeful officer of the Liberating Army, in the pale, weary-looking man, whose brow was troubled and heavy with care. He paused and raised his thoughtful eyes over the splendid lands, stretching like a green prairie back from the river, as the stately trees, which had been the pride of the haughty race whose sole representative he was, waved their hoary branches in mournful whispers to the wind; their murmuring fell like reproaches on the ear of the miserable man. "Lost—all lost," he muttered, "but life, and that hangs like a curse upon me. The home of my forefathers passes into the hands of strangers, and I, the last of the Dudleys, must wander, penniless and alone. God! what a fate! Strange indeed is the problem of life, for this is a terrible infliction consequent on the act whose motive was as pure as the conscience of an honest

man. The act whose performance is still my pride to acknowledge. There
is one thing evident—I cannot remain to see these halls desecrated by
strangers. I will not stay to mark the changed tone that will greet my
fallen fortune; the pitying eyes of my former companions. I will go ere
the blight cankers on my heart, and I curse those whom I have called
friends. *Experience* shall never tell me that human nature is base. In the
fearful struggle that has passed, I found it faithful and true; by that will I
judge it. I have known men devoted and sincere even in suffering and
death. This holy memory untarnished will I bear in my heart as a comforter to the strange land which I must seek—the land of fortune's exiles—California. Genevieve!" an expression of pain crossed his face. "My
angel, Genevieve! There lies the wretchedness of my lot, that gentle, loving woman, to whom my cursed destiny has already brought to so much
sorrow. How am I to leave her? Yet I cannot stay. Would to God I had
fallen in Cuba, or rested beside my buried general! I cannot ask *her* to go;
and then, what the devil would Mrs. Clifton say to me if I did! My own
Genevieve, with her sweet fond eyes and hoping smile! I cannot see her
again. If I do—I shall linger, falter perhaps in my purpose. Gods! it must
not be. My fate is a hard one, but I will bear it with at least a show of
hardy manliness. I will write to Mrs. Clifton, and then prepare to leave
on the morrow all that—" He shook his head with a bitter sigh. With
rapid steps he sought the library, and the letter which Mrs. Clifton read
on the following morning ran thus:

"DEAR MADAM,—I am bankrupt in all things, even in hope. In the cause
of Cuban independence I have wrecked my fortune and saved my life.
The latter I could have better spared. That I regret the adverse circum
stances which have thus thrown me on my own resources I cannot deny,
yet I am still loyal to the noble cause by which I have so severely suffered,
and my arm, which is all I can now offer, will be ready at any moment to
draw its sword at Cuba's bidding. The mere loss of fortune does not affect
me. I am a man young in years and energy, the world is before me, and
labor is honorable. Mine is a greater sorrow, one shared by a people who
mourn the failure of their hope for liberty. A few weeks since, in this very
room, I stood the master of a princely fortune, surrounded by friends of
my choice, the good and brave, who with me listened to one who un-
folded from his mighty heart a scheme for liberty, as sure as that which

throbbed in the breast of Washington. Now there is nothing I can call my own, save despair. I am a guest in the halls of my ancestors. My comrades lie in distant dishonored graves. The hero-strength of my commander availed nothing; he sleeps without a stone to mark his place of rest. This, Madam, is a dark hour in my life. The ashes of hope lie on the past, and the dense fog of despondency covers all the future. This, God knows, is enough, and yet it is not all. There is at my heart a keener grief, whose bitterness is indescribable. The necessity which compels me to seek a distant home, the sense of honor and propriety that restrains me from asking her to share my altered fortunes, forces me to free your daughter from that engagement to which you so reluctantly consented under prosperous auspices. I do not wrong your generous nature with a suspicion that my adversity would cause my rejection. I know she does not care for wealth, nor do you require it; but, Madam, dependence would be more bitter than poverty. I must now be the 'architect' of my own fortune; if I deserve one I shall win it. In thus relinquishing her, who has been for years the shining radiance of my life, I leave my heart dead to all feeling but the gloom of its entire desolation. I could better bear the crushing power of misfortune, did not my own love tell me it brings sorrow to her, whom I would gladly shield with my life from care. Believe me, such is the unselfishness of my love, I would not repine could I feel that my wretched destiny brought pain to myself alone. Though you may not approve, I pray you do not blame. It is by a strong effort I pursue that course I deem honorable and just. Lonely as I am, weary and pining for comfort, it is hard to debar myself from the only sympathy which I might claim. I know depression is unmanly; yet one deprived, by a fell swoop, of all that gave to life its charm—every hope and aim, will pause and gaze on the ruin ere he folds around him the stern armor of endurance. If the future has success for me, then will I lay it at your daughter's feet. Though I free her, yet I cannot free myself. Every impulse of my better nature will, mocking all change, cling to the holy memory of my Genevieve. Dear Madam, I have said I was without hope, yet even while I write, the white-winged messenger walks with silent footsteps through my heart. I measure the strength of her love by my own, and feel an assurance that though I release her yet she will trust me for the future as she trusted me in the past. I enclose a letter, which you will not refuse to

give, nor to believe that I am, under all circumstances, devoted to you
and to her.

"Ralph Dudley."

The letter was written. It did not at all please him, but he folded and laid
it by. He bowed his head on the table and felt very desolate. The blast of
disappointment had left a single light burning in his weary heart, over
which it had no power; that he had now voluntarily removed. Alone, in
the grand old house, he feasted on the bitter fruits of memory. The ever-
waking, ever-watching Scipio stood by his master.

"What do you want, Scip?"

"Uncle Marmion want see you, sir."

"Let him come." The old man entered the room.

"I cum for orders, sir, is you wus 'bout to lef in de mornin'."

"Who told you I was going to leave?"

"Scipio, sir."

"Confound the boy! he finds out everything." Scipio grinned from the
open door where he had safely ensconced himself. Dudley looked on the
grey-headed servant of his father with a miserable sensation of pain; at
last he said, "Yes, Marmion, I am going away for a long, long time; and
what is to become of you all, God only knows; for I have now no right to
be master here."

"Heabenly Father, Marse Ralph! you isn't tryin' to say dis 'state got to
be sole! my blessed ole master's 'cestral halls mus' 'long to strange folk!
Don't say dat—don't disgrace dis ole family servant's grey-head wid sich
talk, Marse Ralph, my blessed master! I ruther be dead 'long him an' Gineral Jackson, Lord knows I had, an' to live to see dis boy what I raze
myself, bring de 'proach of poverty on de name of Dudley."

"Poverty is no reproach, Marmion."

"Not ef you is born to it; but when you jes' throws away a fortune is
you mus' have dun, I calls it a gret disgrace, sir; it's what my master,
nur Gineral Jackson nuther, nuver dun. But, Marse Ralph, you must ha'
managed mighty bad, 'cause 'stravergent is you is, I can't see how you got
through wid everything dis soon. My ole marster lef' a heap of money in
de bank; de 'state cum discumbered into your hands, 'cause your gardene
wus honest, an' nuver fooled you out of nothin'. What you do wid it all,
Marse Ralph?"

"You know it took all the ready money to pay the bond which I signed for Marcell."

"I 'member you put your name to sum fool paper 'fore you wus of age, an' your gardene, Mr. Seaton, as good a man is ever cum frum Veginny, swore you nuver shud pay it."

"Yes—but Mr. Seaton and I had different ideas of honor; I would have redeemed the bond, if it had taken all I possessed, and labor in the bargain."

"I b'leve you would, Marse Ralph; dat's obsternate, jes' like you. Nuver lisnin' to nobody is what brought you to dis. Onruly an' headstrong is you always wus. I can't help feelin' fur my blessed master's chile, now he dun cum to sorrur an' disgrace. You ain't goin' to have nobody hardly to ker fur you now but ole Marmion, 'cause white folks is mighty sateful, Marse Ralph." The old negro looked at the anxious face of his young master with tearful eyes. It is a hard matter to convince a negro that there is anything which a white man cannot do, and then Marmion was perplexed to know "how Marse Ralph could have got through" with an estate, which *he* imagined might easily buy the English crown. So he resumed, "Marse Ralph, maybe things isn't is bad is it 'pears to you. Tell me what de trubble is, 'cause I is 'vised your father 'fore you. What you done wid your property? What is de det dat de 'state's layable fur? sense me on dat subjec', Marse Ralph." Old Marmion had that hard, practical sense which you sometimes find in his race, and he had always known the exact state of Dudley's pecuniary affairs, until of late years, when he avowed "Marse Ralph was too fas' fur his own self, he not goin' to stop tell he crash an' brake all to pieces." Ralph had great confidence in Marmion, and talked openly to the old man, whose strongest feeling was devotion to his "master's chile," so he now said—

"Marmion, it stands so; you know that I endorsed very heavily for 'Swanson & Kyle.'"

"I knows you is always givin' yo' name to enny body dat wants it. You heap too generus fur yo' own good, Marse Ralph. You bin 'nuff better to folk an dey'll be to you. You mind what ole Marmion say."

"Then," continued Dudley, unheeding the interruption; "we have been unfortunate; the negroes have, for the last three years, scarcely supported themselves. We have suffered from cholera among them, and the crevass on the plantations. So when I wanted money for this expedition, in which I have been engaged, I had to get it advanced. My note for the full amount is due. Swanson, poor fellow! as my cursed luck would have it, has failed; with these demands against me, and no other means of meeting them, I must at once give up everything, and though poor, I shall at least feel myself an honest man. Rather a costly pleasure," he concluded, with a sigh.

"Marse Ralph, 'tain't is bad is you seemed to make out at firs'. It 'cisely like you do to git down-hearted an' rekless, an' talk 'bout sellin' out, 'cause you is little under de wedder. I don't see do', how ennybody loss so much in dis exposition, 'cause de solgers nuver got no wagers is dey did in my ole master's an' Ginel Jackson's war. Dese got shot fur dere pay, an' mighty pore pay 'twas, I takes it. But, Marse Ralph, things ain't so desperit; you ken save yo'self frum dis 'tanglemunt. Ef I was white, I knows I could fix it straight fur you."

"I wish to God you were, and in my place; we would see what you would make of this."

"T'ain't," resumed Marmion, with dignity, "like yo' father's son and Ginrel Jackson's god-son, sir, to be givin' up, 'cause you got yo'self in a little scrape. You knows, Marse Ralph, you not goin' to sell dese black ones. How ken you take it off yo' conscience? Sum of dese is ole famly sarvunts an' ain't dun nothin' yers an' yers ago. Now ef dey be put up on de block, sum poor white man'll buy um, 'cause dey go cheap, an' how dese 'spectable ole sarvunts goin' to hard work at dey time of life. Out de question, Marse Ralph; we mus' 'trive sum way to do. I is know'd 'states got out wus differkultys an dis. Dare is plenty of ways ef you would jes' study 'bout it, an' make 'rangements like a man. I knows what's de matter wid you. You grievin' after dat Cubymun, buried in de oak grove. You needn't, Marse Ralph, 'cause Scipio 'forms me he wus brave is twenty lions all turned loose in a bunch, an' a brave man, sir, nuver misses heaben. You members how dem Spanishmun butchered Colonel Critten-den, an' Marse Eugene, an' Mr. Kerr too; an' how dey shot down Ginel Pragi, bless de Lord, he looked an' hel' his head is much like a solger is ever Ginel Jackson did in his bes' day.

"You's had trouble 'sise money matters, Marse Ralph, 'cause de expur-sition turned out bad, and I know you set your heart on berighten' dem heathenish poor Cubymen; but, Marse Ralph, 'tain't right to take it so oneasy; 'tain't becomin' a Dudley, sir, to let his sperit sink down under misfortin'. You feels put out wid de worl', an' 'cause dey is gone, an' de Cuby Ginrel wus treat so 'fernal mean by de Spanishers, you dun got kerless of yo'self, an' 'pears like you don't mind whut cums of ennything; but, Marse Ralph, dis is mighty wrong, 'cause you got to live a heap of yers, an' please God to let you live um is a gentlemun's son oughter. So you mus' rouse yo'self up, an' do somethin'. Jes' think, sir, of all dese black ones at ain't got no 'penunce but you. Look at yo' dead father's ole body sarvunt. You reckon he means to 'long to ennybody but his master's chile? Dat gret river out yonder'll roll over dese poor ole bones 'fore dat day cum."

Dudley sat in moody silence. It was a strange kind of comfort he had in listening to the tremulous tones of the old butler.

"Marse Ralph, is you 'sulted Mr. Seaton?"

"No," he answered, shortly. "Mr. Seaton has already interfered too much with my affairs."

"He wus a mighty good gardene, sir; an' 'twas fur yo' own good he 'jected so strong to sinein' dem skurity papers, an' goin' to Cuba too. You ain't no manager, Marse Ralph; it runs in de blood to spen' money. But, Marse Ralph, we ain't 'cided on nothin'. What'll you do?"

"What I fir\t said. I have contracted debts, which must be paid, and there is but one way to do it."

"Dere's plenty of ways, Marse Ralph. You ken borry de money. Yo' name is good. Dey know you got plenty of property; pay little hush money now, an' dey'll wait. Make 'rangements to pay by 'stalments, jes' tell um how you is fixed, an' dey not goin' to push you. Dey'll give you time. You give yo' note, Marse Ralph; dat's it; Captain Raymond'll sine fur you."

"It won't do, Marmion; besides, Stuart has as much as he can do to keep his own estate from going. And then, I should not ask him, under any circumstances, to do that; for my friendship shall never bring trouble to any man. I will free myself from this, and take the consequences. I don't know," he added, with a cold smile, "that poverty will be so hard, after all."

"You don't know, Marse Ralph; you nuver bin tried it. A gentleman's son can't work, sir; 'tain't born in him."

They were silent for a while; at last Marmion said, eagerly:

'Marse Ralph, dare is one thing you ken do—mortgage de 'state, an' we can 'conermize an' work it out easy 'nuff. Dat's de way plenty of rele Virginny gentlemun duz, 'cause I is bin knowin' to sich cases; do I nuver 'spected my own master's son would be 'duced to dat. It's honerble. You won't mind mortgagin', Marse Ralph."

"And live with a set of hungry creditors watching every movement! I would die first," said the young man, impatiently.

Marmion looked hardly on the irritated face of the speaker, and his dim eyes lighted with indignation.

"Marse Ralph, ef you *does* scatter dese people when you ken keep um, ef you *does* sell dis ole place when you ken help it, ef you wants to, my blessed master'll rise wid his grave close on, to curse you. Fur ginerations an' ginerations dis is bin de home of yo' 'cestors; everthing here is bin born 'longing to de Dudleys, an' now, in my ole age I mus' see stranger folk marster here. Blessed Jesus! Marse Ralph, I'll kindle up de fire under dem whut's hanging' up dare de ole house, ole Marmion, an' dem blessed ole picters'll all go home to heaben together. Marse Ralph," he continued, in husky tones, "if you isn't got no feelin' fur yo'self an' dem what's dead, look at dis poor ole man dat razed you frum yo' dyin' father's bed; he mose in his grave, an' you gwine sell him fur money." Tears streamed down the dark, wrinkled face. "You better uv died, sir, when you wus a little fatherless boy in dese ole arms, 'fore you brung disgrace on you an me too, an' dem dat's gone. God a'mighty hep me! my master's chile dun give me up."

The great, broad chest heaved with heavy sobs.

"Good God, Marmion," exclaimed Dudley, in a voice of indignant sorrow, "I never dreamed of selling you to a stranger! I intended to get Mr. Seaton to hold you and Scipio until I could redeem you."

"Oho! Marse Ralph," chuckled the boy, in a low tone, from his hiding-place, "Scip'll be fas' 'nuff fur you; he knows you; he not bin to Mexico an' Cuby fur nothin'."

"Marse Ralph," said Marmion; "ef de ole house an' de buryin' ground, an' de people is all sole, an' you goes off to a foreign lan', 'tain no marter whut 'cums of dis poor ole sarvunt—he'll soon go to his blessed marster and Ginel Jackson, whut's in heaben."

"Marmion, you talk very strangely. You seem to think I act from choice. Do you suppose I would voluntarily give up everything I possess?"

"'Pears mightily like it, Marse Ralph," persisted Marmion.

"What am I to do, then?"

It was a strange question for the master to ask his slave.

"Morgage de 'state, an' we ken work it out; ole Marmon go to de fiel' hisself, an' be glad to do somethin' fur his blessed marster's chile," persisted the old man, with a ray of hope on his face. "You ken do it, an' not hurt nuther yo' pride nur yo' honer; you ken make de 'rangements wid de crediturs, an' leaf evything in Mr. Seaton's hands. You know, ef money ken be made, he'll make it; an' he luvs you is he luved yo' father 'fore you; and ef you wus his own son, he wouldn't do no better part by you. You's got a rovin' dispersition; you ken go to Callyforny, an' nothin' thought of it; when you cum back, den all'll be straight an' hushed up, an' no hard feelins 'gainst nobody. Lis'en to yo' ole white-headed sarvunt, Marse Ralph, 'cause poor Marmion's bin faithful to you, an', please God, he want to die whar he wus born, in sight of his ole house whar he used to wait on his blessed marster, an' de great Ginel whut's swarin' in glory. But 'tain't fur me to have my way," he said, with a gentle deference.

The devoted old slave had read too long the fitful changes of his master's face not to know his determination was shaken.

"Lem me sen' fur Mr. Seaton, Marse Ralph," he continued, with ready tact; "he ken 'vise you better 'an me."

Dudley was really noble at heart—rash and violent, yet his impulses were good.

"Very well, Marmion," he said, with a faint smile; "but it is devilish hard—you must control me, both as boy and man. You can send Scipio for Mr. Seaton; he will go with me to the city, and we'll see what can be done."

"Marse Ralph, you'll 'zempt Scipio, an' take him wid you?" The anxious face of the sable hero peered eagerly in.

"No, I can't afford to keep a servant now. I will leave him with the rest. Poor fellow! I don't know how he will take it. I don't think I can tell him. Do you see him, Marmion."

"'Tain't no use to lef him, Marse Ralph; he not gwine to be no 'count to nobody in dis worl' but you—'cause you done ruin him, he woulden be wuth his salt on de plantation, an' you can't git 'long widout sumbody fur wait on you."

"I must try, Marmion, for I shall be obliged to leave him."

"We'll jes' see, Marse Ralph," muttered the boy, moving cautiously from the door, "if you lefs Scip, you lefs him dead shore."

Old Marmion lingered. The pale, haggard face of his master grieved him sorely. "Lord bless you, Marse Ralph," he said tremulously, and, with a relieved but still heavy heart, he left the room.

CHAPTER XXX

RALPH DUDLEY WAS decidedly a man of faults. Violent and headstrong, as Marmion had said, quick to despair and eager to hope, his were errors that required no generosity to forgive, they pleaded for themselves. When he found his affairs were entangled, he never thought of trying to avert a crisis; his pride was wounded at the idea of losing his inheritance, of seeing his father's estate in other hands; he was wretched because his worldly position, in his own estimation, debarred him from wedding her whom he loved; and yet he never thought of making any exertion whatever. He had suffered greatly—he had, to use his own words, lost more than mere fortune; about that he was indifferent; if the cup must be bitter, let it be gall. Then the thought of obligation, of a creditor, was torture to him. To free himself was the impulse of his impetuous nature, and then make the best of poverty in a country where he was unknown. But Marmion's reasoning, and Marmion's appeal, changed the current of his thoughts.

So when they reached the city he made, with Mr. Seaton's judicious assistance, all necessary arrangements, and leaving everything in his hands, embarked for the Eldorado of the western world—the gold-breasted shore of California.

It was with mingled feelings that Colonel Dudley stood on the deck of the stately vessel, as she moved like a queen through the star-mirrored waters of the gulf, and watched the isle of so many hopes, glimmering in her purple loneliness through the shadowy veil of moonlight. Like the rose of fabulous beauty she stood, resplendent in her dewy charms; the very stars, drawn by loving admiration, sank down in the waves as they circled melodiously around, and dimmed as they kissed the enchanted shore of nature's paradise. As did the wondrous flower of tradition, so the "Antilles Queen" wears in her bosom a destroyer, which crushes her vitality, and mars even the glory of her surpassing beauty—the canker-worm of tyranny.

Dudley turned with sickening sorrow from the fairy-like vision the brilliant night-lamp gave of her who had robbed him of both fortune and friends. The sacred memory of Lopez burned in his heart, and mingled with recollections of Pragi, Crittenden, Downman, Kerr, de France, and others not less brave, who fell around him on the field of battle. Then came ringing from the past the words, which Lopez had almost implor-ingly spoken, "Be ye faithful to my country when I am no more"; and his spirit silently renewed its vow, that which was sworn over the star which gleamed from the patriot General's grave. The island-gem faded in the mellow light, and Ralph sighed that the last familiar thing which could weave a memory of his by-gone life was past. He loved Cuba, not only with the strong, broad love of a patriot, but with the chivalrous tender-ness that arises within the brave for the wronged and weak. He had a haunting sympathy for her—he loved her as we love those for whom we have suffered and endured. All that lay before him was new and strange; all former ties were broken, and he felt that worst of loneliness—the loneliness of a crowd. As his eye wandered listlessly over the strange forms which thronged the deck of the steamer, the tones of a familiar voice arrested his attention, and looking down on the lower deck, he saw Scipio surrounded by a highly-amused set of deck hands; the boy was with his doubled-fists making the most violent gesticulations towards the fast-fading shore of Cuba.

"Dare you go—'drot you, mose out of sight, thank God! ef I keeps my eyesight ain't no ways 'ticular ef I nuver does see you no more. *I* knows you; you thinks we is comin' dare, but you miss it dis time; got 'nuff of you. Umph! You does look peaceful, but Scip tried you; he knows you got de very ole devil in you, 'sateful Spanish sarpent. I hear Marse Ralph call you a queen. Wonder whut he think of queens now! Ef you's a queen I got 'nuff of um for one. I tries Callyforny awhile myself. Ef 'tis a mixed poplation, is I hear folk say, it better an you, consarn you Queen is you is, you ain't fit fur a colored person to look at; you clear 'neath my notice. I puts my han' in my pocket, I does, an' turns my back on you fur ever

an ever." He straightened himself, and rolled his eyes up, to the great delight of his audience. "God a'mighty—Marse Ralph! Umph! I'll catch it."

"Well, sir—have you got through?"

"Yes, sir."

"Come up here, then."

The boy obeyed, muttering, as he went, "Hopes I is got through wid
Cuby, but I 'bleeged to 'buse the tarnal cut-throat long is I got breath,
shure; ain't furgot Marse Eugene yet." He stood before his master with a
deprecating look.

"Is it you or the devil?" said Ralph, half amused, half angry.

"Dis me, sir; dare de debil out yonder," pointing to the object of his
wrathful denunciation.

"Can I never get rid of you? How did you come, and what for?"

"Nothin' 'tall, sir; jes' cum 'long wid you. Mr. Seaton 'zempted me on
purpose, 'cause he an' uncle Marmion bof know'd I wusn't gwine stay no
how. You can't *nuver* lef me, Marse Ralph; you need n't try no more, tain
no use. Scip ain save yo' life five, six times, fur be 'ceived an' 'posed on,
dis way."

"Well, sir, we will see which will be master; I shall put you on the first
vessel we meet, going either way; then make the best of it, you infernal
scoundrel." Scipio knew what his master's threat meant.

"Don't ker whar you puts me, Marse Ralph; I gwine foller arter you to
de t'other side of Jurden. Ungle Marmion tole me nuver los sight of you,
an' I diden 'tend to, no how. You can't lef me, Marse Ralph, you welse
not try; ef you sen' me 'way I ken cum back; an' when I git to Calforny I
free is you; den you see which sticks closes to you, white folk ur Scipio."[45]

CHAPTER XXXI

THREE YEARS HAVE passed, and we are again at Ellawarre. The grounds
are brilliant with many lights, and the gay forms that fill the spacious

45. The Fugitive Slave Act of 1850, much stronger than an earlier act of 1793, meant
slaves did not become free when they entered into free territory.

rooms that are wreathed in flowers, wear the robes of festivity. A marriage night! It is always one of mirth and gladness, but to me there is a sadness inexpressible in this sealing of destinies; this stepping into a new world, whose regions are yet unexplored; one which imagination and hope have filled with the beautiful flowers of unchanging love; the joyous sunshine of unfading happiness; one in which reality may bring all the bitter grief of disappointment. Though the merry song echoes gleefully from lip to lip; though the dance swims down the flowing hours, and many-voiced mirth thrills forth its mingled tones like a thousand fairy water-falls trembling into one, yet deep in the heart is a questioning fear, an unsatisfied hope, reaching from the inner life toward the mantled future.

A bridal at Ellawarre! Mrs. Clifton stood at the lower end of the long saloon, wearing a robe of dark velvet, over which sparkled the light of jewels; her jealous mother heart throbbed with the quick alternations of hope and fear, for unto the love of another she gives her child.

Mr. Clifton, the same kind-looking "uncle Louis" of other days, was by her, and the hushed silence of expectation reigned in the room. As the guests fall back from the door, the bridal party entered; the holy vows of the mystical ceremony commenced, and the fair was given to the brave. Erect and proud, the noble form of Colonel Dudley stood, giving with his clear musical voice a practical confession, that *all* chains are not galling, and thraldom may, under some circumstances, be united with happiness. Protectingly his dark glorious eyes rested on the timid, clinging loveliness of his Genevieve—for beautiful she was in her bridal robe of white unfigured silk, whose shining folds gleamed through a falling mist of Honiton lace, like moonlight through the vapory clouds of a summer night. No jewels threw their cold splendor over the warm joy-light of her sweet face; a simple wreath of orange flowers lay on "the fairest brow in all the south"; and the long, white veil drooped in gossamer lines about her, like the shadowy drapery of some fairy queen. Beautiful Genevieve! sweet Honey-flower, moved forward a happy bride. With blushing grace she glanced upward to her hero-lover, and smiled to hear her new name from his fond lips. The congratulations which greeted them were suddenly stilled, for the clergyman again commenced the solemn ritual, and before him stood Stuart Raymond and Mabel Royal. The same Mabel of former days, though the eager, brilliant face which came to us sparkling in the glad imperial light of early enthusiasm, sorrow had shaded into repose. With calm, tender beauty, like a dreaming moon-beam, it smiled from the shining waves of hair that lay as a golden crown about her head. The glorious love-dreaming, spirit-conquering eyes were darkened with the hovering shadows of memory, but the radiant soul came from their depths with an earnest, onward look. In firm, trusting tone she murmured the vows which placed all her future happiness in the hands of another, and Mabel, peerless Mabel, was the bride of Stuart Raymond.

The sounds of mirth and music mingled with the merry whispers of falling footsteps gliding through the dance, and by courtesy of observation, all were happy. How we talk of happiness! how recklessly our words dispense it, both in fiction and real life, and yet where is it? Is it in that heart filled with all for which it thirsted? That heart which revels in the entire possession of those things which have formed in anticipation the ideal of happiness, whether it be the smiles and earthly embodiment of heavenly beauty and love; the glory of fame; the elevation of power; the outside splendor of magnificence, or the attainment of long-cherished and noble desires? Is it in the ardor, resolution, and hope of a heart springing forward on an unexplored career, or does it repose in one that has struggled bravely through all difficulties, achieving a glorious triumph in the battle of life? The records of the past give a mournful, murmuring whisper—no. Where then is perfect happiness? High, high above us, like a star whose rays we love and watch, but cannot catch; it mingles its radiance with the spiritual light of the unattainable.

Where, then, is most happiness? Though it glimmers artfully from all these conditions, its beams are surest and brightest in that soul who pursues with steadfast faith and earnest purpose, a lofty aim, whose accomplishment is the good of our common nature, the elevation of humanity.

Apart from the gay crowd who wandered through the illuminated grounds, presenting a scene of brilliant beauty, which imagination might liken to a fairy encampment, good Stuart Raymond and his young bride, no longer Mabel Royal, but always royal Mabel. On the fine, energy-stamped face of the Liberator gleamed a fond smile, as he stroked the white hands, clasped though his arm, like mingling snow-flakes.

"Mine, at last," he said, tenderly. "Look up, my Mabel; tell me, can you think how strong that love must be which was watched through years; which lay silent on my heart, keeping a fond vigil over the holy memory of thy beauty?"

"Yes," she answered.

"Can you know how full is the joy that holds thee to my heart, its best friend; that binds thee to my spirit, its brave, bright counsellor and supporter?"

"Nay, Stuart," she smiled, "not that you are all-sufficient and complete within yourself, your true heart is its own unerring guide to all that is good."

"No," he said earnestly; "I was nothing until I knew you; then I felt that you might make me everything. I loved you not as I had or might love another, but with that entireness of devotion which fills the heart but once. I felt that in all the wide world there was nothing like you; therefore, it could exist for you alone. When you turned from my love and spoke of the past, I did not despair; you were, if possible, dearer to me. I knew that you would be mine; that though you did not then love me with the tenderness of your woman's nature, yet you responded to my devotion, with the mental strength of your being. I felt that my love was your destiny, and you *must* take it. I found in you all for which my spirit had so long pined—the concentrated excellence of your sex—all beauty, all goodness, and truth. Now," he continued, with manly fondness and pride, "you are mine, ever mine, and that is all happiness. The world may fall away, its brilliant light go out, but darkness cannot be with me while you remain; my spirit-light! my heart-legislator! for there shall you rule with absolute power. Your earnest spirit shall act through me; its beautiful influence moulding me into a better man. When I grow weary, and falter even when good is before me, then will your faith and hope urge me forward. The velvet touch of your warm enthusiasm, my beloved, will soften the frost of disappointment which experience has crusted on my heart. You will make me self-reliant and strong; your glorious smile will dispel despair, and point 'ever upward, ever onward.'"

"Dear Raymond, I cannot reach your noble aspirations; they are far above all, but my love."

"Nay, my beautiful! is not your whole sympathy with the one great purpose of my life, that hope towards which every exertion tends—the liberation of the fair land of Cuba!"

A flash, gentle as Aurora's first roseate smile, mantled her white cheek, and her blue eyes flash with ready enthusiasm.

"Hope! Oh! Stuart; must it still be hope? Does not the divine bud of promise swell, ripening, bursting into a maturity of wondrous beauty, which will be the presage of Cuba's glorious future?"

"Ah! even now it blossoms. Fate is lavish; all my happiness comes at once. Thou banded, and Cuba freed! But tell me, my Mabel, dost thou look with smiling eyes to our own future? Wilt thou, my heart-queen, my joy-consort, be happy?"

She raised her large eyes, in which a thousand waking memories beamed, and said—"*When Cuba is free!*"

"Mabel, Mabel, turn hither thy loved face, with the soft moonlight on it; let me gaze one moment on the sweet brow which 'guests a royal dweller'; but thou art already mingling in the throng."

We must glance at the happy, consequential faces of Scipio, Marmion, and Emily, who stood about with great complacency, commenting, with much satisfaction, on the appearance of the fair brides. Scipio contending to Emily's infinite chagrin, that "Miss Genevieve was mighty pretty, but dare wan't nobody like Miss Mabel."

When the guests were around the luxurious table, on which was served the marriage feast, when the fair brides had been toasted in sparkling champagne, when the bridegrooms stood looking proud and happy, there was a confusion just opposite Colonel Dudley, and Scipio Africanus struggled into view, holding above his head a tremendous glass, his face and manner bearing witness to the truth of a former assertion, that sperits was brandy, and brandy was sperits.

"Marse Ralph!" he cried out, flourishing his glass, "I drinks to you; I'se got a right to, sir, an' to me, an' Miss Mabel, an' Miss Genevieve, an' Capin Raymond, an' Ginel Quitman—what 'manded us in Mexico, an' Ginel Lopez—what's dead, an' Jeff Davis, an' all de solgers we took to Mexico an' Cuby; in fac', sir, I drinks to all our boys dead an' 'live."[46]

Ralph laughed because the company laughed, and because he could not well help it, and every one knew that Scipio was, as he certainly deserved to be—a privileged character.

46. Jefferson Davis served in the Mexican War of 1846. Later, of course, he would become president of the Confederate States of America. Lucy Holcombe Pickens was a firm supporter of Jefferson Davis during the Civil War.

Now that my heroes and heroines are as happy as I can make them, it is well, perhaps, dear reader, that I leave them, and thou, which I do sadly, for by the pause of my pen, we are again strangers; thou returning to happier thoughts than I can give thee, I—, but ere the momentary chord of communion be broken, ere these leaves are closed and thrown aside, let us together pledge, The Liberating Army of Cuba! The libation has been poured in wine and in blood, but thou and I will take the silver cup of faith, fill with hope's sparkling nectar, and quaff its every drop to the flag which will wave over the Island Republic—the Free Flag of Cuba.

CHAPTER XXXII

CUBA

CUBA—THE LOVELY and beautiful—rises like Venus from the foam of the sea. As she stands on her ocean-laved pedestal, like the Greek Slave, her charms win our admiration, not more than her chains awaken our sympathy. What wonder then that young America, the nation-knight, who loves liberty no less than beauty, should brave the dangers of war, wave, and garotte, to release the fair thrall.[47] Young America has made the attempt, and though unsuccessful, yet, like a true knight, he stands ready at any moment to resume arms in a cause so worthy his chivalrous devotion. It was hoped that Cuba might have, at least, one arm free enough to assist in the struggle for her liberation; but, alas! every muscle was paralysed, and benumbed by heavy clamping chains. Woe and disaster have attended the gallant efforts to free her; her song of mourning is echoed along Columbia's shore, where fond hearts weep for the "unreturning brave."

The effort to liberate the Island Queen has commenced, and though intermitted, it is not over; for *never* can the struggle between tyranny and freedom cease, while chains are galling and Liberty is dear. Every age has its error; a great error which has all the power and authority of a true

47. See introduction, pp. 7–8, on the Young America movement.

principle. It was thus in the middle ages, when the Pope claimed the supremacy over all temporal powers. While they submitted, he exercised
that control as his legitimate right. During its prevalence, the daring individual who questioned this authority, was regarded as announcing sentiments so preposterous, that they did but prove his madness. Though it
had long been submitted to, the progress of enlightenment at last dis-
pelled this error. So in modern times, not very long since, he who dared
deny the divine right of kings, was denounced as insane, and hung upon
the gallows. In the same light is he now regarded who ventures to assert
the moral and religious beauty, the political justice of those admirable
doctrines of progressive liberty, which the heroic missionaries of freedom
sought to promulgate in 1851. The error of the present day—the one pre-
vailing in our country, is to suppose that our government can by any
national obligation restrain its *constituents* from individually assisting a
people to throw off a yoke, degrading to their moral character, hateful
and oppressive to their political energies. By the progress of freedom and
enlightenment, this error will be removed. Truth must and will ultimately
prevail. With all the power of the rising sun, will she gradually dispel the
mists of error and prejudice which hang around the political world. Then
will it be acknowledged that the liberty-giving principles espoused by the
Cuban Liberators, are morally and politically right; then will it be univer-
sally conceded that men whose generous sympathies are awakened by a
people in distress, whose generous impulses may prompt them to brave
so many dangers to aid them, ought not to be thwarted by their own
government, whose glorious nationality stands on the very principles
which they seek to establish. If our own immediate government be not
extended, it behoves us as freemen to recognise the extension of its free
institutions and liberal spirit. As far as good faith is a motive, it is certainly under stronger obligations to faithfully sustain the great principles
which its people profess, than to maintain the interest of a foreign despot.
Do not monarchs instantly take up arms in favor of their brother monarchs to reinstate them on thrones, from which they have been deposed
by their disaffected subjects? Did not all the powers of Europe unite to
maintain the claims of one family over the rights of thirty millions of
people? Did they not wantonly interfere, and *force* monarchy on the
French people when they had adopted a democratic form of government?
Then why shall not republicans, on the great and noble ground of human

rights, assist a people to regain that power which was always theirs, and which was wrested from them by a usurpation, to which time and tradition alone have given an appearance of legitimacy?

Our sympathy as a people is certainly with those who, grateful for the happy blessing of that liberty, which their ancestors obtained by foreign assistance, emboldened by high and generous example, delight to prove themselves worthy to be freemen by offering the same aid to the Cuban revolutionists, which America so thankfully accepted in her own memorable struggle.

The Liberating patriots, God bless and prosper them, pursue with earnest determination the high aim of their holy mission; the suffering Island Queen is bound by the dark unholy bands of despotism, submissive to the tyrant's will, but there is a link of *blood* which holds her to every American heart. Had our sympathies never before glowed in pity for her wrongs, they would now spring up and cluster with sad vengeance around the land deluged with the blood of our kindred and countrymen. Her mournful wailing touches a chord in our hearts which has never before vibrated, for the blackness of her gloom has cast its shadows around the hearth-stones of America.

Poor Cuba! long has she wept; but a radiant smile is breaking over her sadly-beautiful face, for a star has arisen—a bright joy-promising star—whose destiny is to pour the rays of hope into her sad despairing heart. The night of her degradation wanes, for—

> The day-star o'er her its bright beams sheds,
> Commencing a glorious morrow.

THE END